CRAIG ODANOVICH

AN
EROTIC
ADVENTURE
NOVEL

CAPTURED PREY

BOOK TWO IN THE BLACK WIDOW TRAINER SERIES

Published by River Grove Books
Austin, TX
www.rivergrovebooks.com

Distributed by River Grove Books

Design and composition by Greenleaf Book Group LLC
Cover design by Greenleaf Book Group LLC

Publisher's Cataloging-in-Publication data is available.

Print ISBN: 978-1-63299-526-1

First Edition

To the scores of hardworking and dedicated personal trainers—men and women—and their clients

Acknowledgments

Once again, I would like to thank my wonderful/fun team at Greenleaf Book Group. I never would have believed going through the detailed process of editing could be so enjoyable. Aaron, you were great to work with, and you did a great job of challenging me with your comments. I feel that *Captured Prey* is all the better for it. Lisa, you continue to blow me away with your cover art. You deserve some type of award for your creativity. If nothing else, you have earned my admiration. Bryan, it was a pleasure working with you as always.

I would like to welcome Victor Gulotta to the team. Your public relations blitz will be the key to breaking the Black Widow Trainer series out of the pack. I am well aware of how daunting a task bringing awareness to a new author can be. Of course, your guy Michael Borden (that's an inside joke for all of you that don't know Victor and Michael) can give you a leg up with his adaptation of the first book—*The Black Widow Trainer*—into a screenplay. Hopefully we'll be well on our way to securing a movie contract by the time *Captured Prey* is released.

I would also like to thank Jenny McChesney; the BWT logo you designed is totally awesome! Bobbie Joe Martin, Dave Chaney, and Jessie Stanco: the brochure of the entire first chapter of TBWT was not only gorgeous but unique to the book industry, and Jenny's logo looked terrific on all the BWT merchandise.

I would like to thank Richard Yount for guiding me on the appropriate laws the congressman could have violated in regard to his contract with Misty, as well as my longtime friend Rick Mulinix for customizing the PR campaign for my hometown, Corpus Christi, Texas.

To my posse, Roger Davidson, Wanda Knippa Polasek, and Amy Evans: thank you once again for acting as my focus group and letting me know if I stray from the course. I swear you guys know the main characters better than I do.

To my beloved family and wonderful friends: thank you all for your encouragement. There is no way I could have done this without your support.

And especially to my partner of thirty years: dear Cathie, thank you for unselfishly allowing me to travel the world gathering research. And to my children, Jack Odanovich, Michelle Odanovich, Amy Odanovich, and Stephen Odanovich: your support has meant the world to me.

To the followers of the Black Widow Trainer series: I hope you have enjoyed reading my books as much as I enjoy writing them. Of course, if you do, it means you are fun-loving, adventurous, and open-minded people. What a wonderful way to live life!

1

On Vacation

Misty stood statuesque as soothing warm water cascaded over every voluptuous curve of her well-honed body, washing away the salty sweat left over from yoga class. Tonight she would dine with her best friend, Gabriella, in the quaint little town of Lahaina. Maui offered the girls a sunny escape from the cold June days in Buenos Aires. The next two weeks would be filled with beautiful beaches, exotic tours, fabulous food, and everything else paradise could provide.

"Misty, dear! I'm going downstairs to the bar for a drink so take your time getting ready."

"Okay, Gabriella. I won't take long."

Misty finished showering, toweled off, and then lay on the bed for a short respite.

After what felt like only a few minutes, she was jarred awake by a voice outside the door. "Maid service! Do you need anything?"

Misty groggily reached for her cell phone to check the time and then panicked.

"No thanks! I don't need anything," Misty shouted as she frantically jumped to the floor. *I've been sleeping for ninety minutes! Gabriella must be worried sick. I'll send her a text.*

As she hurriedly threw on some clothes, she wrote, "So sorry Gabby! I fell asleep. I'll be down in a jiff!" Within a minute she heard a beep with Gabby's reply: "Take your time. I met the most amazing man."

Oh really? Misty thought. *Well, good for her.*

On her way to the lobby Misty couldn't help but wonder what Gabriella's mystery man looked like. *Knowing Gabriella, he's smart as well as attractive.*

Misty spotted the two as she walked into the bar. As she drew nearer, she stopped dead in her tracks. The strikingly handsome man looked incredibly similar to an old acquaintance she'd had drinks with at this hotel over three years ago. *It can't be. What are the chances of running into him after all these years?*

Broad shoulders, silky, smooth brown skin, and long, thick black hair. Whoever he was, her old acquaintance was still one of the most magnificent creatures she had ever laid eyes on. His exotic blend of possibly half Hawaiian and maybe half Asian or Polynesian still made him the most intriguing-looking man she had ever known—and the last time she had known him it had been in the biblical sense.

Gabriella said, "Oh, Misty, I would like you to meet—"

Gabby quickly glanced back at her new acquaintance and said, "I'm sorry, what did you say your name was?"

"I didn't say."

Misty remembered how the man she knew long ago had never divulged his name to her, which in an insidious way had made him all the more intriguing.

As she took a seat she studied his every feature before asking, "We've met before, haven't we?"

"Possibly. You remind me of someone I met several years ago in this very same bar."

"So you two already know each other?" Gabriella asked.

They both nodded without taking their eyes off of each other.

The night in his hotel room long ago had been a sexual awakening and was instrumental in setting her free. The thought of that night caused her to cross her legs and pump her right leg up and down vigorously. Now both mentally and physically aroused, she fought the impulse to drag him up to her room and hold him hostage for a repeat performance.

If only Gabriella were not here.

Bemused, Gabriella stared at the two in disbelief. "So you two really know each other?"

"A chance encounter," Misty said.

The man added, "Yes, and what's the chance of being with two beautiful women this time?" He rose from the table as if sensing it would be best to let the women sort this out in privacy. "I'll be right back. Please order another round of drinks when our waitress returns and put it on my tab."

When he was gone, Gabby asked, "What's going on, Misty? There seems to be history between you two."

"Remember me telling you about the man I had an affair with that led to my breakup with Rob? It's him!"

"No way," Gabriella replied. "So what is his name?"

"He never told me. My friend at the time, Becca, referred to him as The Man."

"'The Man!' That has a nice ring to it," Gabriella said. "Then that's what we'll call him."

A glassy-eyed Misty said, "Yes, and what a man he turned out to be. I accompanied him that night, to his room. I can still remember him stopping me before we entered and saying, *this is no place for little girls.* I went in anyway. If there was still any little girl in me I was all big girl when I left."

Now that Misty had confirmed his prowess in the bedroom, Gabriella's pulse quickened. She had fallen under his spell while waiting for Misty and found him off-the-charts handsome and oozing with charisma. But being the practical one, something began to trouble her. Assuming only one of them could score, which one of them would it be?"

"Misty, we need to talk. I'm as enamored with this man as you are, but if we fight for his affections I'm worried one of us will get hurt."

"So what do you suggest we do?"

Gabriella thought it over for a moment before saying, "Why don't we invite him to dinner and see how it all plays out?"

"I'm down with that!" Misty said with a mischievous grin. "After all, we are on vacation, so a little adventure is in order."

When The Man returned to the table he said, "Hey, why the long faces? This is my last night on Maui. What do you say we all go get some dinner?"

Misty winked at Gabriella as she replied, "Gee, why didn't we think of that."

On the way out the door Misty said, "Hey, we still don't know your name. We can't spend a night on the town with a nameless man. Now come on, give it up."

The Man contemplated long and hard before saying, "Teakie. My given name is Teakie."

The girls looked at each other in astonishment before Misty laughingly blurted out, "Teakie? Oh, how darling, we're going out with little Teakie tonight!"

Misty realized her remark had embarrassed him, so she quickly put her arm around him and patted his chest. "I'm so sorry for laughing. I was just joshing you."

A warm smile spread over his face that showed off his perfect row of sparkling white teeth. "That's okay. Now you know why I hesitate to give women my name."

The quality of the food at their restaurant was matched by the quality of conversation. After eating a little too much they decided to take a long walk along the beach to walk off dessert. Gabriella found Teakie to be charming, not a charmer. From her past experiences, a man this good-looking had a propensity to be somewhat conceited. She now understood why Misty had trusted him enough to go to his room without even knowing his name. Seeing how well Misty and Teakie were getting along, Gabriella decided that she would not compete for his affections. Now if Teakie chose her on his own without her trying, that might be another story.

The girls hung all over Teakie as they climbed the steps to their hotel. The message in their body language was clear: "You're not going anywhere tonight without one of us, Buddy." Once in the main lobby,

Gabriella reached around Teakie's back to pinch Misty as she said to Teakie, "Why don't you sit on that comfy sofa while Misty and I visit the ladies' room?" Teakie shrugged his shoulders and plopped on the couch.

Once safely inside the ladies' room, Misty asked, "What's up, Gabby?"

"What's up? Teakie's penis is what's up. I accidentally brushed it while we were walking up the stairs. Well okay, maybe not accidentally." She grinned. "That man is primed and ready for action!"

Feeling both excited and a bit silly, Misty said, "So he's as hard as teak wood?"

"Cute, Misty," Gabriella said. "Why don't you and I discuss which one of us gets to mount that hardwood and which one retires to the room to be bored out of her mind?"

Misty turned on the faucet and splashed some water onto her face. "That's quite the dilemma, my friend."

Trying to delicately deal with their predicament, the girls spent the next five minutes coming up with reasons why the other should spend the night with Teakie.

"Gabby, it's only fair you get to experience Teakie firsthand. I've had my opportunity."

"No, Misty. I could tell during our walk on the beach that you guys have a lot of catching up to do. I should be the one to bow out."

They eventually agreed it was ultimately Teakie's decision to choose, and the unlucky one would gracefully exile herself to the boredom of their room.

Misty hugged her friend tightly. "Now, let's go let the cards fall where they may."

When they arrived at the couch they panicked. Teakie was nowhere to be found. A pall fell over the girls as the disappointment set in. Misty and Gabby held hands in an attempt to console one another, feeling like brides left standing at the altar.

Suddenly, their trance was broken as two powerful arms wrapped around them from behind. A friendly, seductive voice asked, "Why the long faces? Did you get some bad news?"

When the girls realized it was Teakie, their moods lifted and each breathed a sigh of relief.

Teakie said, "I've got an idea. Why don't we all three go up to my room and get to know each other better?" Giving the girls a little squeeze, he added, "Misty knows what I mean, don't you Misty?"

Misty looked at Gabriella with a twinkle in her eye as she said softly under her breath, "Are you up for it?" Gabriella's smile indicated she was.

When Teakie unlocked the door to his room, Misty took him by the arm and said, "I hope you know this room is only for big boys."

Teakie replied, "You can be the judge of that."

2

THE SECOND TIME AROUND

Teakie's room looked the same, but Misty was different. She was single this time. Over the past six months she had refused to take on new clients as she waited patiently for her separation with Rob to be finalized. Misty never felt good about her affair with Teakie four years ago, but that was all in the past now. She could not deny that the affair was the catalyst that caused her to reevaluate her marriage to Rob. The separation was amicable, and Rob falling in love with Amelia allowed Misty to move on without regrets. Remaining friends with Rob helped put the issue to bed. Now it was time to put something else to bed.

To help Gabby feel comfortable, Misty led her onto the balcony.

"What do you think of this view, Gabby?"

"Oh, Misty, the Pacific looks absolutely enchanting. Is that Black Rock down below? It looks magnificent in the torchlight."

"Yes, and when we wake up in the morning, we'll be able to see the island of Lanai just over there." Misty pointed out to sea.

"What a spectacular view that would be. My only regret is we didn't come during humpback whale season."

Misty couldn't hold back a grin. "Well, at least we may see a little

humping, and maybe we'll be on our backs." The girls walked back into
the living room and noticed Teakie had changed into a colorful Hawaiian shirt, string-tied cotton shorts, and flip-flops. Misty got a whiff of
his cologne.

"Obsession, right?

Teakie nodded.

Misty traced his face with her finger. "I just might be obsessed with
you."

Gabby sniffed one side of his neck, and found the fragrance intoxi-
cating. Misty quickly staked her claim to the other side.

Misty whispered in Teakie's ear, "I nicknamed you The Man the last
time we were together, but tonight you can be Our Man."

"I'm at your service, ladies."

They were on their way to the bedroom.

The scented candles, new age music, and king-size bed brought back
fond memories for Misty. She'd spent the most enjoyable two hours of
her life in this very room and now anxiously anticipated the night to
come. Misty turned and began unbuttoning Gabriella's blouse.

"Let's get you ready for bed, girlfriend."

Gabby returned the favor. The Man sat on the bed enjoying the show.
After their blouses hit the floor, the girls reached around their backs and
unlatched their bras. Misty gently removed Gabby's and added it to the
growing heap of clothes on the floor. Perfectly shaped and blemish-free,
Gabby's moderate-sized breasts were in full view with nipples standing at attention. Misty removed her own bra, letting it join Gabriella's.
Gabriella gazed at the breasts she envied. Misty's full, taut C-sized breasts
rested comfortably on her chest. They were so spectacular! Gabriella
often fantasized about spending a full evening of exploration, gawking,
feeling, tasting, and playing with the beautifully shaped twins. When
their panties joined the rest of their undergarments on the floor, the
girls stood in front of their male companion, anticipating his command.
Teakie cupped each of his hands under one of the girls' breasts and began
gently bouncing them up and down. Fully aroused, their nipples became
hard and elongated. Teakie gave each one a little pinch, sending a sensation they felt all the way down to their lower privates.

Sensing they were anxious to begin, Teakie reached under the bed and pulled out a replica of the master massager he'd introduced to Misty during their previous encounter.

"Sorry girls, I only have one so you'll have to share."

Misty reached out and took the magic wand.

Teakie crawled onto the bed and motioned with his finger for Gabriella to join him. Teakie pulled her onto the bed next to him, placed a pillow under her head, and began massaging her temples. The touch of his strong, powerful fingers caused Gabriella to drift off for a moment. Misty placed the head of the vibrator over Gabriella's mound and flipped the switch. Gabriella's legs opened wide, as if instructed to say *ah* by the powerful vibrations from this wonderful device. She instantly felt it pulsating throughout her entire pelvic region—so powerfully at first that her vagina began to itch. Not long after, the itch was replaced with warm waves of sensual pleasure. One at a time the penetrating waves came crashing through her body. As they grew strong and stronger, Gabriella instinctively arched her back and raised her pelvis toward the ceiling. Teakie began tugging on her nipples ever so gently with his teeth. Gabby moaned uncontrollably until her orgasmic climax.

When she got there, she screamed in ecstasy. "Oh my god!"

Settled comfortably into the mattress, she motioned for Misty to come to her and said, "I've *got* to get me one of these."

"Misty's already got one," said Teakie, "so please take this one with you when you leave."

Gabby replied, "That's very kind of you, but leaving is the last thing on my mind right now. I'm just getting warmed up."

The girls turned their attention to Teakie. Working in tandem, they unbuttoned his Hawaiian shirt and pulled off his shorts, throwing them to the floor. Gabby held Teakie's attention with sweet, moist kisses as Misty removed his boxers, putting her face to face with his one-eyed bandit. Misty stole Teakie's attention away from Gabriella by taking him into her warm, wet mouth. She could feel his manhood become larger and harder with each head bob. Teakie's hips began to gyrate, so Misty quickened her pace. She became lost in the moment until he reached down and gently pulled her head off his massive unit. Teakie was't ready for his final curtain call. With only one bullet in his gun, he wanted to prolong the encounter. Teakie took back control, coaxing them on their backs side by side. Once in place he leaned in and gave each girl a sensual kiss before moving into position.

On his knees, facing the girls, Teakie softly rubbed their tummies until they were completely relaxed. He slowly moved his hands down to their pubic hair, drawing circular patterns with his fingertips. His soft, playful motions caused the girls to draw their knees into the air, fully exposing their womanhood. They watched in approval as Teakie coated his powerful hands with lubricant. The sight of his thick, perfectly manicured fingers glistening with gel heightened the girls' expectations to the point of frenzy. He rubbed his hands together in slow, precise movements, like a skilled surgeon preparing for a delicate operation. As they opened their legs wide to coax his fingers toward them, Teakie rubbed the lotion over their inner thighs and continued rubbing until every inch of their privates was drenched in the oily liquid. The feel of his slippery hands was so calming they closed their eyes and drifted into a state of semiconsciousness.

Their tranquility was interrupted by the feel of thick fingers penetrating their sacred hollows. Careful not to cause any discomfort, Teakie backed off and gently massaged their swollen clitorises with the tips of his fingers. Gabriella opened her eyes to the sight of Misty's fully exposed breasts expanding and contracting with each breath she took. It made her mouth water. Noticing the attention, Misty rolled her upper torso toward her friend until they were face to face. As they dreamily gazed into each other's eyes, Misty realized how special it was to share her moment of bliss with her best friend.

Once deep inside the girls, the tips of his fingers skillfully located their G-spots, causing them to abandon their infatuation with each other and return focus to their own bodies. They ground their hips in a circular motion to enhance the experience. Misty found it difficult to take her eyes off Teakie's massive, well-defined pecs. They flexed and rippled with each powerful thrust of his fingers. Nothing turned Misty on more than a well-developed body, and Teakie's upper torso was as beautiful as any Chippendale performer's.

Sensing massive climaxes were on their way, the girls twisted their bodies in an effort to witness each other's facial expressions during lift-off. Gabriella erupted first. Misty watched as her eyes rolled back in her head and her mouth opened wide. Seeing her friend writhing in ecstasy quickened Misty's own orgasmic ascent and caused her to wildly roll her head about the pillow, anticipating her own climax to come. And it was magnificent.

Dripping with sweat, Misty looked at Teakie with crazed eyes and said, "What do you plan to do to us next?"

Teakie replied, "Next! This is the first time I've been with two women. You tell me."

The girls were raring to go, but they struggled to come up with the next move. Misty broke the stalemate. She rolled on top of Gabriella and gazed into her eyes. From Gabby's vantage point Misty's dangling, seductive breasts resembled low-hanging fruit. Her locks of golden hair gently tickled Gabby's nose. From Teakie's perspective, Misty's rear stood a foot in front of his nose, calling him to action. But just as he was about to mount Misty, he noticed how enticing and vulnerable Gabriella looked with knees bent and legs spread apart.

"Hurry up, Teakie!" Misty moaned. "It's time to choose, dammit!"

Misty felt his massive member penetrating her moist pussy from the rear. Had he not chosen the correct orifice she would have rolled over and smacked him. She braced herself as he forcefully rammed her from behind. With every thrust, her melons swayed to and fro, giving Gabriella a delightful show. Misty's moans so stimulated Gabriella that she instinctively raised her head and suckled Misty's breasts. The combination of Teakie's pile-driving penis and the titillation of her nipples from Gabriella's warm mouth caused Misty to erupt with her second full-blown orgasm.

A still-hard Teakie turned his attention to Gabriella. Cupping her tight little butt cheeks with his hands for leverage, he positioned himself for his next assault. Gabby anxiously awaited his thrust. Teakie removed his right hand and guided the tip of his big unit slowly into her crevasse. She felt the head of his penis move around her entrance in slow circular motions. Her fully stretched lips gave way, allowing him to slowly thrust deeper and deeper until hitting bottom. No one had ever so completely filled her. Teakie replaced his right hand under her butt and began driving in and out of Gabriella at a faster and faster pace.

The power with which he drove intimidated Gabriella at first, but the intimidation soon gave way to pure ecstasy. With each thrust, Teakie's chest pounded into Misty's rear, forcing her forward. Knowing how much Gabriella loved her bosoms, Misty lowered them onto Gabriella's face. She wrapped her arms around Gabriella's shoulders and held her tight, being careful not to smother her When the final moment arrived, Misty heard Gabby's muffled moans of pleasure emanating from beneath her own bosoms as she held her girlfriend tightly in her arms. Once the orgasm subsided, Misty continued to hold Gabriella tight as Teakie resumed his quest for his own, well-deserved orgasm. The girls heard his deep groans of pleasure, realizing he had come. Teakie collapsed onto the bed next to the girls. Too tired to speak, they huddled together on the bed. A few moments later, Teakie reached up and turned off the lamp. They fell fast asleep.

* * *

Misty awoke in the early morning and noticed Gabriella and Teakie missing. At first she didn't think anything of it, but then, against her better judgment, she felt a twinge of jealousy. She rose from the bed, wrapped a sheet around her, and walked into the main room. Misty looked onto the balcony and saw a disturbing sight—so disturbing it brought back horrible memories of being chased by the European drug cartel in London.

She drew closer to the balcony to make sure her eyes were not deceiving her. They weren't. There, Teakie and Gabriella stood precariously on the balcony railing, eight stories above the ground. Teakie's hands firmly gripped Gabby's throat in a choke hold. Misty wanted to scream but held it in, fearing she might startle them and cause them to plummet from the balcony to their demise. Petrified and disoriented, she bumped into a vase, which crashed to the floor. Teakie turned his gaze to Misty. She was now a witness and Teakie knew it. Glaring at her with crazed eyes, he broke into a bloodcurdling laugh before falling over the balcony with Gabriella in his arms.

Misty screamed uncontrollably.

3

AUNTIE EM

"Misty! Misty! Misty!" Gabriella's voice was unmistakable, but how could she have survived the fall?

"Gabriella!" Misty yelled at the top of her lungs.

Gabriella shook her vigorously. "Wake up, Misty! Wake up! You're having a bad dream."

Bad dream? This was all just a bad dream? Misty thought.

She opened her eyes and saw Gabriella looking at her with concern. Misty latched on to Gabriella and held her tight, her sweat-soaked nightgown sticking to her body as drops of sweat rolled down her face.

"Oh Gabby, I was so scared. I thought you were dead! Can you believe that? I thought you fell eight stories to your death!"

"Of course I'm not dead, Misty. I'm right here with you. You were just having a nightmare."

Gabby gently stroked Misty's hair while rocking her from side to side. Misty was relieved she had dreamed the whole sequence of events, but she marveled at how real it still seemed to her. As she looked around, she saw the familiar features of her bedroom, and it all came back: she was still in Buenos Aires, on an extended stay at Gabriella's estate.

After Misty gave her friend every juicy detail, Gabriella said, "Well! You have quite the imagination, dear. I'd say we have a pretty exciting blueprint for one wild evening. Now if we can only find a man as fabulous as your imaginary friend."

After the girls had a good chuckle, Gabriella stood up. "Why don't you take a nice hot shower, and I'll have Annabel fix you breakfast? I'll start a pot of coffee."

Over breakfast, Gabriella kept the conversation light, joking with Misty as much as possible. Misty laughed between large bites of pancakes.

"I must've been famished. Could Annabel bring some more bacon?"

Tom, Gabriella's chauffeur, walked into the dining room with Miguel, Misty's bodyguard.

Gabriella winked at Misty. "Do you remember these guys?"

Misty caught Gabby's gist and responded, "Why yes, he's the tin man, he's the scarecrow, and you're Auntie Em. But please tell me this isn't Kansas."

Gabby laughed while the boys stood there scratching their heads. "What the heck was that all about?" Miguel said. "You guys watch *The Wizard of Oz* last night?"

The girls shared a smile but did not reveal their little secret.

"You said last week you were ready to take on a new client," Gabriella said to Misty. "Do you still feel that way?"

Anxious to get back on the road, Miguel jumped in. "You're not thinking about backing out, are you Misty? If you delay much longer your list of potential clients will dry up, and you might not be able to command those outrageous fees you charge."

"Outrageous fees!" said Misty. "I'm worth every penny of that money, buster, and you better not forget it." And she knew she was worth it. She was the Black Widow Trainer. Her clients were wealthy, and they paid handsomely for her training sessions at the gym—and for the promise of the one and only sexual encounter guaranteed in the contract they signed with her. And lately, her job seemed to consistently get her in dangerous situations, which was why this rest at Gabriella's Argentinean estate had been so welcome.

"Ouch!" said Miguel, noticing that Misty had become solemn. "Struck a nerve, didn't I? It's good to see you get some color back in your cheeks. I think you *are* ready to hit the road. Now that the divorce has been finalized, you can really woo those clients of yours. Heck, take on another woman client like Gabriella and I'll help you."

Miguel leaned in and attempted to grab a piece of bacon off Misty's plate, but she playfully slapped his hand.

Gabriella's face became serious. "Do you really think you're ready to take on another client after that crazy dream last night?"

"I'll go stir-crazy if I don't get back to work, Gabby, you know that. The fact that I dreamed about The Man could mean I'm ready. Remember, the real Man is responsible for setting things in motion for me to become the Black Widow Trainer." Misty added, "Besides, I haven't had a man in months."

Gabriella winked at her. "I haven't either. Maybe it's time for both of us to take advantage of the weaker sex."

Miguel and Tom both rolled their eyes.

After Gabriella took a sip of coffee, her tone regained its solemnity. "Promise you'll let me choose your next client. I would like to make sure they are properly vetted. Your last assignment in London almost got you killed. Let's make sure that doesn't happen again."

Misty replied, "Oh, okay. Go ahead and act like my mother."

"You know I'm only looking out for your safety, dear."

"I know, Gabriella. I'm teasing. I appreciate your concern and accept your offer. But *please* don't make him too dull."

4

YEE HAW!

Flying high above the Gulf of Mexico to a destination unknown, Misty turned to her bodyguard. "Come on Migs, open it, Gabby won't know."

"Hey, you promised Gabriella you would wait until five o'clock."

"Miguel, it's already four thirty-four. Aren't you dying to find out who our next client is?"

"Okay, okay. I guess Gabby will never know."

Miguel pulled down the tray in front of him and did a drum roll with his fingers. Putting the envelope to his forehead, he said, "I am Carnac the Magnificent and our ultimate destination is . . . Podunk, USA!"

Misty unsuccessfully tried to rip the envelope from Miguel's hand.

Miguel turned away, holding the envelope securely out of her reach. "Hey, if you don't stop I'm going to make you wait until five."

Misty placed her hands under her armpits, dropped her chin, and looked at Miguel with a protruding bottom lip. Miguel laughed before ripping open the envelope.

Miguel's eyes lit up as he read the first paragraph. "Yee haw! We're going to San Antone!"

"San Antonio, Texas?"

"Yes ma'am. We'll be deep in the heart of Texas."

"That sounds interesting, but just don't start singing that song. Go on, keep reading, Migs. Who's my new client?"

Miguel crinkled his nose. "Mr. Naples?"

"So what does Mr. Naples do?"

"It says he owns a manufacturing plant."

"A manufacturing plant? What exactly do they manufacture?"

Miguel read a little further and then handed the letter over to Misty. "Excuse me, Misty. I need to visit the lavatory."

As Miguel was closing the bathroom door, Misty let out a shriek. Safely inside, he waited for her to cool off.

After a couple of minutes, Miguel returned to find Misty staring out the window. He attempted to settle in without her noticing, to no avail. She whipped around and waved the letter wadded in her right fist at him.

"Do you realize he manufactures frickin' *toilets*! Oh, I'm sure Mr. Naples is a real winner."

Miguel knew better but couldn't help himself.

"Hey, do you think his first name is John? That means one of these nights you could literally be sitting on the John."

"Very funny, Miguel." Misty then reverted to staring out the window.

Misty and Miguel didn't get into San Antonio until almost eleven o'clock that evening. Luckily, the airport was small. The limo driver was there waiting for them, and the trip to downtown San Antonio was a short one. They arrived at their hotel, and after checking in, quickly went to their respective rooms for a good night's sleep.

5

MIXED EMOTIONS

Misty felt terrific when she awoke the next morning. The seven-layer bed, with Egyptian linen sheets and king-sized pillows, made for a wonderful night's sleep. Relieved she had made it through the night without another nightmare, Misty now hoped Mr. Naples wouldn't turn out to be a living nightmare. A further inspection of her 750-square-foot suite revealed stained ebony hardwood floors, white marble in the bathroom, and a separate sitting area. She moved one of the down-stuffed leather chairs onto the balcony and sat admiring her wonderful view of the Riverwalk.

Mid-morning, Miguel joined Misty and they waited to be picked up in front of the hotel. When the limo arrived, the driver stepped out and opened the back door. Inside, they found a young woman in her late twenties. Her brown hair was pinned in a bun, and she wore large quirky glasses and business attire.

The girl greeted them in a friendly but professional manner. "Hi, I'm Stephanie, Mr. Naples's assistant. I trust you found the accommodations to your liking."

Misty took her time looking the woman over before replying. "Yes we did, thank you. I had a wonderful night's sleep. How about you, Miguel?"

More interested in his surroundings than the conversation, Miguel responded, "Yeah, sure. *Great* night's sleep."

"Good," said Stephanie. "I hope you don't mind, but Mr. Naples is a very busy man, so he sent me to be at your service. I'll coordinate everything from scheduling your workout sessions to helping you figure out what to do on your time off."

The last part got Miguel's attention.

"So you can help me find some authentic cowboy boots and a big ol' cowboy hat?"

"Sure, I'd be happy to. Give me time to do a little research first. Most of the real cowboys live in the smaller towns surrounding San Antonio, but I'm sure we can find what you need in town."

"I don't mind venturing out to rural Texas if we need to," said Miguel.

"If you think you might enjoy seeing the Texas hill country, Mr. Naples owns an exotic game ranch several hours west of San Antonio. The wild game ranch started out as a cattle ranch in the eighteen hundreds. Every year they drove the longhorn cattle to market in Kansas. The ranch still holds old-fashioned cattle drives. You'll want to go on one if you're into that kind of thing. Of course you would be in a saddle all day."

"Whoa there, sweetheart! I didn't say anything about riding a horse. Only want to look like a cowboy, not be one."

Misty patted Stephanie on the knee. "The only heifers GQ Cowboy there is interested in are the two-legged sort."

Stephanie gave Miguel a curious look as he stared out the window. It wasn't long before they pulled up to the South Texas Athletic Club. Once inside, Stephanie took Misty on a thorough tour of the facilities. The club was complete with a lap pool, a basketball court, racquetball courts, and two weight areas, and Misty felt it was adequate for their needs. She would wait to meet Mr. Naples before assessing whether she would have him use the free-weight area or the weight machines. She and Stephanie finished their tour at the basketball court, where Miguel was shooting baskets. All she could do now was chill out and wait for toilet man to show.

Misty looked at her watch. "Is your boss usually this late?"

Looking slightly embarrassed, Stephanie replied, "Yes, I'm afraid so. Mr. Naples gets a little self-absorbed at times." Stephanie quickly tried to retract the statement. "Oh, I didn't really mean to say self-absorbed. I meant . . . well, ah."

"Honey, its okay to level with me," said Misty. "I would never tell your boss. I can assure you everything you say will be held in the strictest confidence. Look, you and I are going to be joined at the hip for the next three months, so we need to become comfortable with each other. Maybe you, Miguel, and I can tour the Riverwalk this weekend. Bring your husband if you like."

"I'd love to show you downtown San Antonio! But I don't have a husband . . . or a boyfriend."

"Great! It'll just be the three of us, then."

They began discussing their weekend plans, but soon Misty noticed Stephanie pulling back into her shell.

Turning in the direction of Stephanie's gaze, she immediately understood why.

Oh my god, that can't be him, she thought.

A long and lanky man was walking toward them with a lively gait. His beady little eyes and greasy, slicked-back hair made Misty's stomach churn.

If this is him, god help me!

Misty cringed as they shared a limp handshake. Known for her upbeat mood and take-charge attitude, she suddenly found herself completely out of character. She couldn't believe she'd have to spend three months with this guy. Part of her hoped he'd give up in the first week and give in to the temptation of his one allotted encounter with her—thus ending their relationship, as specified in the contract. But something told her he'd wait till the end of their time together to claim his prize.

Noticing her change in demeanor, Miguel dropped his basketball and walked briskly to her aid. "What's up, Misty?" he asked, looking concerned.

"Oh Miguel, I'm glad you came over. Meet our new client, Mr. Naples."

Miguel shook Mr. Naples's hand with authority, letting him know he had plenty of strength if called upon.

"Nice handshake, Miguel," said Mr. Naples. "I assume you're Misty's bodyguard?"

"Yes sir. I've been Misty's bodyguard for going on four years now. Her safety is my utmost priority."

Mr. Naples redirected his attention to Misty.

"So this is the renowned trainer I keep hearing about. I hope you're as good a trainer as you are pretty."

Misty gave him a half smile, but was unable to keep from looking like she smelled something rancid. Mr. Naples didn't pick up on her trepidation, and before she knew it he had walked past her on his way to the workout area.

"Come on, honey. Let me show you my favorite exercise machines."

Misty walked after him, catching up quickly. "Now, you know I'm here to get you into excellent shape. It's not necessary to see your favorite machines—I'm going develop a routine you're not accustomed to. That's how you'll make the most progress."

Mr. Naples quickly turned to Misty. "Oh, I'm not that interested in getting in shape, honey," he whispered softly. "I'm more interested in you and your special talents, if you know what I mean." With a wink he added, "Why don't you call me Chester?"

Chester headed off, leaving Misty in his wake. Her hands became clammy, and she felt like she was going to puke. *When I get back to Argentina, I'm going to have my attorney do a better job stipulating my contractual obligations*, she thought. *I need to see about putting in an out clause.*

Although repulsed, Misty reminded herself not to do anything that would ruin her reputation. As Misty slowly walked toward the goofy bastard, she thought, *I know Gabriella was only trying to be protective of me, but I swear this is the last time I let her or anyone else select a client for me! But . . . once I sleep with him, I'm free to collect all my money and go home. I could be back in Buenos Aires in no time if I decide to seduce him.*

That thought only made Misty feel ill all over again.

Chester could now tell Misty didn't feel right. "Are you okay, honey? You sure look awful green around the gills. Maybe you picked up something on your flight."

"I don't think so, Chester. Give me a few minutes. I think it's just an upset stomach. I'm sure I'll be alright soon."

Misty bent over, her hands on her knees, and breathed in deeply as she tried to clear her head.

Chester said, "Excuse me for a minute, Misty. I need to spend a few minutes with Travis."

Curious, Misty lowered herself to a seat on the floor, propped herself against the wall, and eyed Chester's acquaintance up and down. Travis was ruggedly handsome, with long, dark brown hair pulled into a ponytail. His tight, navy blue short-sleeved shirt exposed a well-developed upper body. Thick, rounded shoulders, massive pecs, and triceps so ripped she could make out their V-shaped bulge from a distance. His tight-fitting Wrangler jeans were packed with powerful legs and anchored by two well-rounded buttocks. The jeans draped over his cowboy boots perfectly.

Misty couldn't wait to find out how this deliciously handsome man fit into the picture. Snapping herself out of her stupor, Misty popped up off the floor and walked in their direction with her usual confidence and enthusiasm. Travis's dark brown eyes lured Misty toward him. But to her consternation, Chester slapped Travis on the shoulder before she could get there and turned to walk back to the workout machines.

Damn it!

Chester patted Misty on her arm as he walked briskly past her.

"Come on, honey, let's pump some iron."

Before following, Misty took one more look at Travis's retreating figure.

When she returned to Chester, he was curling a whopping thirty pounds. Misty shook her head in disgust.

A seventh-grader could lift as much, she thought.

6

STEPHANIE TELLS ALL

On their way back to their hotel, Misty interrogated Stephanie about Travis.

"So who is that guy Mr. Naples was talking to at the club?"

Miguel raised his eyebrows and settled in for the conversation. He knew Misty's type, and the man fit the bill.

"Travis?" Stephanie said with a gleam in her eyes.

"Yeah, I think Chester did refer to him as Travis."

"Travis comes into town every Friday to go to lunch with Mr. Naples," said Stephanie.

"Why?" asked Misty.

"Travis is the foreman of Mr. Naples's ranch."

"Oh, I see," Misty replied. Wanting to keep the conversation about Travis going, she added, "He seems like a nice guy."

"Oh, yes!" Stephanie replied enthusiastically. "He's my favorite person in San Antonio. Travis is a honey. I used to love it when he came to our headquarters every week." With a quick giggle she added, "Every time Travis came in, the women in our office got so excited they were worthless the rest of the day. I think Mr. Naples figured it out, because he's been meeting Travis for lunch ever since."

Miguel couldn't help teasing Misty.

"Isn't this Travis guy kind of young?" he asked Stephanie.

Misty shot him a look.

Not understanding what Miguel was up to, she quickly responded, "Oh no, Miguel. Travis is six years older than I am. He's thirty-two."

Miguel said, "So he's a little young for the women in the office that are, oh, let's see, in their mid thirties?"

Misty glared at Miguel.

Still not ready to drop the topic, Misty said, "*Travis*. That sounds like a good South Texas name."

"It should be," said Stephanie. "His mother was a distant relative of William B. Travis, the Texas commander at the Battle of the Alamo."

Miguel's face lit up at the mention of the Alamo. "Will you take us to see the Alamo this weekend?"

Stephanie smiled. "Sure, Miguel. I'd be happy to."

After Stephanie had dropped them off at the hotel, Misty patted Miguel on the butt and said, "I think she's hot on you, guy."

"Don't worry, Misty. Stephanie's not my type."

"Why, because she's a nice girl?"

"Yeah, she's way too nice for me. And it sounds like Travis might be way too young for you."

Ignoring Miguel's comment, Misty headed toward her room.

7

TACOS, ANYONE?

On Saturday morning Miguel convinced Misty to join him at a local café for breakfast. He'd stayed up late the night before checking out the local women at the hotel bar. Now he was hungover and needed a big hot bowl of menudo to get him back on track.

Misty found the café colorful, yet plain. They took a seat at a table next to a large sombrero hanging on the wall. She noticed a couple of bowls of hot sauce in the middle of the table, one red and one green. She took a spoonful of one and dropped the red substance back into the bowl. She placed the spoon up to her nose and sniffed. It immediately cleared her sinus cavity. When the waitress finally got around to their table, Miguel said, "Give us one large bowl of menudo and . . . we need an assortment of breakfast tacos. Let's see, make it one potato and egg, one chorizo and egg, and one carne guisada. Oh, and lots of hot coffee."

"Would you like those on corn or flour tortillas?" the waitress asked.

Miguel looked at Misty. "I take her for more of a flour child than a corny girl."

"Come on Miguel," said Misty, "it's way too early for corny jokes. At least wait until I'm caffeinated."

While they waited for the food to arrive, Miguel explained the difference between the red and green hot sauce. He suggested she try the pico de gallo if the others were too hot. Misty played with the bowl of fresh tomatoes, onions, and green chilies with her spoon before declaring it the winner.

When the tacos arrived, Misty said, "Okay Miguel, guide me through this."

"Try the potato and egg taco first. At least you're familiar with the ingredients."

Misty dove in.

"Mmm, that's good. What's in this one? It looks like a . . . meaty stew."

"That's a pretty good description. That one's carne guisada—we're talking round steak in thick gravy spiced with cumin."

Misty smelled it and then took a small bite.

"Oh, that's really good. It's spicy, but not hot spicy. I guess I like cumin."

Miguel looked pleased. "Okay, now it's time for some spicy Mexican sausage."

She looked at the taco warily. "Why is it red and greasy?"

"It's seasoned with dry, smoked red peppers and chili powder."

She cautiously nibbled around the edges. "Not bad," she said. "It's edible. What's that you have? Soup?"

Pretty sure Misty wasn't ready to try menudo he said, "It is, and it's the perfect cure for a hangover. I'll tell you what, if you get a hangover, we'll come back and you can try some. Until then, you're better off leaving it alone."

Once he was halfway through his bowl, the menudo began to work on Miguel's stomach. He excused himself and headed to the restroom. Still curious about his soup, Misty used Miguel's spoon and pushed the ingredients around.

What the hell? she thought. *I've liked everything so far. I'll give it a try.*

She loaded the large spoon with soup and placed it in her mouth. Her mouth was instantly flooded with a horrible rancid taste. First, she tried to swallow the whole mouthful in an effort to get it over with, but when it caused her to choke, she spit it out. With no other option available, she ejected the vile substance back into Miguel's bowl.

A little old Hispanic man at the table next to them had been watching Misty intently. "Ma'am, are you okay?"

"I am now. I ate some of my friend's menudo. *Ugh!* I can't imagine what's in this stuff."

"Menudo is made with tripe," the man said matter-of-factly. "It usually comes from cows, but my mother sometimes used sheep, goat, pig, or deer tripe."

"What exactly is tripe?" asked Misty.

"It's the internal organs of a butchered animal." Noticing the horror in Misty's face, he quickly added, "Don't worry, the intestines are washed and thoroughly cleaned first. They only use unwashed intestines for dog food."

Misty practically knocked Miguel over as she passed him on her rush to the ladies room. Apologizing to the old man, Miguel followed her and placed his ear to the restroom door. The sound of Misty's vomiting was clear. Cracking the restroom door open, he yelled, "Are you okay? What's the matter?"

There was no response.

When she emerged from the restroom, Miguel asked her again. "What's the matter?"

Looking sternly at him, she replied, "What's the matter? I ate some of your menudo. And the old man sitting next to us told me what they put in it. Are you insane? How can you eat that crap?"

Miguel did everything he could to keep from laughing, but his facial expressions gave him away.

"Oh, go ahead and laugh, Miguel. I don't know why I agreed to come here with you in the first place. I should have known better."

By the time Miguel had paid the bill and exited the restaurant, Misty was already down the street, walking briskly back to the hotel. After a good little run he caught up to her.

"You know I told you specifically *not* to try the menudo today. Surely you can't blame me."

"Alright," she said. "Let's just forget all about it. Stephanie will be in the lobby at noon to take us on our tour. We should get ready."

Miguel knew better, but he couldn't control himself. "Okay Misty, but I've got a question for you. When you were face to face with the toilet, did you happen to notice if it was one of Mr. Naples'?"

Misty chased Miguel all the way back to the hotel.

8

STEPHANIE, TOUR GUIDE

Stephanie wandered through the hotel lobby until she came upon Misty and Miguel lounging on the most comfortable looking set of couches in the place. "How's your morning going, guys?" she said cheerily.

"Don't ask," said Misty.

Stephanie looked at Miguel for a clue, but all she got out of him was a shrug.

"So where would you guys like me to take you first? A boat tour of the Riverwalk? Or we could maybe eat lunch on a river barge tour and see the Alamo? Maybe the mall?"

"What kind of food do they serve on the barge?" asked Misty.

"Mexican food."

Misty raised her upper lip. "That's not going to happen. Is there some place more conventional?"

"We can go to a bistro known for their margaritas."

"A margarita sounds good," Misty replied. "Let's do that. We can plan the rest of the day from there."

"Works for me," said Miguel.

Misty and Miguel loved the margaritas, putting down three each.

Miguel, loosened up by the alcohol, noticed what Stephanie was wearing for the first time that day. Her shorts revealed nice, smooth legs and a cute little butt. Her T-shirt was stretched by her ample breasts. Stephanie's conservative business attire had not done her body justice.

After paying the bill, Miguel spoke out of nowhere. "Remember the Alamo!"

The girls both gave him funny looks. "I've always wanted to say that," he explained.

"Well, what are we waiting for? Let's go see it," said Misty.

When they reached the Alamo, Misty and Miguel couldn't believe how small it looked.

"What's up, Stephanie?" said Miguel. "The Alamo looks a lot bigger in the movies."

"Yes—that's what everyone says when they see it for the first time. It's kind of sad there isn't much left of the original compound."

As they got closer, Stephanie pointed out a long metal strip in the rock pavement, directly outside the two large, wooden chapel doors. "Rumor has it that William B. Travis drew a line in the sand here and asked the two hundred defenders of the Alamo to step across it if they were willing to stay and fight. Supposedly, all but one did."

Misty thought about the story for a moment. "That's the same William Travis that our Travis is related to, right?"

"Yes, he's part of Travis's mother's family tree and the reason his parents named him Travis."

At the end of the chapel tour, Misty said, "That was really fascinating, Stephanie. I don't think I've ever been so captivated by a historical event."

Miguel looked across the street. "Hey Stephanie, any history in that hotel bar over there? My margs are wearing off."

"Why yes, there is. It was built in the eighteen hundreds, and the legend is the hotel is haunted."

"Cool, let's go meet some ghosts," said Miguel.

Once they had bellied up to the 150-year-old bar and Misty caught the bartender's attention, she asked his name.

The large, gregarious-looking man replied, "Bob."

"You been working here a while, Bob?"

"Yep."

"Good. Can you introduce us to some ghosts?"

"Not sure if any are here today, but I can try."

"Well then, tell us about the ones you know about."

"Well, let's see. There's the maid, for one. Her husband murdered her on the second floor. People see her roaming the halls on a regular basis. And then there's the lady who shows up for dinner from time to time."

Bob nodded toward some tables in the back of the bar. "Some folks say old soldiers from the Alamo hang out at those tables. I've never seen them, but I've talked to plenty of people who have."

Miguel noticed the large portrait behind the bar. "Isn't that Teddy Roosevelt?" he asked.

"Yes sir. The Rough Riders had a camp in San Antonio around eighteen ninety-eight, I believe. They say Teddy was a regular here when he was recruiting."

Miguel looked fascinated. "What did the bar look like back in eighteen ninety-eight?"

"Actually, most of what you see are original fixtures, if you can believe that. The bar you're sitting at, the fancy ceiling, and all of the wood on the walls are original furnishings. Everything except the chairs."

After enjoying a few drinks, the group left the bar and spent a while exploring the mall on the river. On their way back to the hotel, Miguel insisted on stopping at a local piano bar. Inside, two guys were playing dueling pianos and singing. They stayed for one drink before deciding to head back to the hotel.

Inside the lobby, Misty gave Stephanie a big hug. "Today was fantastic! Thank you so much for showing us around. You're a dear."

Stephanie beamed. "You're so welcome, Misty. I had a great time as well. Good-bye you two!"

Miguel watched Stephanie on her way to the front door. Before she got outside, he yelled out, "Catch you at the club next week, Steph!"

Stephanie turned and gave him a big smile.

Misty patted Miguel on the shoulder. "That girl likes you, dude."

Placing her right index finger on his nose, she added, "Don't even think about taking advantage of that sweet thing."

As Misty walked off, Miguel turned the palms of his hands up and lifted his shoulders. "What! I'll be nice to her!"

9

Back at the Gym

Monday and Wednesday's training sessions with Chester were boring. Chester loved to talk about himself, and Misty did little but repeat "Uh huh" and "Yeah" constantly. By the end of each session she couldn't remember a word he'd said. On Friday morning, Misty kept one eye on Chester and the other fixed on the door. To Misty's surprise, Travis was wearing workout clothes when he showed up.

"So you finally decided to use the membership I gave you?" Chester shouted to him as he approached.

"I've been meaning to for a while now," said Travis, giving Misty a slight nod of acknowledgment.

When Travis headed to the free weights, Misty asked Chester, "So what are you and Travis going to talk about at lunch today?"

"I need to know how preparations are coming along for the fifty Japanese executives we'll be entertaining this weekend. There's a big hunt Saturday morning and meetings in our conference center in the afternoon. We wrap things up with a big party in the saloon after dinner."

It suddenly dawned on Misty: she stood a better chance of getting to know Travis at the ranch than here at the club. She needed an invite.

Springing into action, Misty stepped into Chester's space, taking him by surprise. Only inches away from him, she looked up, making eye contact in a very provocative way. "I think it's so cool you have a game ranch. There must be a side to you I don't get to see at the club." Batting her eyes, she continued. "Why haven't you invited me out to see it?"

Beads of sweat formed on Chester's brow as he measured his response. "When would you like to visit?"

"What's wrong with this weekend?"

"This weekend! But I told you the ranch will be teeming with Japanese businessmen."

Not wavering, Misty replied, "So?"

Chester looked cautious, but she could tell he was warming up to the idea. She held eye contact with him and waited.

"Okay Misty, you can come this weekend, but I need to give you one more piece of information before you decide to come. What I am about to tell you is very confidential, so you have to promise me you won't tell anyone."

Her eyes still locked on their target, Misty said, "I promise."

Chester's eyes darted back and forth. "There's going to be dozens of call girls from Vegas. My clients insisted, you know. Is that a problem?"

"No problem at all. What time should Miguel and I show up?"

Chester sighed in relief. "I'll have Stephanie pick you up tomorrow at noon." Scratching the back of his neck, he added, "I'm not sure if you'll get a chance to meet my wife, but if you do, you can't say anything about the call girls."

Misty placed two pinched fingers over the left side of her mouth and then ran them across to the right side, indicating that her lips were sealed.

With that settled, they resumed their workout. Misty's wandering eyes located Travis, and she marveled at his physique. Oh what she would give to be his personal trainer. At the end of the training session, Chester headed toward the showers and Misty followed. Passing the entrance to the free-weight room, Chester motioned to Travis. He immediately got up from the bench and followed, locking eyes with Misty as he passed by.

Misty's eyes sent a clear message: *You're in my crosshairs now, handsome. It's only a matter of time.*

10

OFF TO THE RANCH

Late Saturday morning, Misty, Miguel, and Stephanie were relaxing in the limo as it headed down Interstate 10 on the way to the ranch. After nearly an hour of small talk, Misty asked Stephanie, "So how did Travis become foreman?"

"You'd better settle in. This is a long story," she replied.

"Go ahead, Stephanie. I'm all ears."

"Well, Travis lost his parents when he was six years old. His Uncle Bud, who was running the ranch at the time, took him in and raised him as a son. They lived on two hundred and fifty acres adjacent to the ranch. Travis loved helping his uncle on weekends and wanted to follow in his footsteps, but Uncle Bud insisted that Travis use his parents' life insurance money to get a good education. Travis was a sharp kid and worked hard enough to make it into the University of Texas's business school. He graduated at the top of his class and took a job with Excelsior Investments in New York. After seven years, things were going well. Excelsior told him he would make partner soon, so he asked his girlfriend to marry him. Emily was thrilled.

"A week later Emily came over to his loft in tears and broke the news that her father was not happy she wanted to marry a Texas boy. He'd told her there were plenty of young men with Ivy League diplomas from well-to-do East Coast families and that she should wait. Emily had her heart set on Travis and tried to talk him into eloping. Travis considered it at first, but later that night realized it would be selfish of him to come between Emily and her family. She disagreed vehemently, and got really angry with Travis."

Stephanie gathered herself before continuing. "As if things weren't bad enough, Travis received a phone call from Mr. Naples saying his uncle had passed away in the night from a heart attack. Travis caught the next plane out of La Guardia for San Antonio and never looked back. Once his uncle's funeral was over, he asked Mr. Naples if he could take over as foreman of the ranch. Mr. Naples accepted. Travis stepped down from Excelsior Investments that day."

Having lost her own parents in a car crash when she was not much older than Travis, Misty at first thought she knew how he must have felt. But then she realized he also lost both his lover and father figure in a matter of days, and it touched her deeply. The group traveled the next fifty miles in silence.

After passing through the front gate of the ranch, they wove their way down a narrow, winding road for another six miles until arriving at the ranch resort. The old rustic cabins surrounding the conference center made Misty feel like she had traveled back in time to the Old West. Once they'd gotten out and stretched, a ranch hand escorted them to their room. The family suite Mr. Naples put them up in had one bedroom with a large single bed and a second bedroom with two bunk beds.

"I get dibs on the big bed!" Miguel shouted.

"No way, José," said Misty, only half joking. "I'm the adult here."

"You expect me to bunk with Stephanie?"

Misty winked at Stephanie. "Why not? It has separate beds."

"Okay," said Miguel, "but I have to warn you. I sleep in the buff, and I plan on doing some drinking this weekend. That means trips to the bathroom in the middle of the night."

"Then I suggest you not sleep in the top bunk," said Misty.

After settling in, Misty decided to go for a long run. Miguel and Stephanie chose to explore the resort, first checking out where the party was to be held. The walls of the saloon were wood, giving the space a rustic feel. The only distinguishing features were a bar that ran along one side of the room and all the animal heads mounted on the walls. Miguel counted over one hundred animal heads, which seemed like overkill to him. The place was perfect for hunters but not much else. An old stagecoach sat outside the saloon. Climbing in the cramped quarters, they marveled at how small people must have been in the old days. From there they walked over to a swimming pool situated on the edge of a cliff. The poolside view was spectacular, allowing them to look out over a large section of the ranch.

"Wow!" said Miguel. "That's an incredible view. What kind of animals are those?" He pointed at a large axis deer.

"There's no telling. The ranch is stocked with exotic game from all over the world. There are antelope from Africa, axis deer, zebra, elk, gazelles, water buffalo, and all types of game indigenous to South Texas. The ranch is a wildlife preserve, you know."

"Man, it's really getting hot," said Miguel. "Why don't we take our shoes off and soak our feet in the pool?"

Stephanie smiled and immediately took off her shoes. The spring-fed pool was cool and refreshing even though they were approaching the hottest part of the day. Stephanie playfully splashed her feet. For the first time since they arrived, Miguel took a good look at her face.

"Hey, where's your glasses, girl?" he said.

Stephanie blushed. "Oh, I don't normally wear them. My eyes were irritated last week, so I dug up those old glasses. They're really outdated, but they're the only pair I have. My eyes are fine now."

Miguel couldn't help but imagine what Stephanie looked like with her hair down. Leaning over, he gently pulled out her hair clip, allowing the long, shiny brown hair to fall softly over her shoulders. Stephanie shook her hair from side to side and then ran her fingers through to free any knots. Miguel was stunned by the transformation; she was indeed a sweet young thing. For the next hour, they sat and got better acquainted, their feet splashing in the pool.

11

MISTY'S MIDDAY RUN

After running the six miles to the front gate, Misty was now on her way back. She hadn't realized how hot the South Texas sun could be in the middle of summer; if she had, she would have brought along plenty of water. Knowing the risk of heat stroke in conditions like these, she slowed to a walk. Although hot and thirsty, she chose not to dwell on her predicament. Instead, she enjoyed the tranquility of being secluded in the country and let her mind wander at will.

Misty was startled by some rustling in the brush close by but quickly settled down once she saw the culprit, a cute little pig that couldn't have been over a month old. Misty walked in its direction.. *I wonder if he'll let me pet him*, she thought.

As soon as Misty laid a hand on him, the piglet let out a series of loud squeals. Then, the entire litter came out of the brush not more than twenty yards away. Finally, an ugly, two-hundred-pound male razorback emerged from the brush. She instantly fixed her sights on his nine-inch tusks. Immediately in fight-or-flight mode, she chose the latter and bolted.

Within seconds she was being followed by a ferocious, mean, and totally pissed-off razorback. Off the main highway now and flying through the underbrush, her mind turned to the night she had been chased by the European drug dealers in London. Being in the crosshairs of a snorting and squealing wild boar seemed just as terrifying. Her central nervous system was being put to the test. Misty briefly looked up from her zigzag course through the brush long enough to spot a ranch house not too far ahead. She set a course for the front door. Her lungs burning and her throat parched, Misty felt like she was running through a blast furnace in the hundred-degree heat. Too frightened to look back, she concentrated on dodging the small brush and cactus plants in her path to the building. But when the seriousness of the situation sunk in, Misty wondered if she could make the house before being overtaken by the beast.

It felt like it was only a matter of time before the horrible creature on her tail struck her down, but just as she was about to give up, she heard a voice in the distance yelling, "Jump into the water tank—now!"

When she located where the voice was coming from, she saw a man pointing to a round water tank underneath an old windmill. It sat to her left only thirty feet away. Misty attempted to change directions on the fly. As she did, the razorback clipped her trailing leg, causing her to fall on a cactus plant. The pain from the cactus was excruciating. Luckily, a rush of adrenaline shot through her body and she sprang to her feet.

Misty reached her target and flung herself over the side, seconds before the boar rammed into the side of the tank. Now totally submerged in water, she lay motionless at the bottom. Exhausted and afraid, the pleasant feeling of cool water on her overheated body kept her at the bottom of the pool until her burning lungs cried out for air. She exploded to the surface, sucking in hot South Texas air until her breathing returned to normal. Just as she was regaining her composure, Misty was shocked by the sound of a big splash behind her in the water tank. *Surely the boar couldn't have jumped that high*, she thought.

In her current state of mind, Misty found it difficult to discern fact from fiction. When she felt something grab her arms, she let out a scream. Misty found herself in the arms of a man who was naked from the waist up. His dripping wet and extremely tanned upper torso glistened in the sunlight. His ruggedly handsome face reminded her of the

Marlboro Man. Once she shaded her eyes, she realized it was Travis. Having traveled to the ranch expressly to run into Travis, she was now in his arms with his full, undivided attention. She couldn't have planned it any better if she tried.

"Are you okay?" Travis asked, sincere concern in his eyes.

"Yes, I think so," Misty replied. But then she felt the dull pain emanating from the cactus needles in her side and grimaced. Looking down to assess the damage, Misty was horrified to see her wet jogging shirt stuck to her bra-less chest like cellophane. Realizing the predicament she was in, Misty quickly covered up her bosoms with her arms. He effortlessly lifted her over the side of the water tank and carried her back toward the ranch house, not setting her down until he'd gotten through the front door and laid her on his own bed. He abruptly left the room before returning with an ice-cold bottle of Gatorade. He held it out toward Misty, but she kept her hands tucked under her armpits.

It dawned on Travis what she was doing. "I'm sorry . . . I don't know what I was thinking," he said. He grabbed a small blanket folded at the end of the bed and covered her with it.

With her boobs safe from wandering eyes, Misty sheepishly reached out from under the blanket and latched on to the Gatorade, gulping half of it down in one go.

"I'll draw you a cool tub of water," said Travis. "Let's get you cooled down before we attend to your scrapes and bruises."

"And the cactus needles in my right side?"

Travis shook his head as he smiled.

"You're a mess aren't you? Here, let me take a look."

Misty lifted the blanket so he could inspect her side. Travis counted no fewer than fifteen needles sticking out of her shirt.

"You are one tough woman," he remarked. "That has to hurt."

Misty decided to play the "poor pitiful me" card, so she gave Travis the look of a damsel in distress. "I'm not that tough. Those needles are killing me."

"I'll get the tweezers and be right back."

When he returned, she watched his every movement as he meticulously pulled the needles out one by one. By the time he was finished, she had memorized all his features. Being attracted to a younger man was a new experience, but an exciting one. She now wanted him more than ever.

Travis looked up from his work. "Okay, that was the last one. I'll go fill the tub now. When you're done, come out to the kitchen and I'll take care of those scrapes."

"But what am I going to wear?"

Travis walked over to his closet, took out his robe, and laid it on the bed. "Here, you can use my robe. Once I leave, take off your outfit and throw it out the door. I'll wash and dry it while you're soaking in the tub. If you get through before your outfit dries, you can wear my robe to the kitchen."

After getting the water in the tub going, Travis returned to the bedroom to find Misty holding out her outfit while still wrapped in the blanket.

Taking her clothes, he left the room with a simple "Thanks."

Misty tiptoed over and locked the door. After folding the blanket and placing it at the end of his bed, she picked up his bathrobe and brought it to her nose. She could tell it had been worn a few times, but that's what she'd hoped for. She now knew what he would smell like in bed. Misty put his bathrobe on and tied it low at the waist, allowing the front of the robe to hang open, she looked in the mirror and wondered what would happen if she joined Travis in the kitchen with her two luscious breasts hanging out. The thought gave her a thrill. Feeling secure in the fact any noise she made would be covered up by the sound of the running water, she decided to do a little snooping. When she opened the closet, her mouth fell open. There must have been a dozen high-quality hand-made suits accompanied by silky white shirts, slick leather belts, and a wide assortment of ties. Misty tried to imagine how handsome Travis would look in one of his suits and a stylish haircut.

Through with her fun and games, she disrobed and slid into the tub. From her new vantage point she noticed the warm and inviting atmosphere created by the knotty pine walls. It felt manly, just like Travis.

After toweling off and putting his bathrobe back on, Misty pulled open the top dresser drawer and took a quick look. Inside she found a BlackBerry still sheathed in a fancy leather case.

I've got to get his number, she thought. *If we start texting, we can get to know each other a little more each day.*

"Is Doctor Travis in the house?" said Misty as she poked her head into the kitchen.

"Hey, don't laugh," he replied. "I got scraped up all the time growing up. I'm pretty handy when it comes to cuts and scrapes."

Travis dressed Misty's superficial wounds and then got her running outfit out of the dryer. "Here you go," he said, handing her the warm clothes. "Go put them on and I'll drive you back to your cabin."

Misty said, "You can drive me back after you shoot the wild hog that chased me."

Travis gave her a funny look and laughed out loud. "Shoot that wild hog! I would never shoot George."

"George! That horrible thing has a name?"

"George has been living out here for over fifteen years. He's part of the family."

"You let a killer hog live on your property?"

"What are you talking about? His job is to protect the litter. There is no way he attacked you unless you messed with them."

I don't care if he is a hunk, thought Misty. *I can't believe he's taking a wild hog's side over mine."*

Not wanting to say something she would regret, Misty walked briskly to the door and shot a look back at Travis. "Well? Come on. You said you'd take me back."

Thinking that Misty was quite cute when mad, Travis did his best to keep a straight face during the quiet ride back to the cabins. When they arrived, she got out of the truck without saying a word. Travis pulled away and never looked back. She felt ridiculous when she looked down and realized she was still in his robe.

12

THE BAR

Misty, Miguel, and Stephanie finished dinner at the steak house located at the resort and prepared to head over to the saloon. Misty's body ached from her harrowing experience with the wild boar, and if it hadn't been for the opportunity to see Travis, she would have elected to retire early and read a good book in the cabin. Instead, she popped a couple of Vicodin and joined Miguel and Stephanie on the walk over to the saloon. All she could think about was the ride to her cabin with Travis. *I can't believe how I reacted this afternoon. I should have at least thanked him for possibly saving my life. Hopefully I'll get a chance to make amends tonight.*

As they entered the saloon, Miguel said, "So where are we going to sit? This place is packed." Japanese businessmen crowded around nearly every table.

Stephanie took charge. "There's Mr. Naples in the back of the bar. Let's find out where he'd like us to sit."

"Sounds like a plan," said Misty.

Never bashful, Misty led the small procession through the maze of Japanese men as if parting the Red Sea. All eyes were on Misty.

Chester was engaged in conversation with a distinguished-looking silver-haired Japanese man, and he looked up once he noticed them standing there. "Well, I see the three of you made it. Have you been here long?"

"Not long," said Stephanie. "Is there anywhere in particular you'd like us to sit?"

The Japanese businessman stepped forward and bowed to Misty. She gave a half nod while looking around for guidance.

"How thoughtless of me," said Chester apologetically. "Mr. Yoshimoto, I would like to introduce you to my assistant, Stephanie, and my guests Misty and Miguel."

The businessman looked Misty over thoroughly before requesting that Chester step away for a short conversation. Misty could see Chester shake his head emphatically. When the conversation ended, Chester rejoined the group as Mr. Yoshimoto walked off.

Addressing Misty, Chester said, "Mr. Yoshimoto wanted to know if you were one of the girls from Vegas. I assured him you were nothing of the sort."

"Well, thanks for setting him straight, Chester," said Misty.

"No problem. Look, why don't the three of you sit at the reserved table by the bar. I'll come by if I get a chance."

Misty leaned toward Miguel and whispered, "Hopefully not."

As Miguel ordered drinks, Misty kicked herself for not finding out Travis's schedule on the ride back to the resort. But of course that would have entailed speaking to him, and she'd been too angry to do that.

Soon, the hired women came busting through the front door, and the noise level went up several decibels. There were blondes, brunettes, redheads, and even one purple-haired woman. The hookers quickly surveyed the bar for men to target. When Stephanie vacated the seat next to Miguel to use the ladies' room, an attractive, buxom brunette quickly took her place.

"Hey there, mister," she said. Miguel looked over at Misty and gave her a "Can I keep her please?" look. Misty shook her head no.

Stephanie returned to find the woman sitting in her seat and chatting with Miguel. She stood there with her arms crossed until Miguel noticed her.

"Oh! Hey Steph . . . uh, this is Candy. She's working her way through college."

Stephanie gave Candy a wicked glare. "Is that right. Well, I'm afraid she isn't going to earn any money for college from you tonight. I saw the guest list, and you're not on the menu, Miguel. Why don't you ask her if she'll give you a freebie?"

Candy pinched Miguel's cheek. "Sorry, this girl needs to make some money, honey."

Miguel was slowly finding out there was more to Stephanie than met the eye.

After taking her seat back, Stephanie turned to Misty. "Miss Candy Cane didn't take a drink out of my glass, did she?"

A thoroughly entertained Misty responded, "No, you ran her ass off too fast."

Realizing the girls were staring at him, Miguel said, "Hey, I can't help it if I'm a chick magnet."

Travis finally arrived, but he spent the first hour visiting with the Japanese businessmen. Stephanie told Misty that Travis took the men out on an early morning hunt and that they were probably swapping exaggerated stories. The laughing and patting of each other's backs seemed to support Stephanie's theory. The businessmen kept offering to buy Travis a drink, but he turned down each offer. At one point Misty thought about walking over to say hi, but she realized the ranch guests came first. When she finally made eye contact with Travis, he gave Misty a slight nod and warm smile. She hoped it meant he wasn't holding a grudge.

When Travis finally headed their way, Misty whispered into Miguel's ear. "Take Stephanie and go back to the cabin before Travis gets here. *Don't* question me."

Knowing when Misty meant business, he took Stephanie's arm and whisked her away.

Travis stopped just short of the table. "So, are we on speaking terms tonight?"

Misty blushed softly. "Yes, of course. But I wouldn't blame you if you didn't talk to me after the way I treated you this afternoon. Sorry I overreacted."

Travis sat down next to Misty and motioned for one of the waitresses. "What are you drinking?"

"Rum and Coke."

"Sally, can you bring us two rum and Cokes?"

"Sure thing, boss." Sally took a couple of steps before looking back at Travis. "But I thought you—"

"Oh no, Misty isn't with the group from Vegas."

The waitress grinned. "Oh."

"So she thinks I look like a hooker, does she?" said Misty. "I'm sorry to disappoint her."

Travis smiled. "And you're not sorry to disappoint me?"

Misty continued to play along. "What makes you think you could afford me?"

"Not sure I could. I have little doubt you could command top dollar."

Suddenly her face took on a serious expression. *If he only knew*, she thought.

"You're not upset again, are you? You know I'm only joking."

Misty changed the subject by pointing to the walls lined with mounted deer antlers. "So did you kill those poor Bambies all by yourself?"

Travis surveyed the wall of horns. "Not all of them. See the big one over there? He used to roam my property. He showed up at my water hole every evening, so I named him Slurpy."

"Slurpy? So what happened to poor Slurpy?"

Travis took a big gulp of his rum and Coke. "Slurpy drank so much water I had my buddy George take him down. When I got to him, there was nothing left but his head."

Misty's eyes opened wide and she gave Travis a good punch in the arm. "Damn you, Travis." But then she quickly smiled. "You got me good."

"That's for not talking to me on our ride here this afternoon."

"Okay, I guess I had that one coming."

The two shared another drink before Travis noticed Chester staring at them. "Listen, I've enjoyed our visit but I better get back to our guests," he said.

"I suppose I've stolen you long enough," said Misty. "Thanks so much for stopping by to visit."

As Travis attempted to rise from the table, Misty grabbed his hand.

"Why don't you give me your cell number so we can text each other once in a while. You know, stuff like, 'Don't forget to feed George his jogger today.'"

Travis cracked up. "Good one. You really are a witty girl." But then his mood became more serious. "Don't take this wrong, but when I left New York and moved back to the ranch, I gave up texting."

Misty acted as if it didn't matter, but her eyes betrayed her . Her look brought back memories of his last night with Emily, and he was struck with a pang of guilt. Uncomfortable, he turned and began walking away. After several steps, he stopped. Knowing it would bother him all week if he didn't do something, he returned to her table.

"Listen, just because I don't like to text doesn't mean I don't enjoy talking to you," he said. Realizing his gesture fell short, he blurted out, "How would you like to go tubing next Saturday?"

Not wanting to look too anxious, she replied, "Yeah, that sounds pretty good."

Travis took his time looking her over from top to bottom, causing Misty to wonder about his intentions. "I could even take you country dancing afterward. But I can't take you looking like that. You'll need to buy a whole country-western outfit, including a hat and boots."

Misty's mood skyrocketed. "Great, I'll have Stephanie take me! I've always wanted to learn how to line dance. Do you think there will be line dancing?"

"You just never know. Hey, got to run, so I'll see you next week."

Misty watched Travis as he walked across the saloon. Saturday couldn't come too soon.

13

WILD RIVER RIDE

"Oh, come on, Misty!" Miguel pleaded. "You've got to take me with you. I'm your bodyguard!"

"Sorry, not today," said Misty.

"But what if Travis tries to take advantage of you? You're going to be floating on the Guadalupe in the middle of who knows where."

She smiled. "Now wouldn't that be something."

Miguel had seen that look before. "Something tells me Travis is the one that's going to need the bodyguard."

Misty handed Miguel her duffle bag to carry to the limo.

"Damn, this thing is heavy," he said. "Whatcha got in here?"

"Just my bathing suit and my country-western duds," she replied.

"You didn't bring the smoking-hot bathing suit you wore in Rio, did you?"

"No way! Well, I did think about it, but there wasn't enough time to get a bikini wax," she teased.

As Miguel watched the limo drive away, he wondered what would happen if she truly fell for this guy.

* * *

As the limo pulled into their predetermined destination, Misty caught a glimpse of Travis leaning against a Chevy pickup. Misty realized the limo looked totally out of place.

When her vehicle stopped, she said to the driver, "Mr. Rodriguez, don't take this personally, but can you let me get out on my own and then promptly drive off?"

Mr. Rodriguez looked at Misty through the rear-view mirror. "I understand. Would you prefer I pick you up in my personal pickup truck?"

"Would you?" said Misty, smiling gratefully.

Travis was standing next to the limo when she got out. "These people gawking at you must think you're someone famous."

Misty patted Travis on the cheek. "Well then I bet they think you are one lucky guy."

Grabbing her bag, he said, "Follow me. You can change into your bathing suit inside the tubing store."

Travis, dressed in cutoff jeans, a maroon tank top, and a straw cowboy hat, waited for Misty outside the changing room. When she stepped out in her light microfiber one-piece swimsuit in a rich green, she could tell from the look on his face that he was surprised. The bandeau-cut suit had an adjustable neck tie with silver hardware at the bust. A stylishly thin strip of material extended from the bottom and stretched to meet the two rope straps draped around her neck, and the top was constructed with side stays for support. The bottom only partially covered her firm buttocks.

Misty looked around to find everyone in the place staring at her. Incredibly sexy as she looked, Misty could tell her attire was out of place. Travis was getting an eyeful, but he wanted more. His eyes followed the two strings of neck tie down to the silver hardware nestled between her breasts. From there, his eyes followed the thin strip of material that stretched down her finely honed midsection to the treasure cove below.

Travis snapped out of it when he heard a loud voice. "Hot damn! I sure hope this is Misty."

Blake offered his hand to her. "I'm Blake. You must be Misty."

Misty gave Travis a puzzled look. "I invited Blake to go tubing with us," he said. "I hope you don't mind. I'll make sure he behaves."

Trying to hide her disappointment at not spending the day alone with Travis, Misty accepted Blake's hand. "No problem! How's it going, Blake?"

While Misty and Blake got to know each other better, Travis sorted through a rack full of T-shirts, pulling a large one down and handing it to Misty. "Why don't you put this on? I don't want you to get sunburned and ruin our night of dancing."

Disappointed he wouldn't be able to ogle Misty's body on the river, Blake said, "That's what sunscreen is for, Travis. They make SPF fifty, you know."

Travis laughed. "Okay, maybe I just don't want you gawking at Misty all day."

Misty grabbed the T-shirt, patted Blake on the cheek, and said, "Sorry Blake, but I better do as Travis says. He's a foreman, ya know."

Misty walked to the closest mirror to try on her new T-shirt. As Blake admired her, he whispered to Travis, "You know you just ruined my afternoon, don't you?"

* * *

Travis, Misty, and Blake walked through the parking lot toward Travis's pickup. Misty looked at the small stream running down one side of the property and said, "That can't be the river we're going to tube, right?"

"Nope, get in the pickup," Travis replied. "We've got about twelve more miles to go."

Blake blocked Misty from getting in the small backseat.

"Oh no you don't. Hop up front with us. You can sit in the middle. That way I can impress any old girlfriends we drive by. I've got a reputation to uphold, you know."

"Now explain to me who invited you again?" Misty said playfully.

Being wedged between Travis and Blake brought back memories of growing up in rural Minnesota. Most Saturday nights she would ride to wherever the party of the week was with a group of boyfriends in a pickup truck. As they drove, Misty focused on Blake, trying to figure him out. Not taking Travis for the talkative type, she assumed he liked having his friend around, knowing he would carry the conversation. She could only imagine the two working the scene at a bar. Blake would approach a table of girls and start a conversation while Travis hung back to gauge their interest.

Blake broke her train of thought when he began explaining how much fun their tube ride down the Guadalupe would be. She inconspicuously looked Blake over as he talked, noticing his lean, wiry frame and long, blond, curly hair framing a cute but not totally handsome face. He was already starting to grow on her.

Travis pulled into a local store and the boys proceeded to rent three large inner tubes, load up their ice chest with beer they purchased there, and grab the life jackets from the back of the pickup. They then boarded the bus that would drop them off under one of the many bridges on FM 306.

Once they'd dropped their tubes into the water and made it several hundred yards down the Guadalupe, Misty looked around at all the people floating on the river with them, guessing there were well over one hundred on the stretch she could see. There were large groups linked together by rope, feet, or hands, turning them into one massive barge. Every now and then someone would jump into the water, swim around, and then come back to the refuge of their floating fortress. Misty found this all very cool.

"This is known as the Lazy Leg," Travis said. "Relax while you can because when we come to the river bend, the rapids will move you along more quickly."

"Yeah, those twenty-foot drops are quite wicked!" Blake chimed in.

Misty figured Blake was pulling her leg but looked to Travis for assurance. His look told her Blake was bullshitting.

When they got to the rapids she found them tame, wishing they had been bigger.

Travis pointed out Party Rock as they drifted by.

"Why don't you tell Misty about some of the parties we had on those rocks?" Blake said.

Travis shot Blake a look, clearly indicating he should come up with another topic.

Now that they were back in calm water, Misty lay back and looked up to the sky. Suddenly she felt two hands on her bottom, pushing her up and off the inner tube. She surfaced to find Blake sprawled out in her tube and patting his mouth as if he were yawning.

Furious, Misty dove back underwater. Blake frowned at Travis, but Travis only shrugged. Although a billboard on the way to the river read "Enjoy the emerald waters of the Guadalupe!" the water was in fact opaque, and they could see no trace of Misty anywhere. Travis began to hum the theme from *Jaws* as Blake scanned the water. "Dun, dun . . . dun, dun."

"Hey! What the fuck!" Blake yelled as he felt someone attempting to yank his swimsuit off from below.

Blake hung on to the sides of the tube while struggling to keep his suit on. Soon, Travis heard Blake shout, "Oh crap!"

Misty shot to the surface gasping for air as she spun Blake's swim trunks in the air above her head. "Okay, very funny, Misty," Blake said, now submerged to his chest in the water. "You've had your fun, so give them back."

Misty's mischievous grin unsettled Blake. "Where are you going!" he screamed as she swam away.

"Looks like she's swimming toward Tree Island," Travis answered.

"What's she doing that for?"

"Beats me. I really don't know her that well, but she's got me curious."

Misty reached the island, got out of the water, and walked to the nearest tree. Climbing a low-hanging limb, she hung Blake's trunks from a branch for all to see. Once back on the ground, she jumped into the river and swam back to the boys. Blake was still hanging on to the inner tube with both arms while his body stayed in the river. He had on nothing but a pair of old tennis shoes.

Misty swam up and rested her arms on his tube. Looking him squarely in the eye, she said, "Go get 'em, big boy."

Blake turned to Travis and pleaded, "Hey man, get my trunks for me."

Travis leaned back on his tube, pulled his straw hat down over his face, and pretended to go to sleep. Drifting farther away from Tree Island by the minute, Blake panicked. "You're not really going to make me get it, are you?"

"You don't know me very well, do you?" replied Misty.

Blake sighed. With a "Go to hell" look, he disappeared into the murky water. Travis tipped up the brim of his hat and positioned his gaze on the receding island. As Blake swam away, all Travis and Misty could see was the back of his head, two flailing arms, and his milky white butt. After reaching the island, he sat in the water for awhile contemplating his next move. He surveyed the hordes of humanity floating by and then gazed upstream to see if he could wait for an opening, but the river was teeming with activity as far as the eye could see.

Like a Navy Seal springing from the ocean and scampering onto an enemy beach, Blake darted for the tree, holding one hand over his package. Misty saw he had a cute, tight little butt. *No flab on that boy*, she thought. Blake let go of his gonads and climbed the tree, freezing for a moment when he saw how far out his trunks were on the limb. Wasting no time, he stretched out and snatched his trunks as his family jewels dangled beneath him.

"I think Blake now knows what it's like to be hanging out on a limb—literally," said Travis.

The whooping and hollering from the tubers was merciless.

"Hey baby, way to hang out on the river."

"Woo hoo! You are one brave man."

"Whatcha doing tonight darling? Jenny, who can I turn to? For a good time, for a good time call 867-5309."

Eventually Blake got back to his tube, which Misty had been kind enough to hang on to for him, and struggled to put his trunks back on. Once he was dressed and back on his tube, he looked at Misty. "I underestimated you, but I can assure you that will never happen again."

Reaching out to straighten Blake's blond locks with her hand, she said, "I wish we had been closer so I would know if you're a true blond."

The trip down the Guadalupe from that point on was uneventful. Misty willingly wedged herself between Travis and Blake on the return trip. By the time they got to Gruene, Blake was back to his usual self.

Travis parked in front of a place called Texas Hall. It sat in the middle of a row of restaurants and gift shops in the little tourist town. Misty thought the rickety old building looked like it was ready for demolishing.

The whitewashed walls tilted to one side and the tin roof was so rusted it looked like it was possibly the original.

Misty laughed. "You're joking, right? I thought we were going dancing. Like to a honky-tonk or something."

"Damn, woman," said Blake. "Don't you know a honky-tonk when you see one? Read the sign."

"Texas Hall? That's a honky-tonk?"

"It's one of the oldest dance halls in Texas," said Blake. "Built in the eighteen hundreds and she's still standing."

Blake jumped out of the pickup and headed toward the dilapidated front door.

"Come on, Misty," said Travis. "I'll tell you all about this place after we change."

14

TWO TONS OF FUN

Travis escorted Misty to the ladies' dressing room, which was in the back of the hall next to a large stage. "Obviously, I've never been in there, but one of my old girlfriends says it's a good place to shower and change after tubing," he said. "Take your time."

Misty found the bathroom accommodating, with several nice showers and a changing area. After taking a hot shower and getting into her new cowgirl outfit, Misty put her hat on and looked in the mirror. She didn't recognize herself. Neither did Travis and Blake when she stepped out of the dressing room. Waving to get their attention, she said, "Well boys, do I look country enough for y'all?"

Travis and Blake were stupefied. Misty's wool felt cowgirl hat was adorned with a floral concho-accented hatband, and a dark maroon choker was fastened around her neck. The sleeveless top was made of a soft, terra cotta–colored suede and laced with a brown suede tie. Her skirt had a small ruffle around the bottom. Misty had done some improvising with her costume and tied the ruffle up on her right thigh, exposing her fine legs all the way down to the top of her heavily stressed python boots. A small crowd of women gathered around.

One of the women said, "Your outfit is absolutely darling! Where on earth did you get it?"

"I wish I could take credit, but a very good friend of mine from Argentina sent it to me," she replied.

A sassy-looking dark-haired woman said, "She sure did a swell job. You're going to be the belle of the ball tonight."

Misty turned to Blake. "How's your reputation holding up now, buddy?"

"Not bad, but if you'll sit on my lap tonight, every woman in the place will want to date me next week."

Misty scratched Blake under the chin with the tip of her fingernail. "You wish."

She then looked over at Travis to see what he had changed into. He wore brownish-yellow ostrich Tony Lama boots and cowboy-cut Wrangler jeans. His white oxford button-down was standard attire, but there was nothing standard about the way he filled it out. He topped it off with a Stetson cowboy hat.

Misty softly stroked Travis's chest with her open hand, pretending as if she was smoothing out wrinkles. "There—now you look perfect, Travis." Her touch was intimate and sensual.

Leading her off by the hand, Travis said, "Let's go get a drink at the bar."

As they walked, Misty noticed the walls were covered with photos of musicians.

"Who are these people?'

"Those are musicians that've performed at Texas Hall through the years."

Misty walked the wall, looking at pictures: Jerry Jeff Walker, Willie Nelson, Jerry Lee Lewis, Bo Diddley, Kris Kristofferson, Merle Haggard, Garth Brooks, Lyle Lovett, Michael Murphy, Asleep at the Wheel, and many, many more.

"Hey, isn't that John Travolta?" she asked, stopping to peer up at one of the photographs.

"Yep. Remember that movie *Michael*? They filmed the dance scene here." Travis pointed. "The picture was taken right over there on the dance floor."

She moved on to the next picture. "Hey, that guy's good-looking."

"That's George Strait. He looks really young there. He got his start playing here in the late seventies."

When they made it to the bar, Travis signaled to the longhaired bartender and ordered. "Give us two rum and Cokes."

"You remember what I drink?" said Misty. "How impressive!"

Something on the wall behind the bar caught Misty's attention. "Look at those license plates." One of the plates read "Tube-N."

"Personalized plates are big around Texas. If you lived here, how would your plates read?"

Misty knew but wasn't anxious to say. Travis egged her on until she blurted out, "BLK-WIDO."

"Why Black Widow?"

Misty grabbed his hand and pulled him toward the dance floor in an effort to divert his attention. "Come on, I hear the band warming up. You promised to teach me how to country dance, remember?"

"Sure, but let's sit and watch for awhile. When you feel like you've got the hang of it we'll give 'er a try."

The band began to play a song called "Kiss the Girl." Men grabbed their partners and headed for the dance floor while single women stood on the sidelines, moving their hips to the beat of the hot little tune. With the strum of a guitar, the beat of a drum, and the powerful vocals of the lead singer, the sleepy old bar transformed into *the* country dancing mecca of Texas.

As they walked across the uneven, rickety boards, Misty shouted above the noise, "What's up with the floor?"

"What? I can't hear you!" said Travis.

Putting her mouth to his ear, she shouted again. "What's up with the floor?"

Travis mouthed the word *old*.

Misty tugged on his shirt, stopping him so she could move closer to his ear. "Who is this band?"

"Two Tons of Fun," he said.

"What kind of music would you call this?" she asked.

"I guess you could say they're a blend of Elvis Presley, Elvis Costello, and Buddy Holly. Some of their stuff is considered rockabilly."

Misty nodded her head to the beat of the music. "Rockabilly . . . *rocks*!"

Travis led Misty to a bench that ran the perimeter of the hall and was tattooed with hand-carved names. The walls, made of hundred-year-old planks that looked hand-cut, had chicken wire covering the areas where old wood had rotted away.

Misty pointed to the wire.

Travis yelled, "Texas air-conditioning!"

She frowned. *Hmmm, no air-conditioning. I wonder how hot it'll get.*

As they sat watching the band, Blake walked up with an old girlfriend.

"Blake," said Travis, "take Sally onto the dance floor so Misty can watch you guys do the Texas two-step."

"Sure thing, Travis. Hey Misty, watch and learn."

As the couple headed off to the dance floor, Travis said, "I'll explain what they're doing as they dance, but first, watch how they come together."

Blake and Sally squared up to face each other. Blake put his right hand on Sally's waist and took her right hand gently into his left.

"Here they go," said Travis. Misty watched intently, tracing the steps in her brain as the couple danced: *Step together, walk-walk. Ok, now the tempo. Quick-quick, slow-slow.*

Travis sat back as she concentrated. At the end of the first song, it all began to click for her.

Leaning in toward Travis, Misty said, "This looks pretty basic. I learned tango and salsa in Argentina last year. I should be able to handle this."

"Tango and salsa? I'm impressed."

When the song ended, Travis walked to the front of the stage and motioned to the drummer. "That's Rick, an old buddy of mine," he said to Misty as the drummer walked toward them.

"What's up, Travis? I haven't seen you out here lately."

"Been busy. You guys still doing the Two Ton Tuesday thing?"

"Yep, all summer long. You should come out."

"Maybe I will. Listen, I need to teach someone how to dance. Can you guys play one of those old, conventional, two-step songs for me?"

"How about Alan Jackson's 'Chattahoochee'?"

The band's lead singer approached and said to Travis, "Sorry, buddy. I need a closer inspection of this young lady before we sing someone else's song."

Travis knew Jimmy was teasing and hoped Misty didn't get offended.

Looking Misty over he fanned himself with his hand. "Damn, ma'am! You are one hot mama! Where'd you find her, Travis?"

"I'll tell you over a beer sometime. Just play my song, will you?"

"Hell, we might as well bring out the ghosts of the past. But 'Chattahoochee' might not be your best bet . . . George Strait must have played 'All My Ex's Live in Texas' over a hundred times at the Hall—let's make it a hundred and one."

Travis slapped him on the side of his arm. "That would be perfect, Jimmy. Thanks, man."

Travis led Misty onto the dance floor and they squared up. Jimmy grabbed his microphone and said, "Ladies and gentlemen, we have a greenhorn in our midst. Misty, will you raise your hand so the rest of these cattle herders don't run you over?"

Misty blushed as her hand went up.

All eyes were on her, and one of the regulars yelled, "I'll show you how to dance, Misty. Travis has two left feet!"

Just then the band began, and Jimmy belted out the first lines of "All My Ex's Live in Texas."

Travis rested one hand on Misty's waist and took her right hand in his other. His palms were rough from calluses he had developed while working the ranch, but for some reason their roughness made her feel safe. Misty followed his lead, at first a little clumsy, but it didn't take long for her to get into the rhythm.

"You've been pulling my leg," said Travis. "You must've two-stepped before. There's no way you picked this up this easily."

Misty just smiled. *If Gabriella could only see me now,* she thought as she glided across Texas's oldest dance floor with a genuine cowboy.

When the song ended, Jimmy leaned toward the microphone. "Damn, little lady. You're good!" Holding his hand up to the crowd, he added, "Well, how do you folks like Misty?"

The place erupted. Men and women alike began patting Misty on the back.

"Now we'll see if Misty can dance to one of *our* songs," Jimmy yelled before turning to say something to the other band members. When he turned back around, the band broke into another one of their originals.

Four songs later, Travis escorted Misty back to the bench.

"That was a ton of fun," she said.

"I'm glad you liked it. Ready for another drink?"

"Sure, I'm really thirsty. Beer sounds good right now."

"Beer sounds good to me too. I'll be right back."

As soon as Travis walked away, Blake swooped in, grabbing Misty's hand and leading her onto the dance floor. She could hear the creaking of the old boards, and she felt for a moment like she was a part of history.

"Just one dance? There's some gals here I want to impress."

Misty put Blake's curly blond locks back in place as if he were a child and then gave him a big smile. "Wrap your arm around my waist tight. Let's get them real jealous."

"Yes ma'am!"

Travis came back, beers in hand. He knew what Blake was up to and was glad Misty played along. When the song ended and they came off the dance floor, Travis handed over Misty's beer. "Drink up so you can replace those body fluids."

Three beers later, Misty found herself sitting alone while Travis visited the men's room. By now her sweat-soaked La Perla lingerie clung to her body. Her brow was aglow with beads of sweat. Sleeveless, she used the hem of her skirt to wipe her forehead. As she bent over, the blood rushed to her head and left her grasping for support, so she leaned against the wall to keep the room from spinning. She got a short respite from the heat when a heavenly gust of wind blew through the chicken wire. When the breeze subsided, she succumbed to the elements once again. *I never dreamed being this hot and sticky could be such a thrill*, she thought.

Back from the bathroom, Travis slugged down what was left of his beer and escorted her onto the dance floor. He drew her into him tightly. Misty's face rested on the side of his neck while her breast pressed flat against his chest. She could feel his hot breath against her skin. The muscles of his back felt taut and firm and she kept a tight grip on his soaked shirt, which was warm to the touch. She wondered how good it would feel to rip his sweaty oxford open and lick every inch of salty dew from his chest. As they glided across the dance floor as one, Misty wished time would simply stop, leaving them suspended in this moment. But before she knew it, the band had fallen silent.

Sweat dripped from Travis's face onto the floor. Suggesting they get a breath of fresh air, he grabbed Misty's hand and led her to a secluded picnic table in the courtyard. When he sat down, Misty pulled the bottom of her cowgirl top out of her skirt, leaned in, and wiped his face dry.

"You're a mess," she said, laughing.

Misty climbed onto his left thigh and placed her hands atop his broad shoulders. The warm breeze did its best to evaporate the moisture from their skin as they gazed into each other's eyes. Travis pulled her to him and they kissed—soft, gentle pecks at first, but little by little they progressed until their warm, moist tongues entered the fray. Misty's breathing became heavy. Pulling away, she grabbed Travis's cowboy hat and set it on the table. She reached around back and grabbed his ponytail, pulling his head back. The force with which she showered his exposed neck with kisses excited Travis. His animal instincts kicked in, and had it not been for the sound of Blake's approaching voice, things may have gotten hot and heavy right then and there. Misty quickly let go of his hair, dismounted his knee, and stood to her feet. Travis stretched his neck from side to side in an effort to act as if nothing had been going on.

As he got closer, Blake said, "There you are! I've been looking for y'all everywhere."

Blake noticed Misty smoothing out her skirt. "Hey . . . did I just interrupt something?"

"Misty and I came out here to catch some fresh air and cool down," said Travis. "It's like a furnace in there."

Had Blake not come on a mission, he may have pressed the issue, but not tonight. Looking at Misty with a pleading face, he said. "My ex-girlfriend walked in. Can you find it in your heart to make her jealous? Please. I'll forgive you for stealing my swimsuit."

Misty sighed, "Okay, but this is the last time. Go ahead without me and I'll be there in a bit."

"Okay, but don't take too long," Blake said as he headed back to the dance hall.

Misty ground her toe into the grass. "Listen, Travis. I don't want you to feel uncomfortable about what we just did."

Travis lifted her chin up and said, "We're both consenting adults."

Misty patted Travis on the chest. "Stay here and cool off while I help Blake. It won't take long."

Travis nodded his approval.

15

MISTY TO THE RESCUE

Misty found Blake talking to three women when she got inside. Two chunky girls flanked a brunette, looking like guardians. She surmised the tall, slender woman in the middle was the target. Misty didn't like the way the brunette was acting: she ignored what Blake was saying to wave at two guys passing by. Steeling herself for the encounter, Misty made her way to the quartet. Strategically positioning herself with her back to the brunette, she gave Blake a big hug.

"Where have you been, babe?" she said. "I've been looking all over for you."

"I'm sorry. I bumped into some old friends of mine and we were catching up on things."

Misty spun around, looked straight into the brunette's eyes, and rubbed the side of her arm. "That's a nice outfit. It makes you look . . . well, thin. Or maybe it's just because you're standing in between them. Nice contrast."

The brunette glared at Misty while her portly companions' mouths dropped open.

Misty swung back to Blake and took him by the arm. "Come on, honey, I want you all to myself tonight."

Glancing over her shoulder at the women as they walked off, Misty said, "I'm sure you understand. Ta-ta."

Blake took a quick peek at the girls before exiting the building. His ex's eyes locked onto him with laser precision while her sidekicks carried on an animated discussion. Blake gulped.

Outside, he turned to Misty. "You don't play around, do you?"

"What for? There's nothing they have to say that I'm the least bit interested in. Trust me, give her a week and she'll send one of her girlfriends to talk to you. Her ego won't be satisfied until she seduces you, but remember this, she'll only fuck you once before she fucks you over. That's twice, so make the first one count."

Blake's eyes opened wide. "Damn, Misty. If she does, I owe you one."

Misty patted him on the arm. "Let's just say we're even for the stunt I pulled this afternoon."

When Misty and Blake returned to the courtyard, they found Travis with a group of his and Blake's friends.

"Here come Misty and Blake," Travis said to the group. "How'd it go, guys?"

"Misty did real good," said Blake.

Misty winked at Travis, and he smiled back at her. "Guys, I'd like you to meet Misty."

Misty smiled, shook hands with the ones closest to her, and waved at the rest.

"Misty learned the Texas two-step tonight," Travis told the group.

"But I didn't get to line dance," she added.

Travis said to the women in the group, "It's almost closing time, so why don't you teach Misty some basic steps and then I'll bring her back next Tuesday."

The women quickly gathered around Misty. For the next ten minutes they took turns teaching her the basic steps, with instructions coming fast and furious.

"Heel out, heel in, tap. Heel together and swivel. Left heel touch, left step back. One, two, three, four, five, six, seven and eight. Twist your feet back and forth. Right leg behind, and touch. Half turn, touch."

"She learns fast!" said one girl.

"I've got an idea," said another, reaching into her purse. She pulled out her iPod and queued up "Boot Scootin' Boogie." She then clipped the iPod to Misty's string tie and handed her the earphones.

"Put them on and hit play. Let us know when the song starts."

Misty put the earphones on as instructed and nodded when the song started. With "Boot Scootin' Boogie" blasting in her ear, she got in line with the girls and danced in lockstep.

The girls danced until they heard someone yell out, "Last call!" Misty hugged and thanked them for their help. When they left, she found Travis standing by the bench, grinning at her. So full of energy she couldn't control herself, she ran to Travis and jumped into his arms. Her legs wrapped around his waist and her arms around his shoulders.

With their eyes only inches apart, Misty said, "This is so much fun. When did you say we were coming back to line dance?"

"Next Tuesday, I promise."

Misty rested her head on his shoulders. "It's a date. Meet me in my hotel lobby next Tuesday at six o'clock?"

"Great, it's a date."

Misty wrote something on a napkin, then reached around and stuck it in the back pocket of his jeans. "It's my phone number, in case you get the urge to text me."

16

BACK TO THE GRIND

Misty stared out the window of the limo on her way to the club Monday morning, with a noticeable glow on her face.

"Misty won't tell me anything about Saturday night," Miguel said to Stephanie, attempting to bait Misty into conversation. "What's up with that?"

"I'm jealous, Misty," said Stephanie. "Travis never took *me* dancing."

"Too bad, honey," Misty muttered. "He's a terrific dancer."

Misty perked up when they arrived at the club. Floating on air, she made her way over to Chester and said, "Ready to rock and roll?"

"You seem like you're in a good mood," replied Chester. "What's going on?"

Misty shrugged her shoulders. "Oh, nothing."

While resting between sets of reps, Chester gave it another try. "Come on now, I'm your boss and have a right to know."

Chester's remark struck Misty the wrong way, causing her to lose some of her tact. "Well if you must know, Travis took me country dancing this weekend."

Chester's mood darkened.

"He did? Where did he take you?"

"Texas Hall. We had a wonderful time."

"Is that all?"

Misty couldn't tell where Chester was going with this, so she tried to think of something plain and factual.

"He also took me tubing on the Guadalupe Saturday afternoon before we went dancing."

Chester's ensuing silence didn't stop her mind from drifting back to her wonderful night with Travis many times throughout the remainder of the workout. When the session ended, Chester walked briskly toward the exit. In a voice so soft only she could hear, Misty said, "Bye, I'll see you Wednesday."

For the rest of the day, all Misty thought about was Two Ton Tuesday.

On Tuesday morning, she felt like sharing her good fortune, so she called Gabriella.

"Hello?"

"Gabby, it's me, Misty!"

"Misty! How have you been, dear? I've been dying to find out how Mr. Naples turned out."

Misty decided to play around with Gabriella to pay her back for picking such a loser. "Well, his first name is Chester and he's the most handsome man I've ever met."

There was nothing but silence on Gabriella's end. A few moments later Misty burst into laughter.

"*Not!* He's the biggest dork I've ever met."

"That bad? Why don't you sound mad at me then?"

Misty giggled. "Because I've met the most gorgeous man. He's so hot he would give The Man a run for his money."

"Really? What's his name and how did you meet him?"

"It's Travis. Mr. Naples owns a ranch, and Travis is his foreman. Well, he's really a big-time businessman who used to work for Excelsior Investments, but that's another story."

Misty spent the next thirty minutes telling Gabriella all she knew about Travis. Gabriella felt more and more uneasy as her story drew on. Misty had just come off her divorce from Rob, and she did not think it wise for her to get involved with another man this fast. Being careful not to pop Misty's bubble, she said, "He sounds wonderful! I'm so happy for you, Misty. Just be careful, darling."

After they hung up, Misty went down to the inner courtyard of the hotel to contemplate. Although Gabriella seemed genuinely happy for her, she couldn't get her last four words out of her head. *Just be careful, darling.*

17

TWO TON TUESDAY

Late Tuesday afternoon, Misty tried on the second cowgirl outfit Gabriella had sent and studied herself in the bathroom mirror. It consisted of an understated light blue blouse and cowgirl jeans so tight they looked painted on. Pleased, she gave her butt a little slap.

I've still got it. That hot ass more than makes up for being four years older than Travis.

She headed downstairs to the lounge area situated between the restaurant and the hotel bar. It was her favorite part of the hotel. She walked to the middle of the enormous U-shaped couches and took a seat amongst the dozens of comfy pillows strewn about. Soft backlighting gave the area a cozy feel and the nineteen candles covering the east wall made for a good focal point. As she sat, Misty began planning her meeting with Travis.

When Travis gets here I'll greet him with a hug and a slight peck on the cheek, and then suggest we have a drink before heading out to Texas Hall. We'll snuggle on the couch . . . and who knows where things will go from there?

Misty's anticipation grew until Travis finally arrived. As he walked toward her, Misty noticed he had on his work clothes, but she figured he would change once they got to Texas Hall. But when he reached her, she wasn't sure.

"Hey, why the long face? If you had a rough day, we can stay here for a couple hours, hang out on the couch, and have a few drinks. I don't mind."

Travis plopped down without giving Misty as much as a hug. It was now clear to her that this was more than just a long day at work. She moved closer and placed a hand on his knee. "Come on now. Things can't be that bad. Let's have a smile."

Travis repositioned himself to face her.

"I'm afraid I've got some bad news." He took her hands in his, pulled back slightly, and looked her over. "You look absolutely spectacular tonight."

His comment pleased her, yet did not appease her. "Thank you, Travis. That's kind of you." She worried about what he might say next.

Travis's face hardened. "Misty, we can't go to Texas Hall tonight."

Trying not to show her utter disappointment, she remained positive. "That's okay, Travis. We can put it off until Saturday."

Travis broke eye contact and stared in the direction of the candles on the east wall. "I'm afraid not."

His words cut deep. Misty sat back, shocked.

What is he saying? Is he dumping me? But I thought we hit it off so well Saturday.

Travis looked back at Misty, but she was too deep in thought to notice. He let out a sigh before continuing. "Mr. Naples called me this morning. He said in no uncertain terms that he did not want us to see each other. I asked him why and he said that you belonged to him. What did he mean by that?"

Misty's head began to spin. Her thought process became convoluted and crazy ideas swirled in her head. *Chester thinks I'm his? I have an obligation to that jerk, but nothing in our contract says he can dictate to me who I can see. Why is he doing this to me?*

Misty exploded. "No! No! No! I do *not* belong to Mr. Naples. He hired me to . . . well, uh, train him. Nobody owns me!" When Travis didn't respond, she continued her rant. "I'll get this all straightened out tomorrow. Come on. Let's go dancing. This is all just a big misunderstanding!"

"I'm sorry, Misty. Mr. Naples is my boss and I have no choice but to comply with his orders."

Misty's temper flared, setting the moment ablaze. "Damn it, Travis, you're not even going to fight for me? You're just going to sit there and take it?"

"I'm sorry, Misty. I've never heard Mr. Naples so angry. When I started to reply, he cut me off instantly. I realized he was in no mood to hear me out, so I told him I understood and hung up."

Misty balled her fists and began hammering him in the chest.

"Damn you, Travis!"

Travis showed little emotion, taking her blows in silence. When her assault ended, he simply replied, "You're understandably upset. I think it's best I leave so you can have time to yourself."

He rose from the couch, placed his hand on the side of her cheek, and said, "I'm so sorry. I hope you find it in yourself to forgive me."

As he walked to the front door, Misty called out, "Will we ever see each other again?"

Travis stopped in his tracks but replied without turning around. "I can't answer that, but I hope so."

With Travis gone, Misty became even more furious. *I'm going to give Chester a piece of my mind tomorrow. How dare he!*

Once in her room, Misty returned to her senses. She needed to calm down before addressing Mr. Naples tomorrow. She understood that if this situation was not handled properly it could cause irreparable harm to her reputation and adversely impact the fee she charged future clients. In no mood to go anywhere, Misty undressed and crawled into bed without brushing her teeth or cleaning her face. Thinking about the possibility that she might never see Travis again, she gently cried herself to sleep.

18

THE SHOWDOWN

Misty placed the bar in Chester's hands as she stood over him. It totaled only ninety pounds, but Chester was nevertheless proud he could bench press it. He lifted the bar six times and then placed it back in Misty's hands. She held the weight over his head for a moment, wondering how much damage ninety pounds would do if she dropped it on his thick skull. She then visualized beating the living crap out of him in the back alley. In her daydream, she dumped his bloody carcass in the Dumpster after his beat down.

"Misty! Come on. Let's move to the next machine. What's gotten into you?"

Misty did not respond.

Chester made his move. "Say, since you like country dancing so much, what do you say I take you dancing sometime?"

Misty's blood was boiling, but she managed to hold it together. "Maybe we should, now that Travis taught me the two-step."

Now that the topic was on the table, Chester said, "I suppose Travis told you I don't want him seeing you anymore."

"He did, but I don't understand why. Our contract doesn't say anything about you being able to decide who I see and who I don't see outside of our training sessions."

"You are correct," he replied sternly. "I cannot tell you who you can't see, but I can tell Travis whatever I damn well please. I don't want his performance to slip, is all."

When Chester could tell Misty wasn't buying it, his temper got the best of him.

"I'm paying you a fortune to pay attention to me. I'm not going to share you with Travis!"

Misty retained her defiant expression.

"Let's talk turkey, girl! We signed a contract. I can order you up to your room right now and demand payment in full. Is that what you want?"

Misty assessed her options. If she said yes, per her contract, she could do the deed, scrub in a hot shower afterward, pack her bags, and go home. Once a client slept with her the contract was fulfilled. It wasn't her problem if he couldn't hold out the entire three months. But then the awful thought of Chester lying on top of her crept in.

She squared up to Chester. "We have fifteen minutes of our workout left. I suggest we get back to work."

On the way back to the hotel, Misty confided in Stephanie, explaining the whole situation and her conversation with Mr. Naples. When she finished, Stephanie said, "Mr. Naples can be an asshole, but I'm sorry you won't be able to see Travis anymore. Not as much for your sake as for his. I've noticed a positive change in him over the last three weeks. You've been good for him."

Stephanie's last comment didn't make things any easier for Misty.

19

AN UNEXPECTED EVENT

Late Wednesday afternoon, Misty called Gabriella. After hearing Misty's story, she wanted to fly to San Antonio and read Chester the riot act.

Gabriella said, "I'm so sorry I didn't do a better job of vetting him, Misty."

"Please don't beat yourself up over that, Gabby. Your heart was in the right place. Who would've thought this guy would turn out to be such a creep?"

Gabriella tried to think of anything she could say to make Misty feel better. "It's probably for the best anyway. You know, falling for a guy could be hazardous in your line of work."

"I know, but I feel so alive when I'm around Travis. It's like being on dope. I mean, I've never been on dope, so let's just say like when your body releases dopamine. Our relationship ended so quickly, I feel like a drug addict quitting cold turkey."

"I know, dear. There's nothing like being around a good man. Listen Misty, I'm on my way to a big meeting and need to go over the agenda before I get there."

"Tell Misty hi for me!" Tom yelled from the driver's seat of Gabriella's car.

"Hey, Tom says hi."

"I really miss Tom," said Misty. "Please tell him so."

"Will do. Bye, dear. Stay strong."

Misty hung up and noticed the red light on her room phone was lit. The message was from Stephanie.

"I know this is short notice, but put on something nice and meet me at the Down Town Bistro for dinner. Reservations are for seven."

I wonder what that's all about, thought Misty. *It's already six—I'd better get ready.*

* * *

Misty walked the short block to the bistro. Arriving early, she sat at the table and admired the wall-length mural. The colorful depiction of movie stars helped her pass the time. She noticed two full-length flags hanging from the ceiling. *Texans must be just as proud of Texas as they are of the United States.*

Stephanie showed up with an attractive woman who looked to be in her mid-fifties. *I wonder who this could be*, thought Misty.

The woman had a firm handshake, letting Misty know she was of strong character. "Hello Misty," she said, "it's so good to finally meet you. I've heard so many nice things about you."

Stephanie quickly chimed in. "This is Brenda. Chester's better half."

Having never met face to face with one of her clients' wives, Misty found herself in uncharted waters.

Brenda sensed her anxiety. "Please sit down, Misty. Let's order some food and drinks. We're going to have a wonderful evening, I'm sure."

Once drinks were ordered and dinner choices were made, Brenda said, "Chester doesn't know this, but I know the pass code to his computer and have read your contract with my husband." She leaned over and patted Misty's thigh. "Don't worry, dear. I'm your biggest fan. If I could have had a gig like yours, I wouldn't have had to marry my dorky husband."

For the first time since they had arrived, Misty began to relax.

"It's a clever contract," said Brenda. "There's only one problem that

I can see. You need to do a better job picking your clients. Why in the world did you choose Chester?"

"I didn't," Misty replied. "A very good friend of mine picked him for me. She wanted someone . . . well, safe and boring."

Brenda broke out laughing. "I would say she did an excellent job. Trust me, you're going to be totally underwhelmed when you sleep with him. And your training sessions—how boring they must be."

The thought of sleeping with Chester, as usual, turned Misty's stomach.

Continuing to control the conversation, as was her way, Brenda said, "Look honey, I like you. I have the cutest house on Mustang Island. Why don't you come with us this weekend to get your mind off Chester—and Travis. I promise you, it'll be a blast!"

"So you know about Travis and me?" she asked.

"Hell, girl, Stephanie tells me everything. Besides, Travis is one hot dude. I can see why you're attracted to him."

Misty shot Stephanie a glance, and Stephanie smiled back. "Come on, Misty. It'll help you take your mind off Travis."

Misty thought for a moment. "Chester's not coming?"

"Hell no!" said Brenda. "I only go to the coast when Chester can't come. Thank god he's finally going out of state this weekend."

"Can Miguel come?"

Stephanie's eyes lit up. "Of course! He's your bodyguard."

"Then to the coast it will be!"

The women hoisted their glasses of wine and toasted. "To the coast!"

20

ON THE WAY TO PORT A

After the luggage was loaded, Misty climbed into the back bench seat. Brenda handed Miguel the keys to her maroon Suburban. "You mind driving, handsome? I stayed up late last night and could use the sleep."

"No problem, Mrs. Naples. I've always wanted to drive a Texas Cadillac. Wow! It's a beast!"

"Call me Brenda, for god's sake. And yeah, most things are big in Texas." She thought for a moment. "Well, except for Chester, if you know what I mean."

Brenda laid claim to the second-row bench, propped her head on some pillows, and closed her eyes.

Happy to ride shotgun, Stephanie said, "I'll give you directions, Miguel."

Half an hour south of San Antonio, Misty realized there wasn't much to see on the flat, featureless terrain so she settled into her seat and zoned out. No matter how hard she tried, all she could think about was Travis. Three hours into the trip she sensed they were getting closer.

Brenda popped her head up. "Oh, good, we're going over Redfish Bay. It won't be long now."

Several miles later, Miguel yelled out, "Hey! We're at a dead end and I don't see a bridge."

Brenda leaned forward from the middle bench. "Don't worry, honey. This is a ferry crossing."

Miguel laughed. "A fairy crossing! Are you still dreaming, Brenda?"

Stephanie punched Miguel in the arm. "F-e-r-r-y, not f-a-i-r-y, silly."

The man waved for Miguel to follow the automobile in front of him onto the flat deck of the ferry, which resembled an old tugboat. Once Miguel turned off the engine, Misty got out, walked to a guardrail, and closed her eyes. A soft breeze swept across her face, easing the sting from the early afternoon sun. She breathed in deep, filling her lungs with wonderful, warm, salty air while listening to the sound of hungry seagulls overhead. When she opened her eyes, dolphins were entertaining the tourists. For the first time in several days her mind was preoccupied with soothing thoughts.

The drive down the main drag of Port Aransas reminded Misty of the sleepy ocean towns dotted along highway 1, north of Malibu. She made special note of souvenir shops, restaurants, and bars she might want to visit. Five miles south of town, Stephanie guided Miguel into Laguna Estates, where they wound their way down residential streets until pulling up to the three-story beach house.

Stephanie announced their arrival. "Here we are. Leave the Suburban in the driveway, Miguel, until we unload it."

Misty got out and looked up to the second-floor balcony. "It's beautiful, Brenda!"

"Wait until you see the inside," she replied.

Misty noticed that the seaside homes all had front porches, and it reminded her of the country homes in Minnesota where she grew up. The inside of the beach house had hardwood floors and a light, airy color palette. Stephanie and Miguel began loading the luggage onto an elevator on the first floor.

As they pushed the button to send the elevator to the second floor, they heard Misty yell, "No way! I can see the Gulf of Mexico from the kitchen on the second floor. Come see!"

From the balcony, Misty looked across the lake to a beautiful waterfall from a community pool. Beyond the pool lay a barrier of sand dunes and, behind them, Gulf of Mexico waves crashing onto the beach.

Misty's tranquility was broken by a man's voice. "My, my, my. Aren't you a cutie pie?"

Misty whipped around to see a man with a gray ponytail and goatee who was grinning from ear to ear. He seemed beyond unpretentious.

Before Misty could say something sarcastic back, Brenda walked up, gave him a big hug and kiss, and then pinched his cheek. "You're my big Mustang Island man, aren't you Buddy?"

Buddy put his arms around Brenda's waist and hoisted her in the air. "I am as long as you're nice to me. Are you going to be nice this weekend?"

"Oh, Buddy. You know I'm always nice to you. Now put me down and go help Miguel carry in the provisions."

Buddy turned to Misty. "Damn, she's already ordering me around."

When he left the porch, Brenda said, "Buddy's my boyfriend. I come down to visit him every chance I get. You see, you're not the only one that can't stand Chester. Shit, if Chester wasn't so rich, or if he hadn't made me sign that damn prenup agreement, I'd divorce the dickhead tomorrow. Fuck, I can't live on two hundred thousand dollars a year."

Misty hugged her. "Don't worry about me. I'm okay with it."

Before leaving, Brenda gave Misty a word of warning. "Now if Buddy hits on you, which he will, just tell him to fuck off. He'll oblige—it's all just bravado, and he's a teddy bear at heart."

Misty gave her a wink. "Don't worry. I can take care of myself."

She looked Misty over and replied, "I'm sure you can."

21

MUSTANG ISLAND

When everything was put away, Brenda stood in front of the master bed-room with an arm around Buddy and said to Misty, "You guys will find a golf cart in the garage you can take to the beach." She patted Buddy on the chest. "I hope you don't mind, but Buddy and I have some catching up to do." Brenda walked into the bedroom and then called out, "Come on, Buddy. Get your butt in here."

Buddy winked at Misty. "Time to service the woman. Don't worry though, there's plenty to go around."

"Hey, buddy, Brenda warned me about you," she replied.

"Hey, you know my name. That's a start."

* * *

Miguel stopped the golf cart on the middle of the crosswalk that ran over the dunes to allow the group to survey the beach ahead. After looking at beach as far as her eye could see, Misty said to Miguel and Stephanie, "If it's okay with you two, I'm going to take a long walk by myself."

Miguel said what a bodyguard should say. "Are you sure you don't want us to come with you?"

"Thanks, but I could use the solitude. I'll be fine. You guys hang out here and have a good time together."

When Misty had walked off, Miguel turned to Stephanie. "Well, what do you want to do?

Stephanie shot him a mischievous grin. "Why, go for a swim of course."

Miguel wasted little time ripping off his shirt and kicking off his shoes. He looked up to see Stephanie drop her T-shirt to the sand. A single thin string holding her bikini top up gave Miguel a full view of her lean, muscular back. She then bent over, pulled down her shorts, and stepped out of them, one leg at a time. The bottom of her skimpy suit left little to Miguel's imagination. Stephanie stood up straight and began running her hands through her hair so it was free to blow in the breeze. He was standing directly behind her, and could see the bottom portion of her sizeable breasts hanging out of the bottom of a bikini top that fell woefully short on coverage. Her breasts jiggled as she shook her head back and forth in an attempt to free the tangles. Stephanie turned around and Miguel's face gave him away.

He stumbled for words. "I, uh . . . wow! You look great, Stephanie!"

Now it was Stephanie's turn to look over Miguel's muscular body. Standing only five foot ten, he was thick and sturdy from the neck down. Every muscle group was well represented from years of hard work in the gym.

Stephanie picked up a bottle of Bull Frog suntan lotion, walked over to Miguel, and began rubbing it on his shoulders and chest.

"The sun here is brutal," she said. "You can get burned even if you are Hispanic."

"Okay, but I get to put lotion on you next."

"I'd be disappointed if you didn't."

Stephanie used slow, measured strokes, being careful to cover every spot. Her hands were delicate and sensual. When it was Miguel's turn, he started on her back where he found toned muscles underneath smooth skin.

Working on her shoulders and arms, he said, "Those business suits you wear don't do you justice."

Stephanie took the suntan bottle out of his hands, threw it on the sand, and led him by the hand into the oncoming waves. Once they had gone a little farther out, a big wave crashed over them, causing them to lose their footing and fall into the warm gulf waters.

After body surfing for awhile, Stephanie said, "Let's go a little further out, where the water's deeper."

Miguel couldn't understand how the body surfing would be any better further out, but he didn't argue.

When the water was up to their armpits, Miguel noticed the nearest people were fifty yards away. He started to say something, but she placed a finger over his lips and peered into his eyes. Caught up in the moment, he placed his hands on her bottom and hoisted her up. Her legs instinctively wrapped around his waist. Only inches apart, Miguel leaned in and gave Stephanie a kiss. Their lips were moist, warm and salty, from the water. When kissing wasn't enough, Stephanie slid off Miguel, dropped into the water, and pulled off her suit bottom. She then dropped below the surface and reemerged with Miguel's trunks in hand. Miguel wrapped his arms around her lower back and lifted her up and onto his throbbing member, delicately working to penetrate her fully. Stephanie laid her face on his shoulder and concentrated on his every thrust.

Miguel did all the work, and Stephanie could feel the muscles of his ripped upper body under her grasp. The warmth of the sun and the motion of the water acted as an intense aphrodisiac, causing Stephanie to come in no time at all. Just before she exploded, she clamped her open mouth on his neck like a vampire to keep from screaming out loud.

Her orgasm was so intense she went limp in his arms afterwards. She felt like a rag doll as Miguel continued to screw her. When it was obvious he was done, Stephanie gave Miguel one last sensuous kiss and dismounted.

After putting their bottoms back on, they worked their way back to the beach. Now fully satiated, Stephanie couldn't believe she had acted so boldly, but never for a moment did she regret her actions.

* * *

As Misty walked the beach, the sound of crashing waves along with the soft, steady, cool breeze on her face brought her closer to nature. She stopped to frolic in the gulf as the mood hit her. The seagulls were out in full force this fine afternoon. Two dozen hovered above a group of children, swooping down each time one of them threw a piece of bread into the air. To the kids' delight, the gulls battled for every tasty morsel. The children's laughter soothed her soul.

I wonder what it would have felt like to have children. If I had been fertile, would things have worked out differently with Rob?

Soon her thoughts moved from Rob to Travis. *Maybe things are working out for the best.*

Misty returned to find Miguel and Stephanie sunbathing in their beach chairs while holding hands.

"My, my. Look at you two lovebirds," she said.

Instinctively, they pulled their hands apart. "Oh, hi Misty," said Miguel. "Did you have a good walk?"

"I had a wonderful walk! I think I'll go clean up for dinner now. Are you two coming?"

"We're going to stay out a little longer," said Stephanie. "When you're ready to shower, use the one in the back bedroom. It has a wonderful showerhead."

"Thanks for the advice, Stephanie. I'll catch you guys a little later."

22

SHRIMPY'S

Invigorated from her shower, Misty climbed the steps to the second floor. The room was filled with radiant energy emanating from her sun-kissed skin. Buddy stood captivated.

Misty broke the uncomfortable silence. "So where are we eating tonight, Buddy? I'm starving."

"Shrimpy's!" he said. "They have great seafood. You'll love it. But first we need to stop by the RV park and pick up my partner, Greg."

"The RV park?"

"Yeah, Pioneer RV. You passed it on the way here."

"Yeah, I do remember that. It looked nice."

"It's only one of a handful of parks in the state of Texas that received a five-star rating," Buddy replied proudly.

"Well congratulations! You must be proud."

An hour later, the Suburban carrying Brenda, Buddy, Miguel, Stephanie, and Misty pulled into Pioneer RV. The park was teeming with weekend RVers, escaping the rigors of their everyday lives to have some fun in the sun. The park was spacious and clean, with two swimming pools, a large recreational center complete with showers, and a walkway through the dunes, giving their patrons direct access to the beach.

"Impressive, Buddy!" said Miguel. "This place must be fun to run."

Brenda rolled her eyes. "Yeah, Buddy gets to look at scantily clad women all summer."

"Need a helper for the next six weekends, Buddy?" asked Miguel. "I could make myself available."

Stephanie dug her knuckle into Miguel's ribs. "Don't listen to him, Buddy. Miguel's weekends are taken."

They all climbed into the Suburban with Greg sitting next to Misty. As they pulled out, Buddy said, "Next stop, Shrimpy's."

Misty found Greg to be extremely polite, engaging, and knowledgeable. Halfway to Shrimpy's, they passed a sign that read "Padre Island."

"Did we leave Mustang Island?" asked Misty. "What's Padre Island?"

"Ask Greg," said Brenda. "His great-granddad used to own the whole damn island, way back when."

Misty looked at Greg. "No kidding. Tell me some stories about the island in the old days."

Greg thought a moment. "Let's see. My granddad, Burton, ran cattle on the island. They had not dredged the Intracoastal Waterway channel yet, so the water was shallow enough to herd the cattle from the mainland to the island. The water on both sides of the island acted as a natural barrier, saving the need for fences. My granddad actually got caught on the island during a hurricane once."

"Why the hell did he stay on the island during the hurricane?" asked Miguel.

Greg replied, "You have to remember, communications of all kinds were limited back then. No cell phones or Internet to warn him of the impending storm."

"How did he survive the hurricane?" asked Miguel. "Or did he?"

"Granddad climbed on top of a large sand dune, riding it out with a coyote and a rattlesnake. He said all three of them were so preoccupied with surviving the storm, they pretty much left each other alone."

"Your granddad must have been one tough hombre," said Miguel.

Buddy egged Greg on: "Tough, I'll say. Tell them about how he cured his hemorrhoids, Greg."

Brenda slapped Buddy on the arm. "Now why did you have to bring that up!"

Buddy chuckled.

Miguel jumped in. "Yeah Greg, tell us about the man's 'roid problem."

"One night around a campfire," said Greg, "he put the end of his cattle branding iron into the fire until white hot, and then handed it to his ranch hand. At first the ranch hand wasn't sure what to do, but then granddaddy pulled his pants down and bent over. No more pesky 'roids after that."

Misty, Miguel, and Stephanie all cried out. "Ow!" "Ugh!" "Ouchie mamma!"

Brenda turned to Buddy. "I hope you're proud of yourself!"

Buddy grinned from ear to ear, enjoying the attention.

* * *

Shrimpy's sat in the middle of Snoopy's Pier, which ran parallel to the Intracoastal Waterway and lay in the shadow of the causeway bridge. The group secured a large table on the back patio so they could watch the sun set. Starving, Misty frantically looked over the menu.

"Oh no! I'm really hungry but all I see is *fried* seafood," said Misty. "I don't eat fried food anymore."

"Hell, I could tell that by looking at you," said Buddy. "No fat on you, girl. Don't worry. I went to high school with the owner. I'll fix you up." Buddy then sprang from the table and walked toward the kitchen.

About fifteen minutes later, the waitress had loaded the table with every type of fried seafood one could imagine. Misty encouraged the others to dig in, and the waitress returned to the table with more food. She placed a large basket in front of Misty.

A wide-eyed Misty said, "What in the world are these? They're huge!"

"Yes ma'am," replied the waitress. "Buddy went through our shrimp and picked out the largest ones he could find. In the grocery store they'd be considered six-count shrimp, meaning there are only six shrimp to the pound."

Misty dipped her boiled shrimp into the cocktail sauce and took a bite. "Yum! I really owe you one, Buddy."

When Brenda recognized the look on Buddy's face, she jabbed him in the ribs. "She doesn't mean what you're thinking. If you don't behave yourself, I'm going to have Greg go get his granddad's branding iron."

Buddy chuckled. "Well, my 'roids *have* been acting up lately."

On their way back to the beach house, the constable's car began following them. When its lights went on, Buddy pulled over. The officer slowly got out of his car and leaned into Buddy's window, grinning from ear to ear.

"Well hey there, what's up?" Buddy said, looking relieved.

Brenda let him have it. "Damn you, Jerry! You scared the shit out of me. I've got a baggie of Mary Jane in my purse."

Jerry didn't pay any attention to her, too busy sizing Misty up. He gave her a wink. "You're a cute one. I haven't seen you in these parts before."

Brenda took off her shoe and threw it at Jerry. He blocked it with his hand and laughed. "Nice try, Brenda. Maybe you'll get lucky and hit me next time."

As Jerry walked away, Misty could hear him singing: *I shot the sheriff, but I didn't shoot the deputy.*

When she gave Buddy a funny look, he said, "Jerry's a *deputy* constable."

They continued driving, dropped Greg off at the park, and returned to the beach house. Stephanie and Miguel went for a late-night walk on the beach while Buddy and Brenda retired to the master bedroom on the second floor. Not sleepy, Misty curled up on the couch in the second-floor living room and cracked open a book, but her mind kept drifting back to Travis.

Around midnight, she noticed a noise coming from the master bedroom. At first it sounded like the bed creaking in a distinct rhythm, but then Brenda's moans drowned out the bed. After Brenda's cries climaxed in a scream, Misty heard Buddy yell, "Yee-haw!"

Misty smiled a moment before going back to her reading. When she heard the bedroom door open, she lowered the book enough to see Buddy walking toward the kitchen. Even in the dimly lit living room, she could tell Buddy was butt naked. Misty quickly pulled the book up to hide her eyes.

Buddy grabbed a couple of Honey Buns, popped the top on a couple of beers, and walked back. Misty lowered her book and said, "I didn't know it was your birthday, Buddy. Nice suit."

When Buddy stopped, Misty slid the book back over her eyes, expecting to hear the sound of him scurrying into the bedroom, but things remained eerily silent. Then, Misty picked up the sound of breathing only a few feet away.

Buddy's voice startled her. "Hey, Misty. I've got two pieces of birthday cake. Would you like one?"

Misty's eyes darted back and forth. She slowly lowered her book just enough to see Buddy standing in front of her, offering up one of his Honey Buns.

Misty quickly raised the book. "That's okay, Buddy. You go share that cake with Brenda."

Brenda's voice rang out from the bedroom, "Buddy, get your butt back in here!"

Buddy chuckled his patented chuckle. "Sorry, Misty. Looks like Brenda's still in an amorous mood."

Misty lowered the book enough to see Buddy's butt cheeks moving up and down as he walked away. Thinking the whole ordeal cute, she jokingly called out after him, "Hey, Bud, those are some nice Honey Buns."

Buddy looked back at her and gave his right cheek a hard slap. When the bedroom door closed, Misty thought, *I wonder how that would've played out if Buddy had offered me a Twinkie . . .*

23

SUNDAY MORNING

Misty leaned on the second-floor balcony railing, drinking her morning coffee, listening to powerful gulf waves in the distance, and witnessing the sun slowly rise above the dunes.

"Good morning, sunshine!"

Misty spun around, spilling some coffee.

"Oh, Buddy, good morning. Did you finish off all of your birthday cake last night?"

"Nope, still got some left. Want me to bring you a piece?"

Misty gently shook her head and took a seat on the couch.

Buddy sat down beside her, seeming serious for the first time. "Brenda told me all about your guy problem."

"She did? What did she tell you?"

"I didn't ask for specifics. They seldom matter. You either feel bad or you don't." Buddy patted her on the knee and added, "I came out here to tell you that you are one terrific gal and any man dumb enough to pass you up isn't too bright."

Misty gave him a big hug. "Thank you so much. That's really sweet of you."

"One more thing before I go," he said. "Guys are at a disadvantage when it comes to relationships. It's programmed into women's DNA, but for guys, being with a woman is like moving to a foreign country and learning a new language. By the time we figure things out, we're usually too old to put it to good use. Don't be too hard on the dude."

Misty grinned. "Thank you, Buddy. I'll take that to heart."

On the trip back to San Antonio, Misty focused on how hard she would push Chester in their next training session. So hard he'd regret hiring her.

When they made it back to the hotel, Brenda gave Misty a hug. "I hope you feel better. If you need anyone to talk to, give me a call. Actually, why don't we plan on having dinner once a week while you're here?"

"Thank you, Brenda. I'd like that very much. You've been wonderful."

24

No Pain, No Gain

Misty set a torrid pace at their next training session, briskly moving Chester from one exercise machine to the next, making sure there was no small talk in between. For the first time, his shirt was soaking wet.

Chester halted on their way to the bench press. "What's gotten into you, Misty? Look at this shirt. It's ruined! I'll have to throw it away."

"Come on, Chester, no one throws away their workout shirt after a little sweat. I thought you wanted to get in shape. No pain, no gain."

Chester mumbled something inaudible on his way to the next station. Misty smiled behind his back. She knew her actions might force Chester to make his move sooner rather than later, but watching him sweat made it all worthwhile.

* * *

Travis came back from checking the herd of longhorn cattle to find Blake's truck in his driveway. Blake had used the spare key Travis let him keep to get in, and Travis found him sitting in a chair in the kitchen.

He walked right past Blake without acknowledgment and threw his hat on the kitchen table.

After a few moments of silence, Travis said, "What's up, Blake?"

"That's what I came out here to ask you, buddy. I thought you were going to take Misty back to Texas Hall so the girls could teach her more country dance steps. They keep asking me where Travis and Misty are."

Blake sat back in his chair, watching Travis move around the kitchen, ignoring his question. Travis opened the refrigerator, got out a pitcher, and poured a glass of iced tea.

Without looking up, Travis said, "Want some?"

Blake didn't answer.

"Okay, suit yourself."

Travis walked over to the chair opposite Blake, removed his boots, and settled in.

"Okay Blake, let's get this over with. What's on your mind?"

"I want to know why you didn't show up at Texas Hall with Misty Tuesday night, and why you haven't been returning my phone calls."

Travis took several gulps of his tea, set the glass on the table, and locked eyes with Blake. "Mr. Naples told me that if I continued to see Misty, he would fire me. There, are you happy?"

"It doesn't matter if I'm happy. The only thing that matters is whether you're happy, and it's obvious you're not."

Travis leaned back, placing his hands behind his head. Blake let some time pass before continuing. "Okay, so Mr. Naples is an asshole. What else is new? All I know is that Saturday night at Texas Hall, you were the old Travis. This girl's the best thing that's happened to you since your uncle passed away. Misty's a godsend, man. She's the antidote for your misery."

When Travis didn't respond, Blake continued, "Look, man. If I understood her correctly, she's only here for three months, max. Use her to jump-start your batteries while she's here." He laughed. "Come on! Hook your positive and negative cables to her bosoms and crank the engine. Have some fun again!"

Travis still didn't answer, but Blake kept pressing forward. "Screw your job, man! You have a business degree. You were on your way to making partner at Excelsior Investments before the sky fell on you. What the heck are you afraid of? Go get her, man!"

Blake knew when it was time to back away and let things sink in, so he stood up to leave. As he walked past Travis on his way to the door, Travis reached out and grabbed his arm to let him know he appreciated his concern. Knowing Travis like a brother, Blake was confident he would give his comments series consideration.

Travis sat in his chair contemplating long after Blake left. When he was done, he rose to his feet and walked into the bedroom. He pulled open the top dresser drawer and located his BlackBerry. After hooking the phone holder to his belt, he plugged the BlackBerry into the charger. Travis searched through the pockets of the dirty jeans he wore to Texas Hall until he found the piece of paper with Misty's phone number.

An hour later, Travis unplugged the BlackBerry from the charger, added her phone number to his address book, and hit the save button. He then slid the device into its holder, like a gunslinger would his pistol.

25

INCOMING

Misty lay on her bed recovering from her eight-mile run through the streets of downtown San Antonio. She replayed the morning session in her head to savor the grueling workout she had put Chester through. Her daydream was interrupted by an incoming text message. *Bleep, bleep, bleep!*

That's probably Miguel letting me know he's going to lunch with Stephanie, she thought.

Misty grabbed her phone from the nightstand and saw a number she didn't recognize.

The message read, "Are you mad at me? —Travis."

Travis was the last person she had expected to text her. Misty felt unsettled, but she couldn't tell whether it was from joy, anger, or a combination of both. She decided to make him wait a while, but once she realized her eyes were glued to the message on her cell she decided it was best to go ahead and reply.

"I thought you said you didn't text," she typed.

His reply came after just a few seconds. "I didn't."

"If Chester finds out we're talking, he'll fire you. I'm not sure I want that on my conscience," she wrote back.

"You . . . have a conscience?"

"Smart ass!"

When ten minutes passed without a response, she began to worry she might have pissed him off.

Should I text back and apologize? she thought. *No, I need to gut it out.*

Misty jumped at the sound of her phone. "You do remember begging me to text you."

"I never begged. That's beneath me," she typed.

"Do you want me to send this next text or not? It's totally up to you."

Misty waited ten minutes before replying. "Ok, send the damn text. Yes, I want you to send the text."

Misty waited anxiously for several minutes. She could feel her heart in her throat.

At last, her phone beeped. "Meet me at the Palladium Theater on I-10. Purchase a ticket to the 3:20 showing of 'The Ugly Truth' in the IMAX theater. I'll be waiting for you in the top row."

Misty wondered if it was all a big joke, but before she could form an opinion, another text came through.

"Be sure to wear something loose and comfortable. Bra and panties are optional."

Misty fell back onto her bed and placed a pillow over her head.

Did he really say that?

She reread the text message over and over.

It finally sank in. *He wants to touch my junk!*

* * *

When Misty pulled into the parking lot of the theater, she looked through the little shoulder bag she had hurriedly put together before leaving the hotel. After inventorying the items, she gave herself one more chance to change her mind and return to the hotel. Feeling her resolve strengthen, she got out of the car, slammed the door behind her, and made her way briskly across the parking lot.

Once inside the massive theater complex, she bought a ticket and walked down the long corridor to the IMAX theater. Reaching the end of the interior wall, she paused for a moment. Her heart was racing. She very slowly peeked into the theater to catch a glimpse of him. *There he is!* Pulling back quickly, she rested her back against the dividing wall, wondering what to do next.

The bathroom stall was cramped, but Misty successfully removed her bra and panties and placed them in her shoulder bag. She glanced in the mirror to make sure her loose-fitting T-shirt and cotton shorts hid the fact that she wasn't wearing undergarments. She then made the long walk back down the hallway to the theater.

Feeling like a teenager about to do something naughty, Misty moved up the stairs to the top row of the IMAX. Travis met her halfway down the aisle, greeting her warmly with a hug.

His words were simple. "I'm so happy you came. I've missed you."

Misty placed her hand softly on the side of his face, making it obvious to Travis she felt the same. He grabbed her around the waist and brought her snugly into his arms. Their lips met with equal purpose in soft, tender kisses.

Misty pulled away to whisper into his ear. "I missed you, too."

She noticed he had raised the armrests of six consecutive seats, forming something resembling a couch. She sat down in the middle and was joined by Travis.

"So, how was your weekend?" Travis said softly, so as not to disturb the movie watchers below.

"Wonderful! I went to the coast with Mrs. Naples, Stephanie, and Miguel." A distant look clouded her face. "It helped take my mind off things."

Travis knew what Misty was referring to and chose to change the subject. Looking at her chest, he said, "Hey, it doesn't look like you're wearing a bra."

"Maybe I am, and maybe I'm not," she replied with a grin.

As Travis leaned in to kiss her neck, he said, "There's one sure way to find out."

Travis pulled the T-shirt from her shorts and moved his hands up until he found the answer he was looking for.

She welcomed the feel of his strong, warm hands exploring the size and shape of her breasts for awhile before playfully pulling back.

"So now you know," she said. Sitting up prim and proper, Misty crossed her arms and added, "I'll have you know, I wasn't wearing a bra when you texted me, so it has nothing to do with you."

Travis cocked his head to the right. "Is that so? Were you wearing panties when I sent you the text?"

"Of course," Misty snapped back. "What kind of girl do you think I am? That would be gross."

Travis flashed a cocky smile. "So if I reach down the top of your shorts, I'll definitely run into elastic?"

Misty scrunched her nose and pursed her lips while her eyes darted back and forth.

"Absolutely!" she bluffed.

"Well then, let's find out."

Misty grabbed Travis's wrist in a futile attempt to stop him. He play-fully struggled and then stopped. Misty breathed a premature sigh of relief, but then he reached around and snatched her bag, successfully shielding it from Misty as she struggled to get it back.

"Keep it down, Misty," he chided. "People are looking at us."

Misty spotted a couple that was indeed looking their way. Not wanting to cause a ruckus, she sat back in her chair, crossed her arms, and looked straight ahead, knowing full well what he would find.

When she got the courage to look, her lacy thong was dangling from his forefingers. "I suppose you keep a spare pair in your bag for emergencies?"

Misty snatched the panties from his hands. Then, deciding the best defense was a good offense, she looked at Travis confidently. "Okay, so what are you wearing under those jeans, buster?"

Before he could reply, she moved in quick as a cat, unbuckling his belt and unsnapping his jeans. Travis instinctively surveyed the audience. Each member of the small mid-afternoon crowd seemed to be intently watching the beginning of the movie, so he relaxed. Misty placed her hand inside the slit of his maroon boxers to survey his private property. The soft touch of her hand caused the big unit to grow into its full manhood.

"Something seems to be waking up there, boy," she whispered.

Giving his package a tap before pulling her hand out, she said, "Well, now we know. I must say, I'm impressed."

Travis's intentions were written all over his face. As she turned to get away, he caught her by the legs, pinning her to the seat. He gave her shorts a quick tug, dragging them down around her ankles, exposing her firm ass. She fought just long enough to give Travis the impression she was attempting to resist. He placed his hand on the small of her back to hold her in place as he moved into position. Once on his knees, he looked into her eyes. Misty smiled shyly, indicating total surrender. He directed Misty onto her side and she willingly obliged, lying down across the row of seats, facing him.

Travis placed his hand under her top leg, just above the back of her knee, and pushed until her knee was as far up as it would go. His fingers now had access to what would soon become his point of entry. He placed the soft heel of his hand over the entrance to her portal, gently applying pressure in slow, circular motions until the lips of her moist vagina opened wide. He massaged her privates in a clockwise motion as her natural juices seeped to the surface. Once wet and moist, Travis probed Misty's sweet insides with his middle and index fingers. He buried the knuckles deep inside.

While Travis manipulated her, Misty used her own hand to massage her clit. As she drew closer and closer to orgasm, Misty's pelvis vigorously rocked back and forth, assisting the many fingers in play. Watching Misty's facial expression intently, he knew she was on the verge of orgasm when her eyes glazed over. Travis gently placed his other hand over her mouth to muffle noise before adding a third finger. Misty worked her pulsating clitoris harder, until she was coming apart at the seams. Thank goodness his hand was there to muffle the sound.

Travis removed his hand from her mouth and put his finger to his lips, playfully indicating she should remain quiet. Misty laughed under her breath. Travis handed Misty her shorts and she wiggled them up until back in place.

"You're pretty good," she whispered.

"Only pretty good?"

"Okay, very good!"

When her shorts were back on, Travis stroked Misty's hair with the hand he had used to cover her mouth, allowing her to lie there and catch her breath. The sensation was so enjoyable that Misty fell asleep. Travis patiently waited for the show to end and the sparse crowd to exit the theater before attempting to wake her.

"Wake up, sleepyhead," he said. "The coast is clear."

Misty sat upright, at first unsure of where she was. Travis enjoyed watching her wipe the sleep from her eyes and attempt to smooth her hair out.

"You were drooling," he whispered in her ear.

Misty slapped him on the arm. "I was not. You're making that up."

Travis placed his hands on her shoulders. "Come with me to Austin next weekend. We'll get a room at the Drake Hotel on Sixth Street Friday night and party downtown. I have friends who'll take us out on Lake Travis Saturday. It's a beautiful lake. You'll love it."

"But where on earth will we stay Saturday night?" she asked playfully.

"I've got an idea, but let's keep it a surprise."

"Sure!" said Misty. "I'm all in. I love surprises!"

26

F L Y   I N   T H E   O I N T M E N T

Preoccupied with thoughts of her weekend trip to Austin, Misty paid little attention to Chester during the early portion of Friday morning's training session. She was okay with Miguel and Stephanie coming on the trip but wanted to make sure she had plenty of alone time with Travis.

Chester was not pleased with her distraction. "Misty, look at me. I need to tell you something."

She snapped out of her trance. "Sure. What is it?"

"Things just aren't working out."

"You're kidding. Do you feel I'm not upholding my end of the contract?"

"No, you're in compliance . . . with the contract. It's just that I'm bored with the process and tired of working out."

"What are you saying, Chester?"

He straightened his posture in an effort to look authoritative.

"I've decided this is going to be our last training session. I'm coming to your room tomorrow night at ten." Chester placed his hand under Misty's chin and lifted her head so her eyes met his. "Wear something nice. I'm partial to red."

Misty's mind raced. *Sleep with Chester Saturday night? I'm supposed to be in Austin with Travis. He said he has a surprise for me Saturday night!*

Misty thought quickly. "That's fine. But if this is our last training session, I want it to be one to remember."

During the remainder of the workout, Misty made frequent stops at the water fountain, mainly to buy herself time to think. On the third trip, something swelled up from deep inside her, pushing out all thoughts but one.

As if possessed, she escorted Chester to the dumbbell rack and placed a pair of thirty-pounders in his hands. She was well aware the weight was more than he could handle on his own. Chester struggled to press the weights into an overhead position. He successfully raised the dumbbell in his right hand to a locked position high above his head but struggled with the one in his left hand.

"Here, let me help," she said as she took the dumbbell out of his left hand and threw it to the floor. Chester's free hand couldn't support the remaining dumbbell on its own, and the weight over his head succumbed to gravity. When the dumbbell was at the level of his chest, Misty jumped in to help, pushing the weight toward Chester's groin as she pretended to gain a grip. Her plan worked to perfection. Misty caught the falling dumbbell after it made contact with Chester, freeing his hands to cover his crotch. He dropped to the floor and assumed the fetal position. Misty showed little emotion as she watched him writhing in pain. Chester looked up at Misty with tear-filled eyes.

She kneeled over him. "Oh my god, I am *so* sorry. Are you okay?"

"No, I'm not fucking okay," he said, holding his testicles with both hands.

Misty tilted her head to one side and peered at him inquisitively. "Does it hurt?" she asked.

"*Hell yes, it hurts!*" Chester bellowed. "Are you kidding me?"

The manager of the club, hearing all the commotion, came running. "Mr. Naples . . . are you okay? Can I call for an ambulance?"

Chester looked up angrily. "No. Just help me get to the dressing room and send in a bucket of ice."

The manager and an attendant put their arms around Chester and slowly led him to the dressing room.

With tongue in cheek, Misty yelled after him. "Chester! What about tomorrow night? It's red you like, right?"

Chester glanced over his right shoulder and snarled at her.

Misty shrugged her shoulders and called out, "I guess we'll make it another week, then."

27

ESCAPE TO AUSTIN

Stephanie talked Brenda out of her Suburban so they could travel to Austin in comfort, and Blake covered for Travis at the ranch, as he had done several times before. If Chester came out to the ranch, the official story was that Travis was in Austin spending the weekend with a couple of old clients from Excelsior Investments. Lying was not something that came easily to Travis, so he was comforted by the fact that Kevin and Bruce were two former clients, and that he had an open invitation to visit them anytime. All three being fellow Texas Longhorn fans had helped them to form a bond beyond their business activities. Travis insisted his clients have their wives accompany them to make Misty feel comfortable.

Taking the back roads to Austin in the Suburban gave Misty and Miguel a good sense of the rolling Texas hill country. The narrow, winding roads made for a fun ride, especially when Travis tromped on it coming out of the curves. Miguel was having a blast, but Misty and Stephanie eventually talked Travis into slowing down. From that point the drive was peaceful, giving Travis time to observe Misty and try to figure out why he was so attracted to her. He began to realize it was her wide range of emotions that made being with her so interesting. Her little temper tantrums were never malicious and always short in duration, just like a child's. Her enthusiasm was infectious, and her forthright honesty a breath of fresh air. Travis stopped his analysis when it dawned on him that the only thing that mattered was how good he felt in her company.

The south side of Austin looked like any other town until they exited along Town Lake. Misty gazed at the hordes of joggers making their way around the lake on one of the finest jogging trails she had ever seen. The path was lined with gravel like an old high school track, and it snaked in and out of tree-lined trails. She made a mental note to come back one weekend and spend half a day on the trail.

Their destination, the historic Drake Hotel, was located in the heart of Austin's Sixth Street district. When the vehicle reached the valet stand, Misty stepped out to admire the outside of the hotel, which was over a hundred years old. She played the game Sammy had taught her in New Orleans and imagined it was the late eighteen hundreds. She envisioned dirt roads with wagon-wheel ruts running down the middle and horses tied up to hitching posts. The outside of the hotel was grand and stately, but the inside turned out to be even more spectacular. Gargantuan columns supported the ceiling several stories above them, giving the lobby a Romanesque feel. Thrilled by her surroundings, Misty admired the massive curved stairway and wondered where it led.

After a brief stop at the front desk and a ride up the elevator, Travis unlocked the door to their hotel room and pushed it open. Misty quickly moved past him to the middle of the room, looking it over in delight. It was exquisitely furnished, yet masculine on a grand scale. *This is Texas perfect!* thought Misty as she twirled around in the middle of the room. Wood-paneled walls, sixteen-foot ceilings, and wood-framed windows—it was all to her liking.

"Which style of room did you chose?" she asked. "This is so . . . Texas!"

"It's called the Cattle Baron's suite."

"I should have guessed!" She sat on the massive bed and gave it a few bounces. "Nice and firm. Just the way I like it." Misty realized Travis had caught her little innuendo. "But there's only one bed. Where are you going to sleep?"

Travis played along. "We could arm wrestle for it, but I've got a better idea."

"Oh really! So what's your big idea?"

"I'll show you later tonight."

"Well, you're just full of surprises, aren't you?"

Misty took a catnap while Travis showered. She drifted in and out of sleep until she awoke to the sensation of Travis rubbing her arm. "Hey, sleepyhead. I'm headed down to meet Bruce and Kevin in the piano bar. When you're ready, go down to the lobby and walk up those curved stairs you were looking at this afternoon. We'll be at the bar."

He leaned over, gave her a peck on the temple, and departed. After the door closed she curled into a snug little ball. Misty couldn't remember the last time she felt this serene.

* * *

About thirty minutes later, Misty climbed the massive staircase as if she were royalty. She couldn't help but wonder which dignitaries had made the climb over the years. Her eyes worked overtime as she walked through the grand lounge area of the piano bar. The room was every bit as masculine as her suite. There was a big star in the carpet and a *D* in the middle, no doubt for Drake. The massive sofas were covered with distressed leather—naturally distressed from years of wear and tear rather than artificially made to look old. *Oh, the stories they could tell*, Misty thought.

She stopped to ponder an intriguing metal sculpture of a horse dragging a man who had one foot stuck in the stirrup. Behind the fallen cowboy rode a horseman clutching his own horse's mane as he leaned over to one side with a Winchester rifle in his free hand. He appeared to be aiming at the first rider's horse, which puzzled Misty.

A dark-haired man with a kind face standing next to Misty said, "It's a pretty spectacular work of art, no?"

"Yes, it's fascinating," Misty replied, "but why is that man trying to shoot the other man's horse?"

He seemed pleased she had asked. "Well, that scene depicts a serious concern in the Old West, referred to as Widow Maker."

"Widow Maker? But that cowboy dude is getting ready to shoot that poor horse. Horses don't get married, so how is he going to be making a widow?"

"Yes," the man said, amused, "but the cowboy being drug to his death may have a wife."

"Oh! Now I get it. Will he shoot the horse in the leg so it won't die?"

Realizing she didn't know horses with a damaged leg get put down, the man paused in an attempt to think up a respectful reply. Fortunately, their discussion came to an end when Travis put his arms around Misty and the man she was talking to.

"So I see you've met Bruce," he said.

"Oh! You're Bruce," exclaimed Misty. "I had no idea."

Bruce offered her his hand. "It's a real pleasure. Can I give you credit for getting Travis to finally accept our invitation?"

Before she had a chance to respond, another man walked up. "So, you must be Misty," he said. "You fit Travis's description to a tee."

Misty looked at Travis and frowned. "And just what description did Travis give you?"

"Actually, I don't remember, but 'hot, bodacious bombshell' would've worked."

Misty gave him a hug. "I like this guy. I hope he's Kevin."

"That I am. I just call it as I see it."

Bruce laughed. "Yes he does. It's a good thing you're not ugly."

Misty didn't understand why Bruce and Kevin took a few steps back until she noticed the two attractive women approaching.

"Hello, boys. Helping a damsel in distress?" one of the women said.

"I think the damsel's in distress *because* the guys are helping her," the other woman added.

"Travis and Misty, meet my wife, Terri, and Kevin's wife, Annamaria," said Bruce. "Girls, meet Travis and Misty."

"Annamaria," said Misty. "What a beautiful name."

"Why thank you," she replied. "It's almost as beautiful as you."

With a polite smile, Misty stepped back a few paces to observe the people she would be spending the rest of the weekend with as Travis and the couples made final plans for the evening. Kevin was a handsome man, with sandy blond hair that gave him a youthful appearance for a man his age. His wife, Annamaria, was trim and cute in the classic Barbie-doll sense. Her olive skin indicated possible Italian descent. Bruce was tall, dark, and handsome and matched up nicely with Terri, his attractive blonde wife. They appeared to be in their forties, but Misty assumed active lifestyles may have helped them defy their age.

Misty couldn't have been more excited about spending the weekend with them.

28

AUSTIN NIGHTLIFE

When Miguel and Stephanie emerged from their hotel room and joined
the group, they all went out for Chinese food. After a light meal accompanied by large quantities of sake, they took to the streets, barhopping,
staying at each bar long enough to enjoy one drink and move on. By the
time they got to a local honky-tonk, Kevin and Bruce were feeling no
pain. The group worked their way through the crowded bar until reaching the dance floor in the back. It was no Texas Hall, but fun just the
same. After thirty minutes of brushing up on her Texas two-step, Travis
led the group through the crowd once again until they reached a wooden
barrier. On the other side sat the mechanical bull.

"Outstanding!" Miguel shouted. "I'm going first."

Travis whispered into Misty's ear, "This is how we are going to
determine which one of us sleeps on the floor tonight. Whoever stays on
the mechanical bull the longest gets the bed."

Misty cracked up. "You're joking, right?"

Looking mock-serious, Travis led Miguel to the bull, leaving Misty
to contemplate what she was getting herself into.

Terri and Annamaria stepped in, flanking Misty on either side. "What did Travis whisper in your ear?" Terri asked.

Misty blushed. "Oh, he wants me to ride that thingy."

"I rode it once," said Terri.

"And?"

Terri raised her eyebrows and smiled, but did not comment further.

Misty looked at Annamaria, hoping she would say something, but she just shrugged. Misty's hands became clammy.

Miguel mounted the bull with a little help from Travis. The operator pulled on the lever and the whole contraption began to move, starting out slow and easy but quickly picking up pace. Miguel's look of confidence was fading by the second. Then, the bull spun violently, throwing Miguel to the padding below. He quickly bounced up with a frustrated throw of his arm.

Travis mounted the mechanical bull next, and it was obvious he knew what he was doing. His movements were effortless, so the operator picked up the pace. People scurried over to watch him, women cheering and men jeering. Travis had a firm grip on the reins, but the rest of his body was fluid, yet stable. Once he'd hung on for a full twenty seconds after the machine reached full throttle, even the men were cheering. When the time came for Travis to fall, he fell gracefully. Women hugged him and men slapped him on the back as he worked his way back to the group. The manager of the club came running over to tell them, their next round of drinks was on the house.

Misty tucked her hands under her armpits, refusing to hug or slap him on the back.

Travis leaned in with a grin. "It's your turn, Misty."

Misty wouldn't look at him. "There's no way I can win back the bed, so why should I try?"

Travis smiled. "Because I might make you sleep in the hallway if you don't."

Misty stormed red-faced through the crowd.

"You're not going to let her get on that thing are you?" Annamaria said to Travis.

Kevin spoke up. "Why not? Misty seems rough and tumble. Besides, she looks madder than any bull I've ever seen."

The girls turned to Bruce, hoping he might have a different opinion, but he tilted his head to the right and shrugged. "There's plenty of padding under the bull. I think she'll be alright."

The girls then turned to Miguel, but by then Misty was already halfway mounted. The group held their collective breaths.

Travis stood at the rail, watching intently as the attendant placed Misty's feet in the stirrups and the reins in her hand. The operator sensed that Misty had never done this before, so he eased the lever forward, causing the bull to gently sway from side to side. After a few moments, he took it up another notch, and the boys were pleasantly surprised how well she handled it. She seemed to have a real knack, and she was becoming more confident in the saddle by the moment. As the operator attempted to nudge the throttle up one more notch, a drunk tripped, falling directly into him from behind. The fall threw the throttle into high gear, and the bull lurched forward violently and then spun full circle, throwing Misty high into the air.

The crowd gasped as the combination of centrifugal force and Misty's slight one hundred and ten pounds catapulted her past the heavy padding and onto the hard wood floor. She landed squarely on her derriere. Travis, Kevin, Bruce, and Miguel all flew over the railing to her aid. When they reached her, she had already rolled over onto her side and was covering her face with her hands. The music stopped and the bar went deathly silent. Although in great pain, Misty was too proud to let Travis know. As she struggled to get up, Travis and Miguel helped her onto her feet. When Misty gave a thumbs-up to the crowd, the place erupted in cheers. With a noticeable limp, she walked back to the girls.

Annamaria, Terri, and Stephanie gathered around, hugging Misty to see if she was okay. One by one they gave the guys dirty looks.

Kevin looked at Travis. "Oops!"

Travis walked up to Misty. "I'm so sorry," he said. "That was my fault."

She stared back at him for a moment before saying, "Get over it. I'll live."

As they left the honky-tonk, Kevin asked her, "So what was racing through your mind while you were airborne?"

Misty looked at Bruce. "Widow Maker."

Bruce smiled.

As they walked onto the street, Terri and Annamaria thought it might be a good idea to get Misty back to the Drake and call it a night. They sensed she was hurt more than she let on. As the group made their way back to the Drake, Misty stopped to look into the window of a club.

"Follow me," she said with a twinkle in her eye.

They walked through frosted front doors, and as they did, large curtains opened automatically, giving them the impression they were walking onto a stage. The bar's dark walls were lined with tall, circular, upholstered booths, filled with Austinites grooving to the Latin beat. Misty had already made her way back to a crowded dance floor. She motioned for Travis to come closer. When he did, she pulled on his shirtsleeve until his ear was next to her mouth and yelled over the loud music, "You're on my turf now! Wait here."

Walking toward the DJ, she thought, *Time for a little payback, cowboy.*

Misty found the DJ accommodating. When she got back to the group, he made an announcement over the intercom: "Ladies and gentleman, we have a request for salsa music. And don't forget we give free salsa lessons every Tuesday night!" The crowded dance floor erupted in cheers.

Misty grabbed Travis by the hand and pulled, but he didn't budge. "No way. I don't know how to salsa," he said.

Misty put both hands firmly on his arm and pulled harder. "Come on! I didn't know how to two-step until you taught me."

Travis did not take to the salsa steps quickly. As he clumsily moved around the dance floor, Misty reveled in his discomfort. When she could tell he was thoroughly frustrated, she told him to wait on the sidelines while she danced with Miguel to demonstrate the moves. She had no problem rubbing it in.

She moved her hips to the music as fluently as Travis had ridden the bull. As she and Miguel danced, she thought about how thankful she was that her adrenaline had kicked in and masked the pain from her fall. Her salsa moves were much more seductive than bull-riding, and they drew all eyes in the bar to her hot bod. Annamaria noticed Kevin was enjoying Misty's moves a little too much so she jabbed him in the ribs. Watching Misty, Terri and Annamaria made plans to drag their husbands to the free salsa lessons next Tuesday night. When Miguel stepped off the dance floor and offered to give the married couples dance lessons, Kevin and Bruce backed out, saying they wanted to go get a beer.

For the next half hour, Miguel gave Annamaria and Terri lessons while Misty made Travis try one more time. She enjoyed watching him struggle as she moved around him seductively. At the end of a song, he put his hands on his hips, letting Misty know she had pushed him far enough.

Trying to rebuild his self-esteem, Misty patted Travis on the chest. "It's okay—you're a great country dancer."

Travis grinned. "All right, you earned your way back into bed. Let's call a truce."

Misty offered her hand. "Truce."

On the way back to the hotel, Travis could tell from Misty's limp that she was still in some discomfort. When they'd said goodbye to the other couples for the night and gotten back to their suite, Travis placed a hand on each of her shoulders. "You're one tough girl. We have a long day planned tomorrow, so I think it best we let your injuries have time to heal tonight."

Misty was pretty certain Travis had had little sex, if any, during his yearlong sabbatical. What he did to her in the movie theater was wonderful, and she had planned on returning the favor tonight, but she knew Travis was right. She needed the time to heal.

Grimacing from the pain in her legs, Misty pushed herself up on her tiptoes and gave Travis a short, sweet kiss. "Don't worry. I'll make it up to you tomorrow night."

29

A Day on the Lake

Stephanie read the directions out loud while Travis navigated the Suburban down the narrow, winding river road.

"There's the marina straight ahead!" Misty yelled out.

Travis parked the car in a lot close to the water and they all exited the vehicle. As Miguel stretched, he noticed a customized, extended golf cart heading in their direction.

"You actually got here on time," Kevin yelled out from the cart. "I'm impressed."

Travis patted Misty on the back. "Well, Sleeping Beauty here was pretty hard to wake up."

Kevin looked at Misty. "Come on, Sleeping Beauty. We've got a full-size bunk on the boat, so you can sleep away the day while the seven dwarfs play."

Misty began counting on her fingers. "Stephanie, Miguel, Travis, Kevin, Annamaria, Bruce, and Terri. Nice, Kevin! You can count. There *are* seven of you."

"Well, I've got fingers too, you know," he shot back.

Misty returned the serve. "I'm assuming you're Dopey?"

"Keep this up and you'll turn me into Grumpy!"

When Kevin pulled the golf cart up to the marina store, Stephanie asked, "Would you like us to buy some provisions?"

"Nope," Kevin replied. "Happy and I bought everything we needed this morning."

Leaving the cart at the store, the group admired the boats as they worked their way along the floating docks on foot. Kevin pointed to a boat several slips away. It was a 58-foot Sea Ray, loaded with all of the latest gear.

Bruce, Terri, and Annamaria appeared on the bridge above. "Hey guys!" Terri yelled. "Don't be bashful, come on up!"

They all broke out laughing at Terri's unwitting use of a dwarf's name. She and Bruce were clueless until Stephanie explained the earlier conversation.

Bruce played tour guide, pointing out all of the features of the boat, which he proudly told them was named *Coconut Joe*. After showing them the plush upper cabin, he escorted the group to the lower decks and sleeping quarters. The master stateroom was equipped with a 32-inch flatscreen TV, queen bed, full-length mirror, and small shower. Bruce cranked up the Bose entertainment system to the sound of Willie Nelson.

When the tour was over, Kevin untied the boat from its moorings and tossed the lines into the boat. Bruce threw the twin V8 diesel inboards into reverse and eased the 58-foot beast away from the dock. Everyone gathered on the bridge except Stephanie and Miguel, who chose to get cozy on the aft bench. Annamaria and Terri played the perfect hostesses, handing out beers from the refrigerator and offering up mixed drinks from the bridge's full bar. Travis and Misty joined Bruce and Kevin in the cockpit with drinks in hand. Once clear of the marina, Bruce let the engines loose, bringing them to a comfortable cruising speed of ten knots. It was a typical August day in South Texas; temperatures would reach ninety-eight by midday.

"Enjoy the morning air," Bruce yelled out, "'cause it's gonna be a scorcher." Misty gazed at the beautiful dark blue water of Lake Travis as a heavenly breeze tousled her hair.

Today is not about Chester, thought Misty, *it's about enjoying Austin and my wonderful new friends.*

Bruce throttled down as they neared their destination. He pointed to a long line of boats up ahead and yelled, "Devil's Cove!"

"What's up with the lineup?" Miguel hollered up from below, noticing a string of vessels strung into a row in the cove ahead of them.

"It's called rafting up," Bruce yelled back. "We tie our boat to the end boat and when someone else comes along, they tie up to us."

Kevin shouted, "It's party time!"

Once *Coconut Joe* was moored to the neighboring *Seducer*, Bruce cut the twin diesels. Shortly after, another boat moored on their other side. Bruce pulled a beer out of the fridge and threw it to Kevin. "Drink up, buddy. Let's have some fun."

"How'd you come up with such a cool name for your boat?" Misty asked.

Bruce pointed to Terri, who happened to be in the process of removing her T-shirt. Her boobs, barely held by her swimsuit top, were amazing. "Terri's middle name is Joe."

A smile spread across Misty's face. "That's so cool! How did you get Terri to go along?"

"Hell, it was her idea," he said.

After putting suntan lotion on Misty's back, Travis said, "Hey, do you mind if I discuss a little business with Bruce and Kevin inside?"

Misty shoved him in the direction of the cabin. "Sure, get me on the high seas and then abandon ship."

"I knew you would understand," Travis said, laughing, as he walked away. "Don't do anything to sink the ship while I'm gone."

With Travis inside and the others talking to the neighbors, Misty decided it was a good time to take a dip in the lake. Armed with some noodles to help her stay afloat, she jumped in. Out of habit, she unconsciously prepared herself for the cold Pacific water of the West Coast, only to find the lake water bathtub warm. Misty put noodles under her knees and neck, imagining she was soaking in a Jacuzzi, and observed the mass of humanity. There appeared to be three fit and attractive women to every guy. Misty realized being a single guy in Texas with a badass boat had its advantages. She then noticed how well Bruce, Terri, Kevin, and Annamaria fit in with the younger set because they kept their bodies in excellent condition. Travis had told her on the trip up from San Antonio that Kevin and Annamaria were avid bike riders and ran half marathons several times a year.

When Misty caught Miguel looking at dancing girls aboard a boat called *Miller Time* and saw that Stephanie looked agitated, she climbed back onboard and playfully slapped Miguel upside the head.

"Hey! What the heck was that for, Misty?" he blurted out.

"You need to quit gawking at the bimbos and pay attention to Stephanie."

With an apologetic shrug, he turned and headed back to Stephanie. Misty could hear him sweet-talking her as they walked off.

Travis made up for his little business meeting by giving Misty his full and undivided attention. They made their way to the upper-cabin sofa, content to lie there and watch the three-ring circus going on about them. Mid-afternoon, a dark, tanned man without a hair on his body climbed on board and walked past them to the galley where Terri stood fixing sandwiches.

"Hey, can I get a drink?" he asked Terri. She graciously opened the fridge without saying a word.

Seeing the lone can of energy drink, he said, "I'll show you my butt if you let me have that last Red Bull."

Terri looked over at Travis and Misty and laughed before replying, "Hell, I don't care. Show me what you got."

Terri laughed hysterically after he did as promised. "You're too much," she said, handing him the Red Bull. "Okay, time for you to go."

When the man lingered, Travis whistled to get his attention. "Hey. You heard the lady. Fun's over."

He gave Travis a glare and angrily walked back to the next boat.

Moments later, there was a ruckus outside the cabin. The guy was standing on the bow of the boat flashing himself to the world.

Not amused, Annamarie walked up to the man, looked him directly in the eye, and said, "Listen, buster, I'm a certified gastroenterology registered nurse, and we perform dozens of colonoscopies each week. I can spot an asshole when I see one, and no, it's not the one you keep flashing. It's the big, fat butthead sitting on your neck."

When everyone within earshot erupted in laughter, the man became belligerent, hurling obscenities at Annamaria. The men hustled over to the other boat. Kevin and Bruce grabbed the man's arms as Travis and Miguel each grabbed a leg. On the count of three they flung him high into the air and then watched him flail wildly on his way down.

The man hit the lake facedown, making a loud slapping noise. "Damn, he looked like a cat falling out of a building," said Bruce.

"Ouch!" said Kevin. "He didn't land like a cat."

Miguel looked at Annamaria in awe. "You were amazing!"

The usually mild-mannered Annamaria blushed. "Yeah, I guess I kind of lost it for a moment." She was the most popular woman on the flotilla after that.

While Travis fixed himself a sandwich, Misty walked over to visit Bruce. "So Bruce, tell me the coolest thing that's ever happened to you on the lake."

Overhearing the question, Terri said, "I know what it is. Go ahead and tell her, Bruce." Terri then turned to Misty. "Just so you know, this was before we met."

Bruce began his story. "Well, I was contracted to build a new topless bar years ago, and the manager was having a tough time recruiting girls. She asked me if I knew anyone with a boat they could use to recruit women on Lake Travis. I asked how many girls the boat needed to hold, and she told me eight. Guess I got caught up in the moment, because I said yes, even though the boat I had at the time wasn't big enough. I called a friend with a much larger boat who happened to be on the lake and he agreed to give the girls a ride. By the time Jimmy arrived, the number of women had grown to eighteen. Our buddy Billy had a boat that held twelve, so we talked him into bringing his as well. When we pulled out of the marina, eight girls were with Jimmy and ten girls were with Billy and me. Billy drove while I sat up front. It was a hot summer day, so the girls decided to take their tops off. Although the rest of the day was a blur, I do remember proudly waving to friends all along the lake."

Misty patted Bruce on the back. "Well, aren't you the lucky one." She then said to Terri, "Looks like you saved Bruce just in time."

"I saved him from acting out his fantasies, but I'm sure they're still rolling around in that noggin of his," Terri said. She walked behind Bruce and massaged his neck. "I wouldn't have it any other way. It takes a good imagination to be as good in bed as he is."

At five o'clock they broke from the chain of boats and headed in. Misty took one more look at Devil's Cove as they pulled away.

"What a fantastic afternoon," she said to Travis. "Thank you so much for bringing me to Austin." She added, "So what's up next? I'm starving."

"First, we're headed to the Yellow Parrot so we can get a bite to eat and watch Kevin and Bruce's band play. I'll tell you after that."

"You're kidding me. They have a band? I thought they were businessmen."

Annamaria was within earshot, and she called out, "They are, but they still think they're kids."

"Hey, what's wrong with that?" said Kevin.

Annamaria patted Kevin on the knee. "Nothing at all, dear, and I enjoy being a groupie."

A charter boat caught Misty's attention as it passed on the port side. It was loaded down with muscular men and hot young women. She could only imagine how wild things would get on that boat tonight.

When they hit open waters, Terri advised them to use the showers to clean up for dinner. Bruce held to four knots so everyone had time to get ready. After finishing her shower, Misty was greeted on the bridge by a wonderful breeze that soothed her sun-drenched body. Travis joined her on the bridge, looking buff in a white Tommy Bahama shirt that accentuated his golden tan. It reminded Misty of how stunning Travis looked the first time she'd seen him at the athletic club. They wrapped their arms around each other, enjoying the breeze together.

* * *

The Yellow Parrot was just up a hill a stone's throw from the marina. The open-air bar had a wonderful view of the lake, serving as a nice backdrop for the band. Kevin and Bruce broke from the group to set up on stage as the others sat at a special table with a great view, having some drinks and reliving the event with the butthead on the lake. When they were finished setting up, the owner of the club stepped to the mic and said, "Please welcome back Against the Wind!"

The band launched into "Badfish" by Jack Johnson. Bruce sang and Kevin played the drums. Later, Bruce dedicated Pat Green's "Carry On" to Misty and Travis. Halfway through the song, Misty walked over to Kevin while he was playing his drums and pushed her index fingers into the middle of his cheeks.

Kevin turned and yelled, "What the hell!"

Misty patted him on the head and mouthed the word, "Smile."

After having dinner and watching a spectacular sunset, Travis grabbed Misty by the hand and coaxed her from the table.

"See you later, guys," Travis said to the group. "I had a wonderful time."

"You two have a nice evening," Terri said, a knowing tone in her voice.

Misty got the impression everyone knew what was going on except her, but she didn't care—she was sure it was finally time for her surprise.

30

A Night to Remember

Travis led Misty back down the hill to the marina, where Bruce's friend Billy was waiting for them in his ski boat. After a quick introduction, Travis and Misty got aboard and Billy taxied through the still water of the marina.

"I really appreciate this," Travis said to Billy.

"Not a problem. I'm used to Bruce calling up and needing my boat when there are beautiful women involved."

"So you must be topless Billy," said Misty.

"Topless Billy?" he replied.

"Yeah, the guy that helped Bruce cruise the lake with a boatload of topless women."

Billy laughed. "One and the same, ma'am."

Misty desperately wanted to ask Travis where they were going but decided instead to let things play themselves out. As Billy took them clear across the lake, her anticipation grew. They approached a different cove, and Billy throttled back. And then she saw *Coconut Joe* moored to a private dock.

Excited yet puzzled, Misty turned to Travis. "How did the boat get way out here?"

"Remember when I had that business meeting with Kevin and Bruce? The meeting's agenda was figuring out how to pull off your surprise, which is, of course, that we're going to spend the night alone in the cove."

A man appeared on *Coconut Joe*'s deck. "That's Billy's friend. He brought the boat out and will ride back with Billy."

Misty threw herself in Travis's arms. "What a wonderful surprise," she whispered into his ear.

After dropping them off, Billy and his friend said good-bye and motored off toward the other side of the lake. Travis and Misty spent the next several hours walking the deck, talking, and looking up at the stars. A few sparse clouds drifted by from time to time, but the stars shone bright most of the night, which one would expect, being deep in the heart of Texas. Their conversation was lively at first but as the time went by it became more subdued. Misty decided against drinking anything because she wanted to ensure that she remembered everything that she hoped was about to take place.

Travis caught Misty yawning. "It's been a long day," he said. "What do you say we retire to the master stateroom?"

"Yes, why don't we, Master Travis?" Misty replied teasingly.

Down in the stateroom, Misty sat on the bed, taking in her surroundings. Travis grabbed the remote control and gave it a click. The sound of rain emanated from the speakers. He sat down beside her.

Misty placed her hand on his. "So Master Planner, where are our PJs? Looks like you didn't think of everything after all."

Travis leaned in and gave her a lingering kiss to let her know that PJs would not be needed tonight. The kissing continued, and they stopped now and then to look into each other's eyes. As Misty slowly unbuttoned her blouse, Travis focused on her eyes and smiled. Her blouse fell to the floor, and she reached back and unhooked her silky black bra. Travis waited until he was certain she had completed her task before slowly lowering his eyes to gaze upon her sumptuous breasts. He had never seen two mounds as luscious as the ones displayed before him tonight, and chances were he would never see their equal.

"I think we should rename the boat *Mount Misty* just for tonight," he said.

"Is that what you want to do? Mount Misty?" she said seductively.

Travis leaned down to fondle, kiss, and suckle her trophies. Misty had dreamt about this moment ever since their affair at the movies, wondering how much better it could get. Now it was time to find out. When Travis was satiated, he placed his hands on the sides of her arms and gently coaxed her onto her back. Straddling her, he delicately rubbed his hand over every inch of her exposed and naked upper body. After carefully exploring each taut breast, he gave the nipples a gentle squeeze and tug. Misty felt each pull in her privates. He finished by circling her mouth with his fingertip before working his way down to her skirt. Nimble fingers quickly and ably unzipped and removed her skirt, with some help from Misty. Becoming impatient, she planted her feet on the bed and raised her hips, giving Travis the opportunity to free her underwear. With her panties now down to her thighs, she lifted her legs into the air, allowing Travis to do the rest. He lifted them up, up, and over her feet. She teased him, clinging to the undergarment with her toes momentarily before allowing him to fling them to the floor.

She watched as he pulled off his shirt and moved into position. Facing her, he grabbed her thighs just underneath the knees and pulled her to him. As he spread her legs open, it gave her a full view of his powerfully built shoulders and well-developed pecs covered with soft, dark brown hair. Misty was so wet now that slow and easy was not going to satisfy her much longer.

Travis began his assault by sloppily mouthing his way down the insides of her thighs, leaving a trail of wetness behind. When Misty hung her legs over his shoulders, Travis put his powerful hands under her buttocks and lifted her to him, proceeding to kiss and lick every inch of her privates. As he split the lips of her vagina with his thick, hot tongue, Misty let out a soft moan. The deeper he thrust, the more she arched her back, pushing herself snugly against his face. By the time she came, the only parts of her left on the bed were her head, neck, and shoulders. Fixing her with an amorous stare, he gently picked her up and laid her entire body back down on the mattress.

As Misty lay with hands to her forehead, trying to catch her breath,

Travis stood next to the bed and took off the rest of his clothes. Misty wasn't sure if she had ever seen a man with buttocks so firm and perfectly rounded. She looked at his thick, muscular legs and understood why he looked so good in his tight-fitting cowboy jeans. He turned around, exposing his long, hard penis that rose so high in the air, it almost reached his belly button. Yearning to touch his instrument, she sat up and hung her legs off the side of the bed. She grabbed his penis with her right hand and directed it into her warm, moist mouth, working on the head with deliciously delicate moves.

Travis braced himself by placing his hands on the top of Misty's head as she moved up and down in a twisting motion. Cupping her left hand underneath his testicles, she massaged them ever so gently. As he became more excited, Travis moved his hands to the side of Misty's head as if to take control and guide her movements, but quickly decided against it. Instead, he tilted her head back and kissed her on the top of the forehead. Then, with one quick, powerful move he lifted her into the air and deposited her not so gently onto the bed. Misty found herself on her back, her knees bent. Travis climbed on top of her, choosing plain-Jane missionary style. But as he guided his manhood inside her, she discovered there would not be anything plain-Jane about it.

Travis worked his pelvis as he ground in and out of her. She observed him as if merely a spectator as long as she could before succumbing to the wonderful sensation racing through her loins and bracing her hands against his chest to support his powerful thrusts. Travis stopped long enough to give her a sensuous kiss, which unleashed a passion deep inside she never knew existed and catapulted her into a string of orgasms back to back to back. They were long, strong, and powerful. Travis, aroused by her sounds of pleasure, arched his back toward the ceiling and let out a mighty groan. She felt his warm ejaculation deep inside and was elated she had made him come with such a powerful explosion. She figured he was unleashing a full year of frustration and was pleased to be the recipient.

In a way, Misty felt as if she had exorcised the demons that had been making his life so miserable.

31

MORNING HAS BROKEN

Misty awoke to the sound of waves lapping against the boat. With her back to Travis, she lay snuggling in his arms. When the first rays of sunlight illuminated the room, she lightly traced the veins on the top of his hands with her index finger. But why did she feel so troubled? Travis was not a client, and this was not the typical morning after. She didn't have to notify the client she had fulfilled her obligation and then return home. Yet somehow it felt the same. After heavy deliberation, she realized there was something she had to do. It was time to explain to Travis that she was the Black Widow Trainer—and risk losing him. She couldn't let him find out from someone else and not be there to explain the best she could.

As she pondered her plan of action, Travis opened his eyes and pulled her to him, hugging her tight. This only made her task more difficult.

"Hey, Sleeping Beauty," he said. "You must've worn me out last night. I'm the one sleeping late today."

Misty rolled over, placed her hand under his chin, and gave him a kiss.

Nothing was said over the next few minutes. Finally, Travis broke the silence. "You're awful quiet this morning. Is everything all right?"

When no answer came, Travis suspected a problem.

Eventually she spoke. "I have something to tell you, and I pray you will understand, but if you don't, I won't blame you," she said without rolling over to look at him.

Thoughts of the horrible night his fiancée had told him her father forbade them to be married shot through his head. He feared the worst but prayed he was overreacting.

Taking in a deep breath, he said, "Okay, I'm ready."

Misty lay back down and stared at the ceiling as she filled Travis in on her profession. "I'm not the kind of girl you take home to your mother." She quickly remembered his mother was deceased. "I'm so sorry. I shouldn't have referenced your mother."

"It's okay."

"Well, what I'm trying to say is that, well . . . I do more than train my clients. I agree to sleep with them—but only once."

At first, Travis felt relief that Misty wasn't blowing him off, but knew he would have to come to grips with her shocking profession. When he lay there staring at the ceiling in silence, Misty decided to take a shower and give him time to think. She arose and left without a word.

Once under the stream of warm water, she found it hard to fight back tears. When finished, she scooted past Travis up to the galley to make a pot of coffee. Misty heard the shower down below and hoped he wasn't trying to wash off any remnants of her from last night.

Sitting on a couch in the upper cabin, her legs curled in a ball as she drank her coffee, Misty could swear she heard him whistling down below.

Didn't he hear a word I said? she thought.

A few minutes later she heard footsteps coming up the stairs. Her breath caught in her throat as she nervously awaited his arrival. Walking over to her, he stopped long enough to give her a kiss on the nose before heading for the coffee pot.

"Are you on drugs?" asked Misty.

Travis poured his cup of coffee. "Nope. I don't do drugs."

"Then why are you in such a good mood after everything I told you?"

He took a seat next to her and sipped his coffee. "You make good coffee."

Misty scrunched her nose.

He patted her on the leg and chuckled. "The only thing wrong with you is that you were born in the wrong century."

"I beg your pardon!"

"You were born in the wrong century. If you lived in the sixteenth century, you would've made a top-notch courtesan."

Travis could tell from Misty's facial expression his comment needed a little more explaining.

"One of my all-time favorite movies is *Dangerous Beauty*. I think it came out in 1998. It's about a courtesan in Venice. Courtesans played an extremely important role in upper-class society in those days. They were well-educated, worldly, and fiercely independent women of free morals. Some were trained artisans of dance, and many were married. It was just a job. They were chosen on the basis of their breeding, social and conversational skills, intelligence, common sense, and companionship. And, of course, their physical attributes. But it was their wit and personality that set them apart from regular women. Sound like anyone we know?"

Misty lowered her head as she sorted through his comments. After a bit she looked up and said, "So what you are saying is, I'm good looking, worldly, independent, witty, intelligent, have common sense, and make a good companion?"

"Yep, that pretty much sums it up."

Well I am an artisan of tango and salsa, Misty thought, *and I'm getting pretty darn worldly these days. I must have something out of the ordinary going for me to get paid what I do.*

She set her coffee cup down, took Travis's cup out of his hand, and took a seat in his lap. Travis knew he would never be able to do anything other than adore her; she was so full of life and fun to be with. For a moment they just sat there grinning at each other like two kids.

Finally, Misty said, "So was I a good courtesan last night, Master?"

Travis pulled her to him. "Misty, no man could ever be your master. You choose your clients, they don't choose you."

"I just love you, Travis," she replied. "I'm so glad we're friends."

"So am I, Misty. So am I."

32

BACK IN SAN ANTONIO

Misty was thrilled when Stephanie informed her that Chester wanted to skip out on this week's training, and she was pretty certain it had to do with his little accident the previous week. But her excitement was short-lived. The next words out of Stephanie's mouth were, "Oh yeah, and Chester sent Travis to a cattle auction in Fort Worth."

"When's he coming back?" she asked.

"Not until late Thursday."

As soon as Stephanie hung up, Misty typed Travis a text message: "So now that you've had me you're riding off into the sunset?"

His reply took only a moment. "Not my choice, Sunshine. Boss's orders, you know. I'm boarding a Southwest flight to Love Field so got to run. Call me Friday afternoon and we'll make plans for the weekend."

"Okay, take care," she texted back.

* * *

On Friday, Misty walked up the stairs of the hotel, on her way back from her mid-afternoon run. She was sweating profusely but wanted to stop by the front desk before heading to her room to shower. She needed to switch to a room with a terrace that overlooked the interior courtyard in the event Travis spent the night. Misty knew she was being a bit paranoid, but the last thing she wanted was to be sitting on her balcony overlooking San Antonio with Travis and have Chester see them.

When Misty approached the desk, the hotel clerk said, "Misty, I'm glad you came by. I have an urgent message for you."

"Who's it from?"

"Mr. Naples."

Misty felt faint, something even the hundred-degree temperatures failed to do, and decided she had better sit down to read his message. After walking over to the nearest bench, she began reading.

Now recovered from your act of clumsiness, I've determined you are dangerous and no longer wish to continue your services. As of tomorrow morning, you will be free to fly away and hopefully never come back. But before you go, we have some unsettled business. Be in your room at 8:00 sharp, because tonight is the night. You are contractually obligated so I expect you to perform to my satisfaction. Consider this your official notification.

—Mr. Naples

Feeling nauseous, Misty lay down on the bench. A passing bellhop asked if she needed any assistance, but she sent him away, saying she would be fine.

I can't believe this is really happening, she thought, but then she realized she should have expected it. After her breathing returned to normal, she returned to her room.

Misty stood in the shower and let the cold stream of water flow over her. The phrases *contractually obligated* and *perform to my satisfaction* kept running through her head. She fully understood her contractual obligation but was extremely upset about his demands to be personally satisfied.

He's treating me like a bimbo, she thought. *Boy, I'm going to set Chester straight tonight.*

But underneath her bravado, Misty knew how detrimental an

unsatisfied customer would be to her business. She thought about how repulsive he was and her hands began to shake. She looked at the clock. Six o'clock. She felt as if she was a prisoner being sent to the gallows. After finishing her shower and drying off, Misty inventoried the alcohol in her room refrigerator but realized none of those little bottles would get her inebriated enough to handle Chester. Nevertheless, she threw back two little bottles of tequila to take the edge off. When her hands quit shaking, she summoned Miguel to her room.

Miguel sat on the bed with his head in his hands as Misty filled him in with every detail.

When she finished, he looked up with fire in his eyes. "What do you want me to do? You know I'll do anything for you."

Misty knew Miguel meant what he said. She placed her hands on the side of his face and said, "There is nothing you can do but stay in your room next door and listen for my knock on the wall if anything goes wrong. If I knock, come running but don't hurt him." She waited until he calmed down before adding, "Have you got the room key I gave you?"

Miguel kissed her on the forehead. "I do, but a locked door wouldn't stop me tonight."

He was on his way to the door when she said, "Just one more thing. Will you buy me a fifth of tequila and bring it to the room?"

He didn't have to ask why. "I've got a full bottle of Anejo Reserve in my room."

Miguel returned with the bottle, pulled out the cork, and took a long swig. "Okay, it's all yours now."

After taking a couple swigs herself and realizing it was almost seven o'clock, she grabbed her phone from the nightstand and composed a text to Travis.

* * *

Travis was sitting in his easy chair wondering why Misty hadn't called when his BlackBerry lit up with a message: "Chester is demanding immediate satisfaction and will be here within the hour. Miguel is stationed next-door so don't worry for my safety. Pray for me my darling."

Travis finished reading Misty's text and came very close to throwing his phone against the wall. When he cooled down he called Misty, but her phone went straight to voicemail. Frustrated, he walked to the cabinet and poured himself a stiff bourbon. With drink in hand, he went onto the back porch and paced back and forth. After throwing down the last of the bourbon in his glass, he picked up his BlackBerry and dialed. He was relieved when the person he was dialing picked up on the other end.

33

COULD IT BE THAT BAD?

Misty was startled by the loud knock at her hotel room door. *My god, it must be eight o'clock*, she thought. *Maybe I should've popped a roofie in my tequila so I wouldn't remember a thing.*

The second knock was harder. When she opened the door, Chester had his hand in the air, ready for a third knock.

"Oh, Chester, I'm sorry. I was in the bathroom when you first knocked."

He walked through the door without a moment's hesitation. "Stephanie didn't tell me I was paying for a room this nice," he said sarcastically.

Keeping her anger in check, Misty responded coolly. "It's nice, but I've stayed in better."

She was proud of herself until she noticed Chester was holding a bag. *Oh, great! I hope he's not a pervert.*

Misty was relieved to see him pull a frilly pink one-piece out of the bag.

He handed it to her clumsily. "Here, put this on."

While changing in the bathroom, she noticed a Target tag still attached. *What a romantic*, she thought.

Misty put the lingerie on and looked at herself in the mirror. Chester was off by two sizes on the large side. The baggy undergarment hid her curves, making her as unsexy as she had ever looked.

She messed up her hair to match her outfit. *There, that's better*, she thought. *Maybe he'll think I'm ugly and send me home.* But she knew better.

Her short respite from Chester was now over. It was time to pay the piper. She pushed open the bathroom door and walked out.

Misty stood in the middle of the room, hands on hips, as Chester looked her over.

A bewildered look came over his face. "I thought you would look prettier. How in the world do you get away with charging what you do?"

Misty fought the urge to rip her clothes off and watch him come in his pants, choosing instead to say, "You know, maybe you're right. I should probably get out of this business. I wouldn't blame you if you changed your mind. In fact, I'm sure we could come to an arrangement on compensation. How about I only charge you for the time I've been here and you can save some money."

Chester shook his head before walking over and giving her an awkward hug. Even though she hugged back as lightly as possible, she could feel how boney his back was.

"Why did you just shudder?" he asked. "Are you cold?"

"Now that you mention it, yes I am."

She quickly crawled into bed and pulled the covers up to her neck. Chester crawled in next to her. A few awkward moments passed as she lay motionless as Chester hesitated, unsure of what to do next. Misty resisted the urge to pull the covers tightly over her head and suffocate herself. Her brow furrowed as he leaned in and gave her a clumsy kiss on the cheek. She smiled nervously as she realized the dreaded moment was now upon her. Chester wrestled the covers out of her grip and slid on top of her. His breath smelled like mothballs. Misty looked into his beady little eyes and let out an internal groan. She felt like she was trapped inside a coffin. Every instinct in her body screamed *Get the hell out of here.*

He grabbed her right breast and squeezed tightly. *Oh my god that hurts! I hope he didn't leave a bruise.*

When Chester's breathing picked up, she couldn't bear the stench. Thinking quickly, she grabbed the back of his head and pushed his face between her boobs. The problem was solved until he started to gag. Misty loosened her grip and he gasped for air.

"What's the matter with you!" he shouted. "Haven't you ever made love before?"

"I'm so sorry, Chester. I don't know what got into me. I guess you just made me so hot."

Chester grinned from ear to ear. "If you think you're hot now, just wait." He grabbed her crotch firmly, and her eyes opened wide.

"I got your attention with that one didn't I?"

She grabbed the back of his hand and pried it from her privates. "Sure did, Chester, but how about being a little gentler?"

He laughed. "I'm pretty strong, right? You made me that way. Besides, I took you for someone who liked to play rough.

If he keeps this up, he's going to find out what rough really is! Misty thought.

Chester grabbed the crotch of her lingerie and popped the snaps open. Misty instinctively put her hands over her eyes and tried not to think about what was coming next. When nothing happened, she looked through the slits in her fingers to see Chester fumbling to get his pants off. The process reminded her of a Three Stooges routine. His pants and underwear were around his knees and his penis was fully exposed. Misty had often heard the expression "pencil dick" but until that moment thought it only an expression.

Oh god, save me from that slimy little thing, she thought.

As if divine intervention, a loud banging filled the room. *Bam, Bam, Bam!* Chester turned his head and looked toward the door.

"Who the hell is that?" he said.

"Maybe I should go see," said Misty.

"No, just ignore it," he said as he continued to struggle with his britches.

Then a muffled voice came from the other side of the door. "Chester! Open this goddamn door! I know you're in there."

Chester froze like a statue and his eyes bulged out. "Crap! That's Brenda! Did you tell her I was coming here?" he asked frantically.

"Absolutely not! I would never do that."

"Then what the hell is she doing here?"

"I don't know. Maybe you should open the door and ask her."

"*Chester!* Open the fucking door!" Brenda yelled.

Chester pleaded with Misty to hide, but she shook her head. "No. She already knows this is my room. How would that help?"

As Brenda continued to pound and yell, Chester wrestled his pants back up and headed to the door. Misty propped up a few pillows behind her so she could witness the upcoming show in comfort. Chester cracked the door open and Brenda burst through. She walked to the middle of the room, stared at Misty, and then glared back at him with her hands on her hips.

"So, is this how we 'work out' these days?" Brenda asked, livid. "Since when did fucking become a goddamn Olympic event?"

"Oh no," said Chester. "I would never do that, would I, Misty!"

Misty tugged on her lingerie until her right breast was exposed.

"Oh no Brenda, we weren't fucking," Chester muttered—just before he turned to see a partially naked Misty.

"Sure you weren't, you bastard!" Brenda said sternly.

Chester walked around the room with his head down as he tried to think of a way out. When his back was turned to both of them, Brenda gave Misty a wink.

Chester raised his head. "I was just saying good-bye to Misty. She's going home as soon as she can book a flight. Aren't you, Misty?"

Misty took her time before responding. "Why yes. Chester came here to tell me I was going home due to his injury." She waited to continue until she got a nod from Chester. "He said he was sorry and that he'd pay me in full for coming all the way from Argentina." Even though Chester's face was turning red, she continued. "He said the contract is paid in full and that there was nothing left for me to perform."

"What was she to perform, Chester!" Brenda demanded.

Chester looked at Misty. "Just training services. Right, Misty?"

"That's right. He was paying me that money because I'm such a good trainer. As soon as the money hits my bank account, I'm leaving San Antonio, never to return." She turned to fix Chester with a humorless stare. "Are we straight about that?"

He nodded weakly.

It wasn't good enough for Misty. "I said, are we straight about that, Chester?"

"Yes, damn it!" he shouted. "We're straight about that."

Agitated by being out-maneuvered, he went on the offensive. "Tell me how you found out we were here, Brenda. Did Misty tell you?" Chester looked back at Misty with a smirk.

"Misty didn't tell me," Brenda replied calmly.

"Then who did?"

Brenda took her time before responding. "It was Travis."

Misty was horrified.

Furious, Chester turned his gaze on Misty. "I'm going to fire his ass as soon as I call human resources. He'll be notified within the hour. If either of you call him first, there will be hell to pay."

With that, he stormed out of the room.

Misty covered her face with her hands. Brenda walked over and sat beside her. "Don't beat yourself up, Misty. When Travis asked me to come to your aid, I told him he would be fired if I did. He told me what happened to him was inconsequential. He said he wouldn't be able to live with himself if he stood by and did nothing."

Misty's eyes filled with tears.

"Misty," she continued. "When Chester talks to HR, he'll find out Travis already called and resigned. He wanted to go out on his own terms. He told me to tell you not to feel sorry for him. He knew this wouldn't work out forever."

Misty got out of bed and gave Brenda a big hug. "Thank you so much, Brenda. I feel like you just saved my life."

"No problem, honey. This was a long time coming. There's a good chance I can use this to leverage a divorce settlement out of the prick for more than our prenuptial agreement. You may have done me and Buddy a big favor."

"I'd be so happy for the both of you if it turned out that way." After giving Brenda one more hug she said, "Do you mind giving me directions to Travis's ranch house?"

"Of course, dear. You can take my Suburban if you let me sleep in your room tonight."

"That's a deal!"

"Here are the keys. Drive carefully. "

34

How Can I Thank You?

Misty stepped out of the Suburban and filled her lungs with fresh, warm country air. Her walk to Travis's front door was illuminated by billions of stars in the cloudless sky. Misty went through three rounds of knocking before the outside porch light came on and the door swung open. The house was totally dark inside, but Misty could make out a silhouette of Travis standing there in what appeared to be his boxers. He rubbed the sleep out of one eye as he gathered his senses.

"Well, are you going to let me in or not?" she asked.

He pulled the screen door open and she walked into his arms. His body was warm from sleep, and his embrace felt like being wrapped in a cozy blanket. With her eyes closed, Misty listened to the pounding of his heart as he stroked the back of her head.

"I'm afraid to ask about your evening," he said.

"I was saved in the nick of time." She pulled back to look at him. "You were my knight in shining armor."

Travis shook his head. "No, Brenda was your knight in shining armor." He pulled her back to him. "The thought of you having to sleep with Chester made me sick to my stomach. I knew I couldn't get there in time, and I was worried about what I might do to him if I got there too late. That's why I called Brenda."

"And how did you convince Brenda to come to my aid?" she asked.

"I promised to sleep with her."

She looked horrified as she backed away from him. "You did not!"

Travis couldn't help himself. "Don't worry, I said I would only sleep with her once because after all, I'm the Black Widow Foreman." He cracked a grin and she knew she had been had. Pounding her fists into his chest, she said, "Damn you, Travis! "

He swiftly placed one arm around her back and one arm under her knees and lifted her off her feet.

Holding her in his arms securely, he said, "If I'm going to be damned, I might as well do something to deserve it."

As he carried Misty to the bedroom, she yelled, "Damsel in distress! Help, Brenda! Come save me!"

After being thrown onto the bed, Misty unbuckled her belt and unfastened her jeans. Travis yanked them off.

Misty looked down at her body. "Oopsie! I guess I was in such a hurry I forgot to put my panties on."

When Misty pulled off her top she wasn't wearing a bra, either. "You really did dress in a hurry," Travis said.

"Well, maybe I thought you wanted me to dress like we were going to the movies."

"Okay, now it's your turn."

Travis dropped his boxers to the floor and stepped out of them.

Misty rolled off the bed and stood in front of him. A soft beam of moonlight kissed his face and she did a double take. "Oh my gosh! What did you do to your ponytail?"

After giving Misty a kiss he reached over to turn on a small lamp, giving her a good look at his fresh, tapered haircut. He looked strikingly handsome.

Misty ran an open hand through his hair. "It looks terrific, but why did you to cut it off?"

"I'll tell you later," he whispered into her ear. "I'm a little busy right now."

Her curious look turned to one of overt passion. She turned Travis around and pushed him onto the bed. He gazed up at her two gorgeous, plump breasts. She crawled over him so that her boobs were hanging over his face like two pieces of fruit, ripe for the picking. Her allure overtook him and he raised his head to suckle her nipples. When she couldn't stand it any longer, she rocked back and down onto his penis. Moist from her fit of passion, she slid on him without the need of a guiding hand. Misty gently eased her way down, taking a little new territory with each descent. When full penetration was achieved, she placed her hands on his stomach and pushed off until she was completely vertical. She then reached behind her back and slid her open palms down the back of his thighs until wedging them under his powerful buttocks for support. She extended her legs until they rested comfortably on his shoulders. Misty rocked back and forth slowly, savoring the moment. Travis marveled at how firm her naked body and delectable breasts looked. Misty quickened her rocking motion, mesmerizing Travis with the tantalizing view of her boobs swaying to and fro, glistening from the light sheen of perspiration. When she came, her screams of passion were loud enough to be heard by razorback George and his pack of piglets.

Having not yet come himself, Travis positioned Misty onto her hands and knees so he could mount her from behind. She placed a pillow under her forehead for support. Sliding into her, Travis began his assault. His thrusts were powerful, and she had to support herself with her arms in order to not fall flat on her face. Travis cupped and fondled her right breast to further his arousal. His final thrusts probed deep, and the slapping on her buttocks stung. Travis only grunted as he released his mighty load. When finished, he rolled over onto his side, pulling Misty with him. He held her tightly with one arm as he used the other arm to cover them up with a blanket. Placing his hand between her breasts, they fell soundly asleep without a word.

* * *

Misty awoke to an empty bed. She found Travis in the kitchen. He poured a cup of coffee as soon as she walked in. He handed the cup to Misty and she rewarded him with a peck on his cheek.

"How'd you sleep?" Travis asked.

"Wonderful! It's so peaceful in the country." Her gaze fell to the floor. "I'm so sorry I caused you to lose your job. I feel horrible."

"Don't be. Excelsior approached me earlier this week and asked me to come back. When you left your message saying this would be your final night, I sent an email accepting the job to their head of human resources."

"I'm so happy for you. This is wonderful!" After a moment she frowned. "But why didn't you tell me last night so I could quit feeling guilty?"

"Last night I had other things on my mind."

He took her by the hand, led her to the couch, and pulled her onto his lap. "I've grown attached to you, Misty, but I'm in full support of the life you live. Being around you has helped me realize I have a life to live as well. You're the best thing that has happened to me in a long, long time, and I will forever be in your debt."

Misty laid her head on his shoulder. Part of her wanted to run off to New York with Travis, but the other part knew better.

"Travis, I have strong feelings for you as well. I'm not sure I've ever cared for someone as much. And that includes my ex-husband. If there was ever anyone I would want to settle down with, it would be you. But I have to be honest, I love my lifestyle and everything it has to offer."

Travis kissed her on the temple. "That's okay. I'm content with us being best friends."

"I'd be honored to be your best friend." She placed her hands on the side of his face. "Maybe someday we'll be more than friends."

"Maybe someday," Travis replied.

35

New Year's Eve in Rio

Sitting with Misty on the veranda, a bottle of wine between them, Gabriella said, "So I suppose you want to pick your next client on your own."

Misty smiled at her, indicating she indeed wanted to resume picking her own clients, but she measured her words, not wanting to say anything to upset her dear friend. After all, Gabriella's intentions were good—even if the results turned out to be horrendous.

Misty set her glass on the table, climbed into Gabriella's lap, and put her arm around her. "I know you meant well, but let me give it one more try on my own. If I screw up, we'll discuss who picks the next client."

Brushing Misty's hair out of her face, Gabriella smiled and said, "Fair enough, dear. I'm not so sure you don't do a better job anyway. You have been home for several months now . . . are you any closer to choosing this new client?"

Misty smiled. "Maybe."

"Will you be here through New Year's?" Gabriella said, crossing her fingers.

"I'll be taking the few weeks after New Year's to choose my next client, but, yes, I'll be here."

Gabriella's face lit up.

"Now what's that smile all about?" Misty asked curiously.

"I have a wonderful surprise for you!" she replied.

"Is it something naughty?"

Gabriella laughed. "No, but it has the potential to develop into something naughty."

"Then hurry up and tell me!"

"Well, I thought a fitting ending to your respite would be for you, me, Tom, and Miguel to spend New Year's Eve on the beaches of Rio de Janeiro. People come from all around the world for the end-of-year celebration, just like they do in New York City."

"Let's do it!" Misty said without hesitation. That would be my perfect send-off!"

"I'm glad you like the idea, because I had to reserve our rooms at the renowned Copacabana Palace three months ago to make sure we would have a room."

Appreciating the effort and planning Gabriella had gone through to make sure their last weekend together for the time being would be a memorable one, Misty leaned in and gave her friend a long, slow kiss.

"You're so kind to me, Gabriella," she said after she pulled away. "I'm glad you tricked me into training you last year."

36

MORE THOR!

As they drove up to the hotel in Rio, Misty marveled at the old-world grandeur of the building's exterior. The elegant, Mediterranean-style landmark sat on a promenade, facing Copacabana Beach. Misty found the inside beautiful and sophisticated. This was truly one of the old, grande dame hotels, and Gabriella had made sure to reserve their rooms in the original wing. High ceilings and tall windows made the room feel spacious, like a real palace. Misty looked out her window and marveled at the magnificent pool and manicured grounds below.

As she lay down on her canopied bed, she thought, *Gabriella really outdid herself this time.*

It had been a long day of travel, so after a nice dinner, Misty, Gabriella, and Miguel retired to their rooms, but Tom was still wide awake. Gabriella had given him a break from chauffeuring on this trip. That was common. He was more than just her driver; he was her trusted companion.

Tom decided to take a walk down to a little bar he had recognized from a previous trip—and a previous lifetime. As he walked through the door to the quaint little pub, the familiar surroundings conjured up memories of old. Tom found a cubbyhole in the back corner of the bar, where he could throw back a few beers and reminisce in solitude.

His Germanic blond hair caught the eye of the waitresses, and one headed toward his secluded table.

She asked Tom what he wanted to drink.

"*Terei uma cerveja por favor. Skol,*" Tom replied, amazed he could still remember how to order beer in Portuguese. He had learned to order beer in over a dozen languages on his tours of duty aboard the USS *Baltimore*. Leaving on the sub's maiden voyage after it was commissioned in July of 1982, the sub became Tom's home away from home for over a decade.

The taste of the drink reminded him why Skol was the most popular beer in Brazil. He was enjoying his second Skol when he noticed a large man in the front of the premises, being very rude to an attractive dark-haired, Brazilian woman. Tom remembered the rule he learned from years of service in the U.S. Navy: never interfere in domestic disputes, especially when in a foreign country. But when the man shoved the woman, he motioned for the waitress. "Do you know this man?" he asked in Portuguese.

"Yes, and he is not a nice man," she said with fear in her eyes. "I'm afraid he may hurt my dear friend."

"So they're not married?"

"She would never marry such a pig!" the waitress said sternly.

Tom shook his head. "Crap!"

On his way to the front of the bar, Tom watched the burly man grab the woman's arm and pull her to him. The man outweighed him by thirty pounds, but Tom's years as the fleet's heavyweight boxing champion gave him the tools to back up his play.

Tapping him on the shoulder, Tom said, "Let go of her arm!"

The burly man turned around, annoyed. After sizing Tom up he shouted angrily, "Why don't you go mind your own business, blondie?"

In his heyday, Tom would have toyed with the man, thinking it all a bit of fun. But that was then. All it took was one swift, powerful right uppercut and the man crumpled to the floor. As he lay there unconscious, Tom turned to the woman. She was exotic-looking, with hair so black it almost looked blue. Her dark brown eyes were a perfect complement to her golden skin. Her large plump breasts and voluptuous hips drew his attention, having always been a sucker for full-bodied women.

"I don't know how I can ever thank you," she said as Tom continued to gawk. "You didn't have to step in."

"Well, I'm here alone and was coming up to ask you to join me anyway," he lied. "Can I buy you a drink?"

"Only if you let me pay."

"That's even better. My table is this way."

Before they could order, the waitress brought a pitcher of beer and two fresh glasses and sat them on the table. "On the house, for taking care of that creep," the waitress said before walking over and giving her friend a hug.

As Tom picked up the pitcher and began to pour, the woman noticed the twin dolphins tattooed on the inside of his forearm.

She looked at him wildly. "Thor?"

Tom had not heard or thought about that name for several decades. His mind raced, conjuring up old memories.

Suddenly his face took on a ghostly look. "Rosie?"

She let out a loud shriek as she climbed over the table and into his lap.

"Thor, I didn't think I'd ever see you again. How have you been? Where have you been? Why are you here?" But before Tom had a chance to answer, she added, "It doesn't matter. Come with me now!"

As Rosie led him out of the bar and down the street, he thought back to his weekend leave, twenty-five years ago. The commanding officer of the USS *Baltimore* ordered their sub to make an unscheduled emergency stop in Rio. He had shore leave for three days, and to the best of his recollection, this was the very same bar where he had met Rosie the first time.

After a short walk, she dragged Tom through the front door of her modest home.

Looking around suspiciously, he said, "You're not married, are you?"

Rosie shook her head. With a gentle tug, she led Tom to the bedroom and proceeded to help him out of his shirt. As he took off his trousers, he watched Rosie undress, tossing garments all over the room. Totally naked and face to face with him, she pushed Tom onto the bed.

When her naked body lay atop his and their faces were only inches apart, she said, "Do you remember how you made love to me?"

"I remember enough to get started," Tom said, knowing he didn't want to do or say anything that would kill the moment.

He sat Rosie on the side of the bed with her feet on the floor and had her lie back.

"How am I doing so far?" he asked.

"Good so far, but don't leave out any details."

Standing on the floor between Rosie's legs and towering over her, he said, "Can you hear the captain? He's saying, dive, dive, dive!" Tom held his nose with his fingers and headed down, down, all the while making the sound of an electric Klaxon: "Ah-oo-gah! . . . Ah-oo-gah! . . . Ah-oo-gah!"

Rosie laughed heartily.

Tom locked onto the target, penetrating Rosie's hull with his tongue, over and over.

She thrashed about the bed as Tom worked to set off her depth charge.

Rosie's orgasm lasted as long as it takes the water displacement from a real depth charge to settle the ocean surface.

"Time to return to the surface for an emergency blow!" Tom yelled.

He took his position, sitting on the side of the bed with feet planted firmly on the floor. Rosie kneeled between Tom's thick thighs. She gasped at what was before her, now remembering how well hung he was. She desperately wanted him inside her, but followed protocol by blowing his big unit until certain it was full throttle.

"Periscope up!" Tom yelled. He stood up, threw Rosie to the bed, and spread her legs. "Man the torpedo, Captain. It's full speed ahead!"

Tom entered Rosie fully and began ramming Herman, the one-eyed German, in and out like a piston in a World War II diesel engine sub. And what a torpedo Tom manned. Rosie was so stimulated that it took only a few moments to detonate her next depth charge.

"Oh, Thor! Oh, *Thor*!" Rosie cried.

When her orgasm subsided, she changed her battle cry to "More, Thor! More, Thor!" And that's exactly what she got.

When finished, Tom and Rosie lay exhausted on the bed. "Thor. You know you ruined me for life. No man can satisfy me the way you do."

Tom hadn't felt this virile in years.

Rosie's tone became more subdued. "Where have you been all these years?"

"I've been everywhere, Rosie. As they say, I've sailed the seven seas." Seeing the distant look in her eyes, he added, "But I never found anyone quite like you."

Rosie refused to look at Tom. "I wish I could believe you."

Tom leaned over and gave her a tender kiss to show he was sincere. Placated for the moment, Rosie got up, picked up a picture from the dresser, and returned to bed. It was a picture of the two of them twenty-five years ago. A sudden rush of guilt swelled over him. How could he make up a name like Thor to keep her from ever knowing his true identity?

Tom became infatuated with the picture. "We looked so young, Rosie. I was in my mid-twenties and you must have been . . ."

"I was only seventeen, Thor. You were my first."

Her statement caught him off guard.

As he continued to look at the picture, Rosie went to the dresser and brought back another picture of a nice-looking young man Tom didn't recognize. He studied every detail of the young man's unusual but striking combination of dark, creamy skin, blond hair, and blue eyes. He began to perspire.

It took a lot of courage for him to ask his next question. "How old is he?"

"Thor Jr. turns twenty-five early next year," Rosie replied.

She gave him time for her words to sink in before continuing. "I tried to locate you through the armed services, but they kept telling me they were unable to find anyone by the first name of Thor."

Tom needed time to think, so he pulled Rosie tight, surprised at how natural it felt to hold her in his arms.

He realized he owed her the truth. "Rosie, I was young and foolish. I hope you can find it within yourself to forgive me."

Rosie's instincts were to forgive him, but she chose instead to remain silent, letting him know he had to earn his forgiveness. He knew what she was doing and didn't blame her. Tom's head was spinning with thoughts as he tried to remember why he never came back to her. When the confusion mounted, he chose instead to hold her snugly in his arms until they eventually feel asleep.

* * *

When Tom woke up, he remembered his commitment to take Misty and Gabriella shopping. Rosie lay beside him, sleeping peacefully with her arms wrapped around him, and he tried to gently free himself from her grip. But the more he tried, the harder she held on. At last he realized she was actually awake.

"Rosie, I'm late for an appointment and need to leave, but I promise I'll come back."

"I want to believe you," she replied softly.

Tom struggled to think of something he could say that would convince her. And then it came to him. He placed the tattoo of the twin dolphins on his forearm in front of her eyes and pointed to the single rose between them.

"I don't remember ever seeing that rose," she said.

"When I left you, our next port of call was the naval base, Rosie Roads," said Tom. "As we pulled into port, I realized what I had to do." He looked into her eyes. "The rose I had tattooed on my arm was in memory of you."

She began to weep gently.

"I'm sorry, Rosie, but I really have to go," he whispered in her ear.

As he walked out the bedroom door, he spoke without turning around. "My real name is Tom."

After the front door closed, Rosie curled into a ball, wondering how devastating it would be if he didn't return and praying she could survive if she lost him again.

37

THINGS TO SORT OUT

Tom ended up being early and took a seat in the lobby waiting on Gabriella and Misty.

As they approached, Misty walked up ahead of Gabriella. "Good morning! Did you get a good night's rest?" Tom asked her.

Misty stretched and yawned. "My word, yes. That was the most comfy bed I've ever slept on."

When she finished asking the concierge for directions, Gabriella led them out of the hotel and down the street on foot. It wasn't long before they entered their first store.

"What exactly are you looking for?" Misty asked Gabriella.

"New Year's Eve outfits, of course."

"But I brought nice outfits with me," said Misty.

Gabriella smiled. "Are your outfits white?"

"White? I thought we were going to a New Year's Eve party!"

Gabriella kept looking through racks of long white dresses as if she hadn't heard Misty.

Finding one she liked, she held it up for her friend to see. "Now that would look nice on you. Why don't you try it on?"

"You're serious, aren't you?"

"Completely. Go try it on in the fitting room."

Gabriella looked at Tom. "If you don't have anything white to wear, we'll buy you something, too."

Lost in thought, Tom didn't reply.

"Earth to Tom . . ." Gabriella prodded.

"What?" Tom said, snapping out of it.

"I asked you if you had anything white to wear for New Year's Eve."

"Oh. No, I don't. Should I?"

Gabriella shook her head. "Men!"

Misty came back from the dressing room looking cute and comfortable.

Gabriella began placing colorful beads over her head, one strand at a time. "The green one's for good health, the gold one's for prosperity, and the blue one is for peace and tranquility," she said.

Gabriella finished by draping a red strand of beads around her neck. "What's the red one for?" Misty asked.

Gabriella kissed her on the cheek. "Why, for romance, of course."

Misty turned to Tom. "Pretty crazy, isn't it, Tommy boy?"

He didn't respond.

"What's up with him?" Misty whispered to Gabriella.

"Something's on his mind," she whispered back. "I've never seen him this out of it before."

38

DOING THE RIGHT THING

The next morning Tom and the girls were having breakfast in the hotel when they noticed he was still troubled.

When Misty left the table to use the restroom, Gabriella said, "Tom, what's going on? Is something wrong?"

Tom shrugged. "I've got a few things to sort out, but I'm fine." He gently placed his hand on Gabriella's arm. "I hate to ask you this, but there's something I need to attend to. Would you mind if I take some time off this afternoon?"

"Sure—remember, you don't have to drive us around everywhere on this trip. Miguel can look after us while you're gone."

"Thank you, Gabriella. I promise I'll be back to normal tomorrow."

Tom spent the early afternoon looking for the perfect flower arrangement for Rosie. He came across a rose so large that it dwarfed all the others. The moment he saw it, he knew a single rose would be perfect.

He then made his way to Rosie's place and sat on the front steps, waiting patiently and wondering when she might return. He was full of excitement and hope one minute and paralyzed with apprehension the next. Late in the afternoon, after patiently waiting for close to three hours, he saw her walking down the sidewalk toward him. Her head was down, as if she were contemplating something important. Tom glanced at the two twin dolphins on his forearm in an attempt to summon his courage. *We protected your rose all these years*, he imagined them saying. *Now it's your turn to protect Rosie."*

Rosie prayed as she walked, asking God to give her the fortitude to remain patient. Lost in thought, she didn't notice Tom sitting on her porch until she was directly upon him. It took her a moment to realize it was actually him. Tom slowly stood up with the most endearing smile and offered up the brilliant red rose. Rosie gingerly reached out to take it from his hands. As she brought it to her nose, the sweet aroma assured her that she wasn't dreaming. She placed both arms around Tom and squeezed so tight he had trouble catching his breath.

"How about going out to dinner tonight?" he said. "We've got a lot of catching up to do, and I've got a lot of questions I'd like to ask you about our son."

Our son, Rosie thought. *Tom said "our" son.*

She kissed him on the cheek. "That's a wonderful idea. Give me time to take a shower. I won't take long."

Inside, Tom settled his tired body into one of Rosie's easy chairs with the intention of taking a quick nap. Just as he was about to drift into a deeper sleep, he felt a soft tap on the top of his head. He opened his eyes to find the culprit was a beautiful, full-bodied woman, wearing a cotton dress that accentuated every voluptuous curve. She looked like an angel.

"Were you asleep?" she asked, her voice soft and sexy.

"I'm not sure, but if I was, this must be heaven—in which case I don't want to wake up."

Rosie climbed into his lap, supporting her knees on his thighs, and wrapped her arms around the back of his head. His face fit snugly between her soft bosoms. The aroma of her freshly bathed body filled his nostrils, and he was instantly wide awake.

Perched there on his lap, she talked Tom into letting her fix dinner for the two of them instead of going out to eat. She knew the restaurants would be packed with partygoers this time of year, and she wanted him all to herself. She also wanted him to know what a marvelous cook she was, so she fixed a wonderful marinated rosemary chicken, a side of fried empanadas, and some *churros* for dessert. Rosie waited for Tom to bring up Thor Jr. as he had suggested, but he was so famished from the long wait that he devoured her meal, leaving little time to mix words in between his bites. After cleaning up the kitchen together, Tom and Rosie retired to the living room.

With Rosie comfortably back in his lap, Tom said, "So why don't you tell me about our son."

Rosie's eyes sparkled. "Well, he's a very special young man. He's big and strong like you. Thor commands attention when he walks into a room. People are intrigued by his sandy blond hair, and blue eyes. Girls can't take their eyes off him, the way I couldn't take my eyes off you when we first met. But like you, commitment comes hard for Thor. That's why he's still single."

He must be my son, thought Tom.

"Thor learned how to defend himself at an early age because his classmates were always teasing him about his name," she continued.

Crap—I never thought that name would get used on a son of mine, thought Tom. *I can't believe that was the first name that popped into my head*.

"But it didn't take long for the little Brazilian boys to understand the name Thor stands for bloody nose, if they upset him."

Tom sat up proudly.

Rosie's mood became somewhat somber. "When can you meet him? I'm certain it will go well. As strange as this may seem, Thor has never shown any disappointment about you not being here. He's proud his father was an American, especially one who served in the armed forces. In high school he saved his money to buy books about submarines, wanting to know how his father lived. He'll be so thrilled to meet you."

"I'd like that very much. What does my son do for a living?"

"He's the assistant manager at a local salsa club. They love him because he can double as a bouncer. He's very bright and always made excellent grades in school, but I never had the money to send him to college. I know he could do so much more if he had a degree."

Rosie's comments about how well Thor did in school made him proud, but it was hard for him to feel too exuberant since he realized he hadn't been around to help him attend college and further his education.

"I've saved up a little money over the years. It should be enough to at least get him off to a good start."

"Oh, Tom!" She threw her arms around him in a show of gratitude.

Holding Rosie felt so natural, so normal, the thought of going back to Buenos Aires and what now seemed like a lonely existence in his one-bedroom apartment terrified him. But how would the others take to her? There was only one way to find out.

"Listen, Rosie, I was wondering if you'd like to accompany me to the New Year's Eve festivities tomorrow," he said as he embraced her. "I'd love for you to meet my friends."

She blushed. "Do you think they will like me?"

He shook his head and said, "I don't think they will like you, I *know* they will love you."

Rosie breathed a sigh of relief.

39

THE EVE

The next morning at breakfast with his travel companions, Tom was just as distant as he'd been the day before, but this time in a positive way. He was practically glowing, lost in fond memories of his encounter with Rosie. Misty pushed her scrambled eggs around her plate with a fork, trying to figure out how to approach him. Dying to know what was up, she asked the first question that came to mind.

"Hey Tom, you sure are in a terrific mood this morning. Did you get some last night?"

He looked at her and raised his eyebrows but did not answer.

Gabriella frowned. "You didn't pick up a hooker, did you?"

Tom shot her a look as Miguel entered the fray. "You met a girl, didn't you?"

Tom grinned.

Gabriella and Misty scooted their chairs on either side of him, pinning him in.

"Give it up!" Misty said.

"You're not going to believe this," said Tom, "but I bumped into a woman I met here in Rio twenty-five years ago."

"Oh, my gosh!" cried Misty. "Are you serious?"

Tom spent the next half hour filling the group in on everything that had transpired over the last two days. The girls' hearts melted as he told his tale of love lost and found again. Miguel wanted to hear more about his knockdown in the bar. Tom came very close to mentioning Thor but didn't want to complicate things. That was a much more delicate matter than gushing about Rosie.

When Tom finished, Misty asked, "So when are we going to meet your Rosie?"

"I asked her to join us tonight," he replied. He then looked at Gabriella. "If that's okay with you, boss."

"Don't be silly!" Gabriella said. "Hey, why don't we go buy you something awesome to wear?"

* * *

That evening, Tom went to pick up Rosie while Gabriella, Misty, and Miguel went to dinner at the hotel's sophisticated Italian restaurant. Gabriella kept the champagne flowing, so by the time the group strolled across the street to Copacabana Beach, they were very much in the mood to party. There was a sea of white as they looked up and down the beach, and Misty was suddenly thankful for Gabriella's little shopping trip. Gabriella had told them at dinner that there would be over two million people from all over the world crammed onto the beach. Large stages lined the water with bands playing everything from carnival music to rock and roll, yet it somehow blended tightly together to form a festive and unique sound. At nine o'clock in the evening it was still hot, and Misty understood why the tradition was to wear something white and loose.

As they stood surveying the packed beach, they heard someone yell from behind. "Hey guys!"

There stood Tom with Rosie by his side. Gabriella immediately approached her, looking her over and taking her hand in hers.

After getting an eyeful, Gabriella said, "You are so beautiful, and what a pretty smile you have! I can see why Tom thinks the world of you."

Rosie patted Tom on the chest. "Yes, but he's not very smart, is he? It took Thor, I mean Tom, twenty-five years to figure it out."

Gabriella grinned. "Yes, Tom can be a little slow at times."

Miguel looked at Tom and mouthed, "Thor?"

Tom rolled his eyes.

After everyone had a chance to greet Rosie, Misty said, "Come on, guys. It's New Year's Eve. Let's walk the beach!"

Misty and Gabriella flanked Rosie and the three talked as if old friends. Misty thought Rosie wonderfully animated and couldn't take her eyes off her. They learned Rosie's ancestors were native Amerindians, a people indigenous to the Americas. Gabriella was mesmerized by Rosie's long, beautiful, jet-black hair that framed her high cheekbones perfectly.

Gabriella drifted over to Tom and whispered in his ear. "You, my friend, are a very lucky man, even if you are a bit slow."

Tom nodded in agreement.

Miguel, fascinated by the sights and sounds of the beach, asked Rosie, "Since you've lived here all of your life, would you mind being our tour guide?"

"I'd love to!" she replied. "I've been coming to these New Year's Eve parties all of my life."

Rosie led them to a group of women in white turbans. They wore traditional *bajana* dresses trimmed with beautiful white lace. The group was enthralled as they watched the women dancing and chanting to the hypnotic beat of drums.

"There are many Brazilian-African cults in Rio," Rosie said. "As you can see, Brazilian culture has a rich African heritage."

"It all seems so magical!" said Gabriella.

Rosie pointed to a long line of people. "We should get in line."

"May I ask what they are in line for?" Gabriella asked.

"To be blessed by the priestess," said Rosie.

"I don't know, that looks creepy," said Miguel.

An elderly woman who had overheard them talking interrupted. "*Tomar um passé.*"

"What did she say?" Tom asked.

"Take a ticket," Rosie said. "See the woman at the end of the line?

She's referred to as a *mae de santo*. The cigar smoke she's blowing takes the bad fluids out of the people around her."

Miguel laughed. "Hell, just show me a bathroom. I don't need any help getting rid of bad fluids."

Misty slapped him on the shoulder. "Be nice."

Gabriella noticed that once each person received the woman's blessing, he or she seemed to have a renewed vigor.

"The blessing takes away past troubles, allowing each person a fresh start to their New Year," Rosie explained.

From there they walked to the far end of the beach to an old historic fort named Forte de Copacabana, where they boarded a giant Ferris wheel. The view as they rode over the crest of the giant wheel was breathtaking.

When they walked back down the beach, people were throwing beautiful white flowers into the sea.

"What are they doing that for?" asked Miguel. "Those are perfectly good flowers."

"They're making an offering to Yemanja, the deity of the seas," Rosie explained. She then pointed to eight firework stations anchored at a safe distance from shore in the horseshoe-shaped bay. "It's almost midnight. Keep your eyes on the barges."

As midnight approached, the crowd counted down. On the count of one, fireworks shot up from the barges, bursting in the air high above. The trails of exquisite colors were coming from all directions. The barrage of explosions lit up the sky with beautiful pictures of hearts and palms. They quickly realized these were no ordinary fireworks; they were exquisite and sophisticated rockets that the ancient Chinese inventors would have marveled at.

"Now we're talking!" said Miguel.

The cascade of fireworks that fell over Forte de Copacabana were the most spectacular of all. As was their tradition, local Cariocas people popped bottles of champagne and poured the cold, sticky liquid over friends and strangers alike. Miguel thought it silly until two beautiful women poured a bottle of champagne over his head and then took turns giving him a kiss.

Dripping with sticky, bubbly liquid, he looked at his companions. "Damn, these Cariocas folks really know how to throw a party!"

Miguel walked off with an arm wrapped around each girl.

"Don't expect us to leave the light on for ya," Misty said under her breath.

It was getting late, so Tom and Rosie said their good-byes and left for her place.

Gabriella smiled at Misty. "Let's go back to the hotel," she said.

Misty was pretty sure she knew what Gabriella had in mind.

* * *

Back in Gabriella's room, they set up shop on the balcony and had room service bring up some more champagne. Gabriella popped the cork and poured some over Misty's head before filling their glasses. The night air was charged with energy from the millions of partygoers below. Misty took a seat on Gabriella's lap and delicately traced squiggly lines over her face.

By now Misty was a little tipsy. "Gabby. You are so wonderful to me. I'm happy we found each other."

Misty gave her friend a big hug. "You're my bestest friend."

Gabriella took her by the hand and led her into the bedroom. She then took a seat and coaxed her toward the edge of the bed. When Misty drew near, Gabriella loosened her white dress and undid her silky red bra. Gabriella lifted the straps over Misty's arms and tossed the bra to the floor.

"What a beautiful red bra," said Gabriella.

Misty lightly bit Gabriella's upper lip. "Red is for attracting romance, you know."

"So you were listening to me at the dress shop," Gabriella said.

Gabriella delicately fondled Misty's breasts, admiring every minute detail. Misty placed her fingertips under Gabriella's chin and raised her head until their eyes met. Misty's gaze was sensual, causing Gabriella's loins to burn with desire. She began showering Misty's neck with moist, open-mouthed kisses, causing Misty to squirm with delight. From there, Gabriella targeted Misty's breasts, playfully kissing over, under, and between them. She braced the small of Misty's back with her arms, allowing Misty's head to fall back. The move pushed Misty's chest out, allowing better access to her breasts. Gabriella's tongue danced around, tickling and teasing Misty's nipples until they stood erect. Grabbing Gabriella by her hair, Misty forcefully shoved Gabriella's mouth deeper onto her swollen breast. Gabriella sucked them as if she were a child.

Totally revved, Misty got up and helped Gabriella out of her clothes. Without warning, she shoved Gabriella onto the bed. Gabriella tried to rise but Misty was too quick for her, taking a dominant position. Now sitting on Gabriella's waist with her knees holding her firmly in place, Misty grinned mischievously while pointing to her flexed bicep.

"Are you going to be a good girl?"

When Gabriella struggled to rise, Misty shoved her back down with one hand while she reached behind her back and found her soft bush. Misty's located her moist opening and played around the edges momentarily before thrusting two fingers deep inside. Realizing she was pinned and helpless, Gabriella succumbed to her aggressor. Misty pulled her fingers out, working Gabriella's clitoris masterfully until her lips dripped with natural juices. Misty reentered with three fingers this time and dug deep in search of her G-spot. Gabriella's eyes let her know when she hit her target before eventually glossing over from the intense pleasure. Misty was captivated by Gabriella's facial expressions as she brought her friend to orgasm, multiple times. Noticing Gabriella's body glistened with sweat beneath her, Misty decided to get off and lie on her back next to her satiated friend.

She looked at Gabriella with a sideways glance. "Now it's my turn."

40

THE MEETING

Sleeping soundly in Misty's arms, Gabriella awoke to the sound of her cell phone.

She cleared her throat before answering. "Hello?"

"Gabriella, it's Tom."

"Tom, we still have hours before we have to leave to catch our plane. You should go back to sleep."

"I know—I'm calling to let you know there's something I need to do this morning, but that I'll be back in time to leave for the airport."

"Does it have something to do with Rosie?"

"Gabriella, I didn't tell you everything that went on the night I met Rosie."

Gabriella laughed. "You're not going to get into the sordid details, are you?"

Tom's tone was serious. "The night I ran into Rosie, she told me I have a son."

Tom gave Gabriella time for his words to sink in.

This was too much for her to deal with alone. "Hold on a minute, Tom," she said, and then shook Misty awake.

Misty managed to open one eye.

"Misty, Tom's on the phone. He said he found out he has a son."

"You're shitting me," she said. "This is so exciting!"

Gabriella resumed her conversation with Tom. "Tom, this is so incredible. Have you met your son? Do you know what he looks like?"

"No, I'm on my way to meet him now," said Tom.

"He's going to meet him now!" Gabriella mouthed to Misty.

"Well, I've got to run, boss," said Tom. "I don't want to be late." After a short pause, he added, "Pray for me, Gabriella. I'm really nervous. What if it doesn't go well?"

"Oh, Tom. You're a good man. It may take him time, but I know he'll grow to love you. Be strong, my friend."

"Thanks for the kind words."

* * *

When the taxi pulled to the curb, Tom paid the driver and got out. Rosie was very religious and had asked them to meet at a historic eighteenth-century Catholic church. Tom had also been raised as a Catholic, although it had been quite some time since he last attended mass. The thought of going to confession before the meeting crossed his mind, but he figured it would have taken all day to absolve himself of past indiscretions.

Once inside, Tom stood in awe before the two spectacular bronze pulpits and German stained glass. He surveyed the pews for signs of life and noticed a young man kneeling in prayer. Summoning all the courage within him, Tom walked down the aisle toward him. When he was directly behind him, he whispered, "Thor?" He waited while the young man finished his prayer, crossed himself, and slowly stood up. When he turned around, Tom was struck by how handsome he was—he fit Rosie's description to a tee. Tom became nervous when the boy's piercing blue eyes locked onto him like lasers. He was at a loss for words.

Fortunately, the boy spoke first. "Yes, I'm Thor, father. Please forgive my delay. I was thanking God for bringing you into my world."

Tom was humbled by his son's words. "Thor, I can't do anything about the last twenty-five years, but I promise to be there for you the next twenty-five—if you let me."

Thor grinned. "So does that mean you'll teach me how to box? I hear you were pretty good."

Tom gave Thor's wavy blond hair a rub. "I would be honored to."

* * *

Lying on the sofa and holding her rosary beads, Rosie heard boisterous voices approaching the house.

When Tom and Thor walked through the front door, arm in arm, Rosie said, "Have you boys been drinking?"

"No, Rosie, we're just high on life!" said Tom.

Thor gave his mother a big hug and kiss. "How have you been, Mother? Worrying as usual?"

"Well, I guess I was worrying for nothing. You two are getting along like—"

"Like a couple of shipmates?" Tom blurted out.

Thor winked at his father. "Now that's an idea. We can add drinking rum like a sailor to our list."

"Aye, aye, mate," Tom replied. "That's something this old salty dog knows how to do."

Rosie settled back to quietly observe her boys carrying on. This was the day she had dreamed about but feared might never come.

Their conversation flowed free and easy, Tom telling old sailor tales, being careful to leave out the women, while Thor filled Tom in on his prowess with the ladies. Rosie, unaccustomed to men's banter, remained quiet and listened. Seeing her son conversing with his true father—someone older, someone who could teach him how to be a man—warmed her heart. But all too soon, it was time for Thor to leave for work, so they said their good-byes.

Giving Tom a firm handshake, Thor said, "Father, until we meet again."

Tom gripped his son's hand just as firmly and placed a hand on his shoulder, saying, "Son, until we meet again."

After Thor left, Tom joined Rosie on the sofa.

She laid her head on his shoulder. "So what's next for us?"

He gave her a kiss on the forehead. "I need to fly back to Buenos

Aires this afternoon, but I promise, it will be the last time we are apart."
He stopped for a moment as if pondering something. "Rosie, would you
ever consider leaving Rio?"

"All that matters is that the three of us are together," she said.

"That I can promise," Tom replied.

* * *

After filling everyone in on his son during their flight home, Tom and
Gabriella moved to the back seats of the Gulfstream to be alone.

"What are you going to do now?" she asked him.

"Well, I was thinking about bringing Rosie to live with me in Buenos Aires."

"Would Thor come too?"

"I'm hoping so, but that would be up to him."

"Tom, I think that's wonderful. I'd like to help in any way I can."

"Thanks, boss. I'm not sure I've even done a good job of taking care
of myself over the years. I could use all the help you can give me."

"Let's get started," Gabriella said with a big smile. "Tell me what
you're thinking."

"Well, first, I would like to find a place big enough for the three of
us but not too expensive. I've got a feeling most of my salary, along with
much of my savings, will go toward putting Thor through college."

"College? That's wonderful! Where are you thinking of sending
him?"

"I'm afraid all I can afford is the University of Buenos Aires."

"Hmmm . . . they have over three hundred and fifty thousand stu-
dents, and their class sizes are enormous," she said. "Do you know if
Thor is a good student?"

"Rosie said he ranked in the top ten percent of his class. He should
have no problem handling the curriculum."

"What do you think he wants to major in?"

"He's an assistant manager at a salsa bar, so maybe business?"

"The University of Catolica has a wonderful business school."

"But that's a private school. I can't afford to send him there."

Gabriella gave Tom a reassuring smile. "Leave that to me. The dean of Catolica has been trying to purchase a tract of land from me—to expand their business school, in fact. Maybe I'll do the deal and negotiate a full scholarship for Thor in the process." Gabby laughed before adding, "I don't know. The dean is kind of sweet on me, so maybe we can get them to name it Thor's School of Business."

Tom laughed heartily. "That would put him on the map, all right!" Then, in a more serious tone, he said, "I don't know how I will ever thank you. You don't know how much this means to me."

*　*　*

It was late afternoon when they pulled into Gabriella's estate. Misty hopped out of the car and headed into the house, but Gabriella stayed behind.

Gabriella said to Tom, "Come with me. I have something I would like to show you."

Tom followed her around the far corner of the house and down a winding, tree-lined walkway that led to the sea. Gabriella stopped in front of the old guesthouse. Her mother loved to spend her afternoons painting seascapes from the upstairs balcony, but the cottage had not been used since Gabriella's mother passed away, eight years ago.

Gabriella took off the padlock and they entered. The cottage was dusty and run-down but it was easy to imagine what it had looked like in its grandeur of old. The quality woodwork, tall ceilings, and massive windows that opened to the sea displayed the same quality as the main house.

"Well, what do you think?" Gabriella asked.

"What do I think about what?" he replied, puzzled.

"What do you think about fixing this old place up so you, Rosie, and Thor have a suitable home? All it will take is some cleaning, painting, and a few new appliances. I have fond memories of sitting in this living room with my mother. She loved to have the windows open so we could feel the sea breeze on our faces. It will do me good to see it in use again."

"But how can I afford the rent?" he asked.

"I've felt for the last year that you were ready to do more than chauffeur me around. I've relied on you as a confidant more and more, and I trust your judgment. I think it's time you add overseeing the operation of my estate to your job description. If you think you're up for the task, I'll have an attorney draft a new employment agreement for your review and approval."

"Gabriella . . . I don't know what to say. I would love to manage the estate."

"Good," she said, "then you can start by overseeing the renovation of the cottage."

41

CONGRESSMAN HENRY

Congressman Henry's aide peeked into his office. "Sir, Rick is here with your campaign advisor. Should I have them wait or send them in?"

"Please show them in, Ginger."

Henry knew something was up the minute they stepped into his office. He looked to his campaign advisor, Jim. "What's up, guys? Rick looks like his dog just died."

Trying to soften Henry up before he gave him the bad news, Rick said, "He did. Who told you, Ginger?"

"Good one, Rick," said Henry. "Now tell me what the real problem is."

The three settled around the small conference table. Rick nodded toward Henry, letting Jim know he should be the one to tell Henry.

"Henry," Jim began, "the midterm elections are less than eleven months away, so I commissioned our first poll to see who your toughest competitor in the primaries is. The good news is that you're strongly in front of Bob. I can't see where he's getting enough traction to be a serious contender."

"That's great!" said Henry. "How can there be bad news? You told me you thought Bob was our only legitimate threat."

Jim squirmed in his chair. "I did. But that was before Molly entered the race."

"Molly, the district attorney? That's very hard to believe."

Henry walked to the window and looked out. Rick placed his finger to his lips, signaling Jim to give Henry a moment.

Henry asked, "So Jim, you've been at this for a long time. What's the chance this is a fluke?"

"Not likely, Henry. The margin of error is plus or minus three points. Even if her numbers are overstated by three points, she's still your closest competitor."

"And how far back is she?" Henry asked.

Rick jumped in. "She's only ten points behind."

Henry exploded. "Don't fuck around with me, Rick!"

"He's not, Henry," Jim interjected. "Molly is a serious contender."

Henry calmly walked back to the table and sat down. "You know, I never gave her a second thought. I figured national politics would be a stretch for Molly. So humor me, boys. What's your best guess?"

"I made some calls and here's what I've come up with," said Rick. He looked at Jim a moment to make sure he was behind him. "Molly isn't just a bright, young district attorney—if you remember, she was Miss Alabama in nineteen ninety-two. Boss, she's way more attractive than Sarah Palin, and look how fast Sarah took off when she hit the national scene. Too bad she's a member of our party. Otherwise we could sic the dogs on her."

Fearing they were right, Henry said, "So how do you recommend we proceed, Jim?"

"I suggest we take another poll to find out exactly what part her looks play in the race."

"Come on, Jim," Henry snapped back. "Nobody will answer that honestly. That would be like asking someone if they cheat on their spouse."

"Don't worry. We have ways to extract their answers without them knowing what we're getting at."

"Okay," said Henry, "get on it right away. Rick, hang around. I've got some things to go over with you."

After Jim left, Henry asked Rick, "Have you got any ideas? We don't want to slide this one under the rug. Let's be proactive, and I mean now."

"Okay, hear me out on this one. There is no way Molly closed the gap this fast without appealing to women voters."

"You're probably right. But unless I have a sex change, we're not likely to get them back."

"I don't think that will be necessary, Henry," he said, grinning. Rick took a picture down from the wall and placed it in front of him.

Henry looked puzzled. "What does my college football picture have to do with anything?"

"You were a pretty good-looking guy yourself at one time."

"What do you mean, at one time?"

"There you go, Henry. You know you've still got it. A little body work and we can start herding some of those women votes back into your camp."

Henry stood up and looked his body over. "I guess I have put on a few pounds lately. You know there's not much time around here for working out, and I'm always eating on the run."

"This is important," said Rick. "Besides, it would do you good to get in better shape and eat a little healthier. What was your playing weight in college? Two hundred pounds?"

"Two hundred and two, to be exact."

"And if I may ask, what do you weigh today?"

Henry played coy. "Uh . . . I'm not sure."

"When's the last time you worked out?"

"Hell, I told you. I'm a United States congressman. I don't have time to work out." Henry sat back with his arms behind his head. Rick knew that was the posture he always took before giving in.

"Oh, what the hell!" he said finally. "I guess I could lose those twenty pounds if I was motivated enough. Maybe I should get a personal trainer."

Rick grinned. "Not just any personal trainer. A Black Widow Trainer."

"Black Widow Trainer? What the hell are you talking about?"

"Henry, remember when you got sick and sent me to the meeting you scheduled with your largest campaign contributors last week? Well, the drinks were flowing that night and the group was talking about a high-dollar professional trainer. A CEO—I'll leave his name out of this—has been trying to hire her for over two years now, but supposedly she has a long waiting list."

"What's so special about her?"

"From what they were telling me, she's hot as all get out, and has an incredible personality. I think these guys get off on the idea of being bossed around by a woman."

"What does she charge?" asked Henry.

Rick raised his eyebrows. "One hundred and eighty thousand dollars for three months' work."

"You've got to be shitting me! I don't care how good she is, that's insane. Who in their right mind would pay that much?"

Always suspicious the office might be bugged, Rick walked over and whispered into Henry's ear. When Rick finished, Henry whispered back. "Now that's what I call motivation. I can't wait to get started. But where will we get the money? My wife would know if I took that much out of our personal account."

"Don't worry. I'll figure it out, as usual."

"Okay, then. Hire her."

Rick frowned. "We still need to get her to accept the job. That might turn out to be more difficult than sourcing the funds."

"Well, tell her . . . what's her name?"

"Misty."

"Tell this Misty gal I'm a U.S. congressman and that this has some-thing to do with national security. Make her feel like she's doing her country a great service. She is an American citizen isn't she?"

"Yes, she is. I'll get on it right away."

42

RESIDENCE OF PRESIDENTS

Misty waited patiently in the lobby of D.C.'s Hamilton Intercontinental Hotel for her new client. She sat in a comfortable chair, intrigued by the colorfully patterned tile floor. A closer inspection revealed thousands of tiny one-inch tiles, and she wondered how many man-hours it must have taken to lay such an intricate design. She let her eyes move up the massive marble column to a ceiling sectioned off in squares, inlaid with decorative patterns. Each quadrant held the name of a different state.

As Misty walked the lobby reading the names high above her, someone behind her said, "Be careful. We don't want you to get a crick in your neck."

Misty turned and saw a distinguished-looking gentleman. He had salt-and-pepper hair and a ruggedly handsome face anchored by a square jaw. If this was Henry, he was more handsome than his picture.

Misty stuck out her hand. "Congressman Henry, I presume."

"I see you've done your homework."

"Of course! I vet my clients thoroughly. Rick sent over twenty pictures of you." Wanting to get off to a good start with him, she added, "I especially enjoyed the one where you were in your football uniform."

"Well, that picture is from thirty years ago. If I looked like that now, I wouldn't need your help."

Misty stepped back to look him over. "You've kept yourself in reasonably good shape. I can't wait to get started, Congressman."

"Please call me Henry. We're going to be spending a lot of time together over the next three months, so let's drop the formality."

"Okay, Henry."

"I hope you haven't eaten anything yet. I made reservations at the restaurant next door so we can get to know each other better."

"Oh! How nice. Let me call my bodyguard and let him know I'll be eating with you tonight."

"And that would be Miguel?"

"I see you did your homework as well."

"Our reservations aren't for another forty-five minutes, so why don't we get a cocktail at the bar?"

"Only if you promise to tell me the history of this beautiful hotel you have me staying at."

"I'd love to. I hope forty-five minutes is enough time."

Misty excused herself when they reached their table, saying she was going to call Miguel and freshen up. After telling her bodyguard about her dinner plans, she gave herself a once-over in the restroom mirror. The realization she was in the presence of a United States congressman was setting in, and she wanted to look her best. Although not dressed as nicely as she would have liked, she was pleased with the girl that looked back at her.

Misty found a martini waiting for her when she returned to the table. She gave Henry a baffled look.

"I'm sorry," he said. "That was rather presumptuous of me. I guess I've been in D.C. so long, I just assume everyone drinks martinis."

Wanting to put him at ease, she replied, "Actually, I was going to order a martini. I was just shocked you could read my mind! I'm going to have to guard my thoughts around you."

Henry drew closer. "Now, that wouldn't be any fun. By the way, I hope you like them dirty."

What does he mean? she thought. *Dirty thoughts? Dirty clients?*

Again, Henry read the dumbfounded look on her face. "Your martini. I ordered you a dirty martini."

"Oh, sure, I like them dirty." *Whatever the hell that means.*

As promised, Henry entertained Misty with some hotel trivia. "Years ago, Ulysses S. Grant sat in the same lobby you waited for me in, drinking brandy and smoking his favorite cigars. Every day people approached him for favors, and that's how the term *lobbyist* was coined."

"That's so interesting!" Misty said.

"Believe it or not, Lincoln received so many death threats after winning the election, a detective named Allan Pinkerton had to smuggle him into the hotel for his own safety. President Lincoln remained in the Hamilton conducting the country's business for the two weeks leading up to his inauguration. And I bet you didn't know that Martin Luther King wrote his famous "I have a dream" speech in one of the hotel rooms upstairs."

Misty wondered if it could have been her or Miguel's room.

"So many presidents stayed in the hotel over the years," Henry continued, "that people refer to the Hamilton as the 'Residence of Presidents.'"

Misty noticed a certain charisma about the congressman as he spoke. It was no wonder he could garner as many votes as he did. Travis had been so quiet and unassuming, never trying to impress anyone, and being in the presence of a man whose career depended on his ability to make people think highly of him was quite a contrast to her beloved cowboy. Misty knew she needed to force thoughts of Travis out of her head if she was to perform at a high level. To help her do so, she pictured herself as the courtesan Travis had convinced her she was—a woman whose job it was to make a man feel special.

If it hadn't already sunk in that she was in the nation's capital, walking into the opulent restaurant drove the point home. Hanging on the long wall to her right were five large painted portraits of the last five presidents. She found the likenesses of Clinton, Reagan, Bush forty-one and forty-three somewhat flattering, but the likeness of President Obama fell short. It seemed the artist had difficulty capturing the essence of the man, maybe because he had not defined himself as a president yet.

Caught up in the moment, Misty gripped Henry's arm as they were escorted to their table. "So when can I come back and see your picture on the wall, Henry?"

The look Henry gave her told her immediately that hanging onto a married congressman in public might not be the wisest move.

Quickly turning his arm loose, she whispered, "I am so sorry. I don't know what I was thinking. Please forgive me."

After glancing around the restaurant to make sure no one was looking, Henry whispered, "Please, don't be embarrassed, I rather enjoyed it. Unfortunately, one photo of a beautiful young woman holding my arm in public could create quite a stir."

During dinner, they were interrupted no fewer than ten times. Henry was accommodating and friendly to each person, regardless of their importance. From the high-powered lobbyist to the gray-haired lady on her first trip to D.C., he treated them as equals. Misty was finding Congressman Henry quite easy to like. When dinner was over, they made plans for their first workout session and then parted ways.

Back at the Hamilton, Misty bumped into Miguel in the hallway as she walked back to her room.

"So, how did it go?" he asked.

"Oh, it was okay. He's a good guy. I don't think you'll have much to worry about."

"That's good to know. I hope I never have to tangle with a sitting congressman."

"Ha, I bet you don't. Catch you in the morning, Migs."

"Get a good night's sleep, Misters."

43

THE WORKOUTS BEGIN

Misty spent the next three weeks training Henry at a massive 100,000-square-foot athletic club equipped with every type of equipment they could possibly need. Misty felt good about the task at hand. She knew that when muscles are developed in a man's formative years, the way Henry's were when he played football, they remain dormant under the surface, just waiting for a call to action. The men she trained always regained 70 percent of their strength during the first three weeks, and Henry was no exception. He was a model pupil and was already strong as a bull after his first few weeks.

As Misty walked into the club on a Friday morning, she caught Henry looking at himself in the mirror. "Admiring my handiwork, I see."

Henry laughed. "Actually I was looking at that guy in the mirror, wondering who the hell he was. I've already lost six pounds, you know."

"Another two months and that guy will be replaced by an even better-looking one."

"I can't wait."

* * *

At the end of their workout, as Henry walked out of the club with Misty and Miguel, he said, "Hey, I'm getting together with Rick and my campaign advisor tonight for drinks. Why don't the two of you join us? Hiring you was Rick's idea, so it would give him a chance to meet you guys in person."

"You bet," said Miguel. "I've seen all the national monuments I can stomach. Do you want to go, Misty?"

"Sure, sounds like fun," she replied.

"Wonderful," said Henry. "I'll call you with the details later."

After spending the afternoon relaxing in their rooms, the pair put on the nicest clothes they had brought and met in the lobby.

"You look nice, Misty!"

"Thanks, so do you. I love your leather jacket."

Miguel smiled. "We're in D.C. You never know who we might run into."

On their way there, Miguel said to Misty, "I've been reading up on Washington in my spare time. The place we are going is the oldest known saloon in D.C. It opened in the eighteen fifties, I believe."

"Isn't that about the same time the bar we went to in San Antonio opened?" said Misty. "The one that was supposed to be haunted? Maybe this one will be, too."

"Maybe we'll see Honest Abe tonight."

Misty laughed. "Well then, you're really going to be glad you wore your nice outfit."

When they reached the saloon, they entered to find the ceiling hung with stuffed wild birds—not exactly what Misty had expected. Miguel spotted Henry sitting at a back table with two other men. When they approached, all three men stood up to greet them.

Henry did the honors. "Misty and Miguel, I would like you to meet Rick and Jim."

After the waitress took their drink orders, Henry said, "Misty, Rick is the reason you are here. Apparently you have quite a reputation among my largest contributors."

Misty smiled. "Yes, Rick is quite the persistent one. He doesn't know how to take no for an answer. But then I guess that's what you pay him for."

"That's what the *people* pay him for," Henry said. "We must always remember it's the people's money we are spending."

Miguel noticed Rick flinch as Henry spoke.

"Jim is my campaign advisor," Henry continued. "We pay him with campaign contributions. Very handsomely, don't we Jim?"

"Indeed you do," he replied. "And apparently I'm worth every penny—you haven't thrown me out on my ear yet."

Henry laughed. "Yes, Jim is very good at what he does. I'm fortunate he's on my team."

Misty reached over and held Henry's beer up to read the label.

"Michelob Ultra. Sticking with low carbs, I see. Good man."

"You need to tell me your secret, Misty," said Rick. "I've been trying to get Henry to listen to me for years."

"Could it be that Misty is prettier and smarter than you?" Jim chimed in.

Rick laughed. "Well, I'll concede to the prettier remark."

Once the waitress returned and everyone had a drink in front of them, Henry said, "Okay, let's get down to business. Jim, why don't you fill us in on the results of your latest poll? Don't worry; consider Misty and Miguel part of the team."

Addressing Misty and Miguel, Rick said, "I need to remind you that what you are about to hear is extremely confidential and is not to be repeated. Are you okay with this?"

"Oh, you can trust us," Misty said lightly. "We don't know anyone important anyway."

"Jim, let me give them a little background before you start," said Henry.

"Sure, that's probably a good idea," he replied.

"Molly, a district attorney in my district back home, is running against me in the upcoming primary. Molly surprised everyone with her polling numbers a month ago, and we're trying to figure out why she's doing so well. Rick, being the chauvinist he is, thinks it's because of her beauty, not her brains."

"Hey now," said Rick.

"Just joking, Rick. You see, Rick may have a point, considering Molly was once Miss Alabama. But let's get on to what Jim has to tell us."

"Well," said Jim, "our data confirmed that Molly's good looks are a contributing factor in the race, particularly with men over the age of thirty-five. And we found that women voters are voting for Molly because, well, she's a woman."

At that point, Misty broke in. "It would be hopeless trying to persuade a middle-aged man to switch his vote to Henry once he's been captivated by Molly's good looks, but don't you guys worry—when I get through with Henry, all the women are going to be swooning over him. Women have hormones too, you know."

Realizing she may have come across as defensive, Misty shifted in her seat uneasily.

"Very nice, Misty!" Jim exclaimed, putting her fear to rest. "Would you like to join my staff?"

Misty sat up tall, planted her butt firmly in her chair, and gave Miguel a *look how smart I am* grin. He rolled his eyes.

Henry surprised Misty by reaching under the table and giving her thigh a gentle squeeze. Flattered, she held up her empty glass and caught the eye of a passing server. "I'll have another martini. And make it dirty," she said smartly.

Giving her thigh a harder squeeze this time, Henry said, "You're my secret weapon, Misty. I'm counting on you."

She threw down the last of her old martini. "I can't see how I'm much of a secret weapon. All of Washington can see me working you out at the gym."

Misty was too distracted by the arrival of her fresh martini to notice the impact her statement had on the men.

The more they drank, the more they praised Henry on how good-looking he was getting from the hours of hard work in the gym, giving Misty great pride. It was all so stimulating.

After a heavy meal and many drinks, they decided to call it a night. They waved good-bye to Jim and Rick just outside the establishment, and Henry walked up to Miguel. Putting his arm around Miguel's shoulder, he said, "I have a few things I would like to discuss with Misty. Would you mind if I walk her back to the hotel alone?"

"No problem," said Miguel. "I'll go on ahead. Misty, you have my cell number on speed dial. Call me if you guys need me."

"Thanks, Miguel," she said. "Catch you in the morning."

For most of the walk back, Misty and Henry engaged in small talk, but as they closed in on the Hamilton, Henry stopped. "I'd like to suggest a change in our workout routine, if that's okay with you."

Misty looked confused. "Change? I'm not sure what you mean. You're not suggesting that you set the routines, are you?"

Henry placed his hands on her shoulders. "At the table you said you couldn't see how you were much of a secret. That was very astute of you. Rick's been hearing rumors that a certain congressman is spending a lot of time with a beautiful female trainer. Needless to say, nothing good can come from the rumors."

"So what are you suggesting, Henry?"

"A friend of mine has a small, well-equipped gym in his basement. He's out of the country until summer and I have access to his apartment. It would give us the privacy we need."

Misty turned her back to the congressman to give it some thought. His request was highly irregular and made her a bit uneasy, but she couldn't think of a good way to back out.

She turned back around. "Okay, Henry. We'll give it a try."

Henry looked relieved. "Good, but I have one more request."

When she didn't respond, Henry went ahead. "It's really hard for me to get away during the day, so would you mind switching our workout schedule to nights?"

"I suppose so," she said, even though she had never trained anyone in the evening before.

"Thanks for accommodating my needs. Now let's get you back to the hotel."

They said their good-byes outside the Hamilton, and Misty found Miguel sitting on a couch waiting for her when she entered the lobby.

"So what did Henry want to talk to you about?" he asked.

Misty sat down next to him. "He wants to change our workout site to a basement in an apartment building. He also wants to move to night-time workouts."

"What!" said Miguel. "What's up with that?"

"He's worried about the media making a big deal out of our training sessions. I guess I can see his point."

When Miguel had no reply, Misty stood up. "I'm really tired. Let's discuss this tomorrow when I can think straight."

Miguel remained seated as she walked away. He sat there for a while trying to sort out the implications of the congressman's request. He had an uneasy feeling about this one.

44

Sixth Judicial Circuit

It was a brisk day in Tuscaloosa, Alabama. Molly's campaign manager, Melanie, bundled up in her overcoat, waited outside the building that housed Molly's office. Melanie was relieved when the taxi she had been anticipating pulled up. The woman who stepped out tipped the cabby as if she were still in Washington, D.C.

"Thanks, ma'am," said the cabby. Then, looking down at the wad of cash in his hand, he exclaimed, "A few more tips like this and I can go home for the day!"

"Hey, Cindy. How was your trip?" Melanie asked as the woman approached the building's entrance.

"Nothing special. Kind of like this town."

"Might be nice if you lose the attitude before I introduce you to Molly," said Melanie.

Cindy smirked. "I've been working in D.C. ever since our college days. Working with politicians will make anyone cynical."

"I need you tough, not cynical," Melanie said.

"So tell me about Molly so I know what I'm getting myself into."

Melanie scrunched her nose. "You, my friend, are going to earn your money. Molly is ruthless. I've tried to handle her, but I'm not having an easy go of it. She's smart as can be, but she's inexperienced when it comes to national politics. Couple that with her hardheadedness, and I'm about ready to pull my hair out."

"Sounds like just another prima donna politician to me. Don't worry, I can handle her. Anything else?"

"Top in her class, strong minded, and aggressive but has been a popular district attorney. They love how tough she has been on crime, so she's not just another pretty face."

"Nice!" said Cindy. "How's she doing in the polls?"

"The latest poll has Molly leapfrogging the top contenders. She's only around ten percentage points behind Henry," Melanie gushed.

Cindy was stunned. "*Wow!* I had no idea. We can really make a name for ourselves if Molly closes that gap."

They walked into the lobby of the eighty-year-old government building and headed for the elevator. Cindy was amazed at the lack of security compared to Washington. Inside the elevator, Melanie said, "So you're not enthralled with the magnificent town of Tuscaloosa?"

"Why, should I be?" said Cindy.

"I guess you didn't catch my sarcasm," Melanie said.

When the receptionist ushered the girls into Molly's office, the district attorney was standing with her back to them, talking on the phone.

"Thank you, Mr. Jones. Your contribution is greatly appreciated. Now if there is anything I can ever do for you, please don't hesitate to ask . . . Okay, I will. Talk to you soon."

When Molly turned around, Cindy saw how beautiful she really was. She stood tall, at five foot eight, with perfect posture from her pageant training. Her close-cut blonde hair gave her the tough look she strove for, but her sleek, shapely body left little doubt she was all woman.

"Molly, this is Cindy," said Melanie.

As Cindy offered up her hand, Molly grabbed her wrist and softly rubbed the top of her hand.

"You have petite, delicate hands, Cindy," she said. "We're getting ready to go to war with a U.S. congressman. Are you sure you're up for the task?"

Cindy gazed into her eyes coldly, and calmly pried Molly's hand from her wrist.

Melanie cringed as she watched the two women hold their eye contact until Molly broke the silence. "I like her, Melanie. You did good. Now, Cindy, tell me what you know about my opponent. What do the other members of Congress think of Henry?"

Melanie breathed a sigh of relief.

"He's known as a straight shooter on the hill and is well respected by the other House members on both sides of the aisle," said Cindy. "He doesn't seem to have any skeletons in his closet, unlike most politicians."

"Only because he's a first-term congressman who's only had three years to become corrupted," Molly interjected. "That doesn't mean he has nothing to hide, however. I've brought many powerful men to justice in my courtroom and I can assure you, they all had their weaknesses. In fact, it's usually dangling between their legs."

"Cindy, tell Molly about the rumor you heard," said Melanie.

"It's only a rumor, but it does have, as you so vividly expressed, dangling qualities," she said.

Molly leaned in. "And?"

"The word on the street is Henry hired a high-profile trainer to help him lose weight and get in shape. If it's true, they must assume your good looks have a lot to do with your polling numbers."

Molly walked to the window and stared into the distance. Melanie nodded at Cindy, indicating she was doing fine. They sat patiently, awaiting Molly's reply.

"That's pretty chauvinistic of them, but unfortunately it has merit," said Molly. "So Henry has decided to fight fire with fire. He's a smart man. He stands to gain a lot if he loses weight and gets back in shape. I grew up watching Crimson Tide football, and I'd guess every middle-aged woman who lived in this district when Henry quarterbacked remembers how handsome he was back then. I was only in my early teens and I remember. I'm sure my mother does as well."

Attempting to lighten the mood, Melanie said, "Well, I think your mother's vote is safe."

Molly whipped around, putting the girls on edge. To their relief, she let out a short, controlled laugh. "I don't know. Two-timer Henry was pretty damn hot!"

"Two-timer Henry?" said Cindy.

A smirk came over Molly's face. "When I pumped my mother for everything she remembered about Henry, she said he was notorious for never staying loyal to one girlfriend. He always had at least a couple on the side." Molly and Cindy looked at each other as if they could read each other's thoughts.

"Find out everything you can about Henry's trainer," Molly said to Cindy. "Who she is, where she's from, and who she's been training. I want you to hire a private investigator. I know plenty, but I'd prefer we use someone who can't be traced to me. Do you know someone good in the D.C. area?"

Cindy nodded vigorously. "Yes, I have a team of two brothers who will get to the bottom of this in no time. How would you like me to pay them?"

"You won't," said Molly. "I'll have someone do it for us. And let's refer to your PIs as 'the boys.' I really don't want to know their names."

"Understood," said Cindy.

"Good," said Molly. "Listen, I'm going to be in the D.C. area in three weeks. We can get together then and see where we stand."

Once Cindy had walked out the door, Melanie turned to look back. Molly's nod meant she could sleep peacefully tonight.

45

STEP INTO MY LAIR

As they walked through downtown D.C. toward the new workout facility, Miguel said, "I don't have a good feeling about this, Misty. You've
always worked out your clients in a public place."

"Are you forgetting Gabriella had a gym in her house?" she said.

Miguel, unable to come up with a good comeback, kept walking in
silence. Eight blocks from the Hamilton, they found the apartment building. A dapperly uniformed doorman greeted them, and another man in a
dark suit lurked behind him, unmistakably a secret service agent.

"Hi," she said to the doorman, "I'm Misty and this is my . . . well, my
companion, Miguel, and we're here to . . ."

"I'll take it from here," the man in the dark suit said to the doorman
as he motioned for Misty and Miguel to follow him inside. "I've been
expecting you."

He led them down a long corridor to the back of the building. When
they reached a thick steel door without an apartment number, the man
pulled out a piece of paper and entered a code into the keypad. The door
let out a powerful clunk, like bolts being released in a bank vault door,
and Misty and Miguel gave each other a funny look. The man leaned

into the door with his shoulder and nudged it open. Inside, they found themselves standing on a small grated landing, looking down a circular stairway that wound its way to the floor below.

"Please be careful," the man said. "These steps are narrow and the descent is steep. Keep one hand on the metal guardrails at all times."

As forewarned, the steps were extremely difficult to traverse. They were so tightly spaced Misty surmised a man with big feet might have to ride down on his butt. When they reached the floor below without incident, a powerfully built man rose from his chair and walked over to greet them.

"Wonderful! I have company," he said jovially. "It gets awful lonely down here, you know. I'll let Henry know you've arrived."

Miguel looked at a wall of surveillance monitors and realized the man's job was to keep an eye on every square inch of the apartment complex. *This place is as secure as Fort Knox*, he thought. *There must be some very important people living here.*

The surveillance man picked up a phone on the wall. "Congressman, your guests have arrived . . . Yes sir, I'll send them right in." Once again a code was entered into a heavy metal door and it clunked open. The door opened directly into the living room of a sparsely furnished apartment. Not the sort of place they expected. No paintings on the wall or decorations of any sort. Purely functional.

Henry rose from his chair and walked over to greet them. "Welcome! I can imagine what you're thinking about now. Please don't let all this spook you. Sorry about all the drama just to use my friend's gym."

"Who's your friend?" Misty asked. "Does he have a price on his head?'

Henry laughed. "No, at least not in this country. I'm afraid his identity will need to remain a secret. National security and all that, you know."

Henry apparently wanted to change the subject quickly; he immediately said, "Come on. Let me show you the gym."

He led them through the apartment to a small door in the kitchen and then down another flight of stairs to the basement below. Misty was pleasantly surprised with how well equipped the gym was. There were no fancy exercise machines but plenty of old-fashioned benches, dumbbells, and free weights. For cardio, there were two treadmills and two state-of-the-art spinning bikes that would have been the envy of any instructor.

Misty looked around approvingly. "I'll bet this is very similar to the weight room you used in your football days."

Henry smiled. "Oh, yeah! It's exactly like our training room. We did things the hard way back then. Heavy metal versus raw muscle. Mano a mano."

I could really get into working out in a place like this, she thought.

Henry sensed her excitement. "Why don't you work out with me?"

"Maybe next time," she said. "Tonight, I need to concentrate on developing a different workout routine with this new equipment."

"What about me?" Miguel said.

Henry calmly addressed Miguel as he pointed to the agent standing in the doorway. "Actually, I thought it might be worth your while to spend some time with agent Mulberry while Misty and I work out. He's graciously agreed to teach you what he knows about the tricks of the trade. Who knows, it could come in handy protecting Misty down the road." Henry looked at the dumbfounded agent. "That's right, isn't it, Agent Mulberry?" he said, nodding his head.

The agent reluctantly nodded in return.

Taking his job of protecting Misty seriously and having always wanted to undergo more training, Miguel said, "I think that's a great idea! After all, this place is so locked down it's impossible for anyone to get to her from the outside. Are you okay with it, Misty?"

"Sure. Go for it."

A very pleased Henry turned to Misty as Miguel and Agent Mulberry exited to an adjoining room. "Now that that's settled, where do we begin?"

She worked Henry out hard for the next half hour. While spotting Henry as he bench-pressed two hundred pounds, she laughed when she thought back to helping Chester Naples bench thirty pounds. She noticed how much more developed Henry's triceps and pecs were getting and began to imagine what he would look like weeks from now. Misty was so into the session that it took her a while to notice the sweat dripping from her hair. "What's up with the heat?"

Sweating profusely as well, Henry replied, "I turned the heat up to simulate my training while in college. I still remember working out in a room with no air-conditioning and running laps in the sweltering summer heat. I need to sweat if I'm going to get back down to my playing weight."

Misty was pleased Henry was taking his training so seriously. She calculated the number of weeks left and the number of pounds Henry still needed to shed. Maybe a little heat would ensure that they met Henry's goal.

At the end of the session, Misty noticed how much better he looked having lost an estimated five pounds of water weight. She was getting a sneak preview of the extremely attractive man lurking under the surface.

* * *

Several weeks later, Misty and Miguel returned for another round of training. She decided training at night wasn't so bad after all as she got into the routine of getting a light snack and crawling into bed after each workout. Miguel was learning a lot from Agent Mulberry. On today's walk over, Misty could tell how aware Miguel was of his surroundings and was pleased he was getting such good training. With Miguel much more attentive, they talked less, allowing Misty time to think about how much more fun it was to train alongside her pupil. It had been quite some time since she last trained with free weights, and she had forgotten how pumped it made her muscles. And Henry had been right about training in sweltering heat. He was down to two hundred and nine pounds and was looking much leaner. The sauna-like sessions were cleansing his skin and returning his youthful look. During their last workout, Misty had pictured Henry in his prime and imagined all the women throwing themselves at him. She had little doubt he was quite an experienced lover.

When Misty and Miguel had been shown in by Agent Mulberry, they found Henry waiting in a revealing tank top and tight nylon shorts. Both Misty and Henry began showing up for workouts wearing outfits with less and less material. They justified the skimpier workout gear by claiming it was necessary to combat the heat. Miguel gave Misty a weary look before heading off with Mulberry.

As usual, this training session began with thirty minutes on the treadmill. As they jogged, they checked each other out in mirrors Henry had installed on the back wall. He used the excuse of being a tad claustrophobic and said it would help make the room feel larger. She didn't buy his story, but she didn't care. Misty was dressed in a frilly tank top. The sweat and heat was causing her inner thighs to chap, so she wore baggy shorts to hide the fact she wasn't wearing underwear. Now if she could only figure out a way to lose the sports bra.

Twenty minutes into the run, Henry asked, "Do you mind if I take my shirt off? For some reason it seems hotter than usual."

"Only if I can," Misty jokingly answered. When Henry didn't laugh, she quickly added, "Just kidding. Go ahead. We don't want you to get a heat stroke, now do we? Your hospital stay might bring attention and blow our cover."

Henry pulled his tank top over his head and threw it to the concrete floor. Misty caught quick glances at Henry's muscled chest, which was covered with a coat of soft, fine hair. His firm pecs moved up and down magnificently to the motion of the treadmill. Misty's temperature was rising, but it had little to do with the heat in the room.

Half an hour into weight training, Misty noticed the muscles of Henry's upper torso swelling as if stung by a bee. She tried to stop staring, but the more he worked out, the more his body glistened under the intense heat. Without panties, the sweat pooled in her pubic hair and mixed with her natural juices. The lack of friction enabled the outer lips of her vagina to slide against one another, causing a sensation that was the equivalent of riding bareback.

They had moved on to lifting weights. After taking a few sips from a bottle of cold water, she poured the remaining liquid over herself to cold-shock her body. It was obvious both of them knew the stakes were rising along with the heat, and that something would eventually come to a head.

Walking back to the hotel, Misty realized the temptation to act on the special provision in her contract was becoming unbearable for both her and Henry, but she desperately wanted to finish the remaining weeks and see Henry in all his glory. Besides, she had convinced herself she truly was his secret weapon, and she wanted the pleasure of feeling like she played a pivotal role in his reelection bid. She decided that she needed something to divert her attention.

"I think we both could use a break," she said to Miguel as they walked. "Why don't you rent a car and drive down to Monticello over the weekend?"

"Thomas Jefferson's place? You bet! I know you're not that interested in history or you'd be coming with me. What do you have planned while I'm away?"

Misty smiled. "Well, I'm interested in the history between Travis and me. I think it's time to pay him a visit."

"I wondered what was taking you so long."

Misty contemplated Miguel's remark. *Why* has *it taken me so long?* she thought. *Maybe I was afraid to make a habit of seeing him. And maybe I'm worried he won't be the same old cowboy I grew to love. He has short hair now, and wears a suit. What if he wants to talk about investing? Yuck!*

Miguel's voice broke her train of thought. "Maybe you shouldn't go. Now that you've been working out so hard, I'm not sure Travis will be able to resist your smoking-hot body. I'm sure he's settled back into his New York lifestyle, and you probably don't want to distract him from his job."

Misty put her head on Miguel's shoulder. "You really know how to push my buttons, don't you?"

"Why, I have no idea what you could be referring to, boss."

46

Things Heat Up

Saturday morning, Miguel accompanied Misty to Union Station, where she would board her train to New York City. Misty felt that riding Amtrak might be a fun experience, just chilling out and watching the countryside pass outside her window. Travis had been ecstatic when Misty called to tell him she was coming. She hadn't told him she took on a client close by, so it was a total surprise. For Misty, hearing Travis's soothing voice conjured up wonderful memories of hot South Texas days, and the even hotter nights—a pleasant reprieve from the D.C. winter.

Inside Union Station, Miguel's eyes were drawn to the incredibly tall ceiling and the grand scale of everything in the building. While Miguel wondered what the story was behind the six colossal statues sitting above the main cornice of the central block, Misty was only interested in boarding the Acela Express to New York. Miguel trailed behind, admiring the marble, gold-leaf, and white-granite train station.

When he caught up with Misty, she was already in the ticket line. "I wonder if they give tours of this place like they do the capitol in D.C.," he said.

"If they do, go for it," Misty replied half-heartedly. "You're free as a bird this weekend."

When it was time to board the train, Misty gave him a hug. "Thanks for walking me to the train. Have a good time while I'm away, okay?"

"I'm looking forward to it, but are you sure you don't want me to come along? New York is a big city."

"It's just a short cab ride from Penn Station to Travis's apartment. I won't be walking the streets alone. I'll be fine."

"Okay. I'll be here when you get back."

Misty patted him on the arm. "Thanks, Miguel."

As she walked off, he shouted, "Say hi to Travis for me!"

"Will do!" she called back.

Misty boarded the quiet car to find comfortable seats with plenty of legroom, and signs forbidding cell phones or loud talking. Her plan to enjoy the countryside was foiled when the gentle sway of the train rolling down the tracks lulled her into a deep sleep.

* * *

Molly walked down First Street on her way to meet Cindy after an early morning breakfast with several of her party's senior legislators. They were all gracious and supportive, but when she asked them about Henry, they had little bad to say about him. That made her upcoming meeting with Cindy and the boys all the more important. Even though they hadn't had any negative comments about the congressman, she did come away from the breakfast with the distinct impression that they found her a worthy opponent to Henry.

Molly found Cindy and the boys sitting in the back corner of the establishment, just where they said they would be.

"Good, you are on time!" she said as she walked up. "We have a lot to cover before I catch my plane back home."

"Nice to see you, too," Cindy said under her breath as the three of them stood up to greet Molly. Cindy handled the introductions. "Molly, I'd like to introduce you to the boys."

Molly was pleased Cindy had remembered not to call them by their real names.

Molly looked around. "This place is a dive. I can't believe so many people on Capitol Hill come here."

Cindy wanted to say she'd picked the place to make Molly feel like she was back home in Alabamee, but she resisted the urge and stayed professional. "I guess it has to do with its close proximity to the capitol. That and the famous martinis."

"Politicians and their martinis," Molly said. "I struck out at my morning meeting, so you better have something good on Henry."

The boys had assured Cindy she would be happy with the investigation. "Take it away, boys," she said confidently.

The older brother, who was the smaller but brainier of the two, took charge. "First, I feel compelled to explain a few things to Molly. Checking up on United States congressmen can be hazardous to your health. One slip-up and we could find ourselves behind bars. We're only doing this because we owe Cindy a big favor."

"Then I'm lucky I hired her," said Molly.

Cindy enjoyed the compliment even though it had little to do with her own talent.

"We have some good information for you, but please do not take any written notes," the older brother continued.

Molly was pleased they were being so careful. "Understood," she replied.

The older man looked to his younger brother, the enforcer of the two, and proceeded after getting his nod of approval. "This Misty dame is referred to as the 'Black Widow Trainer' in certain circles. She hires out to wealthy individuals for three months at a time. We heard that sometimes the client makes it through three months of training and sometimes they don't. Either way, she gets paid in full."

Molly and Cindy exchanged looks, both wondering what caused the training sessions to get cut short.

"This gal not only gets top dollar," he continued, "she gets to choose from over hundreds of applicants. The guys that get selected feel as if they just won the lottery. The fact that someone from D.C. was selected this time around seemed to give the guys something to talk about, resulting in easy access to the information."

What girl wouldn't want a gig like that! Cindy thought.

"She must charge a fortune!" said Molly.

"It's not only the fee," he said. "Someone is footing the bill for a suite in the Hamilton. We have an in at the front desk—"

The elder brother flinched from his brother's kick to the shin.

Grimacing in pain, he said, "Let's just say a little birdie told us that both Misty and her bodyguard are staying at the Hamilton, all expenses paid."

Molly was beside herself. "Bodyguard? All expenses paid? That's an expensive hotel—and why on earth would she need a bodyguard?"

"I'll say it's expensive," the younger brother said. "They've run up almost sixty thousand dollars in bills to date."

"So can we follow the money trail?" asked Cindy. "It would help if we could find out who's picking up that tab!"

"That might be difficult," the younger brother said. "Our birdie says someone shows up every so often and clears their tab with cash. They never know when this person is coming. A guy like that is going to be pretty difficult to track."

Molly repositioned herself in her chair, thinking things over. Cindy slumped back and basked in the glory of pleasing her client. The quality of information was outstanding, which meant Molly had to take her more seriously from now on.

Molly began thinking out loud. "Henry is not a rich man, so there's no way he's footing the bill. Besides, how could he use his own finances and hide it from his wife? Janet may keep him on a long leash, but it's still a leash."

Molly turned to the boys. "What do we know about her past clients?"

The younger brother sat up straight and puffed out his chest. "Misty trained a man named Peter in Colorado, but he is nowhere to be found. Her next client, and I'm not kidding, was an old man named Charlie Brown. Unfortunately, old Charlie is now deceased. After that she trained a businesswoman by the name of Gabriella, in Argentina."

Molly's eyes opened wide. *She trains women?* she thought.

"We don't have any contacts in Buenos Aires," he continued, "and I'm not sure we would be welcome in a foreign country."

"You're right. Who else do you have?"

"After Argentina, she flew all the way up to Alaska to train some guy named Captain Kev. We understand the authorities have been hot on his trail for several years now, but to no avail. The captain and his running mate, Miniature Mike, could be anywhere on the planet.

"From Alaska, she jumped the big pond to London where another birdie tells us she trained a man named Ivan. We've been told Ivan is not a guy you want to mess with, assuming you could even track him down. We're thinking he's some kind of a spook."

Cindy couldn't keep quiet any longer. "What the hell? Whatever she does with these guys seems to make them disappear."

"Well I know what a real black widow spider does to make their mates disappear," said Molly. "We've got to find out what's in her contract."

"You might be in luck," said the older brother. "Her last client lives in San Antonio. His name is Chester Naples."

Molly smiled. "So what do we know about this Naples guy?"

"We hear he's a slime bag," he replied. "Looks like a weasel—greasy slicked-back hair and all. People guard their wallets when they do business with him. What's interesting is his wife filed for divorce a week after Misty left town."

Molly's DA instincts took over. "He's our guy. Since he's not tied to Henry, I'll put some of my staff on it. They can do some quick, detailed background checks right away."

Molly looked at the boys. "Pack your bags—you're going to be on the Monday morning flight to San Antonio. I'd like you to pay old Chester a visit."

When Molly left, Cindy said, "Good job. What do you guys think?"

The younger brother snickered. "I think she's got nice legs."

47

WEEKEND WITH TRAVIS

Misty's anticipation grew as the Acela Express pulled into Penn Station. She only had one day with Travis, so she gave serious thought to hauling him directly to the bedroom upon arrival, but she decided that might seem too tacky. She walked quickly through Penn Station, dodging hurried travelers, on her way to the Seventh Street exit. Flagging a cab was the only thing on her mind; otherwise, she might have realized how much of a dump Penn Station was compared to Union Station.

"Where to, lady?" asked the driver once she managed to flag a cab down.

"Corner of East Sixty-Sixth and Madison."

"You got it."

When they arrived, Misty paid the cabby and stepped onto Madison Avenue. She gazed at Travis's red brick and terra-cotta apartment building from the opposite side of the street. The medieval-looking building conjured up images of the type of sex she wanted to unleash on her handsome cowboy friend. The building attendant who answered the door had little idea there was a barbarian at the gate. It felt pleasantly normal to have him usher her into the building without a secret service agent at his side.

"What can I do for you, ma'am?" he asked once they were inside.

Misty smiled. "My name is Misty and I'm here to visit my friend Travis."

After looking over his guest list, he replied, "Here you are. Travis lives in apartment seven on the eighth floor. The elevators are right around the corner."

Walking along the hard marble floor, she noticed how clean and classy everything looked. It was a far cry from the manly ranch house Travis had lived in the last time she visited him. Once she got to the eighth floor, Misty rang the doorbell and anxiously listened for signs of life inside. She rubbed thumb and forefingers together nervously at the sound of locks being undone. When the door swung open, Travis stood there wearing jeans, a cotton pullover, and a big smile. Misty leaped into his arms, wrapping her arms around his neck and her legs around his waist. She hugged him so tight her boobs flattened into his chest.

Misty leaned back in his arms, looked him in the eye, and said, "So what's with the jeans? I thought you were a sophisticated businessman now."

He smiled. "Not when I'm spending the weekend with one of my best friends."

"*One* of your best friends?"

"Best friend?"

She placed her hands on each side of his face and laid a long, slow, passionate kiss on his mouth. His familiar, manly scent filled her with wonderful memories.

When their lips parted, she said, "That's so you never forget it."

After he let her down, the urge to lead Travis by the hand to the nearest bed or sofa rushed over her.

Noticing the passion in her eyes, Travis pinched her nose with his fingers. "It's a chilly day and I made a hot pot of coffee. Why don't we have a cup and catch up on things before . . ."

Misty scrunched her nose. "Cool, calm, and collected, just like I left you. You're right. Let's take it slow and easy."

Misty checked out the small apartment's living room while he attended to the coffee. She was drawn to a small sitting area with chairs that faced three large windows set at angles that gave her a fabulous view up Madison Avenue and down Sixty-Sixth Street. The middle window allowed her a view of Central Park. The snow-covered park was a refuge in the midst of a sea of high-rises.

Travis handed Misty her cup of coffee. "Cream and two sugars, right?"

"Please," said Misty. "My, my, don't we have a good memory."

After the two took a seat, Travis said, "I see you like the best real estate in my apartment. Isn't the view wonderful?"

Misty smiled mischievously as she glanced at his bedroom door. "I'm sure the view in there would be spectacular as well."

"The longer we hold off, the better it will be," Travis said, which only made Misty hotter.

They spent a wonderful two hours catching up on everything that had transpired since they last saw each other. Travis filled Misty in on how well his job at Excelsior Investments was going. She couldn't help but smile when he told her Brenda had filed for divorce shortly after Misty left Texas. Chester seemed like a cartoon character to her now. Misty had long forgiven Chester, realizing that if not for him, she would have never gotten to know Travis.

She then filled Travis in on her wonderful New Year's Eve trip to Rio and explained why she was in Washington, D.C. Misty noticed Travis seemed a little uneasy when she told him about Henry, so she changed the subject.

"I almost forgot—Miguel said to say hi."

"Miguel. How's he doing? Migs really is a great guy."

"He's doing fine. He's my faithful companion, you know."

"I'm surprised you didn't bring Miguel along to protect you from me," he said.

Misty laughed as she walked to the kitchen to refill her coffee mug. "From the way things have been playing out so far, you're the one that could use the protection."

When she came back into the living room, he said, "I bet you'd like to get settled in. Bring your bag and follow me."

Inside his bedroom, he said, "I sleep on the side nearest the bathroom. You can take the other side."

Misty set her bag down, jumped onto the bed, and grinned at Travis. "Nice and firm. I think this mattress will hold up just fine."

"Actually it's new and could use a little breaking in. But first, I need to feed you a good dinner. I don't want you running out of energy tonight."

Misty stood on the bed, walked to Travis, and placed her hands on his shoulders. "So you're going to fill me up before you fill me up?"

A fully charged Travis replied, "Come on, we better get to the supermarket before I get things out of order."

"Sounds like fun. Can we walk through Central Park on the way?"

"Sure! Actually, there's a shortcut that runs through the park."

The shortcut became a long-cut after Misty insisted they explore this trail and that trail. Travis would have been content walking in the park for hours. Readjusting to the maddening pace of New York City and his old job had kept him running around in circles nonstop. Misty's natural zeal for life lifted his spirits. He knew she would never understand, but walking through the park with her was just as exciting as sleeping with her. He was in no rush to get her into the sack. If only he could bottle her to cheer him up when he got down.

Their journey eventually led them to Columbus Circle. Before they moved on to the supermarket, Misty insisted they stop so she could inspect the statue of Christopher Columbus. Finally, they made it to the escalator that took them down to the subterranean store.

"So this is where they stash their supermarkets in New York. Very cool," said Misty.

"This isn't just any supermarket. It's a two-million-dollar-a-week supermarket."

The dollar amount didn't mean much to Misty. "What are you going to make me for dinner?"

"I make a pretty mean spaghetti."

"I love spaghetti. Let's get some wine to go with it!"

"You wanna pick it out?"

"Absolutely!"

Not wanting to go on any more detours, Travis walked them back along city streets once they had bought everything they needed. They held hands along the way, making Misty feel like she was back in high school, walking with her sweetheart. As they passed a building, Misty began to crack up.

"What's so funny?" Travis asked.

"Look at the address of that plastic surgeon's office."

Travis looked. The side of the building read "800B."

"Pretty sweet address for someone in the boob-job business, don't you think?" said Misty.

Travis laughed. "Maybe we should schedule you an appointment?"

Misty slapped him on the shoulder. "Hey, cowboy. What's wrong with my boobs?"

When Travis playfully slipped the front of her jacket down, she pulled back. "Oh, no you don't. You had your chance to play with them when I got here. You just better pray these babies want to come out and play tonight."

Misty could tell from the look in his eyes that tonight was shaping up to be a memorable one.

* * *

Misty sat on the kitchen counter drinking her wine and watching Travis preparing the meal when the doorbell rang.

"My hands are gross," said Travis. "You mind seeing who it is?"

Misty took another sip of her wine, slid off the counter, and headed toward the door. The doorbell rang again before she could arrive.

"Hold your horses, I'm coming," she said softly.

She swung the door wide open. In front of her stood a well-dressed lady with a look on her face that said *Who the hell are you!* Misty wondered the same thing. She was moderately pretty with stylish short brown hair, hazel eyes, a cute button nose, and a lean body.

Rich bitch, for sure, Misty thought after noticing her expensive jewelry.

Once they had inspected one another thoroughly, the woman demanded, "Who are you!"

"I'm Travis's friend, Misty. Who are you?"

Travis hustled to the door, his apron still on. "Emily! I thought you would be at your folks' place on Long Island this weekend . . ."

The sight of Travis in an apron apparently struck Emily as funny. "My, aren't we the pampered chef? Who's your assistant?"

Misty had never witnessed Travis out of sorts, and it gave her an anxious feeling.

"Emily, Misty is a friend of mine from, uh, Texas. We became friends while we both worked for Chester Naples."

Emily stood there looking suspiciously back and forth at Travis and Misty. "Misty was in town for the weekend and decided to stop by," he stumbled on. "I invited her over to dinner so we could catch up. Why'd you decide not to visit your folks this weekend?"

Emily brushed past them toward the kitchen. "I'm still going. I needed to stop by and pick up a dress of mine."

Travis caught up to Emily and grabbed her by the hand. "I've got some stuff stacked up in the closet—why don't I get your dress? You can get to know Misty while I do."

Emily looked at Travis for a moment before saying, "Alright. It's the red one with the bow on it. You know, the one I wore to your last office party."

"I know just the one," he said as he hurried into the bedroom.

From her vantage point Misty could see into his bedroom out of the corner of her eye. When she noticed him pick her bag up off the bed before heading to the closet, things began coming into focus. Emily was Travis's ex-fiancée. He must have gotten back together with her.

Emily looked Misty over. "Just visiting?"

"Just visiting," Misty replied.

Now sick to her stomach, Misty wished the witch would take her dress and leave so she could sort this out with Travis.

When he returned from the bedroom and handed Emily her dress, Emily said, "Do you mind if I stay for dinner? There's a later train I can catch."

"That would be great!" Travis said immediately. "There's plenty to go around."

He then took control of the conversation, asking Emily questions about her day, her dad, her mom, and anything else he could think of, all in an effort to keep Emily from asking questions. As he did, Misty sat there quietly, but her temperature was rising.

"Enough with the interrogation, Travis," Emily said at last. "Just tell me where Misty's staying tonight."

Misty resented the fact Emily had directed her question to Travis as if she weren't there.

Travis paused long enough to place his foot lightly on top of Misty's under the table. "The Stratford House. She's staying at the Stratford House." He looked at Misty as he added, "You know, a block from Whole Foods."

Travis squirmed in his seat as Misty stared not at him, but through him. He prayed she was not getting ready to hang him out to dry.

To his relief, she calmly looked at Emily and said, "That's right, and actually I must be getting back. I have a big day planned tomorrow."

Satisfied at last, Emily put on a big smile. "I'm sorry you can't stay and visit longer, but if you have a full day planned tomorrow I understand."

Misty despised the patronizing look on Emily's face and used every bit of self-discipline she could muster to keep from slapping her silly.

Misty stood up, placed her napkin on the table, and made a move toward the bedroom to get her things. She turned back and looked at Travis after he loudly cleared his throat.

Realizing his cover would be blown if she walked out with her bag, Misty did Travis a favor. "The walk isn't that far. I think I'll wait to use the restroom until I get there."

Travis followed her to the door to say good-bye, but she was walking down the hall by the time he got there.

Watching Misty walk off under these circumstances may have been one of the hardest things he'd ever had to endure. When the horrific realization sunk in that he had just exiled Misty to the streets with none of her belongings he pathetically attempted to yell after her. "I, uh, I . . ." he called down the hall. He stopped his feeble attempt when Misty shot him the middle finger without looking back.

Travis walked back and took his seat at the table.

Without looking at Emily, he said, "Weren't you a little hard on her?"

"Now, Travis," Emily said in a nonthreatening way. "How am I supposed to act when I find a beautiful woman in your apartment?" Then in a more authoritative voice: "Why didn't you tell me you had a female friend coming to visit?"

Travis wanted nothing more than for Emily to be gone, so he said what he knew would appease her. "Yes, I should have. I'll make it up to you."

Emily accepted his apology with a smile.

In an attempt to move her on her way, he said, "Would you mind helping me clean up the kitchen before you go?"

Emily looked at her watch. "Oh! I'd love to, but I really need to catch the nine-forty train. Will you be a dear and call me a cab while I'm on my way to the lobby?"

"No problem, honey." Travis gave Emily a kiss and said good-bye.

He walked her to the elevator, reached in, and pressed the first-floor button to make sure she was gone before he placed a call to Misty. It rang until he got her voicemail.

"Misty. Emily's gone, so you can come home. You have every right to be mad at me and I have no excuse for the way I treated you, but your things are here and it's not safe walking around the city by yourself."

He hung up and called the cab for Emily before trying Misty again.

After calling her several more times and getting voicemail each time, he began texting.

9:15: "Tell me where you are. I'll come to you."

9:45: "Come on, Misty. It's cold out there. Please call me."

10:20: "Look, I made a horrible mistake. I should have let you know Emily and I got back together a month ago, but I wanted to see you so bad I didn't want to risk you not coming."

10:40: "Come on, Misty. You know I'm just a dumb cowboy. Dealing with two women at one time is way out of my league."

* * *

Misty sat in the Stratford House bar sipping on her third rum and Coke. Each text and each drink chipped away at her resolve to never see Travis again. She knew the reason she kept from getting too involved in relationships had to do with how much she despised moments like this. Her emotions had now run the gamut. Rage had turned to anger, anger to disgust, and now she was headed for a place she refused to go. Self-pity was beneath her.

Grabbing her phone, she composed a text: "When I get back, you have some explaining to do."

When Travis got the message, he breathed a sigh of relief. He wasn't sure whether he could ever make things right again, but at least she was safe.

After about twenty minutes, he heard a knock and hustled to the door. In the hallway stood a woman he barely recognized. Sad but resolute, she coldly walked by him as he held out his hands to her. She sat down on the sofa, and he took a seat on the floor, legs crossed, as he patiently waited for her to say something.

After a few minutes of silence, Travis said, "Listen. You have every right to be mad at me. I have no excuse for the way I or Emily treated you. You did nothing to deserve what we put you through."

Misty's reply was void of emotion. "That's a start. Keep going."

He cautiously took a seat on the sofa next to her, fully prepared to back away at the slightest hint he was not welcome. He was reminded of the time he found a scared, hungry cat on his porch; all it took was one misstep for the cat to run away.

Settled in, Travis continued, "You gave me a lot of time to think things over while I was waiting to hear back from you. I think I reconciled with Emily in an attempt to get my life back to normal. The way it was before she left me and my uncle died. Watching how she treated you is making me reevaluate things. What I did to you was wrong, and I understand why Emily was upset, but the cold way she treated you let me see a side of her I'd never seen. And I'm sick that our wonderful weekend was ruined."

Misty knew Travis was sincere. "I don't want to be mad at you, but we'll just have to wait and see if my affections for you come back with time," she said. "I understand my being here must have been a shock to Emily, and both you and I need to bear some of the blame for that. I never asked you not to see other women, and you never asked me not to see other men. We chose to remain just good friends. So I guess I'm saying it's not your fault."

When Misty picked up on Travis's relief and sensed his next move would be an attempt to hug her, her tone became more serious. "Just don't ever treat me like you did again, or our friendship will end."

Travis gently laid his hand on her knee. When she didn't reject it, he moved it up to her cheek and gently pulled her head toward him, just enough to lean in and give her a kiss. Misty didn't resist, but she didn't kiss back. Travis moved his kisses to her eyelids and finally her forehead. Misty leaned in, and he cuddled her in his arms. Travis could tell she was tired.

He enjoyed their moment a bit longer before saying, "You must be as exhausted as I am. Why don't you go get ready for bed."

When Misty was finished in the bathroom, Travis went in. In the bedroom, Misty looked at the sexy lingerie in her bag before pulling out a baggy T-shirt.

Travis found the bed empty when he emerged from the bathroom, and Misty was curled up on the sofa with a pillow and blanket she had commandeered from his closet. Leaning over, he gave her a soft peck on her temple and then retired to the bedroom. She held a smile until he was gone. *I hope he's kicking himself for passing up on my earlier advances*, she thought.

The next morning they both agreed it would be best for Misty to take an earlier train back to D.C. It would take time to undo the damage, if it could be undone. Misty gave Travis a warm embrace before heading down the steps to the train. When she reached the bottom of the stairs she looked back up. Travis was still watching her. She feigned a smile and then walked off down the sidewalk.

When she got back to D.C., Miguel was waiting at the station as promised. He had sensed something wasn't right when he got the text saying she would be returning early.

"Want to talk about it?" he asked as they walked to the car.

Misty gave him a hug and replied, "Not right now, but thanks for offering."

48

BACK TO THE GRIND

On Monday morning, Henry, Rick, and Jim held a breakfast meeting at the Hamilton.

"I can tell from your demeanor the recent polling data is good," Henry said to Jim. "Am I right?"

"You've still got your touch, Henry. Your press conference at home seems to be paying dividends—you're up two points in the poll. It all came from women voters."

Jim paused so that Henry could savor the good news before he continued. "Your plan seems to be working. Lose another six to eight pounds by this summer and you just might be bulletproof."

"Hey now, that was my plan," said Rick. As soon as he spoke, he noticed Misty entering the restaurant and elbowed Henry.

Henry yelled across the room. "Misty! Over here! Come join us for breakfast!"

Misty was not in the mood for company, but she knew she couldn't ignore a client and walked over to join the trio. Henry rose from his chair and surprised her with an enthusiastic hug. Rick looked around the restaurant to make sure no one had noticed.

The hug lifted her spirits. "What's up, boys? You sure are in a good mood."

"We should be," Jim replied. "Henry's press conference back home added another two points to his lead. And it all came from women voters."

Misty patted Henry on the knee. "Of course it did. Just look at how handsome he is now."

A beaming Henry replied, "And I owe it to your workouts. I can't wait to get them on again; I mean get on with them. Let's take it up a notch, why don't we?"

Misty couldn't help but wonder if he'd just had a Freudian slip. She sat back and enjoyed her coffee while her three male companions enthusiastically discussed the upcoming campaign. She became enamored with Henry's positive energy and found it hard to take her eyes off him. Noticing Misty's attention, Henry placed his hand under the table and gave her thigh a little squeeze. Misty found it comforting in a way that blocked out her disappointment over the weekend fiasco. For a moment, she imagined what it would feel like to be the congressman's girl.

48

East Meets West

The boys' plane touched down in San Antonio at noon on Monday. A cool front had passed through the day before and the weather was beautiful. The pilot informed the passengers they could expect a high of seventy, clear skies, and a soft breeze. Surprised at the mildness of the weather, they checked their overcoats in an airport locker before hailing a cab.

The brothers, Andres and Rubio, were of Mexican decent, but when both of their parents got caught in the crossfire of a gangland shootout on their way to the grocery store and were killed, the boys had been placed in the care of an Italian family after spending time in foster care. Their black Armani suits, dark skin, thick black hair, and heavy New York accents gave the boys a distinct Mafia look—just the look they wanted for their upcoming lunch meeting with Chester Naples.

Molly had used a contact at the local DA's office to set the meeting up. She explained that Chester Naples had information pertinent to an investigation she was conducting and she only wanted to fish for information. After admitting it would be best if Chester assumed he was talking to some heavy hitters from the East Coast, the local assistant DA suggested the meeting be held at a small, out-of-the-way Italian restaurant for effect.

After the boys had been settled at a table, they looked over the menu to pass the time. After that, they looked over the large mural of a city, assumedly in Italy. Just as they began to fear Chester wouldn't show, he entered and walked hesitantly over to their table, late as usual. Andres and Rubio remained seated.

"Sit down, why don-cha?" Rubio said in his thickest East Coast accent. "We've been waiting for ya since noon."

"So, what of it?" Chester said.

Andres, the enforcer, said, "Chester, please do as my brother requested. There's no need to be rude."

After taking a seat, Chester said, "Do you guys know who you are messing with?"

Rubio took a drink of his wine. "Let me apologize for my brother's behavior." Rubio turned to Andres. "You're not in New York. Show this man some respect."

Chester said abruptly, "I'm a busy man. What do you want?"

"Where I come from we make polite for awhile first," Rubio said. "Let's have some appetizers and get to know each other."

As they waited for the appetizers to arrive, the conversation was forced and uneasy. Rubio talked about how much different San Antonio was from New York City, and Chester sat, bored, looking at his watch every few minutes.

When the appetizers finally arrived, Rubio grabbed a platter of lightly breaded shrimp swimming in butter and slid a few onto Chester's plate. "Try this. I hear they're excellent."

Chester reluctantly took a small bite.

"Am I right? How 'bout some nice manicotti?" asked Rubio.

Before Chester could reply, he placed a large serving of manicotti on his plate.

Chester pushed back from the table. "I don't need someone telling me what to eat!"

"We've come here to spend time with you, and we'll be very

disappointed if you refuse our hospitality." Rubio turned to Andres. "Right, brother?"

Andres nodded.

"Let's enjoy our meal first, and then I promise to explain why we are here," said Rubio. "I'm confident you will find the visit well worth your while." He waved for the waitress to come back over. "Please bring two bottles of your finest Chianti. No—make it three. That way we can each enjoy our own bottle."

Chester looked startled. "You expect me to drink a whole bottle of wine at lunch?"

"Wine is good for your digestive system and calms your nerves," said Rubio.

Chester reluctantly stayed, and after awhile the half bottle of Chianti he drank calmed him down. While they drank and ate, Rubio attempted a little levity by telling some Italian jokes. Chester, finding himself more comfortable with the brothers and not wanting to be upstaged, broke out his Aggie jokes.

When the men finished their lunch and the waitress had cleared the table, Rubio laid his hands on the table and cleared his throat. "Listen, Chester. Trust me, there's nothing sinister about why we're here. We represent a client who wants to hire a personal trainer named Misty, who we understand you have recently worked with. He sent us to do a little background check before he submits his application. We were wondering if you could give us an idea of what she's like."

Chester slugged down some of his wine directly from the bottle. After wiping his mouth with his shirtsleeve, he erupted. "Tell your client that Misty is a queen bitch and he's a fucking fool if he hires her prissy ass!"

Rubio pulled out a notebook and began to write, mouthing the words as he scribbled. "Okay, so this Misty dame is an A-one bitch."

Rubio looked up at Chester with the pen still in his hand. "And what might I add that makes her a bitch?"

Chester took another slug of wine. "She didn't give me what I paid for, that's what!"

"And what did you pay for, Chester?"

Chester thought about his nondisclosure agreement and clammed up. "That's none of your business."

"Listen, if you would kindly give us a copy of your contract with Misty, we could go on our way and leave you alone," Rubio said with a large smile on his face.

"Your client should know the contract has a confidentiality agreement attached that carries heavy fees if breached," said Chester. "I can't believe you even asked me to show it to you."

Rubio took a drink of wine and looked at Andres.

Andres took it as a cue to jump in. "Look at me. Is this the face of someone who can't keep a secret?"

Chester didn't think so, and he told Andres so. While the two of them argued, Rubio discreetly checked his text messages. There was one from Cindy: "Molly's getting impatient! How are things progressing?"

Looking up from his phone, Rubio interrupted Andres and Chester's conversation. "Okay guys, we're not getting anywhere with this line of discussion. Chester, I see your point. I'm going to visit the men's room, and we can have a civil discussion when I return." Rubio turned to his brother. "Don't make a scene while I'm gone."

From the privacy of the restroom, Rubio called Cindy.

"Rubio, is your lunch over?" Cindy asked as soon as she answered. "Our client is not in a good mood. She found out the latest polls have Henry increasing his lead. We desperately need a copy of that contract!"

"Sorry, but the skinny-assed freak of nature is putting up resistance," said Rubio. "This Naples guy signed a nondisclosure agreement, and he's not in the sharing mood. Have you got a plan B?"

There was silence on Cindy's end of the line.

"Cindy! Did you hear what I said? We need something on Chester if you want him to talk."

"I know, damn it! Molly has her best investigators all over this case, but they haven't come up with anything yet. Go back and stall for time. I'll let Molly know what's going on."

When Rubio returned, Andres and Chester were still engaged in their little spat. It was plain to see the two despised each other. Rubio poured some of his wine in Chester's glass before sitting down.

"Our friend Chester said he can't let us see the contract, so let it drop," Rubio said to Andres once he was seated. He then turned to Chester. "So tell me about your wonderful city. We've never been to San Antonio."

Always more than willing to explain why Texas is better than the rest of the country, Chester took the bait. Rubio couldn't have been more pleased. Chester went on and on about how great things were in the Lone Star State, and about how much other parts of the country paled in comparison.

When Rubio's phone rang, he jumped up from the table. "Excuse me while I take this call," he said to Chester. "I'll be right back."

Rubio prayed Andres didn't do anything foolish while he was away. He flipped his phone open on the way to the restroom. "Cindy, talk to me. What have you got?"

He listened to Cindy's excited voice. A smile came over his face. "You did hit the jackpot, Cindy," he said. "Thanks. This will be very helpful in our little discussion with Chester."

When Cindy hung up, Rubio put away the phone, turned on the sink, and splashed water on his face. He looked into the mirror and practiced his tough guy look. After a good slap to the face, he stormed out of the restroom and headed back to the table. Andres took one look at his brother and knew it was time to sit back and enjoy the show.

"We've had a nice lunch, some good wine, and an enjoyable conversation," Rubio said to Chester in his best Mafioso accent. "I'm sure you need to be getting back to work, so give us what we came for and we'll call it a day."

Chester became belligerent. In his drunken stupor, he shouted at the brothers for setting up a useless meeting and prying into his personal life, finishing up with, "Fuck you guys!" He staggered up from the table to leave.

Rubio grabbed his arm and yanked him back down forcefully. Andres moved to the vacant chair next to Chester, pinning him in.

Rubio gave Chester a menacing glare. "We're through playing around, Chester."

Chester's beady eyes flashed back and forth between the brothers. With as much conviction as he could garner, he said, "You guys can't rough me up in a public place. There are too many witnesses. This is

Texas." Chester looked around the room at the handful of men in the place and bluffed. "Some of the men in here are probably packing heat. That's the way we do things here."

"No one said anything about working you over," said Rubio. "How barbaric! Of course, we take no responsibility for what your new cell-mates will do to you."

"Cellmates! What are you talking about? I haven't done anything wrong!"

"Really," said Rubio. "So you don't think hiring dozens of hook-ers from Las Vegas, flying them to your ranch, and instructing them to screw every Japanese businessman in the place doesn't qualify as a crime, punishable by serving time?"

Chester's face went pale.

"You don't look so hot," Rubio continued. "Why don't you go freshen up? You can count on us being here when you return." Chester nodded and stumbled off toward the men's room.

"Is that stuff true?" asked Andres.

"The information came directly from our client."

"Outstanding!"

As he threw up in a bathroom stall, Chester noticed the toilet was manufactured by his biggest competitor and began hitting the wall next to him and cursing. After his little temper tantrum subsided, he cleaned himself up and went back to the table.

As he sat down, Chester addressed Rubio in a much more civil tone. "How did you know about the hookers?"

"Our client has very reliable sources. I'm not sure you understand who you're dealing with. Understand this; my client has confirmed everything I just said with Madam Isabel in Las Vegas. She's been offered immunity if she testifies against you."

Chester's shoulders slumped, and Rubio continued his assault. "You may be in some deep shit, my friend. It's your misfortune to be caught up in something much bigger than your little indiscretion with Misty. If you don't give us what we need, our client will have someone from the U.S. Attorney General's office pay you a visit. I can assure you it won't be a pleasant one."

Chester took some time to think things over while Rubio ordered a fourth bottle of wine. When the waitress hinted that maybe they had had enough, Andre took her aside and bribed her with a hundred-dollar bill.

The table was silent until the waitress brought it. Rubio filled their glasses.

"What if there are some things in my contract with Misty that could be construed as illegal?" asked Chester.

Rubio handed Chester his glass of wine. "That's all the more reason for you to work with us. Our client has a lot of sway with the U.S. Attorney General's office. Look, they don't want to prosecute you, Chester. No offense, but you're small potatoes. They're after a much bigger fish."

Chester felt trapped, but he wasn't ready to give up just yet. "What if I decide to fight this? I can afford the best attorneys in the country."

Rubio laughed. "That's your call, but you need to remember that your contract with Misty will come into question. If you are certain there isn't anything incriminating in the contract and think you can work your way out of the prostitution charges, go ahead and fight it."

"Maybe I will," Chester bluffed.

Rubio put his hand under Chester's chin and pushed his head from side to side. "I'm just trying to figure out which side you should offer up for your mug shot." Rubio then leaned back and looked at Chester with something close to sympathy. "Now, if you cooperate with the investigation, our client will do everything in their power to get you immunity, just like they did for your Las Vegas acquaintance. If you do cooperate, it's highly likely those pesky prostitution charges will never be filed."

Chester reached for his phone and called his office. As soon as Stephanie picked up, he said, "Stephanie, make a copy of my contract with Misty and bring it to me."

Andres and Rubio, arms crossed, traded satisfied smiles.

"But isn't that supposed to be confidential?" she said.

"It is, Stephanie! That's why you absolutely cannot read it on the way over here. Now bring it to me as fast as you can."

Stephanie already knew what was in the contract, having made Brenda a copy. She worried that this might in some way harm Misty, but she had no choice but to do as she was told.

50

Doing the Deed

Misty arrived at the underground facility fifteen minutes early to find a shirtless Henry lying on the floor, doing stomach crunches. He had already worked up a nice sheen on his upper torso, making him look hot and sexy. Instantly aroused, Misty threw caution to the wind, leaning over him until their heads almost bumped. Henry stopped just long enough to give her a broad smile and a wink before resuming his crunches. She surveyed every inch of his bare chest as he grimaced his way through a few more. After mouthing "one hundred," he collapsed back onto the rubbery mat. Misty swung one leg over him and braced herself on his chest like a cougar pouncing on its prey.

Leaning in until their faces were only inches apart, she said, "Way to go, Henry! You are doing awesome!"

Henry was breathing heavily from the crunches, and Misty felt his hot breath on her face. Once his breathing returned to normal, she offered her hand and helped him onto his feet.

Misty felt confident and sexy, and it did not go unnoticed by Henry. In a strange way, he enjoyed her telling him what to do and looked forward to obediently following her instructions. Relinquishing control to

Misty gave him the opportunity to put his brain on autopilot. Since it only took ten percent of his mental capacity to follow her instructions, he could reserve the other ninety percent for more important things, like imagining what she looked like naked and what a good lover she might be. Misty often saw a look in Henry's eyes she had seen all too many times with previous clients. No matter how hard her clients tried, there was always a tipping point where they became the captive and she the captor. Was tonight the night that Henry would willingly become Misty's captive prey and leave his fate in her hands?" Fresh off her weekend debacle, she felt a need to reestablish her dominance over men, and training Henry gave her the perfect opportunity.

Henry began putting his shirt back on.

"Don't," she said, grabbing it from his hands. "Leave it off!"

Her demand made him feel strong and virile. He had entered the gym middle-aged, but was now being transformed into middle-aged and crazy. He sat on the bench of the lat pulldown machine, reached up and grabbed the bar above, and began doing pulldowns. From behind him, Misty placed her hands on his taught back muscles and held them there throughout his eight reps. His muscles felt like thick rope underneath his skin.

"Nice work," she said when he finished. "I can really feel the muscle development, but your form could use a little work. Get off and let me show you what I mean."

Misty took his place on the bench to show him the proper posture. Each time the bar came down, she stuck her breasts out to give her back perfect form. She was careful not to look at Henry, giving him plenty of opportunity to look her over without being busted. When her curiosity got the best of her, she snuck a quick peek and reveled in the fact he was taking full advantage of the view.

When she finished, she bounced off the bench and said, "Okay, give it another try."

This time, Henry straightened his back and stuck out his chest. Misty straddled the bench behind him and rested her hands flat against his back. She could feel energy emanating from his brawny upper torso and realized just how powerful he had become. She was becoming captivated herself, and she thought about the consequences of playing this risky game to the end. Was she ready to collect her money and go home? She knew the answer. Her job wasn't finished, and it would be unfair to Henry if she abandoned him now. She thought about how much joy she got out of helping him rise in the polls, but then thought about how much joy she would get tonight from getting a rise out of *his* pole. But their little game of chicken was so stimulating, and she was not ready to be the one to back away.

The stakes grew with each passing moment. Henry moved from machine to machine, working harder than ever in an effort to impress Misty. His muscles were pumped to max capacity. Misty began working out just as hard, giving them a feeling of shared accomplishment. Conversation had ceased, and cognitive faculties were overtaken by sensory perceptions. Visual images of sweaty bodies, the aroma of his pheromones mingling with hers, and the sound of heavy breathing conjured up a concoction of primitive animal passion.

Henry became bolder by the minute, laying his hands on Misty every opportunity he got. They finished up the workout by mounting the stationary bikes for a quick ride. Before Misty climbed on, she cranked up the stereo system, adding auditory to the mix of sensual pleasures. A hard-driving techno tune filled the room. After only a few minutes on the bike, Misty's hot and sticky mound ached with passion from the constant rubbing against the bike seat. To conceal her arousal, she lowered her head, allowing her long blonde hair to drape around her face. She fought the urge to grind vigorously into the leather saddle underneath but soon lost the battle. Close to orgasm, she reached for the Gatorade in the bike's drink holder and gulped down half the bottle. It quenched her thirst but not her desire.

Misty dragged her hand down over her throat to wipe away the sweat. "It's so blasted hot in here!" she said.

Sitting up straight in the saddle, she reached underneath her tank top and freed her sports bra. Henry fixed his gaze on Misty in the mirror. He watched her futile attempt to tuck the bottom portion of her tank top underneath the fold of her breasts for support. Giving up, she let her tight, sweat-soaked top cling to her voluptuous breasts. Henry could see her two firm, brown nipples standing at attention. Looking out from beneath her hair, she saw Henry staring at her chest with crazed eyes.

Hoping to tease Henry to the brink of torture, Misty rose from the saddle and rocked from side to side, as if peddling up a hill. Gravity tugged on her breasts, making them look a full size larger. After a minute of watching them sway back and forth to the rhythmic beat of the music, Henry dropped his gaze to the floor and closed his eyes in an attempt to control the swelling of semen in his testicles. He began pumping vigorously in hopes that extreme exhaustion would take his mind off his enormous problem. The plan was working until he looked up to see Misty standing directly in front of him. Her breasts were only a foot away from his eyes, looking like two large ripe melons. Her head was cocked to one side as she looked inquisitively into his eyes, wondering how much more he could endure.

"Slow down, Henry, or you'll use up all of your energy," she said.

As Henry slowed his spin to cool down, Misty backed against the mirror with a knee bent and the flat sole of her shoe on the mirror for balance. Her pose was as provocative as that of a *Playboy* centerfold. Her body tingled with excitement as she watched his eyes move slowly down from her breasts to her sweat-stained crotch. When he stopped spinning, she replaced her hands on his face and gave him a moist, passionate kiss. Henry pulled away and slowly dismounted his bike.

He squared up in front of Misty and placed his hands on her shoulders. "Why are you doing this to me? You know I can't afford to end our workouts now. We still have much to accomplish."

Misty smiled. "I know, Henry. The last thing I want to do is abandon you before you reach your goal. I just think you need a reward for all the hard work you've put in." She looked down at the foot she was grinding into the floor. "I've decided that tonight won't count, as long as you promise never to tell." Looking back up into his eyes, she said, "Let's just say I'm doing my patriotic duty. Consider it a donation to your campaign."

Misty inched closer and playfully ran her fingers through his chest hair. With the look of someone who just won the lottery, Henry lifted Misty's soaking wet tank top over her head. He brought the shirt to his nose and took a deep breath before discarding it to the floor. Fixated on her beautiful mounds, he reached out with his right hand and lightly fondled her left breast as if testing the ripeness of an avocado. Wrapping his left arm around Misty's lower back, he pulled her to him and then placed a hand under her right breast to help guide it into his mouth. They were way beyond the gentle stage. With his whole mouth over as much of her breast as he could take in, he began to suckle, as if nursing. She closed her eyes and let her head roll loosely from side to side.

When the moment was right, she leaned in and whispered in his ear. "Now, Henry. Take me now."

Henry stood erect, his unit throbbing, as he surveyed the workout facility for a logical place to do the deed. Misty wondered how creative he would be, and she didn't have to wait long to find out. Henry twisted the bolt that loosened the seat of his spinning bike, ripped the seat off entirely, and slung it halfway across the room. After being led by the wrist, she found herself straddling the bike frame, facing the mirror.

Placing her hands firmly on the handlebars, he leaned in from behind and whispered, "Hold on very tight."

Misty clung to the bike and Henry pulled her bottoms off and then removed his. Seeing in the mirror that he was completely naked, she turned around to examine what would surely be inside her soon. His length and girth brought a smile to her face. Misty turned back around in time to feel his hands latch onto the front of her thighs from behind. With a quick, powerful move, he hoisted her up until her back was parallel with the floor. She steadied herself on the handlebars in anticipation of what was to come.

His target was wet and moist, so he swiftly slid in to full capacity. He worked slow and easy at first but then began hammering himself home again and again. She hung on tight as the slapping of his pelvis against her firm buttocks rang through the room, closing her eyes to concentrate on the warm, hot, throbbing member inside her. The sensation was fabulous but the heat was becoming unbearable. Raising her head to better fill her lungs, Misty witnessed her breasts swinging violently with each powerful thrust, coating the mirror with droplets of sweat. Her reflection stared back at her, mouth open wide. When a thunderous orgasm rocked her body, her groans of pleasure could be heard above the music. Watching herself come was one of the most exciting moments of sex she had ever experienced.

When Misty lowered her head to coax the blood back to her brain, she realized Henry was still hammering away. No longer in a heightened sense of passion, she began to contemplate what had motivated her to act the way she had. Was it all about revenge, an attempt to punish Travis? Or was it to prove she still had power over men? Henry's heavy moans broke her concentration as he deposited his massive load deep inside her. He rested a moment before gently pulling out and returning her legs to the floor.

Wanting to leave Henry on a positive note, Misty turned around and held him tight. All she could think about was going back to the hotel, drinking a gallon of water, and falling comatose on the bed.

Misty and Henry dressed in silence. Once she was ready to leave, Misty gave him a kiss and patted his chest before climbing the stairs.

Little did she know this would be her last workout with him.

51

CAUGHT IN THE MIDDLE

Physically and emotionally drained from her workout with Henry, Misty awoke the next morning to a loud beeping sound. Too groggy to roll over, she stuck her arm out and rummaged through the items on the table next to her bed, knocking half of them to the floor before locating her cell phone. It was a text message from Travis. Squinting through one eye, she read, "I woke up at three AM and couldn't go back to sleep. I've never been more ashamed of anything than I am for the way I treated you. I feel like an idiot."

Misty rolled on her side. Travis was not her lover, and he had every right to get back together with Emily. But Emily was such a bitch. How could he stand being with that woman? She rationalized that had Travis come clean from the start, it would have helped prepare her for the horrible events of that night. Travis had treated her with respect before the incident and was treating her with respect after the incident. She was the one who chased him in Texas, not the other way around.

Misty placed a pillow over her face as she tried to sort through her night with Henry. If she was seducing Henry to punish Travis, it made little sense; there was no way she could tactfully let Travis know about the encounter, nor would she even if she could. She admitted that proving she still had what it takes when it came to controlling men gave her a rush and boosted her confidence. She felt no remorse for her actions. She really did consider it a freebie, and she would be back dutifully on the job next week.

Finally, she decided to stop overanalyzing everything and just accept the evening for what it was, one of the more erotic sexual escapades she had ever experienced, which was probably brought on by her tumultuous weekend.

There's nothing like getting a good screwing to alleviate stress, she thought.

Either way, no longer being upset with Travis didn't mean he was totally off the hook. She typed a text message back to him: "You might want to conceal the fact that you're an idiot at work, cowboy."

Twenty minutes went by without a reply from Travis. As she contemplated sending an apology text, her phone rang.

She answered without looking at caller ID. "Travis?"

"Not the last time I checked," a female voice replied.

"Brenda? I'm so sorry. I thought you were Travis."

"I thought you and Travis went your separate ways . . ."

"We did, but that doesn't mean we aren't still good friends. Enough about me. How the hell are you?"

"Never been better! I'm well on my way to getting divorced from Chester. My attorney wanted to go for half his assets, but for the sake of avoiding a lengthy court battle, I told him I would settle for less, provided he doesn't drag this out."

"So if you don't mind me asking, how much do you think you might get?"

"I'd say somewhere between eighteen to twenty million dollars."

Misty gasped. "Oh my gosh—that's a lot of money! Well, good for you. Does this mean you're going to marry Jeff Bridges?"

"Jeff Bridges? Oh, you mean Buddy." She laughed. "I guess he does resemble him a bit."

Misty heard a voice in the background.

"Jeff Bridges! I'm better looking than Jeff Bridges!"

"Is that Buddy?" Misty asked.

"Yep, that's the arrogant son of a bitch. But he's *my* arrogant SOB."

"He's a good guy, Brenda. You better hang onto him." She paused before changing the subject. "So what's up? How did you find me?"

"Oh, I called the number you left me and talked to your friend Gabriella. She gave me your number." Brenda cleared her throat. "Misty, there's something you need to know."

"Okay . . ."

"Look, this may be nothing, but Stephanie told me Chester gave a copy of your contract to two men from out of town."

Misty was instantly alarmed. *Why would he break the confidentiality agreement and risk being sued?* she thought. *Is he so upset with me he isn't thinking straight? And who are those men?*

"Does Stephanie know who the men are?" she asked.

"Steph said someone from the local DA's office arranged the meeting between Chester and the men. Apparently they flew in from the East Coast."

Misty fell back onto her pillow. Whatever it was, it couldn't be good.

"Misty, are you still there?" Brenda asked.

"Sorry, I'm just trying to make sense out of all this. Thanks for bringing this to my attention."

"That's what friends are for. I'm sure this won't amount to anything, but I just wanted you to know."

"I'm glad you did."

"Well, Buddy's pestering me so I've got to run."

"Okay. Thanks again, Brenda. I owe you the next call."

Before Misty could start worrying, she noticed there was a text message on her phone: "I'm sorry I didn't get back to you quicker but I've been tied up in a meeting my firm scheduled for idiots. I can't understand why it was exclusively men. Today's topic was how to referee a catfight between a onetime fiancée and onetime girlfriend."

Onetime fiancée? thought Misty. *Is he dumping Emily?*

She quickly typed a message back to him: "Catfight! If that had been a catfight, your precious Emily would've had her eyes scratched out and fed to the birds in Central Park. I took it easy on her, bud."

"You would have been justified if you had, but I'm proud of you for keeping your cool. You proved to be the better woman," he wrote back.

Misty smiled as she read his text and then typed back: "So what did you mean when you said onetime fiancée?"

Misty drummed her fingers on her thigh, waiting for his reply. Finally it came: "Watching the way Emily treated you, I'm contemplating breaking up with her."

"Oh, really," she replied.

"Well, maybe. Why don't you come back to New York? I could use your help thinking this through."

"Let me see what I can do," she texted back. "I'm in the middle of something right now but will get back with you later. Keep your chin up, boyfriend."

After getting breakfast with Miguel, Misty came back to her room and pulled up a copy of her contract on her laptop. She felt better after reading over the special provision clause and reassuring herself that the language was as vague as originally intended. To play it safe, she called Henry's office and left a message requesting a meeting. An hour later, Henry's assistant called back to tell her Henry could meet her in the Hamilton lobby at five.

* * *

Molly stayed home Tuesday morning to read over Chester's contract with Misty. The terms of their agreement seemed innocuous enough, until she stumbled upon the special provision clause.

> *2.1* Special Provision. *If a mutually agreed upon event occurs prior to the termination date and said event was initiated by the client, services will be deemed rendered in full. All unpaid compensation will be immediately wired to Misty's bank account and she will be free to leave.*

Molly read the provision over and over. The phrases *agreed upon event* and *initiated by the client* kept rolling through her head.

This has to refer to sleeping with Misty, she thought. *The nickname makes sense now. It's symbolic. She sleeps with her client once and leaves them for dead.*

Before Molly moved on to legal issues associated with a married congressman sleeping with a contracted employee, she sat back to contemplate

Misty's profession. Had it not been for Misty standing in her way of defeating Henry in the upcoming elections, she would have chuckled at the trainer's ingenuity. Misty's mastery over powerful men was to be admired.

* * *

Early that afternoon Molly met with her three paralegals. Molly considered the two women trustworthy; they had proved themselves time and again. She wasn't as sure about the male paralegal, as he was relatively new, but she was confident his mild-mannered nature left little risk for her. "I need you all to drop what you're doing for the next day or two and concentrate on some highly confidential research. You are to work independently from one another and show your findings to no one other than me. When I get what I need, you will all go back to your old projects and forget any of this ever happened. I wish I could share more with you, but that's just the nature of this case."

The paralegals nodded their heads in agreement. The women had worked for Molly long enough to know not to ask questions. When their colleague raised his hand, one of the women pulled it back down and gave him a look indicating it was not a good career move.

"You can start by researching the Mann Act," said Molly. "After that, search for any laws that pertain to using campaign funds or public funds for personal use. This is in regard to any public official. Have you got that?"

The three nodded their heads and left the room.

* * *

Misty found Henry sitting in the lobby as promised. As she approached, he motioned for her to follow him into the bar. Once a waiter had shown them to a secluded booth, Henry reached out and took her hands.

"I assume this is about last night," he said.

"I wish it were, but I'm afraid it's about something else."

"Oh, I just assumed . . ."

Misty squirmed in her seat. "It's probably nothing, but I just felt you needed to know."

"Oh," said Henry, somewhat relieved.

"I received a phone call from a former client's soon-to-be ex-wife.

She informed me her husband just handed a copy of my contract over to two unidentified men."

Misty had Henry's full attention. "What do you know about these men?"

"Only that they were from the East Coast. Maybe even D.C." Misty could tell that had alarmed him. "Do you think there's a problem?" she asked.

Henry drifted into deep thought. As she waited for him to reply, the waiter came to the table and she ordered their usual martinis.

Once the waiter had walked away, Henry said, "Misty, I'm sorry but I need to get back to the office."

She reached out and latched onto his hand as he was getting up. "Is there something I should be worried about?"

He leaned down and kissed her on the cheek. "No, if there's anything to it, I will handle things."

Misty sat in the booth alone for a while, the two martinis sitting in front of her untouched, as she tried to decide whether to stop worrying as Henry had suggested. Not able to decide, she headed off to the room for a nap, hoping to escape her uneasy thoughts.

* * *

Henry had his assistant summon Rick as soon as he got back to his office. When Rick arrived, he walked into the congressman's office without knocking and found Henry staring out the window, looking troubled. Rick took a seat without saying anything.

A few moments passed before Henry acknowledged his presence. "Thanks for coming in so fast."

"Sure. What's up?"

Henry sat down and fumbled around his desk as if looking for something. "I just returned from a meeting with Misty. She informed me that one of her former clients had some visitors, and that they may have been from D.C. Apparently her client turned over a copy of Misty's contract to them. Needless to say, we both know what's in that contract."

Rick exploded from his chair. "Is this client of hers nuts?"

"Hell if I know," said Henry, "but we need to consider that he may have been strong-armed. If so, I've got a pretty good suspicion of who they may be working for."

"You're not thinking it's Molly, are you?"

"So that's the first name that popped into your head as well."

"Maybe it's someone else. It could've been any number of people."

Henry looked down his nose at Rick. "Can you think of anyone else who wants to embarrass me before an upcoming election?"

"The opposition party?"

"What the hell's the difference, Rick!" shouted Henry.

Rick slumped back down into his chair. "Nothing I guess."

Henry walked from behind his desk and sat down next to him. Leaning in to look him in the eyes at close range, he said, "Rick, I want you to think real hard about this. You are arranging for Misty to get paid. How much exposure do we have?"

"I wouldn't lose too much sleep over it," Rick said nervously. "We both know the special provisions clause is ambiguous as hell."

"What if they get to Misty? What if they get her to cooperate and tell them what it means?"

Rick paused to think. He scratched his head. "Misty won't talk. She would be jeopardizing her career. No one in their right mind would hire her if she testified against one of her clients. Besides, she would risk going to jail herself—well, unless she copped a plea bargain."

"And then I would go to jail!"

Rick was relieved Henry had said *I* instead of *we*. He loosened his collar and said, "Henry, maybe you should have a talk with Misty, explain to her how much she stands to lose. What do you think?"

Henry shook his head. "Not yet. I need time to think this out, step by step. We can't afford to make a wrong move."

Anxious to leave so he could figure some things out as well, Rick said, "That's a good idea. How about I leave you to think it through?"

"Fine," said Henry. When Rick was almost to the door, the congressman spoke again. "Maybe you should tell me first. Where did you get the funds to pay Misty?"

Rick came to a complete stop.

"You've never questioned where I got the money before. Are you sure it's a good idea to start now?"

"I never asked before because having to explain it to the FBI was never a high probability."

Rick walked back to Henry. "Remember, you didn't want to use personal funds, so I had no choice but to dip into your campaign funds."

"I see," said Henry. He then placed his hand on Rick's shoulder. "It doesn't matter a rat's ass whose fault it is. We're both culpable."

This time the *we* came through loud and clear.

"We're talking a federal crime here, Rick."

Rick simply nodded solemnly before walking out and quietly closing the door behind him.

Once he was gone, Henry canceled his afternoon appointments and called Misty.

"Misty, I'm glad I caught you," he said when she answered.

"Hey Henry. What's up?"

"I wanted to tell you I just found out my wife is coming to D.C. for the next ten days. I'm embarrassed to say this, but if she found out I had a beautiful, younger woman training me, it wouldn't play too well. So I'd like to put our workouts on hold, just until she leaves town."

"Are you sure? We're making such good progress. What about your election?"

"I know, I know, but I'll keep up the workouts on my own. I promise. I might not push myself as hard, but then again, I won't be distracted either."

Misty laughed. "Okay, but what am I going to do?"

"Didn't you tell me you had a friend in New York? Maybe you could go visit him while my wife is in town."

"Hmm, that's a good idea," said Misty.

"Great. Oh, there is one more thing. Do you mind if I cancel your room at the Hamilton while you're away? No sense spending money on an empty room."

"No problem. You can place a reservation for me ten days from now."

"Thanks, Misty. You're a sweetheart. I'll talk to you later."

When she got off, she couldn't wait to compose a text message to Travis: "Still need help deciding whether to dump Emily or not? Well, here I come, ready or not. If you don't feel comfortable having me stay at your place I can always get a room at the Stratford House :)"

"Depends on whether you plan on sleeping on the sofa again or not," he responded.

"You'll just have to wait to find out," she texted back.

A wave of happiness surged through her when she got his reply: "I was kidding. You can stay at my place and sleep wherever you like. I'm just happy you are coming back. I'll play nice this time, I promise."

52

THE SECOND TIME AROUND

Misty booked a room at the Stratford House in her name so Miguel would have a place to stay while she was at Travis's apartment. It would also give her a place to go if things broke down with Travis again.

Sitting on Miguel's bed as he put his things away, Misty said, "So what do you plan on doing over the next ten days?"

"Oh, my good friend Hector lives in the city. We grew up together, and he and I were the only ones lucky enough to get out of the hood. I called him late last night and he's charged about hanging out."

"That's wonderful, but will you come shopping with me first? Travis won't get off work until seven so I have some time to kill."

"You bet. I've got ten days with Hector."

Misty took Miguel to a local department store in search of some sleepwear that would catch Travis's attention. Being a rough-and-tumble girl who wasn't at all into frills, it was challenging. Misty was about to give up when she ran across a Ralph Lauren classic men's shirt that had been converted into a nightshirt for women. Misty put it on and paraded in front of the mirror. The nightshirt, which was rose-colored with white polka dots, had a buttoned front, a breast pocket, and a hem that rested high up on her thighs. She thought it suited her quite well, but she wanted a second opinion.

Miguel was slumped in a chair outside the dressing rooms half asleep when Misty broke his slumber. "Hey Miguel, whatcha think?"

Miguel rubbed his eyes. "Nice shirt," he said in somewhat of a daze, "but where the hell are the pants?"

"It's a nightshirt, Einstein. Who needs pants to sleep?"

"Well, in that case you might need me to protect you from Travis, 'cause you're looking pretty hot, mama."

"Thanks, Miguel, but I can handle Travis just fine."

After they returned to the Stratford to pick up Misty's suitcase, Miguel walked her out and hailed a cab. "Be careful," he said as it pulled to the curb. "Remember, I'm a phone call away."

She gave him a tight hug. "I know. Go have a great time with your friend. You deserve some time off."

* * *

Misty was camped out in the lobby of Travis's apartment complex when he arrived. Not quite ready to let him completely off the hook for last week, she made no effort to greet him.

As he walked up, he leaned over and said, "Excuse me, lady. Is the seat next to you available?"

"This seat is saved for someone handsome, gentle, and courteous," she replied. "Do you know anyone like that?"

Travis plopped down as close as he could without making contact. "Nope, but I know a big handsome fool. Will that do?" Before she could answer, he jumped up and grabbed her suitcase.

"My word," he said. "What are you packing, girl? I could fit half my wardrobe in this thing. You plan on moving in?"

Misty sprang to her feet. "For ten days, if you're nice to me."

"Just how nice would you like me to be?"

"We'll see," Misty said as she walked away.

As she stood in the hallway waiting for Travis to unlock his door, Misty began to feel uncomfortable.

Noticing her change in mood, Travis gave her a smile. "Don't worry. Emily's at her folks' through the weekend."

Misty placed her balled up fist to his nose. "How fortunate for Emily," she said before walking briskly past him. Travis was glad she was back to her old spunky self and that they had gotten off to a good start. He carried her suitcase into his bedroom and set it on a small luggage stand in the far corner. When he came back into the living room, she was glaring at him, arms crossed.

He laughed. "Hey, we can't have your undergarments strewn all over the living room, now can we? Your clothes are safe with me. I'm not a cross-dresser."

"That's too bad. I think you would look kinda cute in women's lingerie."

Travis changed the subject. "Are you hungry?"

"I'm starving!"

"Great. I've got the perfect restaurant."

When they got to the midtown restaurant Travis had picked out, Misty looked over the interior as Travis negotiated for one of the few tables left. The large, two-story establishment was open and airy. The blond wood and leather furnishings stood out against minimalist white walls punctuated by tomato-red panels. She turned her attention to the sleek and seductive bar upstairs, wondering if they made a nice martini.

On the way to their table, Misty placed her hand on Travis's back. "You're off to a good start, cowboy."

Once they had ordered dinner and a couple of drinks, Misty noticed Travis was staring at her.

She blushed—a rare occurrence for her. "What are *you* looking at?"

"You," he said.

She locked onto his eyes. "What do you see?"

"I see someone simple, yet complex. Someone who wears her emotions on her sleeve as a decoy so the sensitive woman underneath can hide in peace. I see someone—"

Misty reached over the table and placed her hand over his mouth. Travis pulled it away and finished. "—that I consider a dear friend."

Misty was saved from the uncomfortable intimacy by the waitress's returning with their appetizers. "You're piling up points pretty fast, buster," she said. "Guess I left you with a lot to think about the last few days."

They ate a wonderful dinner and then moved upstairs to the bar.

"When did you become a martini drinker?" Travis asked after Misty ordered. "I thought you were a rum and Coke girl."

Misty seemed surprised at her own new habit. "I guess I picked that up in D.C. Didn't you know that everybody drinks martinis there?"

"No wonder our country's in so much trouble," he replied.

Worried the conversation would find its way to Henry, she changed the subject.

"So are you ready to discuss Emily?"

Travis picked up his glass of bourbon. "Maybe after a couple of these."

Travis pointed to the tables downstairs with his drink in hand. "Would you ever think about moving to New York? You could be dining in wonderful restaurants every night."

"Why would I want to move here when I have a pad to crash here anytime I want to come?" She smiled at him while adding, "And a tour guide."

"Yeah, I guess I knew the answer to that question before I asked."

Misty patted his hand. "Come on now. Let's talk about you and Emily."

After downing the rest of his bourbon with one gulp, Travis said, "I was honestly shocked at the way Emily reacted the other night. For all she knew, you could have been a cousin."

"Well, maybe she thought I was your kissing cousin?"

"Come on. You know what I mean."

"Travis, forget about the other night. What's important is whether or not you love Emily. Do you?"

Travis seemed surprised by her question.

When he failed to reply, she continued to prod. "Name something that you love about her. Start with something small if you like."

Travis thought for a moment before saying, "Hmm, well, she's good at letting me know the proper attire to wear to social events." He shook his head. "And, man, do I have to go to a lot of those."

"Okay, what else?"

"She's a true socialite, and she knows exactly what to say in every situation."

"What else?" Misty's questioning was relentless.

"She's teaching me to appreciate the fine arts."

"Do you like fine arts?"

Travis frowned. "Not really. Unless it's the art of branding a longhorn steer."

"Travis. Think about all the excuses you just gave. Everything was about making you feel comfortable in high society."

He grinned sheepishly. "I guess you're right. Those aren't things I learned growing up with my uncle on the ranch. I'm perfectly fine with business matters, but I guess going to all the Excelsior Investments functions made me uneasy. As long as I was with Emily, everything was all right."

Misty took her time before asking her last question. "Be honest, cowboy. Are you hot for Emily?"

He looked at her with raised eyebrows. "What kind of question is that?"

"A damn good one," she shot back. "Does she make your juices flow? Is she good in bed?"

He rubbed the back of his neck. I've never given it a lot of thought. My mind is usually on business. When we have sex it's . . . uh . . . I guess, 'civil' would be the best way to describe it. Sex doesn't seem to be a high priority to her."

Travis seemed a little dazed. Misty sat back to let him sort through his thoughts. She thought about how Emily got off to being seen with the most attractive man in the room, knowing she was envied by every other woman who saw her.

"Would you like my opinion?" Misty asked in a softened voice.

Travis shrugged.

"You're not in love with Emily," she said. "You feel you need her at the parties, or she has you convinced you do, but you don't. I'll bet you're fully capable of navigating without her. Why don't you leave her home the next time and give it a try? If you fall on your face, you can decide what to do after that."

"You've given me plenty to think about," he said. "Why don't we go home?"

Hearing him say the words *go home* made her feel warm, the way she felt when she went home with Gabriella. It was then that she realized her relationship with Travis was very similar to her relationship with Gabriella. He was Gabriella's male counterpart.

Back at the apartment, Misty searched through her luggage for something to wear to bed while Travis was in the bathroom. She picked up her new nightshirt and looked it over before deciding this was not the night for it. Travis had too much to sort through, and it was all her fault.

After Travis emerged from the bathroom, Misty went in. When she came out, Travis was resting in bed, looking comfortable on the plush pile of pillows. After giving him a quick peck on his forehead, she said, "Good night, lover boy. See you in the morning."

Misty snuggled up in her makeshift bed on the sofa and, before falling to sleep, thought about how wonderful their evening had been.

53

ANOTHER MEETING

Cindy sat smugly as she waited for Molly in a far back corner of the restaurant. In her line of work, you were only as good as your most recent accomplishment, and she had knocked her first assignment out of the park. The brothers' visit with Chester had been a complete success. As she gave her the good news on the phone, Cindy could tell from the sound of Molly's voice that, at least for now, Molly was extremely pleased she had hired her. Securing a copy of Chester and Misty's contract was no small feat, and it could possibly be the key to defeating Henry in the primary.

When Molly arrived at the restaurant, she made a beeline for Cindy. "Your boys really came through for us yesterday, Cindy," she said as she sat down. "I hope they understand why I asked you to come alone, though. As much as I would like to congratulate them in person, I think it's best I'm never seen in public with them again. You understand, don't you?"

"I completely understand. From now on we'll keep them lurking in the shadows."

"From here on out, it's just going to be you, me, and the boys," Molly continued. "That means Melanie won't even know what's going on. I expect things to get dicey, so I need to know that you're up for this."

"I'm with you all the way, and so are the boys."

Molly smiled for the first time since she had arrived. "Great! Let's get started planning the next steps. I read my paralegals' briefs on the flight here and it looks like we have several options. One option is to provide the U.S. Attorney General's office with enough information to charge Henry under the Mann Act. All we have to do is prove he slept with a prostitute."

Just then, the waiter approached the table. Molly ordered a cup of coffee.

"So what you're saying is, if we can prove Misty does let her clients sleep with her, even once, the fact that she gets paid would make her look like a prostitute," said Cindy.

"Bingo! That would put the last nail in Henry's coffin, but it might be even easier than that. In *Caminetti v. United States* the judge ruled that a noncommercial consensual sexual liaison—consensual extramarital sex, in other words—falls within the genre of 'immoral sex' and is enough to bring charges."

Cindy's face lit up. "So the key is to get Misty to admit having sex with Henry, whether we can prove he paid for it or not."

"Yes, but I don't expect it will be easy. The special clause in her contract is extremely vague, so we need to find a way to turn up the heat and force her to talk."

"What do you suggest?" asked Cindy.

"I suggest we give the U.S. Attorney General's office enough information to open an investigation. You and I both know Henry didn't use personal funds to pay for Misty's services so they'll likely move onto investigating Henry's campaign finances. Willfully converting money from a political action committee for personal use is a federal crime."

"But how do we get the information to the Attorney General's office? Not only is this out of your jurisdiction, but any charges you bring against Henry as his opponent would be a conflict of interest."

Molly surveyed the restaurant before motioning for Cindy to lean in closer. "I have a trusted friend who's an investigative reporter for the *Washington Post*," Molly said in a soft whisper. "You will arrange for the boys to turn the contract over to her, and she'll make sure it finds its way to the U.S. Attorney General's office."

Cindy seemed squeamish about the idea, so Molly patted her on the knee. "Don't worry. She's a reporter. They can't force her to reveal her source."

Cindy nodded in reluctant agreement.

"By the way, what's the latest on Misty? Are the boys getting any covert information from their contact at the Hamilton?

"I'm glad you brought that up," said Cindy. "The informant said both Misty and her bodyguard checked out yesterday morning."

Molly exploded. "They *what*! I need to know where Misty is at all times. What if I need to press her for information?"

"I've got things under control, Molly," Cindy said. "Misty left her cell number and a forwarding address, and she has reservations ten days from now to return to the Hamilton."

"Where did she go?"

"She's staying at a hotel in Manhattan. We've checked it out, and there is a hotel room at the Stratford House under her name."

Molly breathed a sigh of relief. "Nice work, Cindy. Get me her room and cell number when you get it."

"Will do. Anything else?"

"No, that's it for now, but keep your cell phone handy at all times. I expect everything to be up in the air for the next several weeks."

54

THE MEETING

While Molly and Cindy were meeting, Henry was conducting his own meeting with Rick on a secluded park bench along the Washington Mall. His head was still pounding from the half-dozen martinis he had downed the night before.

"So how did you come up with the funds to pay Misty?" Henry asked.

"Misty's fees are hidden in the salary we pay Jim. Remember that night we were all having drinks with Misty and Miguel, when Jim joked about how Misty should be on his staff? Well, Misty *is* on Jim's staff, only she doesn't know it."

"And her hotel room and expenses?"

Rick smiled proudly. "I've been accumulating a slush fund without anyone knowing about it. We're paying her bills at the hotel in cash. There's no way it can be traced."

Henry frowned. "Don't say there's *no way*. There's always a way."

"You're right, but the probability is extremely low," Rick said. "Why don't you send Misty back to Argentina? If things get hot around here, she'd be safe from questioning."

"That's not a bad idea," Henry replied, but he had little else to say. He was trying to sort out what he would say to Misty if he met with her in person. He realized a trip to New York would be necessary. There was no way he could wait until she got back to D.C. Confident no one else knew her whereabouts, he decided it would be best to put the trip off until the weekend, when his absence would be less noticeable.

* * *

Walking down the hall toward his office, Henry was startled by someone walking behind him. "Hello, Henry," a voice said cheerily.

Henry turned around. "Molly!"

"Long time no see, Henry. I was hoping you would stop by on your most recent trip to Tuscaloosa. The town is still buzzing about your press conference. You seem to have made quite an impression with the women voters." Molly eyed Henry up and down. "My goodness, you are looking terrific!"

Henry frowned. "That's nice of you to say, Molly, but surely you didn't come all the way to Washington just to tell me that."

Molly grinned. "Aren't you going to invite me to your office for a cup of coffee?"

"Sure," said Henry. "Maybe I can talk you into dropping out of the race."

The timing of Molly's visit seemed suspicious. Her crack about causing a stir with his women voters, coupled with the observation that he had lost weight, only supported his suspicions. He hoped to discern whether she knew anything about Misty over their cup of coffee.

After picking up coffee at the commissary, Henry led Molly to his office.

"This will be all yours if you win," Henry teased as he showed her inside.

"*If* I win?" She glanced at the wall. "Oh, look at this picture. You in your football uniform." She took the picture off the wall and looked it over. "You know, my own mother had a crush on you back then."

"Are you implying that I'm old enough to be your father?"

"Not unless you'd knocked her up at fourteen." Molly smiled. "Now wouldn't that make for some juicy headlines."

Henry rolled his eyes as he offered her a chair. "Speaking of your mother, I'm sure she's proud of you. I never expected to have someone breathing down my neck this close to the primary."

"Well if you keep losing weight, you might not have anything to worry about. New polling data shows you spiked up a few points after your visit, and it mostly came from women voters."

Henry laughed. "Anything to get a vote, you know." He looked Molly over and added, "It's too bad you're already fit and attractive. Unfortunately for you, there is nothing you can do to improve your appearance."

"Such flattery, Henry. If I'm not careful, you'll have *me* voting for you."

Henry laughed. "Let me know if you can't resist and I'll vote for you to keep it fair."

"So how much more weight do you plan on losing, Henry? Should I just throw in the towel right now?"

"If you like."

"Have you gotten any help?" she asked with a twinkle in her eye. "Most people need a good trainer to motivate them."

Molly knew she had hit pay dirt from the look on Henry's face.

He quickly looked at his watch and stood up. "I'm sorry, Molly. I have a meeting that I need to prepare for. I hope you understand."

With the satisfaction of having struck a nerve, Molly stood up and held out her hand.

"I understand. Good luck, Henry."

"Good luck to you as well. Thanks for stopping by."

When I get done with Misty, he's going to need more than luck, Molly thought on her way down the hall.

55

IN THE CITY

Misty woke up Saturday morning with a stiff back. After two nights of sleeping on the sofa, the thought of moving to the bedroom was looking pretty darn good. Travis had been rummaging around the kitchen for a while and he took her big yawn as a cue to bring her a cup of coffee.

Misty placed the cup of freshly brewed coffee under her nose and inhaled the splendid aroma. "This smells wonderful. You're really racking up points again, you know."

"Good," said Travis. "Maybe I can trade them in for a toaster."

"Clever," Misty replied as she sat up and took a sip of her coffee. "What do you have planned for us today?"

"Nothing big. I thought we could spend a good part of the day at the Embassy Athletic Club."

Misty set her cup of coffee down and sprang to her feet. "No frickin' way! That's one of the most exclusive clubs in New York City. You can't possibly be a member."

"No, but one of our senior partners is, and he owed me a favor. Sam is sponsoring us."

Misty shoved Travis in the chest playfully, causing him to back up a step. "This is like getting invited to play a round of golf at Augusta National. You might have enough points for more than a toaster."

"Well fortunately, the Embassy Athletic Club does allow women—unlike Augusta."

As they neared the club, Misty got goose bumps. Inside, she found the lobby spectacular, thinking it resembled an old historic hotel. To Misty, this was like walking through the pearly white gates of heaven.

They spent the rest of the morning getting in a strenuous work-out. After lunch in one of the club's wonderful restaurants, Travis took Misty down the hall to the billiard room to teach her how to shoot pool. Although Misty already knew how, she played dumb, happy to have Travis wrap his arms around her as he demonstrated the proper tech-nique. He caught on when Misty's competitive nature took over and she ran the table during the third game.

The middle of the afternoon was spent lounging in the library with a drink and fantasizing what it would be like to actually be a member. When it was time to leave, she turned around and took one final look before exiting the building. It was a day she would treasure forever. On the way home they hung onto each other like a couple of lovebirds. Misty couldn't wait to get him back to the apartment.

When they reached Travis's building, two ominous-looking men in long, black trench coats were standing in the lobby. The men followed Travis and Misty to the elevator, and as they waited for the doors to open, Misty felt a tap on her shoulder.

"Are you Misty?" one of them said.

Travis stepped between Misty and the men. "Who's asking?" he said.

The men pulled out badges. "The Federal Bureau of Investigation is asking. I'm Agent Mulroney and this is my partner, Agent Shultz."

"This must be some kind of mistake," said Travis, his voice taking on a more respectful tone. "What could you possibly want with Misty?"

"So this *is* Misty," said Agent Mulroney. "We need to take her in for questioning."

"Questioning for what?" asked Travis.

"Sorry, we're not at liberty to say," said Mulroney. "Look, all she has to do is answer a few questions. If everything goes well, we'll have her back for dinner."

Misty's mind drifted back to her conversation with Brenda, about how Chester had handed a copy of her contract to two men. She wondered if these were the men.

"Give us a moment to sort this out between us," said Travis. "I promise we'll stand in plain view while we do."

When Agent Shultz nodded to Agent Mulroney, Travis and Misty withdrew to the other side of the lobby.

Shultz's eyes remained fixed on Misty. "She's quite the looker. We lucked out on this assignment, buddy."

"I'll say," said Mulroney. "Now explain to me again why we're questioning her."

"The director was contacted by the attorney general's office," said Shultz. "They received a tip about some possible wrongdoing by an unnamed congressman. He wants us to do a quick, preliminary investigation to find out if there's any basis to the allegations. Our tactic is to lay it on her heavy and see if she'll crack."

"Let's take her to the nineteenth precinct," said Mulroney. "That place should be pretty intimidating to a sweet thing like her."

"That's a good idea," said Shultz. "I'll contact the bureau chief so he can give the precinct inspector a heads-up."

A smile broke across Mulroney's face. "Tell the chief we need to use his interrogation room. That should really make her nervous."

Meanwhile, Travis was trying to keep Misty calm. "Are you okay?" he asked. "Do you have a problem answering their questions?"

"I'll be fine," she said. The last thing she wanted was to get him involved. "I'm sure it's just a background check since I'm working so closely with a congressman. This shouldn't take long."

Travis hugged her. "I'll be here waiting for you when you get back."

"Let's order dinner in tonight if you don't mind," said Misty.

"Sure, anything you like."

On her way out the door, Misty turned around and gave Travis a big smile of assurance before nervously heading off with the agents.

* * *

The nineteenth precinct was bustling with officers, detectives, and the largest group of malcontents Misty had ever seen.

"Wait here while we have a chat with the inspector," Agent Shultz said to Misty.

While the agents were away, Misty observed her surroundings with great apprehension, wondering how in the world she ended up in a situation like this. What had seemed like a dream was quickly turning into a nightmare. Luckily the agents were on their way back when several filthy bearded men sitting on the bench across from her began to look her over. She stuck by the agents' side as they led her away.

They ushered Misty into a cramped interrogation room and had her take a seat at a small table in the middle of the room. Mulroney closed the door behind, and Misty immediately felt boxed in. Having never been in trouble before, she relied exclusively on her memory of old detective shows.

"Hey, this is an interrogation room!" she said, trying to keep the mood light.

"Would you rather we sit in the lobby with those sleazebags?" Agent Shultz asked.

"I guess not," Misty replied. "Are you going to read me my Miranda rights?"

Mulroney laughed. "No, Misty. We only do that when we arrest someone."

"Do I at least get to call my attorney?"

"And who would that attorney be, Misty?" Mulroney asked.

"Well, I don't know. I just thought—"

"Do you really want to go through the New York City phone book on a Saturday to find an attorney?" asked Shultz. "Just answer a few simple questions and we'll have you back in time for dinner with your handsome boyfriend."

Misty sighed. "All right. Ask your questions, but make it quick."

The agents handed Misty a piece of paper. She was horrified to see the special provision clause of her contract.

"We understand this is part of the agreement you enter into with your clients," said Shultz. "Can you explain to me what an 'agreed upon event' means?"

Misty took her time reading the clause over and over, her mind racing. Void of anything to say, she went on the offensive. "Where did you get this? That is an extremely confidential document, and it's none of your business."

"So you do recognize it?" asked Shultz.

"I'm not sure. I could be mistaken."

"Oh, now she's not sure? I think she's lying. What do you think, Mulroney?"

"That would be my guess," Mulroney replied.

Completely frustrated and getting a little pissed, Misty took on an assertive tone. "Do you know what I do for a living?"

"You are a trainer of some sort?" said Shultz.

"I'm a damn good trainer, and I'm paid well for my services."

"And how do your services become rendered in full?" asked Mulroney.

"Well, how do you think? I fulfill my contract."

"With fees equivalent to two years of my salary, that must be some service, sugar," said Shultz.

Misty bristled at the comment. "And just what do you mean by that?"

Agent Shultz grinned. "I mean that there's only one profession I know of where you can charge as much per hour as you do, and it's the oldest profession in the world."

"Are you saying you think I'm screwing my clients?"

"Well, are you?" asked Mulroney.

Misty was trapped and she knew it. Smart enough to know you don't lie to an FBI agent, she had been careful to be as vague as possible. That clearly wasn't working; it was time to try the silent treatment. Misty crossed her arms. "I'm through talking," she said.

Agent Shultz figured they would be better off taking a break to rethink their approach. He looked at his phone and fabricated a lie. "Mulroney, looks like the director is trying to contact us. I'm sorry, but we really need to take this call. Can I get you anything while we're away?"

Misty softened a bit. "I haven't eaten anything since lunch. Could you bring me a granola bar and some Gatorade?"

"I'll see what I can scrape up," Shultz replied.

The agents conferred with each other on their way to the vending machines.

"So what's your gut feeling on this one?" said Shultz.

"My gut tells me she's screwing her clients at least once," said Mulroney. "That's probably what 'mutually agreed upon event' refers to. If that's the case and her client is a congressman, this thing's going to get nasty. That's probably why the Attorney General's office moved on this tip so fast."

Agent Shultz gave it some thought. "Let me go back in alone this time," he said. "We'll throw a little good cop bad cop at her."

"Good idea. But don't forget to bring her the granola bar and Gatorade."

Shultz laughed. "Where the hell does she think she's at, a health club? A Snickers bar and a Coke is all she's getting."

Mulroney felt a hard slap on his back and turned around to see a tough-looking Hispanic woman standing behind him. "How the hell are you, Detective Sosa?" he said.

"Not too bad, Mul-dog," she replied. "Hi, Shultz. Are you two still working for that sissy agency?"

Agent Mulroney turned to Agent Schultz. "Go ahead and get started with Misty. I've got a few things I need to catch up on with the detective."

While the agents were away, Misty had spent her time frantically trying to figure out what the heck she was going do next. She was running out of solutions and had decided to think outside the box. Remembering she still had her smoking hot workout outfit on underneath her sweatpants, she decided it was time to turn up the heat.

Agent Shultz entered the interrogation room and placed the Coke and Snickers bar on the table in front of her. "Sorry, this was the best I could do."

Misty was famished, and she downed the candy bar in three bites. After taking a long gulp of Coke, she asked Agent Shultz, "So how fit do you think you are?"

Agent Shultz stood up straight and stuck out his chest. "I'm in excellent shape!" he said defensively, as if his manhood had been challenged.

What Misty did next caught the agent completely by surprise.

Without speaking, she unzipped her sweatshirt and laid it on the table. Then off came the sweatpants. Agent Schulz watched with a look of bewilderment. "What the hell are you doing?" he asked.

"Why, you and I are going to get it on of course."

He knew he should be telling her to put her clothes back on, but he couldn't take his eyes off her. He had assumed she had a hot body, but he never could have imagined just how hot.

Misty now stood in her skimpy outfit, chest out and hands on hips. "Ready to do it?"

The agent gulped. "I'm not sure what you mean."

"Here's the deal. You and I are going to do some working out right here in this room. And I'll tell you what—if you can keep up with me, I'll tell you everything you want to know."

Misty had played perfectly to his ego. "You're on!" he said without thinking. "What's on the agenda?"

Misty smiled. "Let's start out with a little running in place and then move on to isometrics, sit-ups, and push-ups." She patted his little gut. "Your little buddy there can play, too."

In the hallway outside the interrogation room, Detective Sosa was enjoying the fact that she knew an FBI agent. "What are you guys up to?" she asked Mulroney.

Having always wanted to get into Sosa's pants, Mulroney was anxious to let her in on their assignment.

"Come see what we took captive," he said, motioning for her to follow.

He led Detective Sosa to the one-way mirror so she could observe the interrogation. His eyes remained fixed on her face, not wanting to miss her reaction to Misty. When the expression on Sosa's face was not what he expected, he took a look through the glass himself. Agent Shultz and Misty were doing push-ups on the floor. His partner's shirt was dripping wet, while Misty had barely broken a sweat.

"What the hell's going on?" Agent Mulroney yelled.

"I was wondering that myself," said Sosa. "That's the craziest interrogation technique I've ever witnessed, but hey, you guys are supposed to be a step ahead of the rest of us."

Agent Mulroney opened the door. "Shultz, could I talk to you for a second?" he called in. Shultz completed his push-up and got to his feet, wiping sweat from his brow.

Once outside, he bent over and tried to catch his breath. "And what exactly does this have to do with good cop bad cop?" asked Mulroney.

Agent Shultz's words were punctuated with heavy, strained breaths. "She told me . . . that she . . . would tell me . . . what I wanted to know . . . if I could keep up with her."

Detective Sosa cracked up laughing.

Agent Shultz glared up at her. "This is pretty much . . . a bluff . . . so I figured out . . . what the heck. You got a better idea?"

Detective Sosa walked back to the mirror and took a good look at their captive. She resented the fact that Misty seemed confident and in control.

A desire to impress the agents overtook her, along with the desire to put this girl back in her place. "I can handle her," she said. "Lock this gal up overnight and make sure she's in a private cell. I'll change into one of my undercover hooker outfits, throw a little dirt on my face, and drink a little whiskey so it's on my breath. Once she gets comfortable, you can have the jailer escort me to her cell. By the time I get through with her, she'll be crying for her mama. That's when I'll get her to cough up the goods."

"I like it, but what are we going to use to legitimately lock her up?" asked Agent Mulroney.

"You boys are FBI agents, right? Catch her in a lie, and then you can book her on false swearing charges."

"I've got it," said Shultz. "Misty said she would tell us what we wanted to know if I kept up with her. If I claim I won and she refuses to talk, we can say she lied to me."

"It looks to me like she kicked your ass," said Mulroney, chuckling.

Agent Shultz scowled. "No she didn't. Besides, that's a judgment call. No one was counting reps."

Detective Sosa stared through the one-way mirror at Misty and ground her fist into the palm of her hand. "I can't wait," she said.

The agents flung the door open to the interrogation room.

"Okay, you promised to tell us what we want to know," Shultz said gruffly. "Give it up."

Misty laughed. "No way. You didn't win."

"Yes, he did," said Mulroney.

"Prove it," said Misty.

"I was watching on the other side of the mirror, and I kept track of everything. Sorry, but if it's your word against mine, I win every time. It's time for you to tell us about the clause."

"Nope," Misty said firmly. "I'm not telling you."

"Is that final?" Mulroney asked.

"Yep. That's final."

"Too bad you didn't bring your PJs, then," said Shultz, "because you're spending the night in the slammer."

"That's ridiculous!" she shouted. "What are you charging me with?"

"False Swearing," Shultz replied. "You just lied to a public servant. And now I *am* going to read you your Miranda rights. You have the right to remain silent," he began. "Anything you say can and will be used against you in a court of law. You have the right to speak to an attorney. If you cannot afford an attorney, one will be appointed for you. Do you understand these rights as they have been read to you?"

When Misty heard him mention the attorney, she realized that's what she should have done a long time ago.

"I want my one phone call," Misty said when he finished.

He nodded. "Yes, now you get your one phone call."

"I need to call Argentina," she said.

He laughed. "You can't call Argentina from the precinct phones!"

"What if I use my cell phone?"

"If you can get through to Argentina, then go for it. Agent Mulroney will be stationed outside the door while I start on the paperwork."

Misty reached into the pocket of her sweatpants, which were lying on the table, for her phone. Her hands were shaking. She wondered if she should be calling Travis instead, but she worried this could get him into trouble with Excelsior Investments somehow.

As the phone rang she prayed Gabriella would pick up.

"Hello, Misty," Gabriella said, finally answering after six rings. "How are you doing?"

Misty broke down crying. "Gabriella, I am so sorry to call you, but the FBI is charging me with some false swearing stuff and I have to spend the night in jail. I'm staying with Travis and would call him, but I don't want him to get involved."

"Calm down, dear. We'll get to the bottom of this. The legal firm I use is headquartered there in New York. I'll have an attorney arrange for bail first thing in the morning."

"Oh, Gabriella, I may have gotten myself into some really bad stuff."

"What did you do?"

"That's the thing. All I've done is train the congressman. Brenda called me a few days ago to tell me two men talked Chester into giving them a copy of my contract. When I told the congressman, he suggested I come to New York for ten days. He said his wife was coming to town."

It didn't take Gabriella long to figure out that Misty was in the middle of a game of high-stakes political poker, and that the clause in her contract represented the pot they were playing for.

"Misty, do me one favor. Please do not talk to anyone without your attorney present. Do you promise?"

Misty snickered. "Hell yeah, I promise. If I'd kept my mouth shut in the first place and demanded to call an attorney, I wouldn't be in this mess."

Agent Mulroney popped his head into the interrogation room. "Say good-bye, time's up."

"Gabriella, I've got to hang up now," she said. "Do me a favor. Call Travis and let him know what's going on. I'll text you his phone number after you hang up."

"All right, dear," said Gabriella. "I'll call him right after I find you an attorney. I was leaving on a trip to the Bahamas in the morning but I'll have my pilots change the flight plan to New York. I should be able to arrive by tomorrow evening."

The thought of Gabriella dropping everything to come to her aid touched Misty. If there was ever a doubt Gabriella was her dearest friend, it disappeared at that moment.

"Gabriella?"

"Yes, dear?"

"I love you!"

"I love you, too! Be brave."

"I will."

Misty wedged herself against the door so Mulroney couldn't enter until she got her text off to Gabriella. She then walked out of the room with her hands out as if ready for handcuffs.

The jailer escorted Misty to her cell while female detainees in the cell across the way peered at her through the bars.

A woman who looked like an Amazon yelled out, "Put her in here with us so I can kick her pasty white ass!"

Another woman yelled, "Now she's one privileged bitch. How do I get my own cell?"

The more insults they hurled at her, the more pissed off Misty got. Her anger was the perfect antidote; it left little room for self-pity.

56

A Perplexing Situation

Travis was worried sick. It was dinnertime and he had no idea what was taking so long. He roamed his apartment like a caged lion, trying to figure out whether he should try to intervene in some way. But how? He had no idea where they had taken her.

Finally his phone rang. "Misty?"

"No, Travis. This is Misty's friend, Gabriella."

"Oh hi Gabriella. I'm sorry but Misty isn't here."

"I know. I talked to her an hour ago and she asked me to fill you in."

"How's she doing?"

"Not well. They're keeping her overnight in a holding cell."

"You're joking, right?"

"I wish I was. Don't worry though, I've arranged for an excellent attorney to visit first thing in the morning. He'll bring her back to your apartment when she makes bail."

Travis's doorbell rang. "Gabriella, can you hold on for a second? Someone's at my door."

"Sure, no problem," she said.

"Be right back. Don't hang up."

Travis set the phone down and opened the front door to find a middle-aged man with salt-and-pepper hair. "Hi, you must be Misty's friend," he said. "Is she here?"

"I don't want to sound rude," said Travis, "but how do you know Misty?"

"I know her from D.C. I was in New York for the weekend and wanted to stop by to say hi. Is she here?"

"You must be the congressman."

"You got it. And I can tell you, Misty is a first-class trainer. But . . . is she here?"

"Misty was questioned earlier by two FBI agents and now they're holding her overnight. Do you have any idea what this is about?"

Henry was visibly disturbed, even though he quickly tried to cover his concern. "My word! That's terrible. I have no idea what's going on, but it sounds like she could use my help. Do you know where they have her?"

"I'm not sure, but I have someone on the phone who does. Let me go ask her."

Henry panicked, realizing the ramifications of showing up at Travis's apartment. For all he knew the FBI could have surveillance cameras in the building.

Looking down both halls nervously, Henry said, "That won't be necessary. I forgot that I have a very important engagement in half an hour. I couldn't possibly do anything about it now, anyway." He patted Travis on the shoulder and added, "Don't worry, I'll have one of my aides check into it."

Henry turned and walked away before Travis had time to respond, so he hurried back to the phone.

"Gabriella, are you still there?"

"Yes. Who was that?"

"Did Misty tell you who she was training?"

"Yes, the congressman?"

"That was him. He said he was in town and just wanted to stop by and say hi."

"Hmm, that's strange. He told Misty he couldn't train for the next ten days because his wife was in town. Why in the world would he be looking for Misty? Listen Travis, I'm leaving for New York Sunday morning. Can you recommend a good place to stay?"

"I've put several clients up at the Menger Hotel. Would you like me to book you a room?"

"That would be a big help. I'll call after I get checked in tomorrow afternoon."

"Gabriella, I know how close you and Misty are, and I just wanted to say I'm really glad you're coming."

"And Misty's told me what good friends you two have become. It's comforting to know you'll be there for her when she's released."

* * *

Outside Travis's building, Henry walked to the nearest pay phone and called Rick's cell. He caught him out to dinner with his wife and waited until Rick found a quiet place to talk.

"Okay, Henry, what's up?" said Rick.

"I'm in New York."

"What are you doing there?"

"I thought about some of the things you said at our last meeting and decided that maybe I should talk things over with Misty."

"Was she cooperative?" Rick asked.

"I never got a chance to visit with her. Listen, Rick, two FBI agents picked Misty up several hours ago and now they're holding her overnight."

Rick felt like a doctor had just notified him that he had a fast-growing cancer and was destined to die a slow, painful death. He found a chair in the restaurant hallway and sat down.

"Rick, are you still on the phone?"

"I'm here. Looks like things are moving faster than we thought."

Henry looked off into the distance for a moment. "No shit. This is the worst-case scenario."

"What do you think we should do?"

"I'm not sure there's anything we can do until they release her," said

Henry. "If they got her to talk, we have some major damage control to do. Start thinking about how we should handle this if all hell breaks loose, and I'll get back to D.C. as quick as I can."

"You're coming back now?"

"Yes. My departure ticket proves I got here after the FBI picked her up, and if my return ticket shows I left before they released her, no one can say I talked to Misty while I was here."

"Henry, does anyone else know you were looking for Misty?"

"Yeah, her boyfriend and someone he was talking to on the phone."

"Oh man, that's not good."

"Tell me about it. I'll give you his name and address when I see you. Run a background check on him."

"Okay, Henry. I know just the people to use."

57

The Cellmate from Hell

Detective Sosa, decked out in her hooker costume, stood only a few feet away from Agents Mulroney and Shultz in the main lobby of the police station.

"How do I look?" she said.

The agents turned around and did a double take.

"Well I'll be damned," said Shultz. "You look like a sleazy tramp. Good job!"

She frowned. "Hey, you don't have to be that descriptive."

"I'd say you look like a hot tramp," added Mulroney.

She shook her head. "That's better, but why don't we lose the word *tramp*? How about we just say 'lady of the night'?"

"Whatever suits you," said Shultz. "I hope we aren't making a mistake with this whole thing. I spent some time with Misty and she's in excellent condition. How far do you plan on pushing her?"

Sosa stepped up until she was right in his face. "Hard enough to get her to throw the first punch. After that, I'll mop the floor with her long blonde hair." Agent Shultz backed away and directed her to the jailhouse door with his open right palm.

"Come back at three in the morning," the detective said as she walked off, "and Misty will be ready to tell you anything you want to know."

Inside, a female jailer escorted Sosa toward the holding cell. "Nice of you to bring us some fresh meat!" yelled the Amazon woman.

"Not tonight, Roxanne," said the jailer. "Why don't you just get some sleep?"

The jailer coaxed Sosa into Misty's cell by her arm. Sosa yanked her arm away and spat on her. "Take your hands off me, you pig!" she shouted.

The women in the other cell rushed to the front bars and began yelling.

"Don't let her get away with that, jailer!"

"Bash her head in!"

"Bring her over here and I'll make her my bitch!"

The jailer paid no attention to the women as she gave Sosa an angry stare and slammed the cell door shut.

Once safely on the outside, the jailer said to Sosa, "You do that again and I'll throw you in the cell over there with Roxanne."

Sosa walked up to the bars and looked Roxanne in the eyes. "You don't scare me, sister. I think I'm going to talk the guard into letting you come visit me so I can bash your face in."

Misty lay comfortably on her bunk bed while she observed the two women throwing insults and threats back and forth. She was glad the attention was off her and couldn't wait for things to quiet down so she could get some sleep. But her new cellmate had other ideas.

Sosa walked over to the edge of Misty's bunk and looked her over. "You're a pretty little thing, aren't you? What's your name, sweetie?"

Misty removed the forearm she was using to cover her eyes, glanced at the intruder, and then replaced her arm over her eyes without a word. Her calmness irritated Sosa, and she grabbed the end of Misty's mattress and dragged it halfway onto the floor, Misty and all.

The caged women leaped to their feet again and began yelling.

"Catfight!"

"Pull her hair out!"

"Gouge her eyes out!"

"Rip her clothes off! I wanna see what that bitch looks like naked."

Misty sat on the mattress with her back propped up against the bed frame as a slow burn built inside her.

Sosa lifted her right foot and placed it on Misty's upper chest, pinning her to the bed.

Misty glared into Sosa's eyes. "Take your foot off me."

"Take my foot off you, or what?"

"Just take your foot off me."

"You don't get it. You're my little bitch tonight, so strip down and show us your tits."

The caged women began taunting.

"Rip the slut's clothes off so we can see her kahunas!"

"I'll bet they're bouncers."

"No, pull her panties down and show us her pubes."

Sosa's foot was dug into Misty's chest with such force that she had difficulty breathing. She grabbed Sosa's leg, struggling to pry it away, but it was dug in too firm to budge. Gasping for breath, Misty looked around for another way out. She lifted her right foot and swung it across the back of Sosa's left leg, causing her knee to buckle. As soon as her knee hit the floor, Misty easily shoved Sosa's other foot away from her chest and sprung to her feet. Misty grabbed the bars and hung on tight until she caught her breath. Outraged at being outmaneuvered, Sosa walked up behind Misty, grabbed a fistful of her hair, and yanked her head back.

With her face only inches from Misty's, she said, "You need to be taught a lesson."

Sosa felt the time was right, so she released Misty's hair, took a few steps back, and motioned for Misty to throw the first punch. Misty rubbed the back of her head, unable to think about anything but how surreal the situation seemed. Only hours ago she had been on her way home to spend a very special evening with Travis, and now she stood face to face with the woman from hell. Misty had always wondered what a real street whore would look like. As far as she knew, one was in her presence right now. Misty looked over the women's short, tight, zebra-patterned dress, gnarly hair, and face caked in makeup, and pitied her.

When Misty refused to attack, Sosa spit in her face. Misty's fists clenched into a ball so tight the veins in her arms popped out. Sosa snickered at what she felt would be a futile attack by Misty, positioning herself so she could block what was sure to be wildly thrown punches. From her defensive position, Sosa planned to deflect the blows and deliver a knockout counterpunch. Misty, however, had no intention of throwing punches, so she lowered her shoulders and positioned her lower extremities into a sprinter's stance. From there she exploded like a lion pouncing on its prey.

Misty exploded through her target with such force that Sosa slammed into the back wall of the cell. The horrifying thud Misty's right shoulder made as it drove into Sosa's chest was remarkably similar to that of a heavyweight fighter's fist making contact with his opponent's forehead. Sosa dropped to the floor, thrashing around like a freshly caught fish in the bottom of a boat. Misty stood over her and watched her curl up into a ball. She waited until Sosa's breathing returned to normal before she leaned over and wrapped her opponent's hair tightly around her right hand. This time it was Misty's turn to pull Sosa's head back by the hair and look into her eyes.

"I'd make you my bitch if you weren't so fucking ugly," said Misty.

Sensing the fight had been drained from her foe, she released Sosa's hair and backed away. The cell block was eerily silent as Sosa crawled onto her bunk and lay down on her side, facing the wall. Misty climbed up to the upper bunk, making sure she could keep an eye on her temporarily defeated foe. Once her opponent's breathing had remained shallow for a good while, Misty fell asleep knowing the woman was in no shape to retaliate.

* * *

Misty awoke to the sound of her name and quickly sat up in bed. It took her a moment to figure out where she was. When the jailer unlocked her cell, she realized her cellmate was gone.

"Come on, girl," said the jailer. "You've made bail."

Back in the main area of the police station, a tall, well-dressed man with a kind face awaited her.

"Hello, Misty. My name is Kerry, and I'm your attorney."

"That's wonderful. How do I get out of here?"

"Just need to sign some papers. You're being released on a five-thousand-dollar personal recognizance bond."

"But I don't have any money."

Kerry laughed. "Don't worry, honey. It's all taken care of."

Misty walked up to Kerry and shook his hand. "I don't know you from Adam, but right now you're a sight for sore eyes."

Misty began rubbing her right shoulder.

"Looks like your eyes aren't the only thing that's sore," said Kerry.

"Yeah, probably the mattress," Misty said.

"Take a seat, honey, and rest up. I've got to deal with these cabbage heads one more time before we can leave."

Once they were done at the police station, Kerry dropped her off at Travis's apartment building. She made her way inside wearily, took the elevator to his floor, and rang his bell. When the door swung open, Misty fell into his open arms, feeling safe and secure at last.

Travis stroked the back of her head. "Why don't you take a nice hot shower while I make you some bacon and eggs? You can tell me all about your evening once you're fed."

Misty squeezed him tight and then headed to the shower without a word.

58

THE AFTERMATH

Mulroney and Shultz arrived at the midtown emergency room on Sunday morning, shortly after eight. It was only ten blocks from the 19th Precinct, so the agents decided to walk. Things had gotten out of hand last night, and they needed time and fresh air to figure out how they would handle the director. When they reached the hospital, Agent Mulroney flipped a coin to see which of them would get the privilege of giving the director a call. Shultz lost, so Mulroney took a seat on a nearby bench. With legs stretched out and hands behind his head, he gazed into the sky. Just because he didn't have to do the talking didn't mean he wasn't nervous about what the director would say. Every couple of minutes, he peeked at Agent Shultz to evaluate his body language. At one point, Shultz was walking in circles with his head down and his left arm flailing in the air. Mulroney knew this was not a good sign.

As the discussion ended, Agent Shultz put his phone away and walked over to the bench. Mulroney anxiously stood up to greet him.

"Oh man," said Shultz.

"Oh man what? Is he mad?"

"I've heard him madder."

"Well that's good news, I guess. What did he say?"

"He said we used poor judgment last night. All he wanted us to do was explore whether or not there were grounds to investigate further."

Agent Mulroney shook his head. "Crap! What else did he say?"

"He said booking Misty on false swearing charges will bring more attention to this investigation than he would like, and that having Detective Sosa go undercover to intimidate Misty was off-the-chart stupid. He spent twenty minutes on the phone this morning, calming Sosa's inspector down. Apparently he was livid that we involved his employee in the investigation without consulting him first."

Mulroney plopped back down on the bench and threw his hands up in the air.

"It's my fault. I never should have let Sosa get involved."

"Damn you," said Shultz. "You're taking all the fun out of being mad at you." He grinned at Mulroney and added, "Don't be so hard on yourself, partner. Watching Misty's boobs bouncing around during our exercise session was worth the tongue lashing. It's too bad you missed out."

"No, being able to view the catfight in Misty's cell last night would have made it all worthwhile. Let's go find out what happened."

The agents flashed their badges at the hospital's front desk and an orderly ushered them to intensive care. They found Sosa propped up on her bed, eyes closed. Mulroney tapped the doorframe lightly to see if she would wake up.

"So how's it going?" Mulroney asked when her eyes opened.

She didn't reply, but he pushed on delicately.

"Are you okay? You look like you're in terrible pain."

Detective Sosa used her finger to motion him closer before whispering in short breaths, "Bruised breastbone . . . and . . . a bruised lung." She took a few more shallow breaths before adding, "They're moving me . . . to a room soon."

Agent Mulroney patted her on the head. "Get some sleep and we'll be back to see you when you feel better."

That's all it took for her to drift off into a morphine-induced sleep.

"Misty must pack a wallop!" said Agent Shultz quietly as they walked down the hall. "I'll bet she's one damn good trainer."

* * *

Molly was enjoying a Sunday brunch at the country club with her husband when her cell phone rang. It was Veronica, her friend at the *Washington Post*.

"Hi, Veronica," she answered. "How nice of you to call."

"Molly, can you talk?" Veronica asked anxiously. "I just heard back from my contact at the Justice Department."

Excited, Molly put her hand over the phone and said, "Honey, Veronica's on the phone. Why don't you finish your brunch and I'll take the call in the lobby so we don't interrupt the other tables."

"Sure, honey," he said. "I'm just going to check out the dessert table."

Molly briskly weaved her way through the tables to the lobby. When she was situated in a secluded chair next to a large plant, she brought the phone to her ear. "Veronica, you there? What did the agent say?"

"I'm afraid it's not good news, Molly."

"What did you say? said Molly, unpleasantly surprised. "I don't think I heard you correctly."

"My contact told me there would be no further investigation unless I provide the Attorney General's office with something more credible. He said it takes damning evidence to bring serious charges against a sitting congressman."

"This is going to be a lot tougher than I imagined," Molly said calmly. "I guess I'll have to take matters into my own hands if we're going to get to the bottom of this."

"Are you sure that's wise?" Veronica said tentatively.

"It is if I get someone to testify against Misty."

"That would probably do it," Veronica said. "You know I would do anything for you, don't you?"

"I know. I'll show my appreciation next time I'm in D.C."

Molly's determination to become a congresswoman had clouded her judgment. She felt the only way she could win the seat was by implicating Henry in a scandal, and that's what she was determined to do. Realizing she needed to give this her full attention, she told her husband that something had come up and she needed to go to the office for a few hours.

When she got there, she finalized her next move. It entailed visiting Chester Naples personally, so she booked the first flight to San Antonio on Monday morning. Next, she got up the nerve to make a risky call to a small-time local drug dealer she currently had under indictment. His name was Johnny, and he was an old high school classmate of Molly's. The two had been an item their sophomore year. She always blamed Johnny's upbringing for the way he turned out, and she had hoped she could find a reason to let him off. Now she could offer Johnny an attractive plea bargain for a little quid pro quo.

59

TOGETHER TIME

Misty and Travis spent Sunday afternoon holed up in his apartment. Travis doted over her the entire morning, having breakfast ready when she woke, applying an icepack to her sore shoulder, and giving her quiet time to ruminate while massaging her neck and temples. Misty used the time to run the events of last night through her mind over and over. By early afternoon, she was ready to open up.

Lying on the couch in Travis's arms, Misty decided to let him in on her inner thoughts.

"Travis, do you remember the time we were alone on Lake Travis?"

Travis gave her a kiss. "How could I forget?"

"Do you remember what you told me that morning?"

Travis looked puzzled, so Misty continued. "You told me that I only had one problem."

Travis laughed. "Boy, was I wrong!"

Misty gave him a little shove. "Stop it! You remember, don't you? You said I had all the qualities of a sixteenth-century courtesan and that my only problem was that I was born in the wrong century."

Travis nodded in acknowledgment.

"Well, you were right. I feel like a twenty-first-century courtesan, and it suits me just fine. How many women get a chance to travel the world, meet interesting people, and get handsomely paid for it? But all this morning I kept telling myself that if I got out of this jam I would give up my profession."

"And?" said Travis.

"And, I came to the realization that I'm addicted to my lifestyle and will fight to maintain it."

"Then that's what you should do," he said, laughing softly. "You're perfectly suited for your job. And just think about how happy you make men all over the world. How many women can say that?"

Misty laid her head on his chest and squeezed him tight. "I'm so happy you were never my client and that we became friends naturally."

"But your clients are the reason we can never become an item," he said.

Misty sat up abruptly. "Whoa—where did that come from? Have you been keeping that deep inside?"

Travis looked down, embarrassed. "Maybe so. It sure wasn't planned."

"Oh come on," she said, trying to lighten the mood. "I'm four years older than you, Travis! You don't want to fall in love with an older woman."

Still surprised at what he'd just said, Travis welcomed the opportunity to do a little backpedaling. "So, since I've been sleeping with an older woman all this time, does that make me a gigolo? If so, how come you're not buying me stuff?"

Misty reached in her pocket and pulled out a dollar bill. "How much will this buy me?"

Travis grinned. "Let's find out."

Taking the dollar bill in his teeth, he picked Misty up and carried her into the bedroom. Instead of throwing her on the bed, he gently laid her head on his pillow and climbed over her. Misty saw that the pair of eyes hovering above hers were serious and calm, and she became nervous. Things felt too intimate, so she struggled to get up. Travis kept her there and shook his head as he looked deep into her soul.

"No, Travis," Misty pleaded. "We can't do it this way. You know we can't fall in love. One of us will get hurt."

Travis placed his fingers over her lips. "Hush. You talk too much."

When he removed his fingers she said with tears in her eyes, "Please don't. If you make me love you, we'll pay a price sooner or later."

When she closed her eyes as if to hide from his love, a tear streaked down her cheek. Travis kissed the liquid from her skin, starting just below her eye and working his way to the edge of her lips.

Misty's breathing quickened. Her heart wanted Travis to kiss her but her head still said no.

"I have to know, Misty," he said. "I need to know what it's like to make love to you in place of having sex with you. Just this one time, and I promise I will never ask again."

He could feel her tremble beneath him. He knew her well enough to understand he was asking her to go where she had always felt uncomfortable. He waited a while longer and then made his final plea. "You say that I mean more to you than any client." Misty opened her eyes to meet his. With her full and undivided attention, he said, "Prove it to me."

Misty's eyes swelled with tears as she pulled his lips to hers, the taste of his warm mouth in hers.

Misty pulled his head up, breaking their kiss for just a moment. "You mean more to me than any man in the world and I *will* prove it to you. But after we finish, you can never ask me to make love to you like this again. I'm serious."

"I know you are and I agree to your demands," Travis replied. "Now stop talking and kiss me."

Travis controlled the tempo, taking it slow and easy. They kissed so long they began to feel as one. He moved on to her ear, breathing heavily as he nibbled away. Moving back over her, he delicately ran his fingers through her hair and traced her face with his finger. She opened her eyes to keep from drifting off. They held eye contact with each other as if in a trance. He was breaking through her defense mechanism, and she felt naked and vulnerable even though she was still fully clothed. Wanting him more than ever, she reached for the bottom of her shirt to pull it off, but Travis stopped her. She lay there looking at him for direction, which soon came.

After unbuckling her belt, Travis pulled it out and threw it on the floor. He unsnapped the button of her jeans and pulled down her zipper.

With great effort he worked her jeans down to the top of her knees and then pulled her panties down to meet them. She started to speak, but he placed his finger to her lips to hush her. She put everything out of her head and let him be the master. After doing the same to his jeans and underwear, Travis fingered her until he was sure she was moist enough to take him in without discomfort. The entry was slow and easy. He moved in and out of her just as slowly as he had entered the first time. This was not about how fast they could come, but about how long they could extend their pleasure. As his knowing eyes looked deep inside her soul, she began to realize that willing acknowledgment of their shared passion through the wonder of sight was far more powerful than simply becoming hot and bothered at the sight of bouncing boobs or well-developed pecs. When Misty felt the hot rush she always felt before orgasm, she prepared herself to climax. To her surprise, the slow penetration kept her from coming and left her in a euphoric wonderland, sitting just on the threshold of orgasm but never quite coming. But then out of nowhere something swelled up inside Misty and her entire body felt like one large clitoris, and she throbbed in ecstasy for what seemed like hours as she looked into her lover's eyes.

* * *

Misty and Travis fell asleep in each other's arms, emotionally drained from their hour of enlightenment. They would have slept longer had it not been for the ringing of his cell phone.

Travis answered and then listened intently. "Yeah . . . Okay. Thanks," he said.

"Who was that?" Misty asked when he hung up.

"It was the apartment attendant. Someone left an envelope for you and they're sending it up now."

Misty couldn't imagine who would be sending something to her at Travis's apartment.

60

PHANTOM

Travis tipped the courier and took the black, letter-sized envelope to Misty. She was sitting up in bed with her arm out, so he placed the envelope in her hand. Misty looked it over thoroughly, but could find no markings of any kind.

"Open it, Misty."

"But it's so thin. I'm not sure there's anything in it."

Misty tore one end off and squeezed the sides. When the envelope opened wide, she noticed what seemed to be a single ticket. She turned the envelope upside down and caught the ticket with her other hand.

Misty inspected the ticket and a perplexed look came over her face. "Hey, what's the matter?" asked Travis. "You look like you just saw a ghost."

"It's a ticket to *Phantom of the Opera*," Misty replied without changing her expression.

Travis took the ticket from her hand. "Who would send you a single ticket to *Phantom of the Opera*?"

He noticed it was for tonight's performance. "You can't go tonight," he said. "Gabriella will be calling soon. Why don't you let me give it away?"

Misty snatched the ticket from his hands and clutched it to her chest.

"You're not really going to the theater tonight alone, are you?" he asked.

Misty sheepishly nodded in the affirmative.

"But what about Gabriella? What about me?"

Misty stood up and walked toward the bathroom. Before closing the door, she yelled back, "When Gabriella calls, tell her what happened. You should join her for dinner. It would give the two of you a chance to get to know each other."

Travis was about to reply when he heard the shower turn on. He went to the kitchen and poured himself a stiff drink.

Fifteen minutes later, Misty found him sitting in his favorite chair in the living room working on his second glass of bourbon. She was woefully underdressed for the theater but still managed to look spectacular.

She opened her arms wide and spun around.

"How do I look?"

"Why, beautiful, of course."

Misty picked up on the lack of emotion in his voice.

"I'm underdressed, aren't I?"

Travis shrugged.

She walked over and sat in his lap. "Oh, Travis. Don't be like that. You know I love you, but you also know you have to share me. I warned you, didn't I?"

Travis perked up. "I know. Don't worry about me. A few more drinks and I'll be fine."

He looked at her ticket one more time. "Box seats! My, aren't we lucky?"

Misty planted a brief kiss on his lips. "Have a good time with Gabriella tonight. I won't be out late."

As Misty got off his lap, he said, "So, is Gabriella hot? Maybe I'll take her out on the town."

"You better believe it, cowboy." Misty ran her finger under his chin. "If you sleep with her, you have to promise to tell me all about it."

Travis shook his head. "You are really something. Don't worry about me. That just snapped me back to reality."

Just before Misty left the living room, she turned back to Travis and said, "Don't make up the sofa. I'm moving into the bed with you."

Outside, Misty decided she needed to clear her head, so she walked the twenty blocks to the theater. She was so consumed with thought, she walked right through Times Square without even noticing. She knew she had no choice. She needed to find out if it was really him.

After being ushered to her box, Misty took a deep breath before she pulled back the curtain. She was disappointed to find the box empty. She settled in, figuring he would probably wait for the play to begin before arriving. Everything about him always seemed so secretive. She waited apprehensively the entire first half of the play, but he never showed. By intermission the excitement had ebbed, so she decided to sit back and enjoy the second-half performance, hoping it might free her mind.

* * *

Gabriella called Travis looking for Misty moments after she left. Travis explained the strange circumstance surrounding Misty's unavailability and then agreed to meet her at her hotel.

Walking through the heavy doors of the Menger Hotel gave Travis the feeling he was stepping into another era. The velvet-draped lobby was lined with ornate mirrors and peacock feathers. Travis scoured the room for Gabriella but didn't see any women that fit her description. After a few minutes he tired of looking and took a seat and closed his bourbon-heavy eyes.

When his eyes reopened there stood a gorgeous, smartly dressed woman looking down at him inquisitively with gorgeous, brown, olive-shaped eyes. Her smooth, silky hair was draped over her shoulders. The calmness emanating from her made him feel at ease.

"You must be Travis," she said.

"Gabriella. How long have you been standing there?"

"I'm not certain," she replied. "I wasn't keeping track of time."

When Travis stood up and offered his hand, Gabriella said, "I'd prefer a hug. Misty told me so much about you that I feel like we should already be good friends."

Travis opened his arms and Gabriella stepped in. Her hug was strong and firm but not overly long. As she stepped back her wonderful perfume lingered. Less than a minute after meeting her, Travis was already captivated.

"I'm sorry Misty didn't come with me, Gabriella," he said.

She patted him on the arm. "It does seem out of character for Misty, but she's going through a rough ordeal. There is no telling what's going through her mind. I'm certain she will have a logical explanation next time we see her."

"I suppose you're right."

"Travis, I've been worrying about Misty since she called, and I have to admit I don't have much of an appetite. Would you mind if we just relaxed in the bar? They serve some light fare, if you are hungry."

"The bar's fine."

Travis marveled at the zinc-topped bar and the sumptuous velvet surroundings, enhanced by the warmth of the sandstone fireplace. An extremely friendly bartender took their order.

"So explain to me again what caused Misty to leave so abruptly," Gabriella said when he walked away.

"It's kind of crazy. Someone sent Misty a single box-seat ticket to tonight's performance of *Phantom of the Opera*. The ticket was in an envelope without a note attached. After seeing the ticket, Misty's mood changed abruptly. The next thing I knew, she was out the door. Does any of that make sense to you?"

Gabriella had an idea but chose not to share it. "No sense guessing," she said. "I'm sure she'll have a rational explanation when she returns."

Over the course of the conversation, Travis became pleasantly surprised at how well educated Gabriella was in regard to financial matters. Gabriella was impressed with Travis's knowledge of asset management strategies. Sensing he could possibly be making a future client, he told Gabriella all about Excelsior's initiative to train ten thousand women from developing countries in business management. Gabriella knew from experience how beneficial this was for women in South American countries, and she told Travis he should travel to Argentina so they could continue their discussions. He mentioned that Excelsior Investments had a local office in Buenos Aires, but Gabriella would have nothing of it; she insisted that if she was going to invest millions of dollars with his company, she would deal with someone she felt comfortable with.

"Travis, I want to thank you for being such a good friend to Misty," Gabriella said once they had discussed the formalities of how the transaction would work. "As you know, I'm very fond of her, and I worry each time she goes on one of her little adventures. It's comforting to know she had you to lean on."

"She does have Miguel to keep an eye on her, too," he replied.

"Yes, and I am very grateful for Miguel as well, but there is more to keeping Misty out of trouble than having a bodyguard around. So I thank the both of you just the same." Gabriella then glanced down at her watch. "I don't mean to seem impolite, but I think it would be good if you were home when Misty got back. I've enjoyed our visit immensely— we can pick up where we left off next time we get together."

The two embraced warmly and Travis left for his apartment.

* * *

As *Phantom of the Opera* worked its way toward the final scene, Misty's disappointment mounted. The final graveyard scene and the song the heroine sang didn't help.

Saddened by the actress's words, Misty put her head in her hands, wondering what had gone wrong. She stayed in that position until the show ended.

Just as she was getting ready to go, she leaned over in her seat to grab her bag from the floor and noticed a very large foot on the floor next to her. Misty looked up into a ruggedly handsome face and slid into the man's outstretched arms, engulfed in the familiar massive frame.

"Oh, Ivan. It *was* you after all. Of course it was you—who else could it have been?"

Ivan pulled back just enough to gaze into the eyes he had only been able to dream about for the last year. It didn't take him long to remember why he thought of her every moment his mind would allow. Although painfully aware she could never be his, he loved her just the same. Misty, too, was elated to see the man who had showed up in her time of crisis before. After a few minutes of passionate kissing Misty said, "Ivan, how have you been? I've worried about you ever since we last parted." She assumed he had gotten in trouble for hiring her and prayed his punishment was not too severe.

Ivan smiled reassuringly. "I've been fine. A few of my superiors contemplated letting me go, but then they realized no one in the organization was prepared to take my place. I am given the most difficult assignments and I've never minded. It suits my temperament. I'm just a freak of nature, I guess."

Misty was reminded how complex Ivan really was. Her passion for him had often been mixed with fear, but then maybe that's what made being with him so thrilling.

"Oh, I'm so happy for you," Misty gushed, relieved. "That puts my mind at ease. But how did you find me? *Why* did you find me?"

Ivan grinned broadly as he tapped her in the middle of her forehead with his very large index finger. "I came because you've gotten yourself in trouble again. You know it's my job to bail you out."

Misty beamed. "How on earth did you find out I was in trouble?"

Ivan looked around at the crowd that was slowly working its way out of the auditorium, making sure no one would hear his words. "What I am about to tell you would cause me great harm if you ever told anyone, so please keep this confidential."

Misty gave him a quick, earnest nod of agreement. She desperately wanted him to take her into his confidence.

Her enthusiasm pleased Ivan. "I work for the CIA. I'm in between assignments, so I decided to spend a few days at headquarters in Langley, Virginia."

"That's just outside Washington, D.C., right?"

"Yes, and you know that because you've been spending time in D.C. lately, right?"

Misty stared at him. "That's right. But how did you know?'

"Well, we were going through the latest FBI intel during a briefing yesterday and I came across your name."

"But I thought you said you worked for the CIA," said Misty.

"Yes, but ever since the formation of the Department of Homeland Security, all agencies have been encouraged to share information. Still, it was a freak accident that I came across a report with your name in it."

"What did it say?"

"It said an unnamed investigative reporter provided the U.S. Attorney General's Office with information that insinuated improprieties by a sitting U.S. congressman. I think we both know who that congressman is."

"Hey, a girl's got to work," she said.

"The report goes on to say you were to be questioned by a couple of FBI agents. I came here to warn you."

Misty looked at her feet. "Well, you're a little late."

She spent the next ten minutes filling Ivan in on everything that had happened. He asked her to elaborate on the part where she kicked the hooker's ass, just for the fun of it. At the end of her story, Ivan summed things up.

"Okay, don't worry about the false swearing charges. That's bullshit and any good attorney will get you off. The good thing is, you didn't admit to anything." Ivan put his big hands on her shoulders. "Now, I only want to know this so I can discern the severity of your potential legal issues. Have you indeed slept with the congressman?"

"I can't say I technically *slept* with him," Misty's said.

Ivan locked onto her eyes.

"Well, there weren't any pillows involved!" she said, laughing. "Oh, alright! He screwed me on a stationary bike. There, are you happy?"

Ivan sounded amused. "Lucky Henry. You made me use a bed."

Misty slapped him on the shoulder. "Oh, Ivan! That just shows you're not as perverted as the congressman."

Ivan laughed. "Give me another chance and you might retract your last statement."

Misty looked at Ivan seriously. "Get me out of this mess and I'm all yours, big guy."

Ivan smiled. "Consider it done!" He then added, "On a more serious note, I want you to let me know when you have any new information. I'll give you a number to call, but you can't write it down. You have to memorize it."

"That's it? Just call you?"

"No, you'll need to call the number from a pay phone and after you hear the beep, enter your pay phone number and hit pound. I'll call you from a secure line within minutes."

After memorizing the phone number she looked at Ivan sadly. "Will I get to see you again?"

Ivan wrapped his arms around her and squeezed tight. "Don't worry. We'll get together after you are out of danger. It will be much more enjoyable then."

Ivan said good-bye and slipped out.

* * *

Misty returned to the apartment at midnight. By then, Travis was in bed, sound asleep. Misty slipped out of her outfit, crawled in bed, and wrapped her arm around him.

Travis opened his eyes. "You're home. How'd your evening go?"

Misty snuggled up closer.

"It went well. Go back to sleep and I'll tell you about it tomorrow."

61

MESSING WITH CHESTER

Back in San Antonio, Stephanie and a coworker named Beverly had been noticing Chester's strange behavior.

"Has he been like this all morning?" asked Beverly.

"Yep, he's been pacing around like a caged baboon," said Stephanie.

Beverly snickered. "I think caged giraffe fits his description better."

Stephanie cracked up. "Beverly, you're killing me."

"Just calling it like I see it. Hey, gotta run, but fill me in if you find out what's up."

"I will."

At eleven thirty, a tall, attractive woman walked up to Stephanie's desk and asked for Chester.

"Is Mr. Naples expecting you?"

"Yes, he has me scheduled for lunch."

"Have a seat and I'll let him know you're here."

Stephanie entered Chester's office. "You didn't tell me you had a lunch commitment," she said.

Chester let out a throaty grunt. "I must have forgotten," he said, sitting down at his desk and picking up a pen in an effort to look busy. "What are you looking at, Stephanie? Send her in."

Stephanie left and returned moments later with the visitor. "Hello, Chester," said the woman. "I'm Molly. Thank you for seeing me on such short notice."

Taken by the tall beauty, Chester stuck out his chest and said to Stephanie, "Pick up some sandwiches at the deli and close my door when you leave. I don't want anyone disturbing us."

"Yes sir. I'll get right on it."

* * *

It was one o'clock Eastern time when two Russian emigrants left the local pub and headed to the Stratford House hotel on foot. Dmitri was a slender, wiry man with long, mangy hair. His burly sidekick, Yuri, struggled to keep up with his fast-paced boss.

"Dmitri, slow down," Yuri pleaded. "I just ate four hot dogs for lunch!"

"Walking fast is good for your digestion," Dmitri growled.

Yuri bent over and let out a loud belch. Feeling better, he moved as quickly as he could to catch his boss. "So what are our instructions?" he asked, huffing and puffing.

"I'll tell you when we get there."

Dmitri arrived at the hotel first and had to wait for Yuri to catch up. When he did, Dmitri said, "The boss wants us to do a favor for a large dealer in Alabama. Says if we do a good job, his dealer won't have to go to jail and we won't have to find someone else to distribute the merchandise."

Yuri leaned back against the building to rest. "What's the favor?"

Dmitri scrolled through his text messages. "Here it is. Room 412 is registered to a broad named Misty. We're supposed to search her room. It says to bring back any paperwork we find that looks like a contract. Just a fishing expedition, I imagine."

"Easy enough," said Yuri, "but what if she's in the room?"

"Maybe I'll let you slap her around a bit," Dmitri said with a twinkle in his eye.

"I hope she's pretty!" said Yuri.

* * *

Back with the sandwiches, Stephanie placed her ear to the door before entering. There was a lot of laughing and carrying on inside. Stephanie thought nothing of it until she heard Chester mention Misty's name in a diabolical tone. A chill ran down her spine. When she heard Chester say "I'm going to check on our food," she quickly opened the door and walked in.

"There you are. What took you so long?" Chester smiled at Molly and added, "Molly got up very early this morning, and I'm sure she must be starving."

In the sweetest voice Molly could muster, she said, "You are so fortunate to be working for such a marvelously witty man."

Stephanie forced a smile, placed the sandwiches on the table, and left the room without uttering a word.

Misty needs to know about this, she thought when she got back to her desk. *I'd better get a picture of her first, to send along with my text.*

* * *

Dmitri knocked on the door but when no one answered, he jimmied the lock open. Yuri checked out the bathroom, disappointed when Misty wasn't there, and then went through the chest of drawers, looking for her undergarments. He pulled out a pair of men's boxer shorts and held them in the air.

"What the fuck!" Yuri said. "This is one strange chick."

A few seconds later, Dmitri and Yuri heard the door open.

"Who the hell are you!" Miguel yelled as he looked around his room.

There was stuff strewn everywhere. With anger burning in his eyes, Miguel charged Yuri, driving him into the wall with such force that Yuri's shoulder left an indentation. Yuri shook off the blow and glared back at Miguel. Before he could hit Yuri again, Dmitri slammed into him from the blind side and drove him into the dresser. When Miguel bent over from the sharp pain in his rib cage, Yuri used the opportunity to grab him by the shoulders and sling him across the room.

As he lay on the floor, the men's laughter caused Miguel to flash back old gang war memories from his youth on the streets of Los Angeles—memories he had worked hard to keep buried. Miguel stood up and motioned for Yuri to come at him. Yuri ground his massive right fist into the palm of his open left hand, sure that the much smaller man posed little threat. The two men stood glaring into each other's faces, each waiting for the other to make the first move.

When Dmitri yelled, "What are you waiting for?" Yuri lumbered across the room and hurled his fist toward Miguel's head. Miguel ducked, sending Yuri's fist crashing into a picture on the wall. When Yuri tried to pick out a large piece of glass that had lodged in his hand, Miguel drove his fist into Yuri's rib cage, not once, but four times in succession. The room reverberated with the sound of Yuri's ribs cracking. When Yuri bent over to clutch his chest, Miguel landed a crushing blow to the side of his head, sending him crashing to the floor.

Miguel spun around quickly and pointed his finger at Dmitri, indicating he was next. Dmitri scowled, trying to appear unafraid. Not the least bit intimidated, Miguel closed the gap between them. The next thing Dmitri knew, he was lying on his back with blood streaming from his mouth. When Miguel leaned in to grab him, Dmitri quickly covered his face with his arms. Miguel grabbed his shirt, attempting to pull him from the floor. Before he could get Dmitri all the way up, he felt pain shoot through his body, pain unlike anything he had ever experienced. He crumpled to the floor, pinning Dmitri beneath him.

It took all of Dmitri's strength, but he eventually got out from under Miguel and stood up. He first looked at Yuri, on the floor on his hands and knees, and then back at Miguel. Yuri's switchblade was embedded in the small of Miguel's back.

Dmitri helped Yuri to his feet. "Good work, Yuri. Let's get the hell out of here before someone sees us."

"What about my knife?"

Dmitri placed his left foot square in the middle of Miguel's back and with one quick motion pulled out the knife. Worried that someone may have heard Miguel's horrific scream, Dmitri and Yuri headed for the stairwell. Miguel quickly passed out from the pain.

* * *

Chester and Molly's meeting appeared to be breaking up, so Stephanie ducked into the storage closet adjacent to her desk. Peeking through a tiny crack, she saw the two pausing to shake hands before Molly left. Stephanie activated the camera on her cell phone and stuck it outside the crack in the closet door, doing her best to aim where she thought they were standing. Safely inside the closet, she frantically looked to see if the camera had hit its target. Bingo! She had captured a perfect shot of Molly's face. Stephanie composed a text to Misty, attached the picture, and hit send.

62

DAMAGE CONTROL

After Travis left for work the next morning, Misty caught a cab to Gabriella's hotel. When Gabriella opened her door, they embraced.

"Gabriella, I'm so happy to see you. I'm really sorry I couldn't meet last night."

"It's good to see you too, dear. What happened last night?"

Misty walked into the room and lay down on Gabriella's bed. "Do you remember the client I trained in London, the one that got me out of trouble?"

"Yes—Ivan, wasn't it?"

"That's him. Well, Ivan found out I was in trouble and arranged a secret meeting with me at *Phantom of the Opera*. It was so secret he only left me a clue to follow."

"But how did he know you were in trouble?" Gabriella asked, concerned. "Do you think he's in on all this?"

"Oh, no! Ivan would never do anything to harm me, he—" Misty caught herself just before she let out the words *works for the CIA*. "You're just going to have to trust me on this one, Gabriella." Knowing Gabriella deserved a better explanation than that after flying all the way here, she said, "I'm sorry, but I don't want to tell you anything that would cause you harm. Here's the best I can do. Ivan knows someone tipped off the U.S. Attorney General's office about my relationship with Henry. Apparently that's why the FBI agents came to visit me. I'm sure it has something to do with my contract. Ivan is going to do whatever he can to help."

"Well, I'm glad I rushed here then," Gabriella said.

Misty walked over and snuggled up to her.

"You must be worn out," said Gabriella. "Why don't you just lie here with me and rest? There's nothing that can be done right now."

Misty felt secure in her arms. "Maybe I will, but don't let me sleep too long."

As Misty lay on her chest, Gabriella stared out of the massive, floor-to-ceiling windows. She was happy she could support Misty in her time of need, but she also felt helpless to do anything about the situation. She'd gotten Misty out of jail, but what now?

* * *

Misty awoke hours later to the sound of an incoming text. She rolled over and looked at her friend, who was lying by her side.

"Who's it from, dear?" asked Gabriella.

Misty grabbed her phone and then blinked a few times to focus. "It's Stephanie, from Texas. She says, 'Chester is up to no good. He met with a lady named Molly at noon. I overheard them talking about you.' She attached a picture of them." Misty looked at Gabriella. "Molly must be the district attorney in Alabama and Henry's toughest competitor. I wonder if Molly's trying to get a copy of my contract as well. That would be awful bold of her."

"Do you think Chester would give it to her?" asked Gabriella.

Misty showed her the picture of Molly. "Are you kidding? Chester will come apart at the seams in the presence of a woman that beautiful. No wonder Henry wanted to lose weight. She's gorgeous!"

Just as Misty set her phone on the bed, it rang.

"Hello?" Misty answered.

"Is this Misty?" asked a female voice.

"It is. Who is this?"

"Misty, you don't know me but I can assure you, we will become very intimate over the next few days."

The comment about becoming intimate made Misty think it was a prank call, so she hung up.

A few seconds later, the phone rang again. Noticing it was the same number, she decided not to answer.

When her phone rang a third time, Misty was furious. "Who the hell is this?" she demanded.

"Please don't hang up the phone."

"You have ten seconds to explain yourself."

"My name is Molly, and I'd like to meet with you."

Misty put her hand over the receiver and whispered to Gabriella. "It's Molly."

Not wanting to implicate Stephanie, she decided to play coy. "I'm sorry, but I don't know a Molly."

"Look, you don't know me but I'm on my way to New York this afternoon, and its imperative I meet with you. You'll just have to trust me when I say there will be dire consequences if you refuse."

Misty covered up the receiver again. "She says there will be dire consequences if I don't meet her," she said to Gabriella. "What should I do?"

Gabriella walked to the window and looked at the city below.

"Hurry up, Gabriella. I need to say something."

"Go ahead and arrange a meeting, but insist it be in the bar downstairs."

"Okay," Misty said to Molly, "I'll meet with you, but it has to be in the bar in the lobby of the Menger Hotel."

The line was silent for a moment before Molly said, "Can you be there at nine tonight?"

"I can."

"Come alone."

Misty covered up the receiver again.

"She wants me to be alone."

Gabriella nodded her approval.

"I'll be there at nine o'clock, alone."

As soon as Misty hung up, the phone rang again. She answered without checking her caller ID. "Now what!"

A man on the other end said, "Is this Misty?"

"Oh, sorry. I thought you were someone else. Yes, it is."

"Misty, this is Detective Saulsberry. I got your phone number from Miguel just before they took him into the operating room."

"Oh my God! What happened? Is he okay?"

"Apparently he came back to his hotel room and walked in on a burglary in progress," the detective said. "A scuffle ensued and Miguel was stabbed in the back."

Feeling suddenly weak, Misty lowered herself to the bed. "How bad is it?"

Gabriella came over and sat next to her, a worried look on her face.

"It's not good, but I've seen worse," he replied. "The knife went in just under the left side of his rib cage. Fortunately, it missed any vital organs."

"Where is he?" Misty asked.

"Lenox Hill Hospital, but don't get in a wreck getting here. The doctor says Miguel will be in the operating room for several hours."

"Thank you so much for contacting me, detective. I'll be there when he comes out."

Misty dropped the phone and covered her face.

"What's going on, Misty?" asked Gabriella.

"I can't believe this. The detective said Miguel walked in on a burglary in his hotel room and was stabbed in the back. I never should have left him on his own."

"Misty, you can't blame yourself. You had no way of knowing."

"I guess not. The detective said he'll be in the operating room for several hours. I want to be there when he wakes up."

"We will be."

* * *

In the late afternoon, a cab dropped them off outside the hospital. Misty asked Gabriella to go inside and wait for her while she called Ivan. After finding a pay phone and following Ivan's directions, she stood anxiously by the phone until it rang.

"Are you alone?" Ivan said when she picked up.

"Yes," she said. "Ivan, Miguel's been stabbed in the back."

He didn't respond immediately.

"Did you hear what I said?" she asked.

"Yes, just letting it soak in. First, how is Miguel? And second, what do you know about the stabbing?"

"They say the knife went in under his left rib cage but missed all his vital organs."

"He'll be fine," said Ivan.

"That's great to hear, doctor," Misty said sarcastically.

"Misty, I know what I'm talking about. The same thing happened to me years ago. Trust me, he may have a long recovery, but he will be fine."

"I'm sorry, I trust you," Misty said. "Apparently he walked into his hotel room while it was being robbed."

"What else is going on? Don't leave anything out."

"The lady running against Congressman Henry was in San Antonio this morning to visit with one of my old clients."

"Now that's interesting. How do you know that?"

"His assistant tipped me off. She even sent me a picture of the woman."

"What else?"

"You won't believe this, but she called me on my cell phone and wants to meet with me tonight."

"What did you tell her?"

"I told her I would meet her, but only if it was in the bar at the Menger Hotel. My friend Gabriella from Argentina is staying there."

"Smart move, Misty."

"Thanks!" she said.

"Give me a moment to think."

As Misty waited for Ivan's guidance, she realized how lucky she was that he had stumbled onto her situation. Without Ivan, she wasn't sure what she would do.

"Go check on Miguel," said Ivan. "Be back at the hotel by eight o'clock, and I'll arrange for a field operative to wire you for your meeting. He'll hang around and listen in on the conversation and report back to me. Have you got all that?"

"Yes."

"And when you meet with the field operative, show him the picture on your phone."

"Okay."

"Misty."

"Yes, Ivan."

"I can't tell you how sorry I am about Miguel. I really grew to like him in London."

"I know he thinks a lot of you, too."

"Listen, Miguel's a tough guy. He's going to be fine."

"Thank you, Ivan. I'll be sure to let your field agent know how he's doing so he can relay the information to you."

"That's what I was going to ask next. You're one step ahead of me. Hey, I have a lot to do, so I've got to run. Now that we know who's causing the problems, I can run background checks on her. When I was doing some background checks on your congressman, I seem to remember seeing that his opponent was a district attorney from the South somewhere, so I'll need to work outside my usual channels. I know just the guy to use."

"Ivan, I don't know how I'll ever thank you for what you're doing for me and Miguel."

"Don't worry, if you can't come up with something, I'm sure I can."

Misty laughed. "I'll bet you can."

Misty hung up and joined Gabriella in the hospital waiting room. The girls did their best to remain positive, even though they were torn up inside. Miguel was more than a bodyguard to Misty. He had been by her side during every adventure. She considered him family and loved him like a brother. Gabriella was fond of Miguel as well, but the fact that he meant so much to Misty made her that much more concerned about his well-being.

Just before seven o'clock, Miguel's surgeon came out to brief them.

"Are you Miguel's friends?" he asked.

"Yes, we are," said Misty. "How did he do in surgery?"

"Miguel is a tough guy. He did well but I'm afraid he will be in the intensive care ward through the night. I wouldn't be surprised if he was downgraded from critical condition by morning. I'm sorry, but the only thing you can do now is give him time and pray."

Gabriella stepped up and shook the surgeon's hand. "Thank you for your effort."

"Just doing my job. Listen, why don't you ladies go home and get some sleep? Visiting hours start at nine o'clock in the morning. You may be able to see him then, but expect Miguel to be a little groggy from the morphine."

Back at the hotel, while they waited for the field agent, Gabriella called Tom to let him know what had happened to Miguel. It didn't take long for Tom's concern to turn to anger. He asked Gabriella if he could catch a flight to New York and search for the guys who stabbed his buddy. Gabriella tactfully nixed his request, promising to keep him abreast of everything that was going on.

The field agent showed up promptly at eight o'clock. He was a pleasant sort and wasted little time wiring Misty and explaining how the wiretap worked. Misty gave him the news about Miguel and asked him to share it with Ivan. The agent told Misty that Ivan wanted her to get a good description of Miguel's assailants the next time she saw him and relay the information to him. He told Misty not to worry; that he would be in the lobby, just outside the bar, in the event she needed him. He then left.

"How are you holding up?" Gabriella asked Misty just before nine o'clock.

"Don't worry about me. I'll be fine now that I know Miguel will survive."

Misty took a deep breath. "It's almost nine. I'd better get going."

63

TIME TO DANCE

Misty spotted Molly the moment she entered the bar but was careful not to give herself away. Her heart pounded as she walked nonchalantly over to the friendly bartender.

"So, what will it be?" he asked.

"Give me a shot of your best tequila and a beer to chase it down with," said Misty.

The bartender smiled. "That sounds pretty good. I'd pour myself one if I wasn't working."

Misty caught a glimpse of Molly in the mirror behind the bar and resisted the urge to walk over and slap the smug look off her face.

When the barkeep set her drink on the bar, Misty said, "I need to charge it to room eight twelve. Tip yourself five dollars while you're at it."

"I remember that room number from last night. The classy lady from Buenos Aires, right?

"Yep!"

"I had a great discussion with her. What I would give to take a trip to Buenos Aires!"

Misty threw back her shot of tequila, and followed it with a swig of her beer. "Come on down. Gabriella would have no trouble lining you up with a job." She then whispered to the barkeep, "See that lady to my left? She will most likely come over and introduce herself in a moment, and then I'll join her at her table. Keep a close eye on us. If I leave first, take her another drink and tell her I asked you to. Charge it to the room and give yourself a twenty-dollar tip."

"You can count on it."

Misty gave him a wink as he walked away.

After taking another drink of her beer, Misty surveyed the bar as if looking for someone. Instead of walking over to greet her, Molly yelled, "Misty?"

Once Misty turned and made eye contact, Molly said, "Come over here and join me?"

Misty tipped her beer bottle up and drained the rest of it before walking to Molly's table. Molly motioned for Misty to sit down as if in control. Misty gritted her teeth and remained standing. The two took their time looking each other over. Intrigued, the bartender lined up a row of glasses on the bar and began cleaning them one at a time, as he observed their every movement.

Molly was first to break the ice. "You have quite the little career going, don't you, Misty?"

"I do alright."

"I should say. You make more money than I do."

Misty pulled out the chair across from Molly and took a seat. "You're an attractive woman. It's not too late to make a career change."

"No, I think there's only enough room for one Black Widow Trainer."

"You have me at a disadvantage," said Misty. "How do you know so much about me?"

"Let's just say it's a good thing Mr. Naples isn't in the navy, because loose lips sink ships."

"Chester signed a nondisclosure agreement," Misty replied. "I could take him to court if he told you anything."

Molly couldn't hold back her smile. "Chester stands to lose more if he doesn't cooperate with me."

Misty looked at her through squinted eyes. "How so?"

"Let's just say he didn't want to be charged for running a prostitution ring at the ranch. You know, it's illegal to have prostitutes transported across state lines for the purpose of servicing Japanese businessmen. Why, old Chester would get flushed down one of his own toilets if the authorities were to find out, don't you think?"

"That's none of my business," Misty snarled. "Chester can rot in jail for all I care."

Molly sat back and crossed her legs. She wanted to savor the moment before delivering her next line. All Misty wanted was another shot of tequila.

"So what would you think about your precious Travis rotting in jail instead?" said Molly.

Misty was confused. *What could she be talking about?* she thought. *Travis would never do anything illegal.* "Travis didn't have anything to do with those hookers!" she shot back.

Molly cocked her head to one side. "And how would you know that?"

"Because I was there!" Misty said without thinking. "Chester was the one who hired the prostitutes."

"So you admit someone hired prostitutes."

Misty's face was flushed and her mind raced. She realized she was responding without thinking. Not sure what to say next, she crossed her arms and sat staring into the corner. Molly was enjoying herself so much she decided to take a break to sip her drink. Everything was going as planned.

Misty desperately wanted to return to her room. "What do you want from me?" she asked.

"I want you to hold a press conference to explain your special arrangement with the congressman. You know, how he pays you money and you let him sleep with you. Oh, I'm sorry. Let's be more accurate. He only gets to do you once and then you go Black Widow on him."

"And if I refuse?"

The glare Molly gave Misty caused the bartender to drop the glass he was cleaning to the floor. Neither woman noticed.

"If you don't," said Molly, "Chester is prepared to testify that Travis, as foreman of the ranch and the person in charge of the convention facilities, was the one responsible for hiring the hookers."

"But that's a lie!" Misty blurted out.

Molly leaned in until their faces were only inches apart. "Well, we'll just have to let the courts decide, won't we? I wonder what it will do to Travis's career at Excelsior Investments when he gets dragged through the court system. Just think. Travis will be the talk of the firm."

Misty stood up with such force that her chair shot out behind her, causing the bartender to back up and knock a twenty-five-year-old bottle of Chivas Regal to the floor.

Misty balled her hands into a fist. "You're lucky we are in a public place or I'd kick your ass," she said ferociously.

The bartender became so enthralled that he grabbed a bottle of pure agave tequila, popped the cork, and gulped down four shots' worth. After wiping his mouth with his sleeve, he thought, *Kick her ass, blondie! My money's on you, girl.*

As tough as Molly was, her confidence came from her position in life, not her ability to fight. Misty's eyes frightened her, and she looked to the bartender for support.

When he just stood there with a crazed grin on his face, Molly said, "Look. I'm sure you can physically beat me up, but that would only mean you and Travis would both get charged, although for different reasons."

Misty's breathing slowly returned to normal, so Molly continued. "You have a choice to make, Misty. You can admit to sleeping with the congressman, letting Travis off the hook, or you can save the congressman and your reputation and screw Travis. That's what you like, right? Having control over men?"

Misty stood there without saying a word. "Don't forget," Molly continued, "you were at the ranch that night, so we can call you as a witness."

"So call me," Misty said defiantly.

Molly's tone softened. "Give up the congressman and I'm sure the Attorney General's office will be open to a generous plea bargain. They have no interest in you when they can bring down a U.S. congressman."

Misty's head throbbed. She was in deep and she knew it. She also knew she had said too much, so this time she chose to keep her mouth closed.

Molly was happy with her night's work. "Take a few days to think it over. I'll be in D.C. until Friday morning and we can meet again there." Molly reached in her pocket and handed Misty a card. "Here's the address. I'll see you Thursday afternoon at four o'clock sharp. You can give me your answer then."

Misty grabbed the address from Molly's hand and walked briskly out of the bar. Molly sat back slowly, savoring the moment as she finished her drink.

The bartender broke Molly's concentration by setting another drink in front of her. "What's this?" she said rudely.

The bartender pointed in the direction that Misty had exited. "The blonde lady you were talking to bought you a drink when she was sitting at the bar waiting for you to recognize her. She asked me to deliver it to you when she left."

Molly pursed her lips. *That little bitch knew who I was the whole time.* She then settled back and thought, *I wonder what else she knows.*

When she got to Gabriella's floor, Misty used the Menger's heavy brass key to open the room door and walked straight out onto the terrace. When Gabriella joined her, Misty appeared to be looking out over the city, but a closer inspection revealed her eyes to be closed. Standing behind her, Gabriella ran her fingers through Misty's hair and massaged her temples.

"Don't jump," Gabriella joked when she felt the time was right. "This isn't one of your dreams, honey, even if it does resemble a nightmare."

Misty turned around and held onto Gabriella. "Oh, how I wish this was all a dream. What I would give to hear your voice calling out to me from a distance, only to wake up in my bed at home."

"How bad was it?" Gabriella asked.

Misty shook her head. "It's worse than I ever could have imagined. Molly is giving me three days to hold a press conference and incriminate Henry or she'll have Chester testify that Travis hired prostitutes to fly in from Las Vegas to entertain guests at the ranch."

Gabriella pulled back and looked Misty in the eye. "Misty, you would be incriminating yourself if you testified against Henry."

"Yes, and I would be putting my career in jeopardy as well. This case would be so high-profile it would get coverage all over the world. No one will want to hire me after I testify against a client."

"But if you don't testify against Henry, Travis's career will be ruined," Gabriella said, understanding the full scope of her friend's dilemma.

Misty laid her head on Gabriella's shoulder and began to cry. Gabriella wanted to console her, but she could think of nothing to say. Misty was in a catch-22, and no one could make her decision for her.

Gabriella decided to do the next best thing. "Come on, let's get you to bed. Things will look a little less ominous in the morning, after a good night's sleep."

Misty nodded. "Okay, but don't let me oversleep. We need to visit Miguel first thing in the morning."

* * *

Miguel opened his eyes to see his two friends standing before him.

Misty sat down on the bed next to him, put his hand in hers, and said, "So how are you doing, tough guy?"

"Oh, I'm hanging in there. Thank God for narcotics."

"So what happened?" asked Gabriella.

"Not really sure. All I remember is walking into my hotel room and finding two guys tearing the place apart. I probably should have run, but I just wasn't brought up that way."

Misty spent the next few minutes filling Miguel in on everything going on in her life.

When she was through, Miguel said, "And I thought I had it bad. You have an impossible decision, Misty. What are you going to do?"

Misty lowered her head. "I can't decide, Miguel. There is no right answer."

The nurse walked in and said Miguel needed his rest, so the girls prepared to leave. Before Misty got up, she said, "Ivan showed up two nights ago and wants to help."

Miguel looked pleased.

"He asked me to get a full description of the guys who broke into your room," she said. "Be thinking about it, and you can tell me when I come back tonight."

Miguel gave her a thumbs up.

Over the next few days, Misty and Gabriella debated strategy. Unfortunately, they made little ground. They spent the evenings with Travis, but were careful not to tell him too much. Every time Misty looked at him, she pictured him being brought up on racketeering charges and it made her sick to her stomach. Travis asked Misty to stay at his place, but she couldn't bring herself to sleep with him, choosing instead to bunk with Gabriella. Her nerves were so shot that she would frequently wake up in the middle of the night in a cold sweat. She was beginning to think there was such a thing as hell on earth.

64

THE MOMENT OF RECKONING

On Thursday morning, Gabriella and Travis both begged Misty to let them accompany her on her trip back to D.C., but Misty wouldn't hear of it. This was her fight. She also needed the solitude of the Amtrak to delve deeper into her soul in search of her final answer.

By the time she arrived at Union Station, she was no closer to a decision than when she had left New York City. She checked back into the Hamilton, on her own dime this time, and then headed out to walk the National Mall to do some more thinking. She spent an hour sitting on the steps of the Lincoln Memorial, staring at Honest Abe as if hoping he would impart some wisdom. As the time for her meeting with Molly drew near, she began her long trek to their arranged meeting place. Being under another woman's control repulsed Misty, and she swore to herself she would never let it happen again.

Molly had arrived at the restaurant early to secure a table in the back. It was the same one she'd used to conduct meetings with Cindy. She savored the thought of Misty begging her for mercy while promising to do anything she asked. It was the feeling of power that drove Molly to seek high office, and today she would enjoy exerting that power over a helpless woman. The fact that Misty was extremely attractive and used to being in control made it that much sweeter.

Molly's fantasy was interrupted abruptly by the legal-size brown envelope dropped on her table. Startled, she looked up at the imposing figure looking down on her. He stood there in a flowing black overcoat with mangled shoulder-length hair, sunglasses, and a full beard.

"Special delivery," he said in a deep, throaty voice.

Molly exploded in anger. "How dare you walk up on me like that! Who do you think you are?" As she spoke, she scooted her chair away from the man.

The hulking man responded by opening his mouth wide to show Molly his full upper row of shiny silver teeth. The only thing that could have made him more menacing would have been a black patch over one of his eyes.

The man flashed a big grin. "Just delivering a package, lady." He then turned and walked out of the restaurant.

Molly considered following him but then shuddered at the thought. To settle her nerves, she reminded herself she was a district attorney and could deal with him if necessary. Once she regained her composure, her thoughts turned to the envelope lying on the table in front of her. Her curiosity got the better of her, so she opened it. Upon seeing what was inside, she turned as pale as a ghost. *How the hell did he get this?* she thought, her mind frantically trying to figure out what was going on.

After quickly surveying the restaurant to make sure no one was looking her way, she resealed the envelope and placed it under her seat for safekeeping. Molly motioned for the waiter and ordered two martinis. They were both for her.

* * *

Walking with her head down as she attempted to compartmentalize her hatred for Molly so she could be at her best for their showdown, Misty was startled by a low gruff voice. "You own the bitch now. Show her no mercy!"

Misty stared at the large, bearded man leaning up against a building, his right knee bent behind him. "Do I know you?"

When the man grinned, showing off his row of silver teeth, Misty stepped back a few paces. There seemed to be something familiar about his eyes, but she couldn't be sure. "Who are you?"

He showed her his menacing smile again. "I'm Molly's worst nightmare."

An icy calm swept over Misty. Tightening her fists into a ball, she asked, "Are you saying I shouldn't be afraid of Molly?"

He flashed his teeth again. "*You* are Molly's worst nightmare now. Show her no quarter!"

Misty walked into the restaurant with her head held high. She spotted Molly and moved in her direction, her stride self-assured, almost aggressive. Misty could tell right away that Molly lacked her usual confident body language. Misty pulled out the chair opposite her, turned it around, straddled the chair, and laid her arms over the back. Her posture was strong and her eye contact stronger.

"I'm here," she said. "What now?"

Molly didn't seem to know where to begin. She broke eye contact, apparently pondering her next move. Misty smelled fear and it emboldened her.

Misty didn't give her time to think. "Come on, I don't have all day. Let's get on with it!"

Her boldness sparked anger in Molly, which she fought to control. It was obvious she had underestimated this woman and was now paying the price.

Molly decided it was critical that she find out if Misty knew about the envelope. "Are you aware someone delivered me an envelope a few moments ago?"

"Was he a large man in a black overcoat with a row of silver teeth?"

Molly attempted to gain the high ground. "Are you aware I'm a district attorney?"

Misty laughed. "Aren't you a little out of your jurisdiction?"

Misty looked confident, but Molly had to give it one more shot. She sat back with folded arms. "So, what did you decide?"

Misty leaned the back of her chair forward. "I've decided you can go to hell!"

Molly relaxed, showing the look of surrender. "You are something else, Misty. Go on, get out of here."

Misty stood up. Before walking away, she said, "Guess you're going to have to win the election fair and square."

The fresh March air invigorated Misty on her walk back to the Hamilton. She felt alive for the first time in days. Henry's campaign was safe, her career was safe, and Travis need never know his career was once in jeopardy. It was then she realized there was no way she could have ever done anything to hurt Travis. Had things not worked out in her favor, she and Henry would have been the ones to pay the price. Walking past the White House on her way to the Hamilton, she noticed tender green buds forming on the cherry trees and realized everything would be rejuvenated with the coming of spring.

* * *

Molly polished off her second martini and was ordering a third when her cell phone rang. The caller ID indicated it was from Veronica, her investigative reporter friend from the *Washington Post*.

"Molly, I just received a horrible email!" Veronica said in a low voice as soon as Molly picked up.

"Let me guess—a picture of us having sex in your boss's office during last year's Christmas party?"

"How did you know? Oh, you sent it as a prank—right?"

Molly reached under her seat, placed the envelope on the table, and pulled out the picture.

"Sorry," she said, looking it over. "Someone delivered a hard copy of the same photo to me half an hour ago."

"This is terrible, Molly. If these pictures get out, we're ruined. I'll lose my job, you'll lose the election, and . . . and we couldn't be lovers anymore. What are we going to do?"

"We're not going to do anything," Molly said calmly. "I know where the pictures came from and as long as I leave the little bitch alone, she'll leave us alone. Trust me. She has as much to lose as we do if the pictures get out. Calm down. Nothing is going to happen."

"This whole thing's got me freaked out, Molly. I hope you're right."

After taking a big drink of her third martini, Molly said, "I'm looking at your naked body in the picture right now. Can I come over and spend the night?"

"I guess I could use a good stress reliever after this little scare," Veronica said, the excitement apparent in her voice.

"I've still got your key. I'll be waiting for you when you get off work. And Veronica?"

"Yes."

"Let's make sure all the shades are pulled down tonight."

65

A SHOW OF GRATITUDE

Misty exited the elevator when it reached her floor and raced down the hall toward her room. All she could think about was jumping into bed, calling Gabriella, and giving her every juicy detail of her meeting with Molly. After that, she would call Travis and simply say that things had all been worked out and that she would see him soon. Misty flung the door of her room open and ran to pounce on the bed. By the time she saw the man in a black overcoat sitting on the bed, it was too late to stop herself. The man's long, powerful arms pulled her into his chest where he held her tight. Misty thrashed about, and as his grip slowly loosened, she raised her head and looked at her abductor's face. Freeing her right arm, she pulled off his curly, dark wig, revealing a smooth, balding head with soft, short hair around the sides.

She pulled the beard off next. "Ivan! It was you!"

Ivan grinned, showing off his silver teeth.

"Oh, stop it!"

"Tell me the truth," he said. "I had you going for awhile, didn't I?"

She pinched his nose. "Yes, you big baboon!"

"Big baboon? You used to call me an oversized gorilla . . ."

"I called Peter, your alter ego, an oversized gorilla. You're my big baboon."

Misty and Ivan's eyes met. There was no mistaking what was on their minds. She unbuttoned his shirt and began kissing his soft chest hair. Still euphoric from her victory over Molly, she was flush with endorphins, which only increased her desire for him. They took their clothes off as quickly as they could and crawled under the covers. Ivan kissed Misty's lips until her breath became hot and heavy, and then he moved on to devouring every inch of her body with his warm mouth and tongue. She lay there, a willing prisoner, as Ivan owned her like no other man had before. Ivan teased her body, slowly circling the base of her mound until she begged him to take her with his massive tongue. Succumbing to her wishes, he teasingly prodded the entrance of her wet, moist lips with his tongue, plunging his thickness deep inside her nest. Misty pulled her knees to her chest and arched her back to give him open access. He dove in over and over, making sure he dragged up and over her clitoris with each lick.

He brought her to orgasm over and over until she wanted to pass out. As she lay on her back with her arms over her eyes, he came at her again, but this time something was different. Misty uncovered her eyes and lifted her head to see the massive tip of his penis wedging its way into her slowly. Slightly uncomfortable, it wasn't long before Misty felt the head of his penis slam into her interior wall. She looked up to see Ivan above her, using his powerful arms to support his weight and keep from crushing her. Sweat dripped from his chest onto her breasts. Gazing at their privates, she was amazed at how much of him could still not fit inside her. She became mesmerized as his massive penis filled her so full it stimulated everything from her clitoris down to her G-spot. If she owned it, he was doing it.

One after another, the waves of pleasure rose steadily until Misty erupted in one big orgasmic explosion. She placed her elbows by her sides and raised her head off the bed as she came. When the orgasm subsided, she flopped back onto the bed. But Ivan was far from through; he pulled out and rolled Misty over, placing two pillows under her stomach. Eager to please him in repayment for all he had done, Misty drew her knees forward, to make herself more accessible. Once fully penetrated, she felt his right hand clasp onto her right breast. Her left breast was left free to flop back and forth with each powerful thrust. Before long, she heard a massive grunt and the pounding stopped. When Ivan rolled over onto his back, Misty crawled alongside her hero and fell into a deep sleep.

* * *

Misty opened her eyes in the middle of the night and stared at the ceiling, wondering for a moment where the heck she was. When it all came back to her, she sat up and looked around the room. Ivan was gone. She called out, thinking he might be in the bathroom, but she heard no reply. It only took a few more minutes for her to fall back asleep. When Misty awoke in the morning, she found a note on the stand by her bed.

Misty,

My work is done, so I must go. I take your memory with me, as it is the only thing of yours I will ever own. Sweet memories they are indeed. Things may be under control for now, but please heed my advice to leave the country as quickly as possible. Everything will blow over after the November elections. Please keep the phone number I gave you in memory, for you never know when you might need me again. It always feels good to be needed.
Until we meet again . . .

Ivan

P.S. In case you are wondering, I gave Molly an envelope of incriminating pictures before you got to her.

Misty held the note to her heart and relived the night with Ivan one more time in her mind. She then picked up her phone and saw that she had ten messages—six from Gabriella and four from Travis. It was time for her to go as well.

66

LEAVING IT ALL BEHIND

Misty waited for Henry on a bench in a corner of Union Station. She was beginning to worry he wouldn't make it before her train was to leave when she saw Rick appear and motion to someone hidden around the corner. Then Rick disappeared as Henry turned the corner and sat down on the bench next to her.

"I came as fast as I could," he said nervously. "You sounded like it was important we talked now."

Misty patted him on the leg. "It is important, Henry, but it's also good news."

"I could really use some good news about now," he said.

"Henry, I've been through hell and back over the last several days. I'm going to be as vague as I can for your own protection."

"Yes, vague is good."

"Okay then. Molly has been working behind your back to force me to testify that we slept together."

Misty stared into his disgruntled face before proceeding. "I've been interrogated by the FBI, held overnight in the slammer, and threatened by Molly herself."

"Molly contacted you personally?"

"She did. I met with her in New York first and then here in D.C., yesterday."

Henry stared at Misty, afraid to ask any more questions.

"Right before I got to her," Misty continued, "a friend of mine, who will remain anonymous, handed Molly an envelope and basically assured me she would never bother me again."

Henry sat up straight. "What was in the envelope?" he asked with the enthusiasm of a child.

"I honestly don't know, but believe me when I tell you it changed Molly into a pussycat by the time we were finished talking."

A visibly relieved Henry asked, "So what now?"

Misty placed her hand on his cheek. "Now I go home. I think you and I have gone through enough, and nothing good can come from us continuing our training sessions."

Henry nodded. "You're right. But what about our contract?"

Misty stood up, took a few steps toward her train, and stopped.

"What contract? I don't know anything about a contract."

Grinning from ear to ear, Henry replied, "Neither do I. Have a safe trip home."

Once Misty was on the train, she called Gabriella. Remembering what Ivan had written about leaving the country as soon as she could, Misty got straight to the point, filling Gabriella in on everything.

When she was finished, Misty said, "Don't you think we should heed Ivan's warning and skedaddle?"

"Ske-what?" Gabriella replied.

Misty laughed. "Sorry, I guess that's American slang. Don't you think we should go home as quickly as we can?"

"Yes, dear. I will begin making the arrangements the moment you hang up. By the way, I got word from Kerry that the FBI dropped the false swearing charges. Did Ivan have anything to do with that?"

"I have no idea, but I wouldn't be surprised," said Misty.

"It's a good thing they were dropped, because if they hadn't, I would be harboring a fugitive."

Misty flashed back to her night with Ivan and realized he must have left early to work on getting the charges dropped. Ivan had to be smart enough to know she wouldn't have been able to leave the country unless they were taken care of.

"Okay, then I better hang up and let you get crackin'."

"Crackin'?"

Misty shook her head. "Never mind."

By the time Misty got back to New York and crawled into bed, Gabriella had everything arranged. Flight plans had been turned in, allowing them to take off around noon. The hospital didn't think Miguel was strong enough to be released but acquiesced after Gabriella hired a personal nurse to make the trip back home with them. Gabriella even thought to let Travis know he should take the morning off so Misty could stop by and say good-bye. She got a big hug out of Misty for her thoughtfulness.

* * *

The next morning Travis came to the door wearing jeans, boots, and his cowboy hat.

Misty looked him over. "Playing cowboy, are we?"

Travis picked her up, hugging her and swinging her around. "Gabriella told me the good news about the false swearing charges being dropped. I'm so happy things turned out all right. I was really worried about you."

"I know you were, Travis, and you don't know how much I appreciate everything you did for me."

Travis set her down. "Just being a good cowboy."

"So seriously, what's up with the duds?"

"I've handed in my two weeks' notice," he said. "Just making sure my old clothes still fit."

"What! You're leaving Excelsior Investments? Are you nuts?"

Travis held Misty's face with his hands and planted a big kiss on her lips. "I'm going home to run the ranch."

"You would work for Chester again?"

"Not Chester, Brenda. She called me and said Chester mysteriously gave her the ranch in their divorce settlement. Brenda doesn't know anything about ranching, so she offered to give me half of the ranch if

I would come home and run it." Travis's mood became more serious. "That's where I belong. I know that now."

"But what about poor Stephanie?"

"Stephanie turned in her two weeks' notice too. Chester was not happy, but there's nothing he can do about it."

"What will she do?"

Travis laughed. "Steph is going to spend some quality time back home in Wisconsin before returning to be Brenda's personal assistant."

"How cool is that! Tell her hi for me." Misty grinned. "But aren't you going to miss all of those high-society people?"

Travis laughed. "Not in the least."

Misty moved in closer, placing her hands on his sides. "But aren't you going to miss Emily?"

"Not in the least."

Misty looked into his eyes. "But aren't you going to miss me?"

Travis became somber. "You know I will."

Misty began to feel what she had felt the night they made love, so she summoned her defense mechanism. "Hey, I just remembered I left a few things in your bedroom. I better go get them."

While she was rummaging through his dresser, Misty heard the doorbell ring. Figuring it was a neighbor, she continued looking. She stopped when she heard Emily's voice.

"I called for you at work, Travis, and they said you stayed home this morning. Why are you wearing those yucky clothes?"

As Misty listened to Travis's patient explanation to Emily, she grew angry. She looked down at the small stack of clothes in her hand and got an idea.

Misty could still hear the conversation between Travis and Emily as she got ready.

"Travis, you're up to something, I just know it."

"Emily, please calm down. Why don't I take you to dinner tonight and we can have a rational conversation."

"Rational! You think I'm not being rational?"

Emily saw the bedroom door swing open out of the corner of her eye and turned to look. Standing in the doorway was Misty in the Ralph

Lauren nightshirt she never got a chance to wear. She placed her hand over her mouth and let out a huge yawn before throwing her hands in the air and stretching as if waking from a long night's sleep. As she stretched, her shirttail rose enough to reveal that she wasn't wearing panties underneath.

Emily stood in shock as Misty walked over to Travis, got up on her tiptoes, revealing her bare ass, and gave him a peck on his cheek.

"You were really a stud last night, Trav," she said before turning and walking into the kitchen.

Emily slapped his face and then stormed out of the apartment, slamming the door behind her.

Misty strolled back in and grinned as Travis rubbed his cheek. "That was my little going-away present. Trust me, you'll thank me later."

Misty looked so stunning that Travis was ready to thank her now.

He glanced at his watch. "So how much time do you have before you need to head out to the airport?"

Misty grabbed his hand and dragged him into the bedroom. "Enough time to take your mind off Emily, cowboy," she said.

Misty stayed true to her word.

* * *

With good-byes said and everyone on board the Gulfstream, including the nurse, the powerful jet engines lifted them off the runway. Misty was happy to be going home but sad that she was leaving Travis.

Somewhere far below the plane, on West 57th Street, Dmitri and Yuri were on their way to pay a visit to a man who owed their boss money. Dmitri had concealed a crowbar inside his overcoat, just in case. This was their first job since laying low after their run-in with Miguel. They hated being cooped up for so long and were ready to take it out on anyone. An arm came from out of nowhere, grabbing Dmitri, dragging him into the alley, and slinging him to the ground. Dmitri looked up at his assailant. He was a large man, standing well over six feet. Intimidated, Dmitri waited for Yuri to step in but Yuri just stood there, not anxious to provoke the man.

"Well, what the hell are you waiting for?" Dmitri yelled. "Hit him!"

Yuri reached back and swung as hard as he could, but the man caught his fist in midair. Yuri fell to his knees in the man's vice-like grip.

"Which one of you stabbed my friend?" the man bellowed.

"It was him!" Dmitri yelled as he ran further into the alley.

The man released his grip only to drive his fist into Yuri's face. Blood splattered everywhere. Yuri crumpled to the ground and showed no signs of getting up. When Dmitri realized there was no way out of the alley, he pulled the crowbar from his overcoat and brandished it in his hand, hoping to scare off his attacker. Undeterred, the man kept coming. When he was close, Dmitri swung the crowbar at him. The man caught Dmitri by the wrist with one hand and yanked the crowbar away with the other. Dmitri cried out in agony as his own crowbar slammed into his left thigh.

"Damn you!" Dmitri shrieked. "You almost broke my leg!"

"Almost?" the man said before slamming the crowbar into his thigh again.

The crack of bone echoed through the alley.

Dropping the crowbar to the ground, the man said, "There, that's better. I don't like to *almost* do anything."

He waited for Dmitri's screaming to subside before saying, "The man you stabbed was a very dear friend of mine. Consider things even."

Just before the man reached the street, Dmitri's curiosity got the better of him.

"Who are you?" Dmitri yelled.

"You can think of me as a phantom!" the man yelled back before disappearing into the crowded street.

67

HOME SWEET HOME

It was a sober flight home to Argentina. Exhausted from the emotional roller coaster she'd been on, Misty spent much of the journey with her head resting on Gabriella's shoulder, drifting in and out of sleep. The harrowing experience strengthened the already close bond between them. Gabriella let Misty know that Tom and Rosie were now living in the cottage and were to be wed the following month. She told her how handsome Thor was and what a pleasure he was to have around. Miguel spent his time getting to know Maria, the personal nurse Gabriella had hired. Although very attractive, it was her kind, shy manner that commanded his attention. He hung on her every word.

* * *

That evening everyone freshened up from their long flight and gathered poolside for drinks and catch-up. Misty entertained everyone with a blow-by-blow account of their D.C. adventure. Tom's family and Maria *oohed* and *ahhed* with every twist of the plot, even though they of course knew everything would work out in the end. Rosie was enthralled by the relationship between Misty and Travis, Tom wished he could have been there to help, and Maria's heart went out to Miguel as he relived his battle with the two intruders, putting her hand to her mouth the moment Miguel described the switchblade that had been plunged into his body. Thor was totally captivated by Misty and spent the rest of the evening following her around like a puppy. *What a wonderful way to live your life*, Thor thought. Traveling the world had been a dream of his ever since he found out his father had been in the navy.

Later that evening, Tom and Rosie told everyone about their upcoming wedding. It was to be a small, intimate wedding held on the second-floor back porch of the newly renovated cottage. Situated on the ocean side of Gabriella's expansive estate, it provided an unencumbered view of the Atlantic. After the announcement, Gabriella had one of her servants bring in some vintage champagne from her extensive wine cellar.

When they had all been poured a drink, they raised their glasses in the air. "To Misty and Miguel's safe return," said Gabriella.

After several more toasts, Tom asked, "So Misty, who's going to be your bodyguard on your next adventure? It's obvious Miguel won't be well in time."

Enjoying the attention he was getting from Maria, Miguel said, "I'm afraid Tom has a good point. As much as I hate to say this, I may have to sit this one out. Well, at least the first half of it."

Tom attempted to stand up, only to have Rosie pull him back into his chair. "You're not going on any adventures, Tom. You need to stay focused on our honeymoon."

After moving away from his mother so she couldn't latch onto him the way she had his father, Thor stood up. "I'll protect Misty!"

"But you are doing so well at the university, Thor," said Gabriella. "This would not be a good time to interrupt your studies."

"I'd only be out one semester," Thor argued. "School is great, but traveling the world is an education as well." He looked at his mother before adding, "I've never had the opportunity to leave Brazil before coming to Buenos Aires. This would be a great opportunity to experience something exciting in my life." Thor then looked toward Misty shyly. "And I want to make sure nothing bad happens to you, Misty."

Thor's plea was so heartfelt that no one responded for a few moments.

There was something about this young, good-looking kid that appealed to Misty. Maybe it was his passion, maybe his innocence, or maybe just his baby-blue eyes. Wanting to at least show Thor her appreciation for his concern, Misty walked over and gave him a hug.

She stepped away while still holding his hands. "There is no doubt you have the strength, but there's so much more to being a bodyguard, as Miguel can attest."

"But Miguel can teach me," Thor pleaded. Turning to Tom, he said, "You can as well, father. I'm sure you learned much during your time serving in the navy."

Tom laughed. "And I can teach you a lot of things not to do."

"Oh, Thor," said Rosie. "Being a bodyguard is a dangerous profession. Look at poor Miguel."

"But mother, being a bouncer at the salsa club was dangerous, and you didn't stop me. Father was traveling the world at my age aboard a nuclear submarine. Tell me that wasn't dangerous!"

Rosie placed her hand on Tom's arm, indicating that the decision was his. For too long she had made all the decisions. Now that his true father was part of Thor's life, it was time for him to take that responsibility.

Tom scratched his chin a moment. "I suppose school could wait. That is, if Misty agrees to hire you and Miguel agrees to train you."

Thor looked at Misty like a puppy dog begging its master to let it go outside and play. Misty could tell Rosie still did not approve by the look on her face. She also knew that Thor was not aware of the true meaning of her profession.

Hoping to put the decision off for another day, Misty said to Thor, "Train hard and learn everything you can from Miguel and your dad, and then we'll see how you have progressed when the time comes."

Thor nodded politely, but he couldn't conceal the grin on his face.

* * *

It was a crisp day in the middle of May. A small group of friends and family gathered on the back porch of the cottage to witness Tom and Rosie take their wedding vows. Rosie was radiant in her flowing white gown while Tom stood there thankful he had run into Rosie that fateful night in Rio. After the ceremony, Gabriella served cake and punch while the wedding party mingled with the guests. Misty, Miguel, and Maria stood at the railing, admiring the ocean view while discussing how fortunate they were to be with Gabriella and their wonderful new friends. This was their new home, their new extended family. As Miguel began to explain to Maria, his able nurse for the foreseeable future, how he became Misty's bodyguard, Misty leaned against the rail and leisurely surveyed the horizon.

Miguel's concentration was broken by the sound of Misty's cry. "No way! It can't be them!"

Miguel looked out to sea and noticed a rusty, dilapidated ship floating on the horizon. It looked like old Mother Hubbard's shoe. He could see dark black smoke bellowing out of the smokestack and heard the sound of its old diesel engine pistons clanking away in a song of futility.

Misty quickly turned and yelled to Thor, "Grab your father's keys to the limo and follow me!"

Thor excitedly did as he was told.

Misty muttered something under her breath as she headed toward the door.

Puzzled, Maria asked Miguel, "What does Misty mean when she says 'frickin' dirty pirates'?"

Still gazing out to sea, Miguel said, "Well, I'll be dammed! The Captain and his little buddy sure are a long way from Alaska."

Craig Odanovich grew up in Flour Bluff, Texas, only minutes from the beaches of Padre Island. His creative roots are firmly grounded in the muscle car culture of the seventies. As a young music business entrepreneur, Odanovich launched a successful record store at a time when neighborhood record stores were still a prime point of connection between popular music and the public. His genuine affinity for the music and the fans helped Craig's Record Factory build huge customer loyalty, keeping regional and national competition at bay.

Rising to the executive level in the video and home entertainment division of H-E-B, a regional grocery and retail chain, Odanovich led growth for the company in an emerging market space. Later, applying his leadership abilities and insight to other highly competitive business arenas, he built value and increased market share for each of the companies he subsequently served, both in executive posts and as a key consultant.

Through his many stages of career evolution, Odanovich has maintained a constant interest in popular music and film. Three decades of avidly collecting music and seeing movies has provided a wellspring of inspiration for the author. Odanovich currently pursues his writing career in San Antonio, Texas. He and his wife, Cathie, have four children.

1

WHICH WAY DID THEY GO?

Misty peered out the back of the limo as Thor frantically zoomed down the narrow, winding coastal road.

"There's an opening, Thor!" Misty yelled. "Pull in over there!"

Thor turned onto a bumpy dirt road, the thick underbrush scraping the bottom of the limo as he drove. When the car came to a sliding stop, Misty flung her door open and fought her way through the dust cloud to the water's edge. She climbed to the top of a rocky outcropping and peered out. The Rio de la Plata was the widest river known to man and served as the causeway to Buenos Aires from the Atlantic Ocean. Misty motioned for Thor to kill the engine so she could use both sight and sound in her effort to locate her Alaskan companions. Thor soon joined her on the outcropping, and the two took a seat on a small boulder and patiently waited.

"Who or what are we looking for?" Thor asked.

"Maybe we're looking for ghosts," Misty said. "But I could swear I saw a familiar boat from the balcony of the cottage. A boat I last saw leaving Resolution Bay."

"Where's Resolution Bay?" Thor asked.

"Sorry—it's in Alaska."

"What's the name of the boat, just in case I spot it later?"

She grinned. "It's called *Dirty Pirates*, appropriately named after its captain and his running mate."

Thor looked puzzled, so Misty continued. "Captain Kev and Miniature Mike are two of the more colorful characters I've met on my adventures. Are you sure you still want to be my bodyguard?"

"I'm your man!" he said. "I'm up for anything."

Within five minutes, a ship moved slowly up the river on its way to Buenos Aires. As the boat came into view, Misty could tell that it was indeed the Dirty Pirates.

"Let's go!" she said. "Let's drive further up the river ahead of them. I want to be there when they find someplace to dock."

For over an hour, they pulled over at place after place, only to see the boat pass by on its way further up the river. Finally, it set course for shore. Misty and Thor waited for them in an old abandoned marina. Misty smiled when she first heard Captain Kev's voice barking out instructions to Mikey.

"What's taking you so long, Mikey?" he yelled. "Get over here and grab some rope! I told you not to stay up all night."

Mikey slammed his left hand over his bicep as he raised his right arm, giving the Captain the "up yours" sign. Captain Kev broke out laughing. Mikey secured a ramp to the dock below and walked away.

"Permission to come aboard, Captain!" Misty shouted.

Mikey jerked his head around and stared at Misty as if he didn't believe his eyes.

"Well, I'll be damned!" bellowed Captain Kev. "What the hell are you doing in Buenos Aires, sweetie?"

"I live here, capitán," Misty said as she and Thor walked up the ramp. "The question is, what are you doing in Buenos Aires?"

The Captain scratched his chin with his prosthetic right forearm as he always did when not telling the entire truth. "Oh, we're only here for a short stay and then we'll be on our way." Then something occurred to him. "Hey, when we left Seward in the early dawn, didn't you say we should think about coming to Buenos Aires, since that's where the old Nazis hid out after World War II?"

Mikey interrupted the conversation by running up and giving Misty a big hug. At only four foot eight, his face was planted between her breasts. Misty was so happy to see him that she couldn't have cared less. After the hug, he looked up at her with puppy dog eyes and she patted his head.

She pinched Mikey's cheek. "You're a weird one, little fella." Mikey grinned profusely.

"Who's that good-looking young man standing behind you?" the Captain asked.

"Oh, where are my manners?" Misty turned to Thor. "This is Thor, my new bodyguard-in-training."

"What happened to Migs? I really liked that guy."

"Long story, Captain. But Miguel was stabbed while we were in New York."

She could see the look of concern in Mikey's eyes. Miguel had been like a big brother to him in Alaska.

Misty placed her hands on the side of his face. "Not to worry, Mikey. Miguel came through it fine and is well on his way to recovery. But if he isn't healed by the time I hire my next client, Thor might be taking his place."

"Well, that's a frickin' relief," the Captain said.

Mikey walked over to Thor and raised his arms to show off his biceps. Thor looked at Misty, dumbfounded.

"Show him your biceps, Thor."

Thor gave her a funny look but did as she requested. Unbuttoning his shirtsleeve, Thor pulled it back, exposed his full arm, and then flexed. Mikey's eyes widened at the site of Thor's cantaloupe-sized biceps, and Misty reevaluated her stance on bringing Thor with her on her next adventure.

Mikey patted his other bicep, so Thor pulled back the other sleeve and raised both arms. Mikey reached up, placing a hand on each bicep, and began doing chin-ups. Thor just stood there like a rock and shook his head.

A voice behind them said, "My, my, my. What a strapping young man!"

Misty turned around to see a woman emerging from the deck below.

She had gorgeous, silky, jet-black hair that hung all the way down to the middle of her back. She glanced confidently at Misty with her catlike greenish-blue eyes. They were framed by lush eyebrows that were even blacker than her hair. The woman turned her head and set a course for Thor. Her body was exquisite in every way, from her firm, protruding butt, anchored by muscled thighs, to her powerfully built arms. Although she was clearly strong, she looked more like a finely honed athlete than a bulky female weightlifter. Her movements were smooth and agile, like a gazelle. Her breasts lay heavy on her chest, an overflowing D-cup, Misty presumed. Misty looked down at her own body and then back at the woman's. *Surely I can't be jealous!* she thought.

What troubled Misty more was Mikey intercepting the woman along the way and giving her a hug every bit as tight as the hug he had just given her.

"Hey there, Mikey, doing some chin-ups I see."

Mikey grinned when she patted his head, just as Misty had done. The woman continued over to Thor until her face was inches from his. Her captivating eyes held him hostage.

"My, aren't you the strong one?" she said.

Misty walked over to Thor's side and tapped the woman on the shoulder. When the woman whipped her head around, the two stood face to face.

The Captain gulped before hurrying to the women's side. Mikey took a seat on a large crate and settled in for the show.

"Uh, Misty . . . I would like to introduce you to Monique," said the Captain. When neither responded, he added, "And, Monique, this is Misty."

Misty extended her hand and Monique gripped it firmly, each letting the other know her full strength.

"What brings you to Buenos Aires?" Misty asked.

Captain Kev spoke up. "We met Monique in the Virgin Islands. She introduced us to a friend of hers that has a bar for sale. When we buy the bar, Monique is going to be our partner."

"I see," said Misty. "So you have money to invest, Monique?"

Monique moved next to Captain Kev and placed her arm on his shoulder.

"Well, no, she doesn't," said the Captain. "But we're giving Monique a share of the bar and in return we will get a share of the treasure that—"

Monique pinched Captain Kev in his side.

"It's okay, Misty is like family. It's not like I showed her the map!"

"I'll go get the map so we can show Misty!" yelled Mikey.

"Why don't we just put it on the Internet for everyone to see while we're at it?" Monique said. She walked over to Thor and patted him on his chest. "Of course we could always use a strong young man like Thor. I'll bet you would make a great digger."

Misty took Thor by the arm and pulled him away. Looking directly at Monique, she said, "If there's a gold digger on this boat, it's not Thor!"

They all turned to Mikey as he came back waving a folded, wrinkled piece of paper in his hand.

"Put the map away, Mikey. Now is not the time," yelled Captain Kev.

Mikey gave Captain Kev an angry stare and then stormed off.

The treasure map had piqued Misty's interest, but she didn't want to give Monique the satisfaction of knowing. Instead she said, "So what are your plans, Captain?"

"Well, we need to find someplace to moor old *Dirty Pirates* while we're here."

"For how long?" Misty asked.

"Not sure. We need to find someone, but we don't know exactly where he lives. Could take some time, but if we get lucky, we'll be leaving soon."

Realizing how matter-of-fact that probably sounded to Misty, he walked over and put his arm around her. "Of course, I hope it takes a while, because I've missed you. We have a lot of catching up to do."

His smile and hug brought a smile back to Misty. "Hey," she said, "why don't you take your boat back down to the mouth of the river? My friend has an estate that sits on a cliff overlooking the Atlantic. Not too far off shore is a tiny island. Actually, it's pretty much just a bunch of rocks, but you could moor your boat there and then row to shore.

The Captain scratched his chin and said, "I like that idea. We won't draw much attention way out there."

Misty gave him a sly look. "So you're still running from the law?"

"Yep, and we're doing a pretty good job of staying a step ahead."

"So how are you going to buy a bar? Aren't you afraid they'll find you if you put it in your name?"

"You're still smart as a whip, Misty. That's why we're here. Monique knows someone she thinks will agree to put the bar in his name for a piece of the action. He's a quiet guy. Likes to keep to himself."

"Probably why he's so hard to find," Misty said. "Well, that's your business anyway. Listen, why don't you head back out to sea? Look for me on a small peninsula where the river meets the Atlantic. I'll point in the direction of the rock island. You'll be able to see it from there with your binoculars."

Monique and Misty locked eyes one more time before Monique turned and walked away without saying good-bye. As she passed Mikey, she snapped her fingers and he followed her.

Misty turned to Captain Kev. "Nice gal you got there, Captain."

"Hey, hey. She's definitely on the rag today, but don't worry." He raised his infamous prosthetic right forearm and grinned. "She loves my attachments. I'll calm her down tonight."

Misty thought back to the night she spent in Captain Kev's quarters, while training him in Alaska. Shaking her head, she said teasingly, "You are just too much."

Misty motioned to Thor, and they headed out. The Captain pulled up the fake eye patch he always wore to get a good look at Misty as she walked down the plank. She was still as gorgeous as ever. He wished she and Monique could find common ground and get along, but deep down, he knew they had about as much chance of being friends as did two feral cats.

When she was out of sight, he yelled, "Get up here, Mikey! Time to shove off!"

The Black Widow Trainer
Book One in the Black Widow Trainer Series

$14.95

978-1-934572-59-7

Bored with the tedium of her passionless marriage, Misty's life explodes after a weekend of mind-blowing sex with the man of her dreams. Exploring the physical limits of her newfound desire, she combines the lure of her honed, disciplined body with cunning business acumen and redefines herself as the Black Widow Trainer, a high-priced personal trainer/escort.

Negotiating an open relationship with her husband is the easiest part of her career move. Adjusting to the whims and demands of her well-heeled and imaginative clients, however, requires Misty to expand the limits of her sensual being.

The genre-busting novel features a cast of original, gritty characters, including an Alaskan sea captain, a pint-size satyr, and a gender-bending woman. Misty's fantastic sexcapades in exotic locations around the world are hot enough to fire up anyone's sex life.